Margaret Cezair-Thompson was born [...]
She is the author of the highly accl[...]
Daughter, which was a Richard & Jud[...]
History of Paradise was her first novel a[...] the IMPAC
Award. She is a professor of English at Wellesley College, and lives in
Massachusetts.

Praise for *The True History of Paradise*:

'The colourful and dramatic history of Jamaica is stunningly encapsula-
ted in this complex first novel ... Seductive ... powerful ... a heart-
breakingly rich, beautiful story whose characters hauntingly embody their
country's travail. A very accomplished debut' *Kirkus Reviews*

'A strong debut ... robust and authentic ... Cezair-Thompson depicts
with vivid immediacy Jamaica's terrors and seductions ... a setting of
paradisal beauty' *Publishers Weekly*

Praise for *The Pirate's Daughter*:

'Thompson's evocations of Jamaican life ... are a joy to read, at once
humorous, touching and poetic ... *The Pirate's Daughter* charms as surely as
any dashing film hero' *Sunday Telegraph*

'A wonderful confection ... The breathtaking pace and verve of *The
Pirate's Daughter* make it a delight; a touch of summer reading in a cold
winter' *Independent*

'A love song to a slice of paradise that's teetering on the edge ... This
novel is both a complete joy, and a subtle exploration of colonialism'
Daily Mirror, Book of the Week

'A languid, exotic story, full of depth and well-deserving of its many
plaudits' *Sunday Express*

'A heady mix of love and loss, treachery and post-colonial politics'
Guardian

'Cezair-Thompson creates a potent atmosphere, combining the tropical
scents and sounds of Jamaica with Hollywood glamour, and balancing
romantic intrigue with the more serious issues of race and illegitimacy'
The Sunday Times

By *Margaret Cezair-Thompson* and *available from Headline Review*

The True History of Paradise
The Pirate's Daughter

The True History of Paradise

Margaret Cezair-Thompson

headline
review

First published in paperback in Great Britain in 2008
by HEADLINE REVIEW
An imprint of HEADLINE PUBLISHING GROUP

First published in this paperback edition in Great Britain in 2009
by HEADLINE REVIEW
An imprint of HEADLINE PUBLISHING GROUP

I

Cataloguing in Publication Data is available from the British Library

ISBN 978 0 7553 4704 9

Typeset in Centaur by Avon DataSet Ltd, Bidford-on-Avon, Warwickshire

Printed and bound in Great Britain by Clays Ltd, St Ives plc

Headline's policy is to use papers that are natural, renewable and
recyclable products and made from wood grown in sustainable forests.
The logging and manufacturing processes are expected to conform
to the environmental regulations of the country of origin.

HEADLINE PUBLISHING GROUP
An Hachette UK Company
338 Euston Road
London NW1 3BH

www.headline.co.uk
www.hachettelivre.co.uk

For my parents,
Genevieve Cezair-Thompson and Dudley Thompson

Acknowledgments

I would like, first of all, to thank my devoted friend L. T. Tyler for his meticulous reading of every draft; and to acknowledge the late Alfred Kazin, critic, teacher, and mentor, whose passion for literature and for history continues to be a guiding force. I also wish to thank the following friends for their help and support: Judy Clain, Marilyn Sides, Amanda Clay Powers, Byron Loyd, Rufus Collins, Zia Jaffrey, Jesse Browner, Karen Williams, Marjorie and Mac Dobkin, Adlai and Judy Murdoch, Kathryn Lynch, Peter Josyph, Isobel Smith, Trudy Smith, and Crispin, my cat and companion extraordinaire. Also special thanks to Vicki Mutascio at Wellesley College, the staff of the Wellesley College library Special Collections for their help in finding rare historical writings on Jamaica, Ifeanyi Menkiti, Moyo Okediji, and former Wellesley students Ann Ochsendorf and Michelle Li.

The epigraph is taken from V. S. Naipaul's *The Middle Passage* (© 1962), and appears with permission.

Author's Note

While some of the events in this book are based on historical facts, and while many of the places described are real, this story is a work of fiction. Certain Jamaican words and phrases recur throughout the novel, and a glossary has been provided for those who might be unfamiliar with the dialect.

1494
Columbus
arrives in
'Xaymaca'

LANDING

Don Alejandro D'Costa
(1612–1661)

General Crawford——m.——Antonia D'Costa
(1630–1690)   (1641–1728)

Anne Gilbert——m.——William Crawford
of Monmouth   (1630–1700)
(1633–1694)

1655
English capture
Jamaica from
the Spanish

Rebecca Crawford——m.——Sir William Landing
(1682–1751)   (1680–1710)
                     Absentee planter

Frances Gilbert——m.——Edward Landing
(1707–1782)   (1704–1773)
                     Absentee planter

Lydia Watson——m.——William Landing——Stella
(1762–1800)   (1739–1809)   (c.1785–1831)
                   Planter   Ashanti slave

1831
The Christmas
Rebellion

William Landing II   Benjamin Landing——m.——Eliza Campbell
(1786–1844)   (1800–1860)   (1810–1883)
Planter   Free woman of color

1838
Emancipation

Lucy Williams——m.——**Moses Landing**
(1838–1901)   (1838–1865)
                     Baptist preacher

1865
Morant Bay
Rebellion

Gloria McDonald——m.——John Landing   **Mr Ho Sing**——m.——Pamela
(1867–1943)   (1865–1938)   (c.1866–1962)   (1875–1909)
                     Small farmer

George Landing——m.——Cherry Ho Sing
(1883–1951)   (1898–1979)
Bakery owner

Vincent Landing   Winston Landing   **Roy Landing**
(1915–1955)   (1922–)   (1918–1963)

1962
Jamaican
Independence

DARLING-STERN

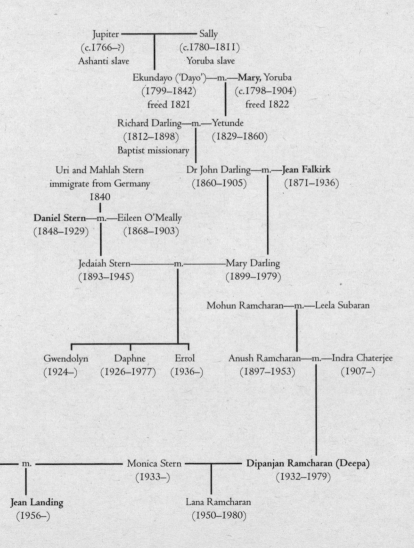

The history of these islands can never be satisfactorily told.
— V. S. Naipaul

Part One

I

It's Easter, and Jamaica is in a state of emergency.

A woman looks out from her veranda. Like most verandas on the island, this one has recently been enclosed in iron grillwork, and this grillwork also covers every window of the house. It's a hot, bright afternoon without breeze. Inside, a transistor radio is playing, and now and then she hears the dogs bark at a stray goat wandering past the garden gate. She wears a faded red housedress and diamond earrings. Her eyes are light brown, an unusual color for someone of such dark complexion ('Where dis black pickney come from?' her own mother asked, examining her at birth).

She lives on Bonnieview Terrace in the suburban highlands of Kingston. To her east are the Blue Mountains, air-blue at the horizon.

But that isn't where she looks now.

Spread out before her, between the broken circle of mountains and the sea, is the capital: corrugated tin roofs, leaning shacks, high-rise hotels, flamboyants she can name from this distance by their colors, the irregular geometry of city houses and lawns, swimming pools, great bushy treetops, animal and vehicle pausing and proceeding, and the corrugated tin roofs repeating themselves all the way out to the corrugated gray water of the harbor.

Since morning she has counted six fires. They continue

blazing, barely luminous on such a bright day, adding no noticeable heat to the already insufferable air.

She telephoned her mother earlier, having heard about a fire on Molynes Road not far from the family business. The moment the secretary answered Jean regretted making the call. Her mother was busy. 'She talkin' long distance. Hol' awn a minute—' Her mother's assistant, Miss Wong, shouted across the room to a delivery man, something about Easter buns. 'Jean, you can cawl back later?' 'It's all right,' Jean said, feeling pointless, realizing it was all business as usual at Island Bakery. Still, she fumbled on, saying she had heard on the radio about the fire across the road at Mr Mahfood's shop and—

Monica Landing got on the phone:

'What happen? You 'fraid?'

Monica has never been afraid of anything and is openly contemptuous of anyone who shows fear. She considers her daughter weak-minded, like her late husband, Roy Landing.

Roy died when Jean was seven. But memories of him surface so often that he continues to live with her in a bright, episodic way. One of his paintings – one of the few he ever finished – hangs in the National Gallery, and a story of his, published posthumously, turns up now and then in anthologies.

Another fire now blazes, near the university, just a few miles away. The firemen won't come. They've been on strike since the King Street fire, when they were shot at by men with machine guns.

You 'fraid?

She unlocks the veranda grillwork and walks down the long paved driveway to the gate. The gardener, Hilston, is late. She knows what he has to go through to get here from his part of town. Roadblocks and soldiers are the least of it; there's the danger of ambush on every unguarded lane. The city has been divided into war zones marked out by graffiti. The name

4

MANLEY or SEAGA, or letters, PNP or JLP, are painted on sidewalks and walls in their respective party colors, orange and green. No graffiti means you're in No Man Land and you take your chances.

She peers down the road, hoping to see Hilston making his way up the hill. A few days ago he told her about an incident he saw on his way to work.

'Dem chop down a man on Birdsucker Lane dis mawnin'.'

'What you mean "chop down"? They stab him?'

'No, ma'am. Chop 'im 'ead off clean-clean.'

He has never been this late. He must have decided it was too dangerous to go out.

She looks at the red ginger growing in front of the veranda. It's overgrown and is bringing lizards into the house. She has wanted for some time now to dig it up and plant roses there instead. Hilston said he would help her even though he has the day off. He has worked for them for twelve years and thinks of it as his garden.

Something must have happened, she thinks. He won't come.

He doesn't realize – how could he? she can barely admit it to herself – that the red ginger has to be done today because tomorrow, God willing and nothing standing in her way, she will leave this house, this garden, this city.

She goes back inside, locking the grillwork, securing the chain and padlock around it.

The kitchen smells of onions and thyme. Irene is marinating fish and listening to her radio drama, *Portia Faces Life*. The story has been on the air for as long as Jean can remember. She would like to tell Irene that she is going away, to sit and talk with her in this honest kitchen with the hum of the refrigerator and crackle of the transistor radio.

'Fire at the university,' Jean says.

'Eh-eh! Look like dem wan' bun down de whole country.'

Jean pours herself some lemonade, pink, sweet, and so cold it chills the glass.

'No sugar in de supermarket,' Irene drones.

A month ago, Irene sprained her ankle in a riot at the supermarket over a shortage of rice. 'Miss Jean,' she said, recounting the incident, 'me neva see anyting like dis from me bawn.'

She has worked for the Landings for almost twenty years and, in the face of the recent hardships, has finally assumed the culinary martyrdom to which she always aspired. Every dish of rice-an'-peas that reaches the family table is due to her cunning market strategy and fearlessness. She also provides an ongoing political commentary: 'Me neva see anyting like dis from me bawn. Prime Minista 'im na know people ha fe put food ina dem belly . . .'

Jean walks back through the living room. It's dark and cool this time of day. She's tempted to sit down, and, while she can, quietly take in the things around her. Only recently has she come to realize how much she likes this room with its gleaming wood floor and bright Armenian rugs, and her mother's piano, which is rarely played. But she is determined to dig up the red ginger; the roses are outside, ready to be planted. On her way out she passes the small brass table where the old family photograph stands, the faces in it distinct only in her mind since the morning sunlight has long been whitening away the features of all four – Roy, Monica, Jean, and Jean's sister, Lana.

She's on her knees pulling up the red ginger, the sun scorching the back of her neck, when her own voice jolts her: 'Why are you doing this? Why are you bothering with this *now*?'

She goes on digging, uprooting several plants at a time. The effort of her hands and the smell of the soil steady her. Upstairs in her bedroom drawer is a US passport with her photograph and someone else's name. She's leaving. She's made up her mind.

There's nothing more to think about, she tells herself and brushes the crawling ants from her arm.

She's still digging, and there's a heap of red, waxlike flowers beside her, when she hears the dogs come tearing around from the back of the house and sees the white pickup truck at the gate.

It's Paul, a day early. Has something happened?

'Jasper! Cleo! Down!' she shouts at the Alsatians, who carry on as they always do when anyone arrives, barking like crazy and lunging at the gate as if they're out to kill. She opens the gate so Paul can drive right up to the house. The dogs run barking alongside the vehicle, a compact Japanese model that cost him dearly in bribes, import taxes, and patience ('But in the long run is well worth it, man, the Japanese build these things to last'). The dogs quiet down, wagging their tails and sniffing the warm body of the pickup, waiting for Paul to get out.

Jean walks up the driveway. She has known Paul since childhood and it is to him that she's always turned for company, solace, safe passage. His habits are well known and dear to her. By now he's usually comfortably sitting on his favorite veranda chair or is inside chatting with Irene, helping himself to a cool drink from the refrigerator. It's odd that he's still sitting in the truck. Is he waiting for her? Does he want her to leave with him now?

One of the dogs begins to whine.

She reaches the top of the driveway, and Paul gets out of the truck. Something has happened.

He tells her, 'Lana is dead.'

2

They bury Lana the next morning because, as someone explains to Jean, burned bodies decompose quickly.

There will be no nine-night for Lana, no tambourines, drums, singing, fried fish, sugar cake, no sprinkling of rum, no glass of water left out at night for the spirit, no time to grieve or seek an explanation or explain. There's the immediate matter of shoes: The mortician needs a pair. Should they buy new ones? Should they cover her burned scalp with a scarf, her hands with gloves? What does it matter? The coffin will be closed. It matters to Lana. It would have mattered to Lana. They're not sure what tense to use now when they talk about her.

It's raining lightly. The funeral takes place in the city's Catholic cemetery at the shrine for the Blessed Virgin. Jean expected graffiti and smashed walls. She's surprised to see how well tended it is. So there's still something the gunmen respect and fear – duppy.

Jean watches her mother, mesmerized. Monica stands by the closed coffin of her elder daughter – the daughter she has not spoken to in over fifteen years – stroking the wood with a manicured, jeweled hand. Her black hat and veil cover her face completely. One of her nephews walks up and puts his arm around her. At his touch, she starts to cry. He says, 'Hush, Auntie, is awright,' and signals Father Thomas to begin.

*

Every funeral takes Jean back to that time in her great-grandfather's grocery shop when the family gathered to pay respects to the dying patriarch. She was only five, and yet the shop is one of her clearest memories: its smell of dried herring and carbolic soap, and its neatly arranged tins.

Mr Ho Sing (whom everyone, even his family, had always called Mr Ho Sing) was not ill, but his third wife had died a few months earlier in a car accident, and he decided it was time for him to go. He was thought to be about a hundred years old when he lay dying. He himself was unsure of his age. According to his indentured-servant papers, he was twenty when he came from China in 1884 on the *Prince Alexander*. He had been orphaned when his village was destroyed and had spent most of his childhood begging and stealing around the docks of Macao.

He wanted all his children, grandchildren, and great-grandchildren around him at the end. There must have been close to a hundred people there. He had never spoken much about China or been known to speak Chinese. But during those last, confused days he had been speaking, or rather grunting, some gibberish that led his children, who had never heard a word of Chinese, to believe he was speaking in his native tongue.

Mr Ho Sing had not written a will, and although he lived in three rooms at the back of the shop, he was a wealthy man. At the age of eighty or so, assured that his children were financially secure, he had finally indulged in the great, secret wish of his life: he had bought a racehorse, Marshal Bloom. At the height of his career, Marshal Bloom had been worth over fifty thousand pounds, and at the time of the old man's death, the horse's filly, Twice Bloom, was worth three or four times more.

The family contacted the Chinese Benevolent Association, which sent someone to translate Mr Ho Sing's dying words. He arrived, the Chinese Benevolent Association man, heavyset, wearing a white polyester suit and a flower-print shirt, looking, as Jean's grandmother said, 'like a real pappy show – a wonder if him can speak Chinese fe true.' He sat around all day with the Ho Sing men, whose preferred beverage, like his, was rum, and joined them in a few games of dominoes.

As relatives wandered in and out of the death room, Cherry, Jean's grandmother and Mr Ho Sing's only daughter, fussed around her father, fixing his pillows and shouting questions at him the way people do sometimes to people who speak another language.

'You feel awright, Mr Ho Sing? You need anyting?'

He waved his hand; it was an incomprehensible gesture.

'What about de horse?' Cherry shouted.

Mr Ho Sing looked startled: 'House?'

'Horse! Twice Bloom!'

Mr Ho Sing blinked and looked thoughtful. He seemed to understand and to be formulating a reply. The Chinese Benevolent Association man was hastened from the dominoes table to the bedside: 'Quick, man! Come quick! Mr Ho Sing wan' fe say someting.'

Mr Ho Sing recognized him and began to grunt.

The translator bent over the bed to listen more closely; Mr Ho Sing clutched the man's shirt.

'What 'im say? What 'im say?' everybody began asking.

The Chinese Benevolent Association man released himself from Mr Ho Sing's grasp and chuckled. He took a pack of cigarettes from his pocket and lit one, immensely pleased at being able to hold everyone in suspense.

'Him say, "Gimme one a dem Benson an' Hedges."'

A ripple went through the room, the hilarity of it all, the old man begging a cigarette, not in Chinese, but in the Jamaican patois that they all spoke. Even the small children tittered, without fully understanding, when they saw the grown-ups laughing.

And it was then, as he had his last smoke, that Mr Ho Sing looked at Jean. He had recognized very few people that day, and it was impossible to tell whether he recognized Jean, but for a moment she, out of all the children, held his attention. It might have been because she was the youngest, or it might have been that, among the varying shades of white, yellow, and brown faces – the mixed-up progeny of the old man's oceanic urges – Jean's was the only one that could unquestionably be called black.

Lana's funeral is barely a funeral. The priest didn't know her, but he knows Monica, and so he speaks vaguely about 'a mother's suffering' and reminds everyone to attend the Easter vigil later that day. Only a dozen or so mourners have turned up. There was not enough time to tell people. And there's another reason. Jean counts and names the missing: Roy, Daphne, Cherry, Mary, Deepa – they're gone. Skeletons and spirits.

It isn't until she's walking with the others, following the coffin to the grave, that Lana's death hits her: Her sister is being carried, yes, carried; Lana's footsteps are not among those she hears trampling the wet grass.

She smells something – perfume – and turns around to see who it's coming from. It's no one. It's a hedge of jasmine, the small white flowers drenched with rain, drooping from the branches.

It's over. Someone takes Jean's arm, leading her from the grave. She looks for Paul. He's way ahead of everyone, walking alone to his truck. She looks back and sees the gravedigger shoveling dirt into the open grave. Will Lana be all right? It seems wrong to leave her like that with a stranger. Again someone touches her arm, gently urging her to move forward.

The jasmine is there, involved, enclosing. She thinks it a lovely thing to plant among the dead.

3

She catches up with Paul after the funeral. 'Can we go now.' It's not a question.

'Now?'

She knows what he is thinking: Lana is dead, and one moves slowly after a death, even a sudden death, even in a state of emergency; there are steps, tolls; among other things, the after-funeral gathering at Bonnieview; Monica expects them; but most of all there is Lana's death, how it stuns them.

She gets in the truck; that is her answer.

'But – do you have everything you need?'

'Yes.' She hopes he does not see her trembling.

All she has with her is what she's wearing, a black funeral dress – how fitting, she thinks, to leave the country in mourning clothes – the fake passport, and two hundred US dollars. Alan told her to take as little as possible. All week she's been changing her mind about what constitutes 'as little as possible,' vacillating between the most sentimental and most practical things. She woke up one night from a dream in which she walked part-naked and barefoot through the streets of a new city. Kind strangers kept approaching her with things of hers that they had stumbled upon – among them, a favorite hand-painted perfume bottle. Waking, she realized that she would not be able to take any of the objects returned to her in the dream; they were all already lost or broken.

Paul will take her across the country to Trelawny, where he has a farm. From there she'll go to a small private airfield, then fly to Providenciales, where Alan will meet her.

The Kingston airport is too risky. A diplomat and his wife have been killed. The US embassy has been overrun, and immigration officers have become monsters. It's impossible for Jamaicans to leave, and nearly impossible for people with foreign passports. Besides, someone is bound to recognize Jean. The airport security officers know her; they've arranged VIP passes for her when she's been there on government business. Driving across the country on a holiday weekend will not arouse suspicion, even if she is recognized.

She is sure that the government will fall within days, if not hours. It doesn't seem as though things can get any worse ('Never say never and never say things can't get worse,' her maternal grandmother, Mary Darling, used to tell her). However things turn out here, it will be bad for her. She has no interest in politics, no ideology, no allegiances; but it doesn't matter; everyone has had to take sides. Lately, gunmen wearing no identifying party colors have been abducting children on their way from school, taking them to deserted places, and asking them which party their parents belong to. As if playing a kind of Russian roulette, the children have to choose. Jean has had nightmares where she gives the right answer to no avail because someone recognizes her: 'Is Roy Landing dawta, she a PNP,' or 'Is Monica Landing pickney, she a JLP.'

She looks at Paul. His face, as usual, reveals nothing; it belongs among those expressionless yet alert faces on ancient Egyptian papyri, the face of some palace servant with large tranquil eyes, an almost pointed chin, and skin that is smooth shaven, brown like an old penny. His looks have never changed; his tightly coiled hair has always been close cut like a smooth carpet, even during the proud years of Afros; he has never lost or gained weight as far as she could tell. She looks at his hands on the steering wheel, slender hands, not the kind one expects on a farmer.

'Lana is dead,' he said yesterday, so softly she wondered for a moment if she had heard correctly, but knew that she had. 'I just called the hospital, Jean' — The hospital? She had no idea Lana was in the hospital. — 'The nurse said she was gone. "Gone where?" I asked. I didn't think she could get up and leave so soon, but you know Lana. "Gone to the morgue," the nurse said, cold, just like that. Can you imagine?'

A police jeep overtakes them. The policemen sitting in the back look lethargic, their limbs overly relaxed, as if they aren't actually holding weapons.

'Can't get much hotter. Sorry 'bout the air conditioner.' It's the first thing he's said since they left the funeral.

A wasp flies into the truck, buzzes around Jean, then frantically attaches itself to the windshield. Paul pulls over. The wasp starts buzzing around her head again. She's allergic to insect stings.

'Hold still.' Paul's eyes follow the wasp.

The jeep turns around and heads back to them.

Paul squashes the wasp in a paper napkin.

Two policemen saunter over. They don't say anything; they just stare at them and at the truck with the authority they've been given to stare.

'Step out,' one of them tells Paul.

Jean tries not to look anxious.

'You too, miss. Come on, step out, step out.' The policeman gestures with his rifle. 'Stan' up over there!'

They stand at the side of the road as they're told.

The policemen in the back of the jeep assume an alertness they didn't have before. They look at Jean, then Paul, then back at Jean, trying to figure out their relationship. Lovers? Or brother and sister? It's a bold, libidinous look.

The two policemen search the truck. One of them looks through Jean's bag. She's glad she's got the US dollars hidden in her clothes. He opens the passport, then looks at Jean.

Paul decides it's time to say something: 'A wasp got in the truck, Sergeant. We just stopped to get it out. Didn't want to have an accident, you know.'

The sergeant looks at them as if he doesn't speak their language. There is no sign of comprehension at all. It's clear to Jean that they have no idea what they're looking for. They take the passport back to the jeep and discuss it with the others.

'Jesus Christ,' Paul mutters.

Two small boys appear and the policemen send them to the corner shop for cold sodas and patties. Jean and Paul find a shady place on the sidewalk and sit down.

Almost an hour later, the sergeant brings back the passport. 'Alright, g'wan.'

The police jeep takes off. Paul and Jean get back in the pickup. He sighs heavily. She's afraid he's going to back out, that he'll say, Let's turn back, this is too hard, too dangerous, but he starts up the engine and says with mock bravery, 'Forward.'

I might never see him again, she thinks. They will take the usual roads today, roads they've taken together many times, and that's why it feels so odd: Jean and Paul driving to the country — too familiar to be called a tradition, too enjoyable to be thought of as routine. From Kingston to Trelawny and back again, how many times, over how many years?

When she asked him a few days ago for his help, his unwavering yes assured her that she was doing the right thing. But is she? She is leaving her country. There are people here, souls, whom she never thought to be without. Her sister is dead; her dearest friend, Faye, lies in the hospital.

I can't change what has happened, she tells herself.

She is merely a passenger. After Paul there will be unknown

drivers, pilots, and finally, Alan, waiting for her. A passenger. She falls on the word like a penitent falling to her knees. It's out of her hands. Pray, pray for a safe passage.

Paul turns on the radio. The American evangelist Reverend Peyton F. Peyton reads from the Bible – 'My kingdom is not of this world.' Paul curses under his breath and changes stations. A cheerful locally made commercial for deodorant comes on, followed by another American evangelist. Paul turns off the radio.

The sky is clear and there is no sign of the morning's rain. In a matter of hours everything has become parched and dusty again. She looks at her city, pressing its image to her mind to last a lifetime, and as she does so it becomes a ghost city. In spite of everything, she loves it, the way one might love a dangerous, delinquent brother: the stunted shacks beside the affluent walls, the resilient street goats, and the bright hedges of bougainvillea. It's Easter weekend, the rain has stopped, and Kingston's million inhabitants all seem to be outdoors. Teenagers, liberated from school uniforms, walk the streets and shopping plazas, flaunting American styles. They seem oblivious to the state of emergency. Roadside higglers weigh, measure, and sell, in a disgruntled fashion, everything from hair ribbons to yams. A couple of dusty boys with sticks run through a gully, chasing a rat.

At a stoplight Jean watches a fire burning in an empty lot. A goat tethered to a nearby fence tugs at its rope. It is at a safe enough distance from the flames but is nevertheless in a panic. The one-legged beggar who works this intersection limps deftly between the cars. His hair is matted and his bare chest is encrusted with dried mud. He stinks so badly that drivers throw coins on the sidewalk to keep him at a distance. Jean is momentarily stunned by the odor as Paul hands him something through the window. He puts it in an old Ovaltine tin and limps away, but not fast enough. The light changes. 'Move outa de way, man!' 'Chu man! Move you rass!' The drivers cuss and blow their horns. The beggar hollers back and threatens them with his stick. A driver swerves out of his lane and rams into another car. Everything breaks down. The light changes again. She will be caught here forever, some random violence making her a ghost in the traffic of this embattled city. She is jolted as Paul steps hard on the gas and speeds through the amber light.

They come to a roadblock. Not police this time, soldiers. But whose soldiers: PNP? JLP? She never imagined living in a country where she wouldn't be able to trust the people in uniforms.

An army tank rests at an almost comical angle on the grassy roadside, its gun aimed point-blank at the blossoms of a poinciana. In the middle of the road, a man lies facedown with his hands bound. Another man with bound hands is being pushed into an army truck. Meanwhile, a Rastafarian carries on the business of selling Sno-Kones from a cart on which the words 'No Worry Jah' are painted.

A country bus approaches, blaring its horn and sending black fumes into the air. It leans precariously to one side, heavy with passengers, human and animal, mostly market women on their way to the city. The shouting begins. They're intrepid, the market women. They have a reputation for vile cursing. The soldiers know and don't want to be laughed at. So the minute the women begin – 'G'way soldier-bwoy! Chu! Mek we pass. You cock only good fe piss' – they let the bus through. Then to save face, they turn on 'No Worry Jah,' forcing him into the army truck. A group of ragged children descend on his Sno-Kone cart and drag it away.

A fat, sweaty soldier, who seems to be the only one actually checking vehicles, peers into Paul's truck and waves him on.

At the crossroads Jean sees three john-crows perched on a telephone pole, smelling new death in the new day. A sign says 'Spanish Town.' The old capital. It occurs to her that she is taking the same route the Spanish settlers took three hundred years ago when they fled from the English invaders.

The road cuts through flat, leafy fields that smell perpetually of burnt cane and molasses. They pass the old, defunct sugar mill; it used to be the first of many milestones for Jean when she and Lana were on their way back to boarding school after holidays. These fields were once part of a big slave plantation, and though cane still grows here, Jean has never seen anyone working in the fields. As a child she used to stare at the thick rows of cane and imagine slave ghosts, cutlasses in hand, working pitifully in a realm deaf to change.

A burnt-molasses wind blows through the truck. The scent of enearthed history breaks the air at every landmark, and every familiar thing is a landmark for her today, not in the way of an edifice proudly drawing attention to itself but with the air of a forgotten ruin.

They pass the Arawak museum, and she remembers a family outing. Lana had not wanted to go and showed it by lagging behind. Monica kept warning her: 'Stop draggin' you foot-bottom 'round de place.' Jean was scared by the silence, the sense of desolation around the broken, colorless pottery. The outing ended when Lana struck her forehead against a glass case displaying a stuffed iguana and the glass cracked. The two girls were shoved into the car, which in those days always smelled of sweet pastries. 'Why you cyaan behave youself?' Monica scolded Lana, then turned on Roy: 'We shoulda neva come here. All dis badda-badda over a dead iguana, you woulda tink is Queen Elizabet' crown.' The parents started arguing and Lana sang out: 'Is jus' a big fat lizard.' Roy said that the iguana had been in Jamaica long before Columbus and was a reminder of the island's early history. 'I can't stand history,' Lana said.

As a child, Jean found it hard to believe that the Arawaks, who gave the island its name, Xaymaca, Land of Many Rivers, had been wiped out by the Spaniards. She thought there had to be a few surviving Arawaks in remote caves and mountains, men and women who were centuries old in their ways. For years she played with an imaginary Arawak boy she called Kawara. He spoke the sleeping language of volcanoes, and showed her how to hunt iguanas, build canoes, and pound cassava as his people had done before the Spanish discovery. She smiles to herself, grateful for the memory. She hasn't thought about Kawara in years.

They're moving away from the hot, heavy air of the city, beginning their ascent into the green hills where there will be intervals of shade. She looks, as always, for the sign that says 'Dove Hill' at the bottom of a dirt road, a road they will not take today. Her father took her there on one of their many impromptu expeditions. They had to leave the car at the bottom of the steep road and walk. It was a burning-hot day and the climb was draining. 'Ancestry!' her father said when they reached the top of the hill. She had never heard the word before and thought he was talking about ants. Ahead were some broken walls in the overgrown foliage, with weeds and tufts of grass growing in their cracks. A plantation house had been there, he told her, and they might find buried silver. 'Come, I show you something.' He led her by the hand through the tall grasses alive with lizards and insects, to the gravestone of their ancestor General Crawford, who had fought against the Spanish for the island. This was a *true* story, he said. Not many people could trace their family history so far back. His great-aunt used to show off silver goblets engraved with the letter 'C' for Crawford. For Jean the persistent memory of that day was not General Crawford's grave or the hope of finding silver, but something she came upon all by herself. Walking back, she felt something hard under her feet. 'You find something, Jean?' They pushed aside the tall scratchy grass and saw a small gravestone. The words were whole and clear in the sun:

SUSANNAH CRAWFORD
1687–1692
beloved daughter and sister

She was also part of this true story, a white English girl who lived and died in this black slave country. Jean had no words at the time for how it captivated her, finding that buried daughter and sister among the green interstices of history.

They are climbing high into the mountains. Smoke rises from the forest like burnt offerings: allspice, cedar. Lana is dead.

Her sister's death saturates everything. It is crucial that she go now. It is terrible now to go. Should she let herself be run out of her own country, her sister unquiet and confused in the grave? No one is more confounded by Jean's decision to leave than Jean herself. She has always been of a slow, patient disposition.

She looks out the window at the mountains as if something out there will convince her to stay or encourage her to go.

Speak to me.

Silence. Trees. Green, irreverent green, overgrowing centuries of secret ruin.

Ghosts stand on the foothills of this journey. She smells their woody ancestral breath in the land's familiar crests and undulations. She has heard them all her life, these obstinate spirits, desperate to speak, to revise the broken grammar of their exits. They speak to her, Jean Landing, born in that audient hour before daylight broke on the nation, born into the knowledge of nation and prenation, the old noises of barracks, slave quarters, and steerage mingling in her ears with the newest sounds of self-rule. On verandas, in kitchens, in the old talk, in her waking reveries and anxious dreams, she has heard their stories.

4

Rebecca Landing (née Crawford)
1682–1751

I lived in Dove Hill until the age of eleven. I did not realize, at first, that I lived in a paradise as lovely as that one in the Bible. Flowers outbloomed the seasons; fruit ripened on the trees all year long. The rivers were cool and fresh. We were children of the sun, my sister, Susannah, and I. She was my sole companion. We were not permitted to play with the Negro children.

Like that legendary garden, ours had a Forbidden Tree. This tree bore neither fruit nor flower, only small black pods. Seba, our nurse, picked one of these pods one day, rubbed it vigorously against her apron, and placed it in my hand. It burned horribly, and I dropped it.

'Satan's eyeball,' Seba said. 'Hot like hell.'

Seba said this was the Punishment Tree, and if we misbehaved we would be lashed by tongues of fire like the wicked slaves who were punished there.

There were so many unforbidden pleasures on the plantation however, that this Satan tree (as Susannah and I often called it) held no temptation. I spent countless hours playing with Susannah and riding with my father. We rode daily to the river. The waters were considered excellent for our health, as they contained medicinal salts. We went to the river early, before it became too hot, to a special pool where white, lanternlike flowers provided privacy and shelter. The water was so pure that we saw our feet and the pebbles beneath. I must seem to you to be describing some fairy scene or peep into Elysium. It is possible, of course, that these images appear more radiant through the mist of remembered happiness, but I do not think so.

On the seventh day of June, sixteen hundred and ninety-two, the world changed.

We woke that day, before sunrise, dressed, and drank our morning chocolate in the darkness. It was the day before my tenth birthday. We were going to visit some friends of my parents and stop at my grandmother's home in Spanish Town on our return. She was to come back with us to Dove Hill for my birthday. There was to be a celebration. The Negroes would be given a half-day holiday, and my father had promised them a hog and some rum. Dove Hill had been under a cloud for several weeks and it was hoped that this celebration would lift all our spirits.

There had been a punishment: A slave had been whipped to death. I cannot remember what his crime was, but it must have been abominable because for several days there had been much talk about it among my father and his friends. I heard him say that it was a miserable thing to have to lose a whole man, but in the long run better than inviting insurrection. This punishment, while merely inflicting wounds of a corporeal nature upon the Negro, sorely affected the minds and domestic tranquillity of our family. You see, I accidentally witnessed the punishment. The slave's face impressed itself upon my inward eye and caused me great distress. I had seen that pitiful expression before, in illustrations of the Scriptures. To think that a Negro, a slave, who was by no means innocent, should remind me of our Lord's suffering! My mother scolded Seba for not protecting me from that brutal sight. My father disagreed with my mother and reminded her that I was not an English girl but a Creole like him and had sooner or later to become accustomed to such things. Their contrasting views, as usual, erupted in bitter arguments which threw the entire household into disturbance.

But this trouble was now behind us, and the plans for my birthday had an uplifting effect upon us. I was especially looking forward to seeing Nana, my father's mother.

It was uncommonly hot for that time of day, and within hours the sky was glowing red. We feared a hurricane, but were already too far on our journey to turn back.

At Caymanas, we stopped at a public house for some light refreshment while my father went off on some business. It was a great relief for my mother, Susannah, and me to escape the suffocating heat. Susannah had been irritable all morning, whimpering and insisting that my mother hold her like a baby even though she was five years old.

The owner of the inn, a Mulatto woman, was very talkative. She lavished many compliments upon our pretty Susannah. I was accustomed to being excluded from such compliments, being quite plain to begin with, and furthermore having the disadvantage of being born with my eyes severely crossed. Persons were inclined to turn their gaze from me, and I understood that it was disconcerting for them not to know whether I was looking at or beside them. She said her daughter had just given birth to a son and was having a difficult lying-in. There were several nearly White children around who were apparently the Mulatto's grandchildren. She served us limeade, and she and my mother spoke about birthing, or rather, the woman spoke to my mother. She said, 'It is astonishing, ma'am, how fast the Negro gals on the island do breed and how quickly they recover from their lying-in.' It was quite different with the Colored ladies, she said. My mother said that she had heard physicians make similar observations.

You might think it strange that I should remember something so trivial as this, but it was the last morsel of ordinary life to gain my attention before the extraordinary occurred.

First there was a deep, terrible rumbling, which knocked over the pitcher and glasses. Then the building shook suddenly and with such force that we were thrown from our chairs. The walls crumbled. The rumbling sounded like thunder breaking from the bowels of the earth, a sound so hellish that I knew whatever calamity had befallen us was being visited upon the entire land. My mother held us tightly, shielding us as well as she could. Susannah would not stop screaming, and I was certain that we would die.

I do not know how long we remained like that, and to this day, I cannot understand how or why we were spared. The Mulatto woman and children were struck by the falling roof and buried in the rubble. My father appeared, and seeing him, my mother began to scream like Susannah.

Outside it was far worse. The world appeared to be breaking into many pieces. The sky was dark, yet there were no clouds. Rocks and trees fell before us. Fires raged everywhere. We drove through the wreckage, hurrying first in one direction and then another. My father was for going out to shore, to Port Royal. My mother felt it safer to go inland, to Spanish Town. The thunder was mortifying and came from above and below. But louder still, and unforgettable, was Susannah's screaming.

After some time of speeding back and forth directionless, we stopped at a point of elevation. From there we were able to look out to sea. Oh, it was horrifying. Port Royal sank before our very eyes. Houses, ships, and living creatures dashed against each other. Everything fell into the roaring fire. Even the sea appeared to be on fire. And though it seems impossible, I heard human cries in the distance.

We eventually reached Spanish Town. The destruction was not so great there, though fires had broken out in many places and the inhabitants were running in great alarm through the streets. A tree had fallen upon the roof of my grandmother's house but the house itself stood firm. Nonetheless, we felt it safer to take shelter outdoors in a shed where she kept rabbits.

My father left us in order to search for his cousin, Pietra, who lived in Port Royal, though my mother pleaded with him not to go and threw herself upon him with such violence that I also began to plead and cry.

He came back days later, without his cousin. How he managed to escape, and exactly what he saw there, I can only imagine from the ghastly descriptions others have given, for my father never spoke of it. Port Royal, where so many had been made rich, was made desolate in a day. I heard that as the famous city sank, many of the doomed inhabitants ran about wildly, stealing whatever they could get their hands on, stabbing, shooting, and even strangling anyone who stood in their way.

We remained with my grandmother for several weeks because the roads to Dove Hill were impassable and because my father left us again to search for his cousin. By the time he rejoined us, our Susannah had died of the dengue fever which had spread throughout the land for lack of clean water.

When we returned to Dove Hill we were astonished to see that our home was intact, for all we had heard were stories of death and ruin. The plantation of our cousins in St Ann had washed out to sea and the entire family had drowned.

It was not until I went riding with my father the following day that I saw what the earthquake had done to our plantation. Much of our livestock had disappeared or been killed, many trees uprooted, and a good number of our slaves had run away. Strangest of all, the river, our river, was nowhere to be found. We rode across the altered countryside, searching for it. We finally came to a muddy pool whirling between large rocks. That was what was left of our river! Rocks and trees had tumbled from the hills, changing its course and nature forever.

I had thought till then that rivers outlived men. But here I saw dry land where there had been water, rock where there had been forest, and valleys where there had been hills.

My father changed. He became unkempt and grew a savage beard. He would ride about the plantation at strange hours of the night, no longer like a master but a trapped animal. Worst of all, he stopped speaking to us. He stared through me at times as though he had forgotten who I was. My mother could not be comforted. She, too, seemed at times to forget who I was. I came to prefer her phases of forgetfulness to those of recognition. For when she remembered me, she would clutch me in a manner that frightened me. Days passed without my talking to a living creature or hearing the talk of others. My parents had become strangers to each other and to the world, their souls unhinged by their tragedy.

The slaves were neglected, and they in turn neglected their work. I was served my meals on filthy dishes, and oftentimes not fed at all. The Negroes laughed at me and talked about how ugly I was. Food, clean clothes, baths, all depended on Seba's feeling benevolent toward me. The house was dark because the slaves stole our lamps and our candles, and I was afraid to fall asleep. I missed my sister. I was so miserable that I prayed to die, too.

One night my father found me by the Punishment Tree. I must have cried myself to sleep there, because I only dimly remember him picking me up and carrying me into the house. After that, Nana came to stay with us. She sold Seba, who had taken over the household during my mother's infirmity and had, as Nana said, 'become too big for her britches.' The house was bright and clean again. Nana took good care of me and talked to me. But she could not stay forever. It was decided that my mother and I would go to England.

We went to live with her brother and his wife, the Gilberts of Monmouth. Immediately upon arriving, my mother went to bed and never got up again. I later learned she had become overly reliant on opium. I learned something else, the full cause of her desolation: she blamed my father for Susannah's death. She could not forgive him for abandoning us in Spanish Town while he searched for his cousin, Pietra. Pietra had been his mistress for many years, even before his marriage. My mother knew. Everyone in Jamaica knew — even the slaves knew — and their knowing humiliated her. Her family, when they learned, turned against him. His name was not spoken except by the gossiping servants. And how they gossiped! They said my father's mistress had put a West Indian curse on my mother. Another rumor had it that disgruntled slaves had worked obeah spells on my poor mother. I, too, began to suspect these things were true, for the physicians could find no cause for my mother's illness, and she grew weaker and died within a year. After her death I asked if I might return to my grandmother in Jamaica, but I was made to understand that even if these tragedies had not occurred, it had been my mother's wish for me to live in England once I was of a certain age. Few white families remained long in the colonies, my father's family being a great exception. The climate was considered particularly brutal for females.

My father came only once to England to see me, and that was at my request, for my wedding. I admit that I, too, had borne some anger toward him, but I could not erase my early, happy memories of him. There were stories that he had grown savage and lunatic and it had been hoped, among my mother's family, that he would not respond to my invitation. But he did. Neither savage nor madman was he, but obviously ill. He died on his way back to Jamaica.

Though I lived in England most of my life, I remained a Jamaican lady. I received letters regularly from my Nana till the day she died, and she alone kept the island alive in me. My uncle and aunt felt obliged to eradicate my early memories, and to reform me into an English girl. They had no children of their own and were extremely kind to me. But at the slightest mention of my childhood in the colony, this saintly couple would appear so distressed that I avoided the subject in their company. The subject of my West India inheritance was not so easily avoided. After my father died I inherited the sugar estate at Dove Hill and the large income from my late cousins in St Ann. At the age of seventeen, I was heiress to a great West India fortune. My husband, Sir William Landing, became a powerful man with the wealth I brought him. For that, at least, he showed gratitude.

My husband's family, indeed many in England, scorned me, not only because I was a Creole, but because my father's mother was a Spanish Jew. I was often questioned about the West Indies, but I soon discovered that these interrogators had no interest in my answers. They merely wanted to display their own knowledge of the colonies.

— I've heard the air is so unhealthy that our English women cannot survive there long.

— And, tell me, for I find it too ghastly to be true, do those black devils still try to eat each other on occasion?

— B'Jesus! Hurricanes, snakes, and fevers; you are most fortunate to be here, Miss Crawford!

It may have been my skewed eyes that confused people and made them converse with me as though I were not actually present. I became a quiet person filled with uneasy and unspoken thoughts.

My grandmother had given me Mimba, a Quadroon girl my own age, as a parting gift. Mimba stayed with me many years, a faithful servant and my only friend. When I first arrived in Monmouth she accompanied me everywhere. Her skin looked white but her lips were large and she had Negro hair. To my horror, people who had not yet made my acquaintance often mistook her for me. There is a preposterous idea among the English that the climate in the colonies alters Whites who are born there and causes such modification of feature that we are practically become Darkies.

Upon meeting me, a friend of my uncle's, a Mr Southerne, exclaimed: 'Why, she's as pale as any English girl,' as if he had expected a blackamoor! This same Mr Southerne wrote a play about Suriname, based on Mrs Behn's book *which I did not read. It is supposed to be a True History based upon some time that she spent in the colony. I am certain every word is a lie. I have never read a true thing in any book except for Mr Defoe's* Moll Flanders.

I have read widely on the subject of the West Indies. Indeed, I am considered bookish. I search for facts equal to my memories, and I search in vain. I read in one of these books, which are called Histories, that Creole women are cruel and that they indulge themselves in licentious amours. These books hurt me. They are cracked mirrors which break the paradise in my mind.

My grandmother, Antonia D'Costa Crawford, was a true Creole. No one remembers her or her stories. The forest has eaten her grave. Her father, Don Alejandro D'Costa, a converted Jew, brought twenty horses and fifteen mares from Spain. In spite of his great wealth and his conversion, the Catholics treated him with disdain. He welcomed the English invaders, among them General Crawford my grandfather. Don Alejandro informed them of a counterattack planned by the Spanish. Even so, the English might have confiscated his land and horses had it not been for General Crawford, who had fallen in love with Antonia. She became his wife at fifteen. He was kind to her except in one respect: He was a Puritan and would not allow her or their children to worship as Catholics, and so she was forced to give up her religion for the second time.

Nana told me that it had dismayed her parents to see her embrace the Catholic faith so devoutly. In turn, it broke her heart to deny her children her own beliefs. 'My soul has been divided by a sword,' she told me. 'I have twice lost my religion.' I thought to lose something meant simply to search for it until it was found — like a lost glove — and I remember saying to her, 'Don't worry, Nana, we shall soon find it again.'

My grandfather the General did not tell me stories, though I am sure he had many to tell. He read to us and recited verses:

> *What should we do but sing His praise*
> *That led us through the Watery Maze*

He died at the hands of rebellious slaves on a neighboring plantation. My uncle and aunt Gilbert did not believe this or the other things I told them. They said I had a morbid imagination.

The history of our island is a history of hell. It is also a history of grace terrestrial. I lived in a brightness beyond description, and did not know true darkness until I came here.

I alone survived my family's hardships, and being alone, I was without commiseration. When I came here, no one cared to hear my story. It was uncomely. So was I. I learned my own way of seeing, like one who is blind. I performed the part of an odd, quiet woman, and performed it to everyone's satisfaction. When others slept, I was awake; when they woke, they found me quietly occupied. I took walks by myself. I read and sewed or sat in the garden with my own self for company. I was not missed. I have never been missed. I had all the manners and necessities of other women of my society, yet I was without society.

I was a widow and an old woman at the age of twenty-eight. After my husband died I drew the curtains around myself. I did not follow my mother's way and take to bed. I simply surrendered to that brute unhappiness which had always been close at hand. I no longer made the effort to appear civil, for by then I loathed civilization from the bottom of my heart. Solitude, after a while, becomes the worst kind of savagery.

I never returned to Jamaica. No one in our family visited Dove Hill for years. A manager was engaged to look after the plantation. In the year seventeen hundred and twenty-eight, my son, Edward, visited the island and met his great-grandmother, my Nana, before she died. When he returned, he brought back a Mustee, a pretty girl, to be a servant for his wife. I am no fool and can see that the wench has the face of a Crawford. However, I do not pass judgement. It is possibly God's plan to whiten the Africans and so better their race. Though this means our men fall to degeneracy, we must accept, as Sarah accepted the Egyptian handmaiden, Hagar. I have often felt that it might one day be said of me, as it was said of that other Rebecca in the Bible: 'Two nations are in thy womb, and two manner of people shall be separated from thy bowels,' for I see in the face of my son the father both of free men and of slaves.

That day in Spanish Town as we waited for the earthquake to end its devastation, I heard someone cry: 'Who has cursed us? Who has cursed this land?' God must indeed have a special purpose for us and for our seed to have dragged us through such salamandrine fire.

Like my grandmother, I remained a Jamaican lady, a true Creole. My soul, too, was divided by a sword. That day we left for England the ship whistled so loudly it drowned out my cries.

Know what I know: Time has shaped you from a hundred histories which will never be told; our voices are not welcome among the living. Stay and die there, unaccounted for. Or escape, live, and be silent among the migratory whose lives are like a discontinued letter. What do you expect? What consolation do you seek from the eternally disconsolate?

5

'. . . a mistake.' Paul startles her.

She feels as if she's been woken from the anxious soliloquy of a dream. What does he mean?

They cross Flat Bridge. The Rio Cobre is high from the rain, and the current sweeps branches and other broken things violently downriver. Some women sell fruit and roast corn along the roadside. Paul pulls over.

'Want anything?'

'No.'

The women rush. They all have the same kind of fruit in their baskets, making it impossible to choose. One overzealous woman splits a pineapple down the center to show how ripe it is.

'Chu man!' Paul reprimands her. 'Who tell you fe cut it? Is not pineapple I want, is star-apple. Awright, awright. Gimme de pineapple. How much you want fe it?'

The woman begins peeling the pineapple while he bargains with the others. He hands Jean a naseberry and she bites into its flesh, sweet, brown, and granular like brown sugar.

Paul walks over to the woman roasting corn. 'A mistake,' he said and his saying it had seemed to her like something involuntary, like a sea creature gulping air, not the beginning of a conversation. She believes he was talking about Lana. She watches him standing over the coal pot. The smells of ripe fruit

31

and burning coal and the clean face of the world around her don't suggest anything hidden or terrible; but Paul's words do. Suddenly she feels as if she's going in the wrong direction; not a geographical wrongness, but as if she's being pulled back to some inexorable sadness. What happened to Lana? It's like a question blurted out in a nightmare; she wants to ask but is afraid to.

He comes back, biting into the steaming corn, and starts the pickup. Two army trucks come round the corner, speeding downhill one after the other, and Paul has to pull over as far as possible. 'Dem crazy like hell,' he mutters to himself.

Jean glances at him. He has avoided looking at her all morning like someone who cannot trust himself with a lie.

'What happened to Lana?'

'You tell me,' he says bitterly. 'You're her family.'

6

They probably did seem like a family when Paul first met them, the widow, Monica, and her two daughters. But she would have to go much further back to explain the unruly kinship.

Lana was five when she discovered that Monica was her mother. Until then she had assumed her mother was the woman she called Ma, her maternal grandmother, Mary Darling. She lived with Mary in a country village called New Hope. Monica visited on weekends. It was on one of those visits, while they were having dinner, that Lana found out. Monica told her to take her elbows off the table.

'Why?'

'Because I'm your mother and I say so.'

Monica Darling-Stern was seventeen when Lana was born and there was no hope of her marrying Lana's father, Dipanjan Ramcharan, known as Deepa. She named the baby after Lana Turner, the movie star, whom she herself resembled and whom she did her best to continue resembling way into middle age, copying Turner's wavy hairstyle and once even bleaching her hair blond.

Monica had always felt trapped in New Hope. So had her sisters, Gwen and Daphne. They were yard poor — they had food from their own small yard and were never hungry. What their mother went through to school and clothe them was never talked about. Not even by Daphne, who would talk about anything, especially when she was drunk. They were full of family pride and race pride, those three girls, particularly Monica.

The girls shared a single bed in the tiny three-room cottage. Their brother, Errol, the youngest, had a room to himself. The cottage had been built in the previous century by an emancipated slave who had also given the village its name. Except for the recent addition of electricity, there were no modern conveniences. They collected rainwater daily from a nearby catchment, and there was a pit toilet outside in a shed with a corrugated tin roof; it stood next to a mango tree which dropped its fruit on the roof with a loud clang.

The children were up before sunrise to do housework and yard work before they went to school. Monica would wake up earlier than her sisters so she could lie undisturbed and daydream. She daydreamed about the Indian boy, Deepa, who took piano lessons on the same day she did and who always walked her partway home. The piano, which had belonged to Mary's mother, was the most important thing in the cottage. It distinguished them from the other people in New Hope and reminded them and everyone else that they were the grandchildren of Dr John Darling and his revered wife, Jean Falkirk Darling. Once a year, on Empire Day, Mary invited all the children of New Hope to the cottage, handed out sweets, and played the piano while everyone sang 'God Save the King.' Deepa was not among them. He lived in his Hindu family's compound and was not supposed to mix with the local children.

The girls harbored secret memories of their father, Jedaiah Stern, and talked often among themselves of the way they had lived before their parents' separation. Errol was too young to remember. They had been happy in the town of Black River, a proper town, not as big as Kingston, but with glass-fronted stores and a cinema. Their house had been bigger, with a proper indoor bathroom, and their father used to take them for a drive every Sunday in his motorcar. They remembered with bitterness the day their mother left Jedaiah and brought them to New Hope, a place on a country back road where cars never stopped.

They hated the six-mile walk to school with the other children, whom they secretly called Blackies. The Sterns stood apart partly because they wanted to and partly because they just did. They were 'fair-skinned' and had 'good hair' like White people, and they spoke English better than the others did. They were the only children who wore shoes every day, not just on Sundays.

Once a week they had to suffer the humiliation of walking with produce on their heads, like common higglers, carrying yams, avocados, and other provisions to Miss Drusilla, their mother's friend, who lived near the school and cooked lunch for them.

Mary knew her children were vain, and though she was entirely without pretensions herself she didn't begrudge them their elevated opinion of themselves. She managed to find the money to send Monica for piano lessons, and to send all four of them for extra lessons in reading and arithmetic with Mr Peartree, the school's headmaster. Once a month she put them on the bus to Black River and gave them a shilling each to spend at the cinema.

The girls got out of New Hope as fast as they could. Gwen met a young country dentist, married him, and eventually moved to Kingston. Monica left Lana with her mother and moved to the city of Mandeville about fifty miles away. She got a job as a salesclerk in a shoe store, took typing classes, and after completing the course began working at a bauxite mining company.

Daphne went farthest of all – first to Kingston, where she worked at the radio station, then to London on a broadcasting scholarship. She stayed for six years, wrote radio plays for the BBC, and with her striking looks and generous nature she found herself at the center of a smart, lively group of West Indian émigrés. At some point she fell in love with Peter, an artist from the Dutch Antilles, got pregnant, married him, then realized she had made a terrible mistake. The separation was brutal and draining; she grew to hate London and was relieved to go back to Jamaica with her daughter, Astrid.

In Kingston, Daphne's old exuberance returned. She started a small press, Kyari, which published the island's first arts magazine. She produced radio shows and became one of the founders of the National Theatre. Like her old flat in London, her pink-walled house on Jacaranda Road drew the island's writers, artists, and politicians. People would say to one another, 'See you later at Jacaranda,' or 'I goin' meet the fellows over by Daphne.' She was famous for her good country cooking – curry goat, mackerel-an'-banana, stew peas. She had a well-stocked bar; in fact, she was hardly ever without a glass of rum and Coke in her hand. There was a never-ending supply of gossip at Daphne's, and best of all there was Daphne herself, who was a great mimic and teller of shocking tales.

It was the 1950s, and Jamaicans were talking about seeking independence from Britain. A lot of that talk went on at Daphne's. Many felt Jamaica should be part of a West Indian Federation with the other English-speaking islands. But others were against this; they felt that the smaller islands would hold Jamaica back, and that it would be better for the country to seek its own sovereignty.

Roy Landing was one of the regulars at Daphne's. He had been a fighter pilot in World War II and had seen quite a bit of the world. After the war he took some journalism courses in England, then traveled through Africa as a freelance reporter for a British leftist paper. Back in Jamaica he worked variously as a teacher, painter, journalist, and labor activist, and once as a banana picker.

Roy's two older brothers were also regulars at Daphne's. Vincent, the oldest, was a quiet man who ran the family bakery. He was exceptionally handsome; people compared him to Clark Gable, and women fell for him easily, but he took his marriage vows seriously. Roy, who was not as handsome, was the womanizer. Winston, the other brother, owned a coffee farm in the country and was involved with the Jamaica Labour Party, Bustamante's party. He was adamantly against Federation. Roy was for it, and he was a founding member of Norman Manley's party, the People's National Party. When the two brothers were at Daphne's there was rambunctious arguing that went on till three and four in the morning. One night the shouting was so loud the neighbors called the police; they were sure someone was being murdered. This kind of carrying-on was typical at Daphne's. When Martin Luther King, Jr, was assassinated there were people in Kingston who learned about it from the shouts coming from Daphne's house, with Daphne's voice louder than all the rest: 'Dem kill Martin Luther King! Oh, Lawd, dem kill him!'

Daphne invited Monica to Kingston, and Roy fell for her right away. Daphne, who had seen him with his arms around countless women, noted that this was no mere flirtation: Roy directed all his energies toward courting Monica and convincing her to be his wife. To Daphne's surprise, Monica wouldn't take him seriously, even though she was desperate for a husband and Roy's family had money.

Monica thought he was ridiculous. He begged her to let him paint her and spoke rapturously about her racial heritage and Nubian limbs. In the corner of a sketch that he drew of her, he wrote: 'Monica, a West Indian beauty, burnished by centuries of fiery couplings of Africans and Europeans.' He didn't realize that the race pride of the Sterns, especially Monica, was based on how White they thought they looked. Monica's father was of German descent; her maternal grandmother was *pure* White, from Scotland. Monica didn't think there was anything beautiful about Africans, and she didn't want to hear about Nubian anything in her bone structure. As far as she was concerned, her good looks came from centuries of washing Black people out of the family's blood.

Monica told Daphne, 'Roy too dark-skin for me.'

His mother was half-Chinese, but his father was Black, and Roy took after him. Vincent, with his wavy hair and light complexion, was the one she had her eye on. Too bad Vincent was married. She encouraged Roy so that she could see more of his brother. Within weeks she had grown so close to the Landings that she moved to Kingston and got a job in the family business.

Roy's father, George Landing, started the wholesale and retail bakery in 1910 as a small country business. He was so enterprising, the family boasted, that before he had the money for a delivery van, he used to deliver bread and cakes on his bicycle. By the 1950s the business had moved to the capital and supplied bread to more than half the island's population. Vincent was in charge of the business. Monica became his secretary.

A month after meeting her, Roy proposed to Monica. She asked for time to decide. She hadn't yet told him about Lana. But that wasn't the reason for her hesitation. She wanted Vincent, and she thought she could get him. She had no qualms about breaking up his marriage to Enid, a woman he had known since the age of fourteen and with whom he had three sons. Vincent was not unaffected by Monica's beauty. As a married man he had been attracted to women before, but never to anyone who worked by his side and took a daily interest in him and his business, and not to anyone as compelling as Monica. Honest, quiet Vincent became so overwrought by his feelings about Monica that he did an uncharacteristic thing; he confided in his friend Daphne. He didn't want to leave his wife, but was so tantalized by Monica that he considered having an affair with her. Monica also confided in Daphne: Vincent was handsome, kind, and financially sound, the kind of husband she deserved, and she was close to getting him.

One morning, Monica dressed for work in her favorite brown skirt, which showed off her slim waist and womanly hips. She pinned a lovely brooch on her blouse and slipped on her brown-and-tan high heels. On her way, she stopped to pick up some office supplies, so she got to the bakery later than usual. When she arrived, the ambulance had come and gone. Vincent was dead. He had been electrocuted while trying to fix the faulty wiring in one of the new electric ovens.

Monica married Roy a month later, and immediately became pregnant. Neither Roy nor Winston was interested in running the bakery. Monica took over.

She was certain that the baby would be a boy, and she picked a name for him, John Anthony. The day she went into labor, the contractions stopped altogether; her body locked tight, and Jean had to be delivered by cesarean. To add to her disappointment, the baby girl was not, in Monica's opinion, beautiful. She was scrawny and dark, darker than anyone in Monica's family, and she had a deformity: a strange flap of skin on the side of her head that looked like a third ear.

'She'll be a musician,' someone said.

'A poet,' said another.

'She'll hear the voice of God.'

The doctor removed it.

On the whole, Monica found babies disgusting – their dribbling, their screaming, and, worst of all, their smells. She had caught chickenpox from Lana when Lana was a baby and since then had worried about catching diseases from children. The chickenpox had left faint scars on one side of her face; they could not be seen except under close scrutiny, but she was self-conscious about them. She always turned that side away from the camera and did not give up hope that the scars would disappear with the daily application of bleaching cream and cocoa fat.

From the first moment he saw her, Jean was the joy of her father's life. His feeling for her surprised him because he had not especially cared about having children. He found himself enthralled with each pleasure and distaste she expressed in her comical, inarticulate gestures. He lit her imagination with stories, took her along with him almost everywhere he went, never tired of showing her things, and taught her, with barely containable zeal, how to read and write long before other children her own age.

Family. She might begin here: her father leaning over her shoulder one afternoon, watching her write out the letters in red crayon, the way he had taught her, JEAN LANDING, 13 BELMONT ROAD, the sunlight streaming in through the windows around them. She looks back often on that day and sees its radiance like a marker in the life of her soul, and knows there was a time when she experienced the grace of a father, without variableness or shadow or turning.

7

We weren't that close, Jean thinks of telling Paul. It is a comfortless thought, made worse by Lana's death. She wants to say, 'You were closer to her than I was,' but there is no way of saying it that would not sound accusing. She is aware of a breach between them, and the breach is Lana.

She thinks about Alan, whom she doesn't feel that close to, but to whom she can admit anything, including a certain want of feeling toward him. Like a weatherbeaten sailor, he has seen and heard too much to be hurt by her honest admissions; she is the best thing life has offered his worn-out heart. 'I'll meet you in Providenciales,' he said. Syllables of hope.

She wants Paul to understand: 'Lana and I were never close.'

8

Visiting her grandmother at New Hope, Jean shared a bed with an older girl named Lana. She felt that they must be related because Lana called Grandma Darling 'Ma.' Jean was five, and it was her first time away from home. She had cried a little the first day because she missed her father, but soon got over her homesickness. There was so much to do and see in the country, and other children to play with. Along with Lana, there were Marcia, Uncle Errol's daughter, and Linette, a skinny girl who suffered from intestinal parasites and skin infections. Marcia said Linette was her half-sister, that she was Uncle Errol's 'outside child.' Jean imagined Linette living in the backyard of Uncle Errol's house like a servant or a dog.

'You mean she stays in the maid's room?'

'She don't live with us. She live with her own mother.'

Lana, being the oldest, took charge. The little girls were in awe of her. She was beautiful beyond belief, with long, shiny black hair; the younger girls fought for the chance to play with it and brush it. And Lana knew a lot of things: how to catch crayfish in the river, and how to pickle green mangoes. She was Grandma Darling's favorite, but that didn't mean she was spoiled. Lana worked hard to please Mary. She woke at dawn and her sweet, girlish voice could be heard rousing the chickens and goats, and giving orders to Etty, the girl who helped with the cooking and cleaning. By the time the others were awake,

Lana had organized breakfast: steaming cornmeal porridge and cocoa. She loved housework. It made her feel grown-up. She gave the smaller children tasks, teaching them how to grate coconuts and how to lay clothes out in the sun to bleach them.

'I'm the mother,' she told them, 'you're my children. You and you. Not you, Linette, you full a ringworm an' you smell bad.'

It was the ointment Mary Darling put on her skin that smelled bad. Strangely, Linette took these insults without any sign of discomfort. They called her 'chupid' and 'fool-fool' and 'coco-head' all day long, and she still wanted to hang around them. Every now and then Lana would have a surge of sympathy and would let Linette brush her hair.

The hair-brushing always took place in front of an old-fashioned dressing table with a round mirror and a cushioned stool. Mary had given the dressing table to Lana, and Lana was as proud of this piece of furniture as she was about herself. She had arranged her hairbrush, talcum powder, and ornaments on it around a starched white lace doily. She kept everything in impeccable order and would notice a speck of talcum powder on the shiny wood. The things on the dressing table fascinated Jean – in particular, a tiny perfume bottle painted with purple flowers. It was empty and purely decorative. Lana caught her admiring it one day, and Jean almost dropped it in fright.

'You like that?'

Jean wasn't sure how to respond. Lana was so unpredictable.

'Is ole. I don't like it,' Lana said. 'You can have it.'

When Roy came to take Jean home, Lana and the dressing table went with them.

After a few weeks, Jean asked her father when Lana would be leaving. Roy said that Lana would live with them from now on, whenever she was on holiday from boarding school. He saw her confusion and went on to explain that although he was not Lana's father, Monica was Lana's mother, and that made Jean

Lana's half-sister. That was when Jean realized – though it was hard to believe – that Lana, imperious Lana, was an outside child.

It was Roy who pressed to have Lana live with them. Monica had been uncertain; the circumstances of Lana's birth still burned her. But she was soon happy with the arrangement. She was proud of her eldest daughter's beauty. No one else in the family – in fact, very few on the island – had such long, straight hair, and pretty movie-star features. Lana's fair complexion delighted Monica: just brown enough not to be considered pure white.

Lana made herself supremely useful to Monica, taking charge of all the household business just as she had for Mary Darling. She could iron a shirt to perfection in a few minutes; she cleaned, cooked, and polished better than any of the servants; the servants were more afraid of her than they were of Monica. Once, she took it upon herself to dismiss the washerwoman. 'She slovenly,' Lana said.

Her concern with grooming and cleanliness had a ferocious quality. Roy said it was her Hindu blood. She often grabbed hold of Jean's hands to check her fingernails. 'Nasty-nasty,' she'd say if she found dirt under them. In restaurants she checked under the plates and glasses.

'But we don't eat off the bottom of the plate,' Jean said.

'Nasty somewhere, you nasty everywhere,' Lana replied.

Monica depended on her for manicures, eyebrow tweezing, hairsetting, and hairdos. They spent a lot of time together in front of dressing table mirrors primping and preening, looking at themselves, at each other, and at themselves in each other.

But they did not quite trust each other.

On Saturdays Lana usually went to a matinee movie with friends. Once as she was heading out, Monica stopped her. She noticed that Lana was wearing makeup. Lana was not quite fourteen.

'You t'ink you a big woman now?'

'What?'

'Don't *what* me, you likkle wretch. Go to the bathroom an' wash that foolishness off you face.'

'What foolishness? I don't—'

Monica didn't let Lana finish. She dragged her off to the bathroom. Roy and Jean stood helplessly by the bathroom door. They heard the faucet running and Lana's garbled, choked shouts while Monica scrubbed her face.

'You not walkin' outa my house lookin' like a whore.'

Roy sighed and looked at Jean. 'Come, let's go outside.'

He took Jean's hand, but she wouldn't move from the door.

They heard a slap, and then Lana, who was by then almost as tall and strong as Monica, managed to shove her out of the bathroom and lock herself inside.

'Open the door!' Monica shouted.

Lana began to smash things.

'Monica, leave the girl alone now,' Roy said.

'Open this door or you sorry!'

'Monica!' Roy spoke firmly.

'Fine. Stay there all day then.' Monica walked away.

'Lana?' Roy knocked gently.

They heard nothing for a while, then the sound of her crying and banging her head against the wall.

'Oh God,' Roy moaned. Jean started to cry.

Roy convinced Lana to let him walk in. He stayed in the bathroom for some time, talking in a soothing voice. 'I tek you and Jean to the drive-in later. Okay? They showin' Elvis Presley.'

When he came out, he went to Monica: 'You goin' kill the girl?'

There was a bench in the garden under the lignum vitae tree. Lana and Jean used to sit there in the evenings and watch people and cars go by. That was where Lana found Jean later that day.

'Dolly' – it was her pet name for Jean – 'you sleepin'?'

No. Yes. She had fallen into one of her peculiar reveries. She looked up and saw Lana hovering over her.

'I tell you a secret,' Lana whispered.

Jean knew this was an effort to comfort her.

'I have a boyfriend.'

'Who?'

'Tony Curtis. None of you business who. An' if you say one word to Monica, I tell her how you did wee-wee outside in the bush the other day.'

'I never wee-wee outside.'

'Oh, yes you did. T'ink I wasn't lookin'? Nasty.'

'The chile has a mouth on her,' Jean overheard Monica boasting; she meant that Lana, like herself, always spoke her mind, and that she could cut people to shreds with her words.

Lana had no patience with schoolwork. Her report card was full of C's and D's and 'Lana could do better if she tried.' Lana loved to sing, but piano lessons were a disaster. The piano teacher begged Monica not to send her back. She disrupted the one ballet class she ever took. 'Dis-re-spek-ful,' Madame Sasso, the ballet teacher, said. Lana had called 'Madame So-so' a 'fish-face-fart' and had entertained the class with a riotous monkey imitation.

'The child is out of control. Spoiled,' Monica's friends said.

But she was so pretty. 'Is this you daughter?' strangers would stop Monica to ask. 'Lawd, she pretty like pretty-self.'

'Pretty enough fe a prince,' Monica said one day. 'When you grow up you can marry Prince Charles.'

'Ha! You want to be Queen of England?' Roy joked. 'Queen Lana. What you want to be when you grow up?'

'I dunno,' she answered listlessly. 'Maybe a hairdresser.'

She was in one of her 'moods,' as she called them, when nothing interested her and she was quiet, sullen, and sleepy. These moods would last for several days. Roy had a theory about them: Most of the time, Lana had the energy of two people; occasionally her 'battery' would run out and she would need 'recharging.'

'She can enter Miss Jamaica when she's nineteen,' Monica said, planning ahead. 'She win easy-easy. Then she go on to Miss World.' She added, 'Jus' keep you likkle tail away from the boys.'

Roy teased Lana: 'No boyfriends till you thirty, you hear.'

Monica turned to Roy: 'You tek life fe one big joke.'

Lana cared for Jean like a favorite ornament. She enjoyed dressing her in pretty clothes and tying ribbons in her hair. Sometimes she let Jean sleep with her, lulling her to sleep with songs she made up herself:

> Come back, sailor boy, come back,
> There's a brown girl crying.
> Come back, sailor boy, come back,
> You stay away too long . . .

It was thrilling for Jean to have a big, beautiful sister fussing over her. Unfortunately, there was another side to Lana.

The family ate breakfast in a room they called the back veranda, a latticed porch beside the kitchen. Monica and Roy never had more than coffee and toast in the mornings; it was Lana's job to stay behind at the table with Jean to make sure she ate all her breakfast. Lana would cut animal figures out of the toast and coat Jean's porridge with an extra layer of sugar.

But one morning after Roy and Monica left, Lana glared at

Jean then blurted out: 'Who tell you you could use my Noxzema?'

Before Jean had a chance to answer, Lana hurled a glass at her, cutting her above her eye. Jean had to get stitches, and it was years before the scar faded.

Lana was angry about the Noxzema, not because Jean had used something of hers, but because she had left the jar open: 'You come in me room, come mess it up.'

A few days after this incident, Jean stole into Lana's bedroom and took the tops off everything – Noxzema, Vaseline, hair oil, talcum powder – and scattered hairpins all over the dressing table. Then she went into her own room and waited.

Lana stormed in. 'I goin' wring you likkle neck!'

Jean was ready. She let out an alarming scream, a scream that sounded as though it would never end.

When Monica and Roy rushed in, they found Lana shaking Jean violently by the shoulders.

'She won't stop screaming.' Lana was by now crying hysterically. 'Make her stop screaming.'

After both children were silenced and threatened with a lashing they would never forget, they were ordered to stand in opposite corners of the room with their faces turned to the wall.

Lana refused: 'I not a child. You can't make me stand in the corner.'

Monica slapped Lana so hard she fell down.

'Jesus Christ, Monica!' Roy said.

Stunned, Lana went and stood in the corner and turned her face to the wall.

'And not a damn word from either of you, or you stand there all night too!'

When they were sure their parents were far enough away, the sisters turned around and looked at each other. It was a look not of anger but of assessment. Lana studied her sister. This was not the Jean she thought she knew; this was not her 'Dolly.' She had never thought of her sister as having a will of her own.

Jean noticed Lana's lips trembling as if she was about to say something mean. She braced herself. She would stand up to Lana no matter what. But Lana began to cry.

Jean was surprised. Then sorry.

'Don't cry,' she whispered, 'they'll hear us.'

Hours later, Roy passed by the room and heard the girls talking softly. He peeped in. They had obediently stayed in their corners at opposite ends of the room, but sat on the floor facing each other, in hushed, animated conversation.

9

Jean sat on the zebra-skin rug in her father's study, turning the pages of a storybook. The study was cluttered with photographs and mementos of Africa, among them a Masai spear which her father told her had been a gift from a Masai chief and had been used to kill a lion. She was especially glad to be in the study that day. Her parents were quarreling. The argument kept getting louder as it moved with them from room to room.

'. . . spend all my hard-earned money on you friends.'

'I don't need you damn money.'

'Then get out.'

'Is my house. You get out.'

Jean looked up as her father rushed into the study. Monica followed him. Neither of them seemed to notice she was there.

'Get out,' Roy said to Monica. 'Go on. Leave.'

'All right! See how you manage on you own.'

'I manage fine before I married you.'

'Did I ask you to marry me? Remember is you beg me to marry you. I neva ask you for anyt'ing. Come, Jean, we goin'.'

'You not taking my daughter.'

'*Your* daughter? Fine. Keep you little wretch then—'

Roy threw her against the wall and grabbed the Masai spear. 'So help me, Monica, I never lay hands on a woman before. But so help me God—'

Monica, pinned to the wall, laughed: 'You goin' kill me, Roy?'

'Daddy . . . ?' Jean began.

He released Monica.

'Just leave. Leave us,' he said quietly.

'You goin' sorry—' Monica said as she walked away.

'I sorry already,' he said.

He picked Jean up and sat her on his lap. They heard Monica walking up and down, banging doors, packing. Jean wondered if her mother would come back into the study to take her. Her father held her so tightly, she could not turn around and see his face. She was full of questions that she didn't know how to ask. After a while she heard Monica get in her car and drive away.

Minutes later, she heard her father's light snoring. He had fallen into an exhausted sleep, holding her.

After a week or so, Roy realized he couldn't manage Jean by himself, so he took her to his mother.

Cherry Landing, formerly Cherry Ho Sing, was the family matriarch, the mother of three sons and the eldest sister of eight brothers whom she had raised almost single-handed after her mother died. At sixty-two, when she took in her granddaughter, she was a plump, energetic woman with dyed-black hair and finely penciled eyebrows. The fat hanging from her upper arms as she moved about was formidable. But Cherry was not formidable. She was a kind, efficient woman who loved cooking and was famous for her Chinese recipes. She believed, like most Jamaicans, that fatness was a sign of health. So the first thing she said when Roy brought Jean to her was 'You so mawga, chile. Don' worry, Cherry go mek you nice an' fat.'

The first night there, Jean burst out crying while she was having supper. Cherry picked her up and sat her in her huge lap. 'What happen? You miss Daddy? You miss Mummy?' Yes, she did. No, she did not. Cherry was far more affectionate than Monica. It was the strangeness, that was all, the new evening routine – Ovaltine and toast with marmalade – and the intimation of other new and strange things to come.

'You soon-soon go home, baby, don' fret.'

But over the next few weeks, it didn't seem to be working out that way. Roy began talking about going to Ghana and taking Jean with him. He wanted to work for Kwame Nkrumah's regime.

'Ghana!' Grandma Cherry said. 'You mussee jokin'.'

When Roy came to take Jean for her passport photograph and vaccinations, Cherry realized he was serious.

'Is a backward place,' Cherry wailed.

'Ghana,' he informed her, 'is moving the entire continent forward.'

Cherry went to the bakery to talk to Monica. She liked and admired her daughter-in-law; Monica had proved to be an excellent businesswoman and utterly dependable.

'You hear Roy takin' Jean to Africa?'

'I hear so, but he can't be serious.'

'Serious as the day he bawn. Him all get passport an ting.'

'Him is a madman.'

Cherry let this pass.

'Monica, you cyaan let you pickney go Africa fe run wild wid lion an' chief an' Lawd-know-what. Talk to him. Chu, is high time you two get back together. Him will listen to you.'

Monica was flattered that Cherry thought she had influence over Roy; also, she didn't want to jeopardize her amiable relationship with Cherry Ho Sing Landing, head of the family and chief shareholder of Island Bakery.

'Him is a madman,' Monica repeated, then sighed. 'Awright. Is true we cyaan let him tek de poor chile so far.'

The fights between Monica and Roy were never quite so vicious after that. Though they still disagreed about everything, they kept out of each other's way. Roy managed to be out most evenings when Monica returned home from the bakery. He went to PNP meetings and did a lot of chauffeuring and other errands for the party members. It pleased him immensely to be relied on by Norman Manley.

'Why you don't ask Mr Manley to give you a real job that pays real money?' Monica asked.

For real money, a pitiable amount, Roy wrote for the *Daily Gleaner*. He traveled throughout the islands and reported on President Trujillo's assassination, the effort to create a West Indian Federation, and the Cuban revolution.

On the day of the Bay of Pigs invasion, Roy woke everyone in the house at dawn and gathered them around the radio — Monica, Lana, who was home from boarding school, Jean, and Delia, the maid who was the latest in a long line of servants Monica kept hiring and firing. Jean had never seen her father look so grave. He told them:

'This is the beginning of World War III.'

The radio stayed on all day while friends came by to discuss the situation and drink rum.

'Chu, Castro go beat dem Americans to rass.'

'England goin' send de Royal Navy.'

'Imagine a world war in we own backyard, eh?'

'How long you tink it goin' last — two, three years?'

'I tell you, Castro go lick dem rass.'

Among his friends were several Rastafarian musicians and artists. The Rastafarian community, which was small then, knew about Roy's love of Africa and his travels there, and Roy's Rastafarian friends often came by to discuss African history, or to ask his help with their 'repatriation.' Jean liked them because they called her 'Ethiopian Princess.' They were not like her father's other friends; they did not drink rum, and did not eat pork, shellfish, or salt. Sometimes as day sank into evening, they sat on the veranda beating her father's African drums and chanting.

Monica opposed Roy in everything. She said Castro was a dangerous, bloodthirsty Communist who would take over Jamaica given the chance. She supported Manley's opponent, Bustamante. 'Rastafarians,' she told Jean, 'eat children. Especially girls. They goin' grab you the minute you father not looking.' She warned Roy against 'letting those kind of people in the house.'

She was so rude to his friends that he often took them, along with Jean, over to Daphne's. This was always a treat for Jean. There was always a lot of good food at Daphne's. And her teenage cousin, Astrid, played records for Jean and let her try on her cosmetics and jewelry.

Roy glowed at Daphne's. There were always people there eager to talk with him.

'Hey! Roy man, wha' go on?'

'What you think 'bout Manley's speech the other day?'

'Tell us wha' really goin' on in British Guiana?'

There was a woman named Louise Martin who came often to Daphne's. She had been Roy's girlfriend before he met Monica. On the rebound she married one of Roy's friends. She was a plump, attractive woman, part Chinese like Roy. Sometimes Roy left Jean for an hour or so at Daphne's and went away mysteriously with Louise. Once when Roy took Jean to the drive-in, Louise came along. Jean knew instinctively that she shouldn't mention this to Monica; she had heard Monica and Roy quarreling about 'that woman.'

To live with her parents was to live in two worlds, to always get two different answers to any question, and to expect the opposite of everything to reveal itself.

On one side: her father, Africa, Cuba, revolution, world maps, world leaders, Rastafarians, salt in her nostrils from the Caribbean where he taught her to swim, and panoramic views from hilltops where he would park and point out landmarks. All her life she would remember her father's hands, pointing out something to her.

'Who is this?' he would say, pointing to a photograph.

'Jomo Kenyatta.'

'Look, Jean, over there, a doctor bird, you see the red beak, it's only in Jamaica you find that bird.'

On the other side: her mother's indomitable blend of elegance and practicality. Life-is-rough-chile-an'-you-betta-get-use-to-it. Monica was sure about everything, afraid of nothing. She was tough, tallawa.

Jean thought they were both splendid, her parents, but as different as two people could be.

The sad thing was how disappointed they were in each other. When Monica and Roy were alone together without the usual relatives or friends to buffer them, the silence between them was terrible. Each made a point of being overcareful about whatever the other one was careless about: Monica painstakingly put the records back inside their covers after Roy left them out, her annoyance made obvious by her long, cold silence; Roy would drop everything to properly buckle Jean's shoes or fold her socks down around her ankles, seething, under his breath, about how Monica didn't seem to care how Jean looked. They carried on furious arguments with each other inside their minds, now and then absent-mindedly muttering out loud:

'—at least make an effort.'

'What?'

'Nothing.'

They lived in the heart of Kingston, near a Catholic Church and school. The house was an old, modest shingle-roof house on a fairly busy street with similar houses. In those days, the front verandas were wide open. There was a small garden with lime and ackee trees and a purple bougainvillea hedge. Neither

Monica nor Roy had any interest in gardening. They hired a boy, Neville, to tend to it.

Neville, the 'boy,' was a grown man in his late twenties, with a close-shaven head. Roy had hired him; Monica didn't trust him.

'Look like him jus' come outa jail wid him bald head.'

'So what if him outa jail? Him do a good day's work.'

Jean agreed with her mother. Late one afternoon she saw Neville in the backyard, smoking ganja with another man. When he saw Jean, he beckoned to her in a lewd way to join them under the shady bushes.

She told her parents what she had seen, not the lewd part, which embarrassed her, only about smoking ganja with his friend.

'I tell you that man is trouble,' Monica said.

Roy blew up at Monica, calling her a snob and saying that the man had a right to have a smoke in the middle of the day with his friend; after all, slavery had long been abolished.

But when Monica came home early one afternoon and caught the gardener in the house, she fired him immediately.

'An' if you think you getting today's wages you can forget it. I don't pay you to walk around inside my house.'

He said something obscene, and stood there trying to look intimidating. To most women, he would have been.

'You tink I 'fraid a you?' She went to the telephone to call the police station. 'I get police to lock up you rass!'

'You goin' sorry, you an' you pickney-dem,' he said, and as he left he turned to look back at Jean.

Afterward, Monica and Roy began to notice several things missing, and they wondered how often Neville had been in and out of the house. Monica questioned Delia, the maid, and, not getting a satisfactory answer, she fired her, too. 'The two of them in it together.'

It was some time before Roy realized his Masai spear was gone. He was so hurt that even Monica, who had it in her to say

'I told you so,' felt sorry for him and kept the thought to herself.

In 1962, Bustamante's party, the JLP, won the general election, and Jamaica was granted independence from Britain. It was to be official on August 6. Busta, as he was called, would be the new nation's first prime minister. Jean knew Busta would win, because he was the one Monica voted for.

In the weeks leading up to Independence, Daphne's house was noisier than ever. For once no one cared which party had won. JLP or PNP, what did it matter? Jamaica was going to rule itself. Even Monica, in her own way, got caught up in the excitement.

'Well, I still don't think we quite ready fe independence,' Monica said. 'We need another ten, fifteen years.'

'We ready, man, we ready.'

'Go live in Englan' if you want queen tell you wha' fe do.'

'I hear Busta plannin' to build high-rise hotels like in Miami.'

'I don't altogether trust Busta an' I definitely don't trust Seaga. I hear him practice obeah.'

'Seaga is a Harvard man. Oonoo 'fraid a him 'cause him smart.' Monica defended him.

Roy explained to Jean what the colors of the new flag stood for: 'Green for the land. Gold for the sunshine. Black for the people.'

'Which people?' Monica protested. 'Chu man, no teach the chile none of this Black people—White people nonsense. We are *Jamaicans*.'

'So what I mus' tell her the black stand for?'

'I don't see why we need a new flag anyway.'

'Awright, awright. Black for our dark and painful history, and' – he whispered mischievously in her ear so Monica couldn't hear – 'fe we Black people.'

He continued: 'Lignum vitae is the national flower. Blue mahoe the national tree. Doctor bird the national bird. Ackee—'

The national fruit.

*

Monica woke Roy up in the dead of night.

'Roy—' she whispered, and nudged him.

He rolled over and saw her point towards the bedroom window.

Somebody was climbing through. At first it looked as if the intruder was carrying a long pipe or pole; then Roy recognized his missing spear.

'Tief!' Roy shouted, and lunged after him.

The thief went back through the window, ran around to the back of the house, and disappeared into the dark bushes.

Roy woke the neighbors with his shouting. Monica woke the children, huddled them into her bedroom, and told them to keep the door locked until she came back.

'What happened?' Jean asked Lana.

'I think Castro tek over Jamaica.'

They didn't catch the thief or recover Roy's spear. Jean heard her parents and the neighbors out on the veranda talking.

'Him come back fe avenge you. Jus' like a savage. Come fe kill you with you own spear,' somebody said.

'These people gettin' entirely outa hand,' Monica declared.

'The funny thing, you know,' Roy began. 'Most nights I fall asleep out here on the veranda, and Jean sometimes out here with me. Suppose I did do so last night, eh? I might be a dead man now and Lord knows what woulda happen to Jean.' Then he turned to Monica, unable to resist teasing her: 'You see wha' kind a ting go on when you party in power? See what you man, Busta, doin' to the country? Nex' ting we ha fe put iron bars round the veranda an' live like prisoner in we own house.'

10

'Remember this day,' Roy told his daughters, 'August 6, 1962. Today is Jamaica's birthday.'

They were in the car, moving slowly along a pedestrian-filled road on their way to the national stadium where the Jamaican flag was to be raised for the first time. On the radio was a running commentary on Princess Margaret's visit and descriptions of the floats and marching bands in the Independence Day parade. Suddenly another commentator interrupted with an important announcement: Marilyn Monroe had committed suicide.

Suicide — it was the first time Jean had heard the word. Lana told her what it meant and said it was a mortal sin and she didn't see why you would kill yourself if it meant going straight to hell.

'Suppose,' Jean asked, 'you start to kill youself, then you get 'fraid, but it's too late to stop?'

'Don't worry about it, darling,' Roy said. 'Look, look over there—' He pointed to a man on stilts, weaving through the crowd wearing a papier-mâché likeness of the new prime minister. He blew his horn and the man on stilts waved at the car. 'Wave, wave to Busta,' Roy said. Jean and Lana stuck their hands out the window and waved their tiny Jamaican flags. Pedestrians with flags cheered and waved back and some of them ran alongside the car.

'Independence today!' Roy shouted.

＊

Jean's sixth birthday came a month after the Independence celebrations. Her parents gave her a party. There was a cake with pink and white coconut icing and her name written on it in silver letters. But as Roy was bringing it to the table with all the candles lit and everyone singing 'Happy Birthday,' it fell. That was all right, because the family owned the nation's largest bakery. By the time the children had played a few more rounds of musical chairs, another cake, exactly like the first, arrived.

But it was not all right with Roy. That night the doctor came to the house. Jean went to her father, who remained in bed after the doctor left. He asked her if she had enjoyed her party and said he was sorry about the cake.

'The second one was nice, too. Daddy, you sick?'

'Yes, darling.'

'Sick where?'

'Jus' a headache. I have to go hospital for a few days.'

'You 'fraid?'

'No, no. Nothing to be 'fraid of. Come, lie down nex' to me an' I tell you a story. Ready? Ears wide open? Long ago, there was a big hurricane. Big-big. A hurricane so big that it ran all over the world. But before the hurricane, God warned some of the people. Actually it was jus' two people he warned. A man named Noah and his wife.'

'What was his wife's name?'

'Betty. God told Noah and Betty big hurricane comin' an' they mus' build a boat . . .'

It rained; it poured. All over the world, the torment of rain. That night she dreamed of rain drenching the trees and pounding on the windowpanes, a night so chaotic with the noise of rain that she could not hear the knocking on the door, but saw the old man enter, wiping his feet and taking off his wet hat:

I come to say good-bye.

It was Mr Ho Sing in the brown suit he wore in the photograph Cherry had shown her.

I goin' North Coast fe a sea bath. 'Bye darlin'.

Next morning, as soon as she woke up, she told her father.

'Mr Ho Sing? You sure?'

Yes. She had a clear memory of her great-grandfather. Roy used to take her to visit him at the shop. Mr Ho Sing would lean down and pinch her cheek. She remembered the brown age spots on his hands and how he had smelled of Pears' soap — a smell that would always remind her of him and of old age. Whenever she went to see him, he reached into the big glass canister on the counter and gave her two Chinese sweeties, one salt, one sweet.

'Mr Ho Sing is dead, sweetheart, he's in heaven.'

'Last night he came and said good-bye.'

'Don't worry,' he said gently.

One day, Jean brought the dinner conversation to a halt by mentioning that dead people sometimes spoke to her. Irene had just brought the hot serving dishes to the table, and she gave Jean a strange, almost conspiratorial look. 'You mean in dreams,' Monica said; it wasn't a question. Jean realized she had said something peculiar. 'Yes, that's what I mean.'

Later that night, in the room where the ironing was done, Irene oiled Jean's hair and said, dream or no dream, she had always heard that people who had eyes like Jean's, with the white showing under the iris, were not afraid of duppy, and 'duppy-dem know dis an' no bada fe trouble dem.' She rubbed and pulled vigorously at Jean's scalp. This oiling and plaiting was supposed to be good for her hair. When Irene finished, there were about a dozen plaits, so tight a needle wouldn't be able to pass through them, and Jean's head was slightly sore.

She could hardly wait to get back to her room and look at the whites of her eyes in the mirror. People always commented on her eyes. They were slanted like Cherry's, but unusually large and hazel-colored, subtly changing from brown to green. 'Puss-eye,' people sometimes called her. There was a madman who often sat under a tree in the vacant lot near the house, smoking a pipe. Actually, Jean wasn't sure that he was a man, because he wore a skirt and had a scarf tied around his head like a woman, but he had a beard. One day he called out to her: 'I goin' come a you house a night when you sleepin' an' pull out dem pretty eye.' From then on, she walked on the other side of the road. But he still called to her: 'Pull out you eye.' She looked in the mirror and saw what Irene meant about her eyes. But it was not entirely true about her not being afraid of dead people. That night she slept with the light on.

The doctors told Roy he had a brain tumor and gave him three months to live. He lived for six. The house became strangely peaceful and happy during those months. Lana came home more often from school; Cherry cooked more than usual, and Monica stopped arguing with Roy. He was never bedridden, nor did he go back to the hospital. There were symptoms. He forgot where he had put things. He stopped talking in mid-sentence. He lost all sense of the value of money, a sense that Monica said he had never had. One day he paid the fudge man ten pounds for a tuppence icicle and told him to keep the change. But it was more embarrassing when he underpaid and had to be called back by befuddled vendors.

They went to the beach often because, more than anything else in the world, Roy loved a sea bath. He was a powerful swimmer, often going out so far that they would lose sight of him, and they would watch until they could see him heading back to shore.

Daphne visited nearly every day. She was helping him finish a story he had started writing years earlier. He died before finishing it; Daphne wrote the end and published it post-humously. They would stay up late, Roy and Daphne, working, playing cards, talking. Monica, who always went to bed earlier than everyone else, left them alone.

Roy decided to paint a family portrait. Monica bought new dresses for Jean and Lana, and she posed in a favorite evening dress, a low-cut, white satin gown. Daphne took the photograph of the family that Roy worked from. Jean found the unfinished painting years later, and placed it on her bedroom wall. The only one Roy had finished painting was Lana. Monica was half-finished. Jean was just an outline; so was he.

Daphne was with him the night he died. They were playing cards. He got up to fix himself a drink and fell down. Daphne rushed over to him. He lifted his hand to his head, then smiled, as if embarrassed at having fallen, and closed his eyes. She woke Monica, and they called the doctor even though they knew that he was dead. It all happened so quietly that Jean and Lana were not woken.

Did Jean know her father was dying? No one told her outright, but she felt the change in him the day he dropped her birthday cake and told her the story of Noah's Ark. She had seen Mr Ho Sing leave the world. She understood with a sad heart that her father would also leave. But she was not prepared for it to happen so abruptly. She had said good night to him as usual; the next day he was gone.

The quietness that would become so characteristic of her began at this time. She became a solitary, independent little girl, never expecting anyone to pay as much attention to her as her father had. Lana would try to comfort her, a gesture that came from her own need for comfort: 'Come here, Dolly, mek me give you a big hug.' But Jean had decided that she no longer needed caresses. 'You must try to be a big girl now and take care of yourself,' Monica had told her the day after Roy's death. She became cautious, too, at this time, trying to keep out of harm's way when it came to those two volatile members of her family – Lana and Monica – from whom her father, in so many different ways, had protected her.

Within a year of Roy's death, they moved to the new house on Bonnieview Terrace. The move amazed everyone; women who lost their husbands were expected to 'small-up' themselves, not live more lavishly.

'She mus' miss him, what with the girls both at boarding school now,' Gwen said, the minute Monica went inside to speak to Irene. 'I would feel lonely in this big house. It too big.'

Daphne and Errol glanced at each other, hearing a note of jealousy in Gwen's words.

They had come to visit Monica and had found her on the veranda by herself, a drink in hand, staring out at the view.

'What a wonderful view you have here,' Gwen said to Monica when she returned. 'Something to lift you spirits. Keep you company.'

'Yes, is good company. Nice an' quiet,' she said without mournfulness.

'You miss Roy?' Daphne was the only one who would ask.

'I never realized till now how much he made me laugh. What a dreamer.' Monica sipped her drink and looked out as the evening deepened and lights began to be visible across Kingston. 'He would certainly have liked this view.'

11

Another roadblock.

'What's happening?' Paul asks a policeman.

'Man dead up a road.'

'Dead how?'

'Shot dead.'

Jean and Paul get out and join the onlookers and stalled drivers by the roadside. At a glance Jean sees that the young man lying dead in the road is, by the look of his clothes, not a country boy. She looks away. An old man, strong and wiry, is gesticulating and shouting to the policemen and the gathered crowd, while the policeman in charge yells back even louder, threatening to arrest him and everyone in sight.

'Gang from Kingston,' one of the onlookers explains to Jean and Paul. 'Dem come shoot up de place, an' dem shoot de man goat.'

'That man there?' Paul points to the old man shouting.

'Yeah. Is him goat.'

'So him shoot de one who kill him goat. Wha 'appen to de res' a de gang?'

'Run 'way.'

'PNP,' someone says. 'PNP boys passin' thru mekin' trouble.'

Others in the crowd agree and mutter 'PNP.' Jean sees the torn, graffiti'd campaign posters on a nearby shop; the windows are smashed, the walls riddled by bullets.

Suddenly, there is the sound of a gunshot. The policeman in charge, tired of the old man's shouting, decides to restore order by shooting into the air. 'Jesus Christ, we goin' dead here today!' People begin running, screaming, and taking cover in the bushes. And then, unexpectedly, adding to the confusion, thunder. No one wants to be out in the rain, least of all the policemen. They handcuff the old goat-owner and some others and push them into the jeep, and begin lining up others along the roadside. A baby howls in her mother's arms.

No one has moved or covered the dead man. A stray dog, so thin the ribs show through his skin, approaches warily and begins sniffing him. A policeman stones him; the dog yelps and runs to the roadside, where someone kicks him. 'Leave de dawg alone, man,' somebody says. The dog returns to the middle of the road and sits dazed.

Paul looks at Jean and shakes his head: 'Worse thing used to happen in a place like this is somebody steal a breadfruit.'

It begins to drizzle.

'Let's wait in the truck,' he says.

A policeman comes over. 'Who gi' you permission fe leave?'

Paul doesn't answer.

'Who gi' you permission?' He sprays saliva in Paul's face.

Paul's lips curl slightly as he wipes the spittle from his cheek. 'I hear you, sir.' And in a softer tone he asks, 'Can you give us permission?'

The policeman seems to weigh the question. Another policeman joins him: 'Wha' g'wan?'

'*Homo* no *sapiens*,' Paul whispers to Jean.

The policeman hears this. 'Come ova here,' he says. They take him around to the side of the shop, and stand under the roof eaves, protected from the rain.

The road has become quiet except for the gentle sheet of rain. The bystanders huddle under the trees and wait for the police to tell them what to do. After a few minutes Paul comes back to Jean; the policemen watch him.

'You have any US dollars?'

'How much?'

'Gimme a twenty.'

He goes back over to the policemen. They argue. They want more. Paul reaches into his pocket, offers some Jamaican currency, and continues talking to them. He smiles and stands in a relaxed way with them, palavering. One of them laughs at something he says.

He comes back. 'Let's go.'

They drive past the same two policemen, who are now giving their full attention to another traveler. Jean takes a last look at the people standing along the road.

She cringes as an army truck comes speeding around the bend. It is so full that soldiers hang onto the truck's sides, their weapons and limbs dangling. The policemen must have sent for them. For what? An argument over somebody's goat?

What will happen here today?

They drive on, and the rain falls more heavily. A squealing group of children dash for cover, some of them holding banana leaves over their heads. Everyone disappears from the flooding road. Doors close. Sheets of rain lash the truck's windows, blurring everything. All is rain, winding road, and storm-battered foliage, and principal is the rain, a sound and a force engrossing the island. Yet *it* won't change anything.

Her mind goes back to the people she just left behind. Her memory of them, frozen and framed like a snapshot.

She remembers a newspaper photograph of Cambodian soldiers, the Khmer Rouge, executing prisoners. There were rows of people kneeling, waiting to be killed, perfectly arranged like sheafs of grain in a field. One man knelt in the foreground, the executioner's gun at his head. His eyes were wide open, but he was without expression, the photographer picturing him already among the dead.

The reality of casual annihilation frightens her. No longer does she ask herself, 'Could that happen here?' It is here. It could be her. Fate? That kind of death is no one's fate, not even the executioners'. The mass graves of history are not history; they are pages torn from it.

She remembers names muttered uncertainly on veranda evenings — Moses? The Morant Bay Rebellion? — thrown out with a self-deprecating smile. For who were they to have a Moses or a rebellion in their past? These rags of history haunt her. She wonders what it is like to become, at most, a doubtful utterance, a faltering grin in family lore.

12

It was lore, it was history; and it was nightmare. There had been a state of emergency in 1865; she had read of it as a schoolgirl—

No attempt has been made in this account to depict the alarm which prevailed: the bare facts, as recorded by the Royal Commissioners, have alone been referred to. But it ought not to be forgotten that the white population of the entire parish was only 282 persons, of whom many were women and children; there were 23,230 blacks. That many of these were on the side of law and order is unquestionable, and noble instances of devotion on the parts of servants were frequent; but . . . until the arrival of troops the insurgents did whatever they desired.

—but it was a long, time before she saw the connection between those voiceless words, the veranda talk, and the voice of her nightmare.

13

Moses Landing
1838–1865

I know more about the Israelites and their departure from Egypt than I do about the captivity of the Africans. I cannot tell you the history of our people, but I can tell you the history of a soul.

Her name was Faith, and she was sixteen the day she was baptized in the Plantain Garden River. Twelve were baptized that day. I was their parson.

> *There is a fountain filled with blood*
> *Drawn from Emanuel's veins;*
> *And sinners, plunged beneath that flood,*
> *Lose all their guilty stains.*

She wore a white head-wrap in the old African way, and that was strange because the women of that time went to great lengths to follow the English fashion. She saw me looking at her, and she smiled and looked away.

I was shepherd to a congregation of fifty to sixty souls at the Jordan Baptist Church in St Thomas. I could read and write as well as any Englishman and was respected throughout the eastern part of the country. I was far from rich but lived better than most. I owned a good pair of shoes; so did my wife. We had been married five years, and had two daughters. Lucy was pregnant for the third time. She was a good woman, a good mother. 'Better is an handful with

70

quietness, than both the hands full with travail and vexation of spirit.' Ours was an honest but joyless bed.

I was raised by Christian parents and educated, as they were, by English Baptists. My father was a Mulatto slave, freed by the Emancipation Act in 1838. He was the son of an Ashanti woman who died during a slave uprising at Dove Hill. She was hanged by his white half-brother. My mother was also born a slave in this country. She was the daughter of a woman brought here from Africa of the Mande tribe. Though my grandmother had ceased speaking her old language, she taught my mother a few words, and my mother in turn taught these words to me, but I have forgotten them. What use are African words to us in this country?

The medicines my grandmother and those old Africans used, these I remember, and I will tell them to you because this is useful knowledge. To cool the body down take lime or pineapple, and to bring on heat, take nutmeg or pimento. Here are the bush teas:

For diarrhea, star-apple leaf.

For headache, guinea weed.

For blood pressure, the yellow leaf of breadfruit.

I have spoken about history after all. But it is a subject of no interest to me. I cannot see the Gold Coast from even the highest promontory of this island. Jamaica is our country now. Anyway, I want to tell you about the girl, Faith.

There was a picnic luncheon for the newly baptized. My wife left early. She was due to deliver in a month's time and was tired. Faith was easy to find; her white head-wrap stood out like a tower. Every time I looked at her, she returned my look and smiled. Her smile was pure. She was like a soft, new leaf. She stood with the other girls her age, laughing at the boys' antics, at their efforts to impress them, but her eyes followed me everywhere.

I cannot say this was the first time I had enjoyed looking at a beautiful girl since my marriage. I often looked, but never yearned for forbidden pleasures. I had never broken any of the Ten Commandments. I believed in them.

When the luncheon was over, I went back into the church to lock up. I had been there a short while when she came in, closing the door behind her. I asked *her if I could help her with anything. She said, No, Preacher, then Yes, Preacher, all the while looking down at the floor. I was enchanted.*

'What is it?'

She could not answer.

'Is something troubling you?'

Her voice trembled on the word: 'Sin.'

'But you have been saved,' I said, putting my hands on her shoulders, 'by the precious water of baptism.'

She knelt at my feet. I felt stirred, potent, and wrong.

'Me weak, preacher.'

'Weakness is not a sin. God chose the weak among us to confound the strong.' I touched her young cheek and was surprised at how hot, almost feverish, her skin felt. 'Go home and pray to the Lord who loves you.'

I saw her often. She waited for me on the church steps or at her gate where I passed every evening. Her hair was always hidden under the becoming white cloth, so mysteriously wrapped, closed white petals of a white rose. Her skin smelled of sweet soap and of a light dusting of talcum powder. Sometimes we walked together a bit, and once I took hold of her hot hand. At first I told myself that this was innocent. But the more I saw her, the more I needed to see her and I looked for her everywhere. I smelled her in our country air, and imagined the soft skin of her bosom. One day, hurriedly and part naked, as though this made it only part sinful, I brought myself the pleasure she seemed to promise — a sin that should have weighed heavily on me but didn't; instead it lightened me and sped the hours.

Understand: I had walked such a long way in sureness. Eternal salvation had seemed just an ordinary step away. All I was sure of now was this daily longing. I became distracted, unaware of what was around me. I lost and found things like someone in a dream.

Then came the blood, the terror that seized the whole country, and the confusion in my soul was magnified a thousand times by the confusion all around me.

The rebellion began as a mere scuffle outside the Morant Bay courthouse. My fellow pastor Mr Bogle and some of his friends were outside the courthouse, protesting the mistreatment of a prisoner. That was the immediate cause of the protest, but they had been angry for a long time. Jamaica was still a White man's country. Slavery had ended, but there were still men who were owners and men who were slaves.

I was in Morant Bay that day. I went by mule cart to collect Lucy, who had been visiting her sister. My first errand in town was to stop at the shoemaker's to buy new bootlaces; strangely, the shop was closed. I noticed then that all the shops were closed. As I drew nearer the town center I heard the rioting.

Mr Bogle's men were shouting 'War! War!' and stoning the courthouse. The constables guarding the building raised their rifles and fired on the crowd. But Mr Bogle's men, instead of fleeing, charged at them fearlessly, overwhelming them with sticks, machetes, bottles, stones. Many of the soldiers ran back into the courthouse.

'Bun dem out! Bun dem out!' Bogle's men shouted.

Soon the courthouse was in flames.

I stood under a tree in the school yard and watched.

Men, and women too, ran about in a frenzy, beating anyone in their way, throwing rocks into the shops and houses, shouting, 'White man country fe we now!'

They pulled a White man from his carriage and beat him. I saw a well-dressed Colored man rush past the school gate. I recognized him; he was a court messenger.

'Look de Black genkleman,' someone said, and they descended on him.

'No, don' kill 'im. We fe kill White people, not Black.'

I stepped out from my hiding place.

'Look another one,' someone said, taking in my well-made clothes and shoes. 'Is Parson Landing, Mr Bogle friend.'

I did not want to take part, to choose sides, believe me, but I found myself saying, maybe in order to save the man, maybe to save myself: 'Leave him. He is one of us.'

'Him skin Black but him heart White,' a man shouted, and plunged his knife into the man and laughed. They all fell on him, beating, stabbing, tearing at the poor man, who cried out. Have you ever heard a grown man crying for his life?

I went by Mr Bogle's church that night with a heavy heart. I went because he was my friend, and because I had seen some of my own congregation with him that day. Faith was at the meeting, sitting with her family. I sat next to her.

Mr Bogle was a fiery speaker. He began by giving thanks to God for being on their side and read from the Psalms:

'For thou has girded me with strength unto the battle . . . Then did I beat them small as the dust before the wind . . .'

I found myself strangely swayed by his words and by the spirited response of those around me. I don't know why. I started to shout with the rest.

Hadn't the slaves of Hayti triumphed over the White men? The Lord had strengthened them. Amen. And were we not more advantaged than those Haytians, being free men? Free men, amen. God was with the righteous; if we did not fight now, then when?

I agreed, yes, I agreed to go with them the next morning, armed with stick, rock, or machete.

As it happened, I did not go.

Lucy, stricken by what she had seen in Morant Bay, became ill that night and seemed about to deliver before her time. I feared for her life and the life of my child. I rode to Morant Bay to fetch a doctor. He was an English surgeon, new to the island, and he came promptly back to the cottage with me. After many hours of labor, my wife delivered a boy the next morning, and we named him John after the kind surgeon.

The child's early delivery was a stroke of good fortune for me because Bogle and his stick-and-stone army were captured by the English that day.

A state of emergency was declared. Governor Eyre sent soldiers and three battleships to Morant Bay. The fighting was bloody; the Queen's soldiers decimated what remained of Mr Bogle's army, and the eastern part of the country was under military siege. To make matters worse, there was heavy flooding – the worst I had ever seen. For days it poured. The rivers swelled and became impassable, and this, along with the difficult, unknown terrain, crazed the White soldiers. They fell upon the Negroes of our parish, innocent and guilty alike, shooting and hanging them on the spot. Hundreds of homes were burned to the ground, hundreds of Negroes arrested and flooded, and many innocent people executed.

Now one hundred years later, another state of emergency; this time Black against Black. You want no part of this. You don't want to take sides. You think you have a choice? Listen.

One morning the rain stopped. The sky, however, remained heavy with clouds. I decided to step outside and dig up some yams between the rains. I looked around at the wet hills and the valley in which we lived. There was a cool, pleasant feeling in the air. It felt like mercy.

What were Mr Bogle and this war to me? And all my turbulent feelings about Faith? I had no answers. But the questions themselves, like the cool wind before the rain, were a promise of deliverance.

As I began digging up the muddy yams, I felt the first drops of rain on my back. Then I heard the slow gallop of horses. I looked up and saw them, the White soldiers. They stopped at my gate and asked if I was Preacher Landing. I answered yes, and they arrested me for treason. Treason? They did not give me time to go in and speak to Lucy, to put on my shoes, or clean the mud from my hands. They tied my hands behind me and marched me barefoot across the mud and stones.

I heard Lucy at the door, crying out. But I was too far from the cottage by that time to comfort her. It would be all right. I had taken no part in the Rebellion. The rain fell harder. I thought of the yams I had dug up and laid to one side, and hoped perhaps I would be back home by afternoon.

They brought me to Stoney Gut, where there was a barricade. I saw another man, bound like myself, leaning against a tree. There was a cut above his eye and it was bleeding. He had a scornful, remorseless look like someone who is guilty. But I was not— Before I finished the thought, I saw, in front of me, Faith, her familiar head-wrap unraveled and trailing the ground, her head hanging limp to one side. She was dead. Dead and swinging from a rope.

Questions and cries rose up in me, but my voice was locked tight: What is happening here? Aren't you taking us to jail?

'Trial' was all I managed to say, but no one heard.

They cut her down and she fell into the mud. I saw another body beside hers.

'Trial,' I said again, louder.

The soldiers laughed and pushed me forward.

'Baptist, you are guilty of treason,' a soldier said as he put the rope around my neck.

Like this? Lord in heaven. Quickly. 'Forgive us our trespasses as we forgive . . .'

I thought of Faith. Was it really her? Maybe I had gone mad. This is a mistake, I wanted to say.

'Say your prayers, preacher,' the soldier said.

The man standing against the tree looked up at me.

'This was how they killed my grandmother!' I wanted to shout, because I suddenly understood.

I had fallen into this helplessness, history.

My body would swing barefoot in the rain.

14

She does not want to die like that, unaccountable. An unknown face in a foreign newspaper picture, a number among numbers: 'Sixteen People Shot in Night of Jamaican Unrest.' Alan had sent her newspaper clippings from America, as if she needed convincing.

It's stopped raining, and a ray of sunlight washes her arm. It feels wonderful. She thinks about Alan. She closes her eyes, smells him, imagines lying naked on top of him, her breasts loose on his chest. The mere thought of touching him again keeps her from falling apart with fear. Not love but the promise of sex, with all its graceless lurching, reassures her.

At first, the vigorous demands of her body surprised her. Good sex has changed the course of her life. No, more than that, it may save her: 'For the grave cannot praise thee, death cannot celebrate thee . . . The living, the living . . . shall praise thee.'

Should she be thinking about sex at a time like this? If Alan were here he would call her thoughts naughty. So silly, the English. How had they managed an empire? Huge, hulking, poorly coordinated, middle-aged, sex-hungry Alan calling her erotic thoughts naughty.

Before Alan she thought that something was, not wrong, but different about her. Sex had seemed like a battleground where somebody won and somebody lost. It surprises her that a man who is a stranger in every sense, foreign-born and a foreigner to her soul, can offer such hope. While Paul . . .

She looks at Paul driving expertly through the winding, dense hills. She can almost fool herself that this is no different from the hundreds of trips they've taken together back and forth. 'Familiar,' she thinks, is a word that has lost its warmth in English, and there is no precise way to describe how this road has become like a vein they both share. No word to describe their knowledge of each other and of all that lies between them and the burning road.

15

Paul's family lived across the street from them at Bonnieview Terrace. Roses grew in their garden, and Jean often saw Paul outside, watering them. But they never spoke, not until the day her puppy ran out into the street and was struck by a car.

Paul saw them from his veranda: Jean and Lana bending over the wounded animal in the middle of the road. He came over to them. Jean was a skinny little girl with plaits sticking out untidily from her head in every direction. Lana was sixteen, a year younger than Paul. She wore shorts and a midriff blouse that was then in fashion. Years later, he told Jean, 'I had to force myself not to stare at her. Her hair. She had the most beautiful head of hair I ever saw.' He did not stare; he did not seem the least bit impressed by Lana.

'Your puppy?' he asked.

'Yes,' Lana answered. 'Car knock him down, poor ting.'

'You need to take him to the vet. You mother home?'

'No.'

'Lemme see if I can borrow my mother's car.'

While they sat in the vet's waiting room, Paul read a magazine he had brought with him. Lana kept trying to make conversation. She already knew a bit about him from friends. He was a handsome loner, a high school cricket star, and a 'fabulous' dancer.

'You go to Calabar, don't you?'

'Uh-huh.'

'You know Phillip Bell?'

'Yeah.'

'He used to be my boyfriend. I go around with Peter McKenzie now. You know Peter?'

'Yeah, I know Peter.'

'You goin' 'round with anybody?'

'Uh-huh.'

Not even Lana was brazen enough to ask with whom. He sat there so relaxed and nonchalant. She was used to having an impact on boys. She got up and started pacing up and down. 'What the hell taking so long, eh?'

After this, Jean noticed Lana spending more time in the garden. Whenever Paul pulled out of his driveway in his mother's Austin, Lana happened to be on the veranda or on the front lawn where he could see her. He usually waved. She took an interest in picking dead leaves off the bougainvillea hedge, and often sunbathed on the front lawn, listening to the Drifters on her portable gramophone. She forced Jean to spy on him when he had his girlfriends over; he had more than one. Then at some point Lana decided she had seen enough to be able to tell her friends that she 'knew' Paul Grant.

He stopped by the gate one day while Jean was watering the garden. Lana was not around.

'How's the puppy?'

'Growing big.'

'I see you watering the garden all the time. You like gardening?'

Jean nodded, overwhelmed that an older person was interested in anything she was doing.

'My grandfather has a farm in the country. Whole lot a trees. Orange, coconut, banana. You like bananas? Next time I bring some for you. What's you name again?'

'Rex.'

'I thought that was your puppy's name.'

The blood rushed to her face. 'My name? Jean.'

A year later, home again for the holidays, Jean was riding her bicycle up and down the sloping roads near Bonnieview. She did this every day, and every day the same group of boys – street urchins, Monica called them – tormented her with teasing and shouting; sometimes they even threw stones. She kept finding new routes, but they always managed to turn up. They came from the shantytown at the bottom of the hill, boys who were three or four years older than she was, barefoot and almost naked except for khaki shorts.

One day they suddenly appeared at the bottom of her favorite downhill ride. She was going so fast that all she saw was a blur of limbs and khaki. They knocked her from the bicycle and fell on her, grabbing her hair and tearing at her clothes. One of them spat on her.

'Hold her down.'

'Cover her mouth.'

A boy pulled down his shorts and straddled her.

'Hey! What you doing over there?'

The boys took off. Jean saw a bright white figure looming over her as the boys ran away – Paul in his cricket whites.

'You all right?'

He could see that she was, and so he left her to chase the boys. She saw him running with his cricket bat and heard shouts and screams as he caught the first one.

'I wish I could a see it wid me own eyes,' Irene said. 'Batsman Grant. Man-a-de-match! An' not a wrinkle in you cricket whites, eh!'

He sat in the kitchen with Jean as Irene put iodine on her scrapes and cuts.

'This is the brave one,' he said, smiling at Jean, 'not a sound, eh, an' I know this iodine stings.'

'Jean, she no crybaby,' Irene said.

As soon as they had spoken, she burst into tears.

'Those boys not goin' trouble you again, you hear. You like ice cream?'

'I like milkshakes.'

'Want to go to Monty's for a milkshake?'

Sitting in the car outside Monty's Drive-in with a vanilla milkshake, Jean felt much better. Afterward, they went for a short drive through Hope Gardens, and she found herself chatting to Paul about all kinds of things.

That summer he taught her how to play chess, and he played his favorite records for her. Lana was too caught up in herself to notice that her little sister was spending a lot of time with one of the best-looking guys in Kingston. Monica was similarly self-occupied. She referred to him as 'that nice boy across the road,' but didn't give him much thought. Irene adored him. He was forever giving her a lift up and down the hill, and whenever he returned from his grandfather's farm he brought her fruit and vegetables.

It surprised everyone when Paul decided to become a farmer. He had good grades and was captain of Calabar's cricket team. He was a likely candidate for a Jamaica Scholarship, and his father expected him to go abroad and study medicine as he had. 'It don't take a whole lot a brains to grow bananas,' his father said.

Brains was exactly what it took, Paul explained. Banana was no longer the king of tropical crops. By 1964, when Paul's grandfather died, the property, which had once over a thousand acres, had been sold off piece by piece until only about a hundred acres were left. And much of that had been abandoned to squatters. After a few years, Paul turned things around. The farm was making big profits and employing a lot of local people. Along with bananas, citrus, and coconuts, he began growing spices for export.

He lived in a cottage on the farm during the week and came into the city on weekends. In Kingston, he rented an apartment in one of the first high-rise apartment buildings.

The apartment was Jean's first impression of a 'bachelor pad.' It was essentially undomestic; to find a clean glass to drink from was a feat. Everything was black – the couch, the dining table, even the towels and shower curtain. He had *Playboy* stacked with his agricultural magazines and catalogues. Framed black-and-white photographs of a nude Scandinavian woman decorated his walls. And on the wall facing the bed he had placed hundreds of tiny mirrors glued together like tiles. Jean pretended to be as enthusiastic about the decor as he was, but actually, she didn't like the undulating waterbed and found the broken-up image of herself in the mirrors disconcerting.

She wondered about the women he brought here. She knew there were many. Lana said that Paul had a girlfriend for every night of the week. Didn't they feel as if they were competing with the big-breasted blonde on the walls and with each other? Paul made no secret of his reluctance to commit himself to one woman: 'I not fallin' into no trap.' Marriage, just talk of marriage, petrified him. But he liked women immensely and treated them well. To the women who went out with him, he was a great catch: handsome, financially sound, and fun – apparently a lot of fun in bed, according to Lana's sources. His sexual reputation – a side of himself he did not show or hint at around Jean – fascinated her. He reminded her of James Bond.

At some point Monica began to rely on Paul to drive Jean to boarding school, since it was on the way to his farm. And so it began: the journeys with Paul, the road north, and a knowledge of the road that etched deeper with each journey. Paul knew and marked the events of the landscape: the hurricane that uprooted a great tree and left it growing miraculously on its side, the old bus perched on the hillside where that crazy, rich American woman lived with so many adopted children, the breadfruit's voyage from the South Pacific to Jamaica on Captain Bligh's ship, terrestrial tales of the lost and found.

16

'I, poor miserable Robinson Crusoe, being shipwrecked, during a terrible storm . . . came on shore on this *dismal* island which I called the Island of Despair,' she read in a deep, gravelly voice, an unusual voice for a child.

Faye loved *Robinson Crusoe* and could recite entire paragraphs by heart. Jean met her on her first day at Mercy – the Sisters of Mercy School for Girls.

It had been such a long drive that when Jean got there she knew she was very far from home. There had been nothing but miles of green, and then suddenly a white building with blue trim as pretty as icing, the same shade of blue worn by the Blessed Virgin whose statue graced the front lawn. It was the greenest place Jean had ever seen, the apogee of green. For the rest of her life she would compare all green places to this part of the country. It wasn't as wild and teeming as the rest of Jamaica; it was lush, but orderly. When Jean saw the tidy pastures and low stone walls, she thought of pictures she had seen of England and of names like Cotswold and Somethingshire. Even the cows looked English, white with pretty spots like cows on the labels of condensed-milk tins. And there was mist. 'Mist!' she pronounced the word in wonder that first early morning; this, too, was something she had read about in English books.

In this well-tended garden of coconut trees and pink oleander, the Sisters of Mercy ran a boarding school with

English teachers, English food, English uniforms, and English talk. Rain boots were galoshes, the toilet was the loo, and goat was mutton. Every afternoon at four, the Sisters took tea on the trellised veranda and the girls took theirs in the dining hall with Marmite sandwiches. Jean had not known such a thing as Marmite existed.

On that first day, Sister Pauline, the headmistress, accompanied Monica and Jean to Jean's room. Sister Pauline had large masculine hands and wore sandals with her nun's habit; Jean noticed tufts of hair on her toes. She brought them to a room with four narrow beds and four small chairs. Everything was white except the bedspreads, which were blue.

A girl sat reading.

'This is Faye Galdy,' Sister said. 'Have you been sitting here by yourself all morning, Faye?'

She had startling, big blue eyes and straight blond hair cut in a pageboy style. Her skin was so translucent that her veins showed, and there were deep shadows under her eyes. Jean had never seen anyone so white. She assumed Faye was English, but when she spoke it was clear she was Jamaican.

'Yes, Sister.' Then, to Jean and Monica, 'Good afternoon.'

She started to get up and Jean noticed the crutches.

'It's all right, dear. Don't get up.' Sister Pauline turned to Monica and said softly, 'Faye suffers from a congenital disease.' Her voice rose, and she spoke with nursery-rhyme sweetness to Faye: 'But soon you'll have an operation and play games like all the other girls, won't you?'

Faye glanced down at her book.

Faye left the room while Monica helped Jean unpack; then they went to see Lana in the big girls' dorm. Jean, who could not stop thinking about the girl with crutches, asked what 'congenital' meant. Lana said it was when people were born with something wrong with them, and Monica said she thought it was when you inherited a disease from your parents, and they both thought it meant something that was incurable.

Jean's bed was next to Faye's. There were two other girls in their room, identical twins, Penny and Paula, who became uninteresting once Jean was able to tell them apart. They were rowdy, athletic girls who fell into a deep sleep the minute they went to bed. Jean was bewildered by Faye's unfriendliness until she realized that Faye was not friendly to anyone. Everyone accepted her taciturn behavior just as they accepted her crutches, as if it were a necessary accompaniment to her disease.

During Jean's first week at school, her classmates were tremendously nice to her because she was the new girl. The following week they were mean to her for exactly the same reason. 'The new girl did it': she took the blame for every wrongdoing. They spilled cold juice on her at breakfast and did everything they could to provoke her until they ran out of mean things to do. Then they 'sent her to Coventry'; no one was permitted to speak to her.

All through this Faye kept her distance and seemed not even to notice when Jean cried quietly at night, except once when she said, 'Go blow you nose, for heaven's sake.'

On the third day of Coventry, Faye hobbled over and stood quietly behind her: 'That's a good drawing,' she said.

Bossy Shirley Fitzgerald said: 'You're not supposed to talk to the new girl!'

'The new girl has a name. Jean. And I can talk to her if I want.'

Jean was ecstatic. A friend! Faye was going to be her friend. But afterward Faye went back to being as aloof as before.

Then it dawned on Jean that it took all Faye's concentration just to move her body from one place to the next. Every step seemed to cause her pain. A hundred times Jean wanted to ask, 'Can I help you?' But she could see that Faye planned each thing she did in advance and that any interruption would throw her off course. Jean watched her, fascinated. Her actions seemed propelled by a mysterious wisdom, as mysterious as the word 'congenital.'

Jean had never been so lonely; she imagined that she would be friendless for her entire school life. She wrote sad, melodramatic letters to Cherry, and burst into tears when she saw Lana.

'Poor Dolly!' Lana would say if she was in a good mood, and she would involve Jean in one of her schemes, schemes Lana lost interest in during the early planning stage: they were going to steal Sister Bonaventure's van and go on a picnic; they were going to write a book about Monica's cruelty. But if she were in a bad mood she would snap at Jean: 'Chu man, get outa me room. You neva use to be such a damn crybaby.'

Mercy was a boarding school for upper-class girls: Syrians; old white Jamaican families; White expatriates; a few Chinese; and a small scattering of mixed-race girls like Lana and Jean. There were also several day students, Black country girls who had won scholarships and who were exceptionally bright. The day girls were highly appreciated by the boarders for sneaking in banned substances ranging from chewing gum to cigarettes. Wealth, class, and whiteness were what counted at Mercy, and that was partly why the nuns overlooked Lana's illegitimacy. Her father, Deepa, was a rich Indian. Her mother was light-skinned and prosperous. But mainly they overlooked it because of Lana herself: she was so beautiful. Jean soon realized that at Mercy being Lana's sister was like being related to royalty.

Lana's looks were of such a sensational quality that it seemed as if no ordinary future could contain her. No one would be surprised to see her photograph one day in some glossy foreign magazine. In a country where 'good hair' was worshipped, Lana had the best: shiny, black, and falling below her waist. Her clothes and jewelry were mesmerizing, far more than she needed – presents from her father, who visited every month. It was like a holiday whenever Deepa drove through the school gates in his black Mercedes. Along with the beautiful clothes and Indian bangles for Lana, he brought food for all her friends: roti, tamarind balls, Bombay mangoes. Occasionally Lana dressed herself in a new sari sent by Deepa's mother or sister, and she would invite some of the girls for Indian tea, making and serving the sweet milky tea the way she had learned from Deepa's sister, and playing Indian music on the gramophone. She dressed in Indian clothes only in the secrecy of her room. Monica could not stand anything that reminded her of Deepa, and in spite of their fondness for Lana, the nuns would not allow such outlandish dress.

It got to the point where Jean could think of nothing but Faye. She didn't want just any friend. It had to be Faye. They were both quiet, friendless girls. But Faye's solitude was deliberate and unchildlike. Their similarities, however, kept throwing them together. Faye was excused from P.E. and allowed to read in the library during that period. Jean hated P.E. and did everything she could from week to week to get excused. So she often got to sit out the class in the library, too. Faye would look crossly at her whenever she appeared.

The one form of exercise open to Faye was swimming. There was no swimming pool, but there was a stream on the school grounds, about twenty minutes' walk from the dormitory. It was shallow and not considered dangerous. The girls were allowed to swim there as long as there were three or more of them and they were accompanied by an older student. This precaution was mainly because of boys from the surrounding countryside who occasionally peeped at or called to them from the other side of the barbed-wire fence. Jean knew that Faye always went there alone. Sometimes she quietly followed her.

One day while Faye was swimming, Jean stole her crutches. She didn't stop to think why she had done such a mean, crazy thing or what she was going to do with the crutches, but they had been lying there on the riverbank along with Faye's shoes and clothes. Jean could not resist snatching them. She hid behind the bushes with them. Faye's crutches! She examined them, noticing that the white rubber tops where Faye's weight rested were grimy and worn. Jean rested her own weight on the crutches. She lifted both feet off the ground. The mechanics of it eluded her. She tried to move forward but couldn't. With her weight upon them, the crutches sank into the damp soil. She was stuck, and she felt, not like Faye, but like a child with a circus toy. And then she heard Faye's cry. She looked at her through the bushes and was filled with shame and desperation. What had she done? And now what was she going to do? She threw down the crutches and navigated her way behind the bushes till she reached the bottom of the footpath, then she walked back up to the river, pretending that she just happened at that moment to be taking a walk. Her heart was pounding. Faye was on her hands and knees. She looked dazed.

'Somebody took my crutches.'

At first Jean tried to help her to her feet, with the idea of Faye leaning against her and using her as a crutch. But this wouldn't work. Faye was too heavy. Jean would have to get help. She ran to the infirmary and came back with Nurse and one of the sisters. Another pair of crutches was found, too large for Faye, but better than nothing.

For the rest of the day everyone talked about the theft of Faye's crutches and naturally blamed it on trespassing country boys. Faye was given the rest of the day off and allowed to go to her room and rest.

After supper, Jean ran back to the bushes where she had left the crutches and threw herself facedown in the dirt beside them.

It was sundown, and she was determined to stay there through the night to punish herself. She wished the earth would open up and swallow her. She could not make herself low enough. God had seen. Terrible things would happen to her, and she deserved the very worst.

She brought the crutches back to Faye.

'I found them in the bushes.'

Faye began to cry. She was happy and unhappy and mostly exhausted.

'I'm sorry this happened to you.'

Faye's body was in spasms. 'So-so-somebody think is a joke to see me crawling like that.'

'No. I don't think so.'

'You don't think so? I do.'

Faye glared at her. Jean couldn't bear it.

'If it happen again, I jus' goin' sit there till somebody come find me. I not goin' let anybody laugh at me.'

'It won't happen again.'

'I rather dead than crawl around like any damn cockroach.'

When she had exhausted herself crying and wiped her eyes, she noticed that Jean was still there, and she made an effort to smile. Jean had never seen her smile.

She picked up the book she was reading and showed it to Jean. 'This is a good story. You ever read it?'

It was *Robinson Crusoe*.

They invented a game which they played together for months and talked about for years: Crusoe and Friday. They acted out scenes based on the titles of chapters: 'I See the Shore Spread with Bones' or 'We March Out Against the Cannibals.' It was like acting on a radio show, since Faye couldn't move about easily, their play was nevertheless quite energetic and loud. Jean felt there should be a female in the story, so they invented a native girl named Monday. Eventually they got rid of Crusoe altogether, although every now and then, they came upon his footprints and searched for him in vain.

The summer before Faye went to England for her operation, she and her mother, Dr Catherine Galdy, visited Jean in Kingston. Monica had heard of Dr Galdy, and was interested in cultivating a friendship with her. She invited her to sit awhile on the veranda and have a glass of lemonade.

'It's been nearly three years since Roy died. You know how it is, raising a daughter alone.'

'You have two, don't you?'

Monica looked at her blankly.

'Two daughters?'

'Oh, yes. But Lana is quite a grown-up. Jean, being so small when her father died, you know, needs *a lot* of attention. I often think about giving up the bakery so I can stay home and look after her.'

Jean was astonished to hear this.

'Let me know if I can do anything to help,' Dr Galdy said. 'You must come visit us up at Gordon Town one Sunday. Bring bathsuits. We have a river near the house, fresh and cool.'

'That would be lovely. I'm glad Jean has made such a nice friend at school . . .'

Dr Galdy had the same pale, almost translucent coloring as her daughter, but there the resemblance ended. Faye had obviously inherited her large body and big blue eyes from her father. Her mother was a thin, neat woman with small, piercing, brown eyes and the quick, precise movements of a bird. She was a reserved, efficient woman, one of the first women doctors in Jamaica, a successful pediatrician who had survived two sad marriages. Her first husband, Sam Galdy, had been an alcoholic who had beaten her and who had died mysteriously of a gunshot wound (there was a rumor that he had been killed by his crazy half-brother). Her second marriage, to a notorious gambler, was brief and ended in divorce. Since then she had thrown herself entirely into her work, the raising of her daughter, and visiting her first husband's aging mother and all the other decrepit Galdys who depended on her.

While she was in England, Faye wrote frequently to Jean, describing the 'upstairs buses' in London and the cold weather – 'The sun here is like the moon, it doesn't make you warm.' When she returned, she wore braces on her legs. She went back to England the following year to have the braces removed and for several months of physical therapy.

From then on she was all movement, able for the first time to walk, run, and jump like other children. At the age of twelve, she already had the shape she would have as a woman: flat-chested, with wide hips and long legs. She reminded Jean, in an endearing way, of a giraffe. She developed a long, swift, but ungraceful stride, never looking where she was going, and forever bumping into things. It wasn't just her body that had new energy. She had outbursts of rapid, excited speech between long periods of her old, contemplative silence. Having shed the restraints of painful disease, she began to revel in unruliness.

There was a history teacher from England, Miss Locke, who favored the White girls and was especially fond of Faye. The students called her Raincoat, not because she wore a raincoat but because she had a saliva problem and spat so much when she spoke, especially when forming an s sound, that the girls in the front row felt the need for rain wear.

They were studying the Roman conquest of England.

'Who were these tribes of Angles and Saxons? Our ancestors who came to be known as Anglo-Saxons.'

'*Our* ancestors?' Faye's voice boomed across the classroom.

'You don't consider yourself *Jamaican*, do you, dear?'

'No. I don't *consider* myself Jamaican. I *am* Jamaican.'

There were titters from the class, followed by silence as everyone waited to see how Raincoat would respond.

'Stand up when you *speak* to me.'

Faye stood up.

'And remain standing for the rest of the class.' Raincoat continued with the lesson: 'The Roman conquerors built——'

'Excuse me, Miss Locke——' Faye interrupted.

Everyone, including Miss Locke, gaped.

'Since this is a history class, I thought we might continue our discussion of my ancestors.'

Raincoat realized she would have to punish her favorite if she was going to keep the class in order. 'Bring your chair to the front,' she told Faye. It was the usual classroom punishment for speaking rudely to a teacher: standing on a chair facing the class. It was meant to be humiliating.

Faye brought up her chair and stood on it in front of the class. A wicked grin crept across her face.

'There's a plaque in old Port Royal commemorating Lewis Galdy,' Faye began. 'He was that famous Frenchman who fell into a crack during the Great Earthquake of 1692 and was spat up alive some time later——'

Some of the girls giggled.

Jean watched from the back of the classroom and saw the effect Faye was having on her audience. She had seen this histrionic side of Faye even back in the days when she had crutches, but no one else had. The class stared at her amazed.

'That's my ancestor, known in our family as Baldy-Galdy.'

The whole class laughed.

'The Galdys have lived in Jamaica since then, Miss Locke.'

'Get down. *Stop* behaving like a lunatic.' Miss Locke's voice shook.

'I come from a long line of lunatics. *Jamaican* lunatics.'

The class roared.

'Go down Marescaux Road in Kingston and you see an ole pink-face man on the street corner, preachin' Bible an' givin' away bars of soap. That's my uncle, Willy Galdy.'

The class broke down; students doubled over laughing, others banged on their desks and hooted and cheered.

Faye was sent into detention for the rest of the day. It did not seem to perturb her in the least. She took a novel with her and spent the hours quietly reading.

Later as Jean and Faye were entering the dining hall, one of their classmates caught up with them and said to Faye: 'You don't *consider* yourself Jamaican, do you dear?'

Faye snapped back: 'Wha' the hell you know about it?'

'Jesus! I was jus' joking.'

Faye walked on, muttering, 'It's not a joke.'

17

The land changes from riotous to serene. They drive by a private estate with tidy pastures and stone walls. Jean sees, like something from an ancient tale, a black horse prancing in a field.

The Spanish settlers brought horses to the island, rare and expensive breeds. Did this beauty carry the blood of one of those originals? For years the Spanish hid in the mountains and made counterraids on the English settlers to recover their confiscated horses.

Jean went riding with Alan one day. She had not wanted to go at first but realized that she must seem quite lazy to him; she had not wanted to play tennis or go scuba diving or sailing. So they got horses and rode around Portland. The island looked different from horseback. She imagined she was seeing things as women of earlier centuries had. *We rode every day, my father and I, to the river, our river.* There were still places that were inaccessible except by horse or mule. She told Alan about a place called Nonesuch. Of course he wanted to go. They rode for hours, stopping now and then to ask directions, until a steep track through the forest brought them to a cliff. From that height they saw the northeast point of the island, pricked with coves, white ribbons of sand, and bright blue shallows.

'You realize you live in Paradise?'

'Only because you've told me a hundred times.'

'But it's sad, as sad as Ireland.'

He looked battered; his shoulders were hunched over as if he carried all the unredeemable sins of his race. We are not so different, she thought. Ghosts stood in his way; she could see that.

'Is it Paradise you're looking for?' she asked. 'Some unspoiled place to start all over from scratch?'

'I used to.'

'What happened?'

'The usual. I got shipwrecked.'

'I thought you had to be shipwrecked to find Paradise, that only castaways got that kind of chance.'

'You're very wise. And cynical.'

She watches the black horse running alongside the stone wall as if obeying some secret purpose, and remembers that there is a riding school around here. She went once with her father to see a competition. 'A horse is all nerves and spirit,' her father told her. 'It's one of the toughest creatures.' Roy loved horses, especially racehorses. There was a picture in the family album of Roy and Mr Ho Sing posing beside a racehorse and jockey. They would go together every Saturday to watch the races. Jean has a cloudy memory of going with them, of Mr Ho Sing picking her up in his old, lean arms so that she could see better.

To think of Mr Ho Sing is to think of a better place, a respite from the whirlwind scattering and destroying them. Would Mr Ho Sing recognize this island now? He had sought out this country that she now seeks to leave; as a boy in the dangerous streets of Macao, he had dreamed about the West Indies. A city boy in the Old World, he became a city man in the New, untantalized by the paradisiac countryside, anchoring himself in the dusty commerce of the colonial town. Mr Ho Sing – taking his nightly walk on Kingston streets, hearing piano music inside the houses, tipping his hat to the women sitting on their verandas. Whose memories are these? Who speaks to her of this gentle time that she is too young to have known herself? There was hardship then, certainly, but not hearts chained and heavy with fear. Who is it that laughs with aged lightheartedness and suggests that this is still a place of promise?

18

Mr Ho Sing
c. 1866–1962

It was the same year Dark Star win the Kentucky Derby. Roy, him say to me, 'What a horse, eh? Imagine if you was to own a horse like dat, Mr Ho Sing, how you woulda feel.'

We neva really did see Dark Star fe true, we jus' read 'bout him and see him picture in de newspaper. Roy an' me go Caymanas Park every Sat'day. Him don't call me Grandfada or Poppa or any a dem ting. Everybody call me Mr Ho Sing from time I reach Jamaica.

You see, me was 'fraid fe give me family name to de ship agent because I was Hakka, and a lot a people don't like Hakka dem days in China. I want bad-bad to reach Cuba. So I give the ship agent the name of a crimp I used to work for in Macao.

But that is another story.

I was telling you how me, Mr Ho Sing, who own a grocery shop in Vineyard Town, did come to buy a thoroughbred racehorse. Not no face-boy horse fe breed and parade 'round. No sah, a real champion, Marshal Bloom. From de minute Roy say dat to me 'bout Dark Star, the idea just snap! *so in me head, and I don't stop till I bring-de-horse-come from Ireland.*

I never tink 'bout racehorse till I turn ole man, after I meet Miss Rema.

Before Rema, was Lim Su. An' before Lim Su was Pamela. Pamela was wife numba one, an' Lim Su was wife numba two. An' before dem, was China.

Awright, awright, I goin' tell you how I reach Jamaica.

But keep in mind what I really want to tell you 'bout is Miss Rema and Marshal Bloom, an' how a 'ooman an' a racehorse did mek an ole man life sweet.

I come from de people in Kwantung wha' dem did call Hakka. 'Hakka' mean 'visitor' an' is so dem did call us because we did come down from the North. One day some people come an' bun down de whole village. Everybody dead. Only two a we escape, me sister and me. We run an' hide fe a long time. Sometimes she carry me on her back, an' we go from place to place till we reach water. I remember me sister face, but I don't remember her name.

In Macao, we live 'pon street. Different street-dem. Beggin' an' stealin'. One day she gone. A lot a kidnappin' an' killin' goin' on. I tink she goin' come back one day, but no, and after a while I feel she gone fe true.

I start work fe a crimp. Ships tekin' Chinese people to Cuba and Sout' America to work in de sugar field because African slavery done. A lot a crimp, dem beat up people and put dem 'pon de ship.

Some people in Macao have plenty money in dem pocket. If you have money you can get anyting in Macao, even get outa trouble. Jail, beatin', killin' — nuttin' bad happen to you as long as you can pay. One day, out 'pon street, I see a crimp beat a man till him dead. I feel I going dead too if I stay in Macao. So I mek up me mind fe go Cuba.

I get on a ship, but de ship don't reach nowhere. It start fe sink a sea. Plenty people drown. I swim back to Macao. When I was a chile, I used to dive fe money wha' de sailors t'row us. Dat's how me learn fe swim. Two years pass before I can leave again.

I hear de Prince Alexander tekin' Chinese laborers to Jamaica. When I reach Jamaica, I will find a boat goin' Cuba. I don't 'fraid even though I hear some bad story 'bout what happen to indentured people.

Indentured Chinese is jus' like African slave, I hear. Me no believe it. Anyway, I not staying in Macao. I sign up wid de ship agent, an' same time, I feel like a human, not a stray dawg lookin' food every day.

Almos' seven hundred Chinese 'pon de boat goin' Jamaica. Right away I see is true: I sign meself ina slavery. We down in de ship bottom and we don't see daylight. Hakka an' Cantonese too. People fightin'. People sick. People hungry an' t'irsty.

One night dem put a sack over a man head and cut him t'roat right in front a me. Why? Me no know. Me feel like me a travel tru hell. Me wonder if me goin' reach anywhere.

Wha' people dem suffer on all dem ship from China, from India, from Africa, nobody know, nobody can say. Too much people. Too much story.

When I reach Jamaica, I see daylight first time in two months. Dem send me to Luck-and-Field Estate in St Thomas. Overseer tek us to de barracks where we to live, six man to a room. Him explain de rules: We work fe t'ree years fe one shilling an' sixpence a day. If we leave Luck-and-Field widout we papers, we go jail. If we gone more than one day we go jail an' we pay five pounds fine.

Me say to meself, me not no slave. I not use to field work an' me get sick. I run 'way and tek bus go Kingston. When I reach, me so sick wid fever me almos' dead. Me fall down in de middle a de street and somebody carry-me-go a poorhouse run by Jesuits. I stay an' dem feed and look after me, even gimme new close fe wear. I 'come Roman Cat'olic.

Mr Hanna on King Street gimme me a job in him haberdashery shop, sweepin' an' doin' messenger-boy work. I get a bicycle an' one pound five shilling a week. You listenin'? One pound five shilling, an' one shilling extra fe buy lunch. I mek up me mind to save all but de extra shilling. I still want fe go Cuba.

I live in a shantytown place out by Kingston Railway Station. Ten years' time, me save plenty money, but I change me plans. José Martí fightin' over in Cuba, so I decide to stay in Jamaica. I know me way 'round Kingston an' it seem like an awright place. I see some Chinese man start shop. So I tek me money, buy meself a new shirt and trousers from Mr Hanna at ten percent discount, an' I pay down on a likkle shop in Vineyard Town.

I get a man fe paint a sign: Ho Sing Grocery. An' I find a 'ooman fe help me wid de sellin' because me English not good. Now listen how it go: I sell likkle bit a dis, likkle bit a dat to poor people who cyaan buy a whole heap. I sell penny wort' a cheese, quarter-pack a cigarette, quattie wort' a salt fish. An' I wrap it up nice in brown paper, no matter how small. Dat is how Chinee people succeed in Jamaica. You hear me?

De 'ooman who help me in de shop is Pamela. She 'ave schoolin' and she good-good wid de customers, so me marry her. We have five pickney, a girl, Cherry, an' four boys. Miss Pamela was a good 'ooman. She know how fe hangle de customer-dem. Dem respeck her and call her ma'am. She work as hard as me, plus she raisin' five pickney. I feel sorry when she pass away. The youngest only two years old when she gone.

Cherry, she de oldest, and she try tek her mother place. She work in de shop an' cook an' tek care a de boys. But I want Cherry fe go school. So I decide fe get a secon' wife.

I go to de Chinese Benevolent Association. A lot a Chinese people sendin' fe dem family. One man tell me 'bout him sister in Kwangtung Province. I say awright and pay money send fe her.

Lim Su was 'bout fifteen when she come here. She come off a de boat sick an' crawny. Twelve pickney was in her family and dem so poor dem start drown de girl-chile-dem. She like Jamaica, and after a while she get fat. But she don't speak English, and she 'fraid a Black people. Anyway, she do awright.

She tek care a Pamela five pickney-dem and she gimme four more sons. Is ten pickney I have in all, five half-Chinese, four Chinese, and later on, Noel, Rema's son.

Tings was good-good until dem bun down me shop in de Anti-Chinese Riot. But I build it back up an' I add two more rooms fe me family.

Dem say Black people turn against Chinee shopkeeper. So dem say, dem history book an' history teacher. But is not true. Syrian shop-dem don't give credit to Black people. Only Chinee give credit and sell small-small fe Black people. Is not true dem hate we. You know what really cause de riot? 'Ooman.

A Chinee man catch him 'ooman in bed wid a policeman and him beat him up. Policeman start tell people lie 'bout how Chinese people goin' tek over de island, tek over govenment an' bank, an' turn Communist. Dat is de true story behind de Anti-Chinese Riot: man an' 'ooman.

All me pickney go school and grow up same like Jamaican pickney. Dem don't talk Chinese. Cherry, she go Cat'olic school till she turn twelve. Den she start help in de shop. She good wid customers and smart like Pamela wid money. Plus she have some good ideas, like fe start sell lunch food — patty an' coco bread, bun an' cheese. Cherry, she a bawn business-'ooman.

One day a man come wid some nice bread fe show me, say him want to do some wholesale business. Him name George Landing an' him have a bakery in Morant Bay. I decide to give him some business, an' I let Cherry work out de figures wid him. Every time him come, I notice him and Cherry doing a whole lot a palaverin'. She buy up him bullah an' plantain tart and all kind a ting. I not surprise when him come one day and ask fe marry she.

I see him is a good, sensible man, but Cherry, she only fourteen.

I say, 'Ask me again in two years.'

Him come ask me again one year later.

I tell him, 'Look, I cyaan do widout Cherry fe help me in de shop. You can bake bread anywhere. Move to Kingston an' we can talk 'bout weddin'.'

When him gone, I say, 'Cherry, how you feel? You wan' go Morant Bay?'

She say, 'No, Mr Ho Sing, I don't wan' fe live in de country.'

'You like him, Cherry?'

'I like him but I don't wan' fe leave Kingston.'

'You tell him so?'

'Yes, me tell him.'

Dat is how Mr Landing bakery come a Kingston. Him start fe sell bread all over Jamaica. Him get rich and give bread 'way to poor people. And Cherry, she give me t'ree grandson.

Time pass, an' I know I gettin' ole in age, but I don't feel no different from before. Lim Su, she feelin' ole, an' she tired all de time. So Rema come fe do some washin' an' ironin' fe help out Lim Su.

First time I see her I tink, what a nice, honest smile she have. She like to chat an' laugh. Lim Su like a ghost, she so quiet. She stop sleep wid me long time. Long time I don't feel like a man.

One Sunday, I go Pentecostal church meetin' jus' fe see Rema. When church done, she tek me over by where she live. Is a bad place in Denham Town, a real shanty yard. Right away, I tell her how I feel. Me a ole man, 'bout eighty years ole, and I feel a likkle foolish talkin' sweetness to young 'ooman. She listen and look at me wid her big eye-dem, an' she don't laugh at me. I tell her I will tek care of her and find her a nice place to live. She say yes. One year later we have a son, Noel. Is no secret. Cherry, she come to Noel christenin'. Even Lim Su know, but she act like she don' know.

Rema brother-in-law was a jockey and him give her free tickets to Caymanas Park. First time I go racetrack, I win five pounds an' I tek it buy Rema gold bangle. She say is her lucky bangle and she wear it every time we go racetrack. We start go every Sat'day. Rema, she all dress up in hat an' ting, sitting in ten-shilling seat. She a 'ooman what like to laugh and enjoy life, an' she don't allow any chupidness fe trouble her. I never know anybody like she. Me grandson, Roy, start fe come wid us every week. It get to be a regular outing. And when we not at racetrack, we readin' racing paper, following Belmont and Kentucky Derby. I tell you, horses like Citation an' Count Fleet we not goin' see anyting like dem again. It wasn't bettin' I like so much, it was de racehorse-dem.

It tek almos' four years to bring Marshal Bloom to Jamaica. By then me have plenty money save up. Shop still mekin' good money. All me pickney have big house an' car. Rema, she have a nice house. Lim Su, she not complainin'. I wearin' de same hat I buy in 1924, an' I don't need no new suit. Cherry, she say, 'Why you don't take you money and buy youself a proper house?' But Lim Su don't like change, an' I don' mind livin' behind de shop. How much longer I goin' live anyway? I decide to tek t'irty-t'ousand pounds, dat is everyting me have in de bank, an' buy racehorse. Me pickney-dem say I mad. Dem say Rema mussee turn me into one big fool.

Now, I not a super-stitch-ous man, but night before me go bank someting happen fe make me start worry.

Me hear Lim Su in de kitchen, sayin' 'Shoo, shoo,' an' I hear whole heap a commotion. A black cat follow her in de house and she t'rowin onion, orange, knife, fork, an' everyting at it, fe mek it gone. No cat ever come in de place before. I wonder if is a sign. I tell her, 'Leave de puss alone because good luck or bad luck I don't know, an' anyway it will keep 'way mouse.'

But I worry so till I cyaan sleep and nex' day I go church to pray. I say,

'Lord, if I doin' a bad ting, mek someting happen to stop me on de way to de bank.' I leave church. Sun shinin' bright. Bus come. Everyting awright.

When de ship come from Ireland wid Marshal Bloom is jus' my bad luck, dem havin' a dockworker strike, so I ha fe bribe de union leader and pay whole heap a money fe get him off a de boat. What a beauty! I don't know what I want to do more, laugh or cry, when I first see him.

First week of racing season, Marshal Bloom show him is a superior horse. Him come in first or second in every race. People asking: 'Where dis horse come from?' Newspaper write up story. Priest an' government minister come to me shop to shake me hand. But the best feeling come from seeing de Marshal fly 'round de track.

T'ree weeks in a row him win. Big bet 'pon him now. Him name on radio. Is a celebrity horse!

Week number four, I see Marshal Bloom fallin' behind. Two, t'ree, four horse pass him. I feel he mussee sick. Race after race him losin'. Doctor check him out and say him okay. Week number five, him come dead last every race. I feel somebody poison him. Doctor check him again. No poison. Week after week him comin' last. People start laugh when announcer call out Marshal Bloom.

'Lim Su mouth run faster dan dat horse.'

'Horse cyaan beat him own shit outa start.'

An' I hear some people say, 'Chu man, what Chinee-man know 'bout racehorse. Dem fe keep shop.'

I run him de whole season and him don't pick up. I know someting wrong because him is a prize thoroughbred from Ireland, not no mix-up local breed. I wonder if somebody put obeah on him. But Roy, him tell me dat you cyaan put obeah 'pon horse.

You know is nearly two years straight Marshal Bloom come last in every race. It come like a joke. Me horse turn out to be a bawn loser. I sit in de bleachers, me head bend down. Roy him try to cheer me up, but even him cyaan find nuttin' good fe say.

Him say, 'Life is one hell of a ting, eh? You cyaan be sure 'bout anyting.'

Roy talkin' sense. For is not de money wha' mek me want to bawl, *is de* mystery *a de ting. I cyaan eat an' I cyaan sleep. I feel bad luck goin' kill me.*

Cherry suggest we tek him to a bush doctor. Him boil up bush tea an' give it to de Marshal an' Marshal spit it out. Him give him bush bath an' rub sorrel on him foot. Marshal don't like dis kind a treatment at-all. Him start mek noise and move like him goin' kill somebody. Bush doctor say jockey Sylvester need bush tea an' dat it will cost me ten more shilling.

Dat no mek sense to me. I say to him 'Nuttin' no wrong wid de rider, man, is de horse.'

Bush doctor say him have twenty year hexperience wid jus' dis kind a ting. Jockey Sylvester mus' drink bush tea an' tek bush bath, fifteen shillings.

De bush bath don't do Marshal Bloom no good. Him still come last. I don't even know why I bother race him. And jockey Sylvester stomach runnin' all day long. Him bend up an' can hardly walk, much less ride. Chu, I vex, you see!

Rema say, Is not bush *bath him need, is* sea *bath. So we lock up shop for a week an' go Oracabessa. Whole family an' horse go beach.*

Who tell me fe go Oracabessa in jellyfish season? We almos' lose de horse. After him get sting, Marshal nah *go back ina de water. Him si' down in de shade. Cherry an' Rema, dem cookin' up food an' ting, say we havin' picnic. Me losin' me patience now. Me say, 'Look. Is no picnic dis. Is a serious ting.'*

Rema she say, 'So we cyaan enjoy weself likkle bit? Come, relax, Mr Ho Sing.'

'How me mus' relax when racehorse lie down so 'pon beach? You tink dis is a nawmal situation?'

Roy say, 'Look, Mr Ho Sing, mek we stop try now. We jus' confusin' de animal. Not every horse is a winner.'

But dat is exactly what I cyaan understand — why my horse should lose. Me who God know work hard an' never trouble nobody, who go to church and raise ten good pickney — why my horse ha fe lose?

I vex now. I vex wid God, horse, man, an' 'ooman.

When we go back a Kingston I decide fe let him run out de rest a de season den send him a country fe breed him.

But in me heart every time I see him on de track I hopin' him will come in even t'ird or fourt'. Just so him don't finish like one big joke.

I find meself talking to him. Sometimes I lose me temper an' shout: 'I spend me life-saving on you. What else you want? You want money? You want me girlfrien'? You want rum? You want lay down in bed beside me? You want me grocery shop? Me pickney?'

I tell him 'bout him father and mother in Ireland and how him is a prince of horses.

All dis I jus' saying in me head and mostly in Chinese. All day long I keepin' quarrel wid Marshal Bloom.

I feel like life drainin' outa me. An' one day Rema say, 'Mr Ho Sing, you getting ole. Time you stop work.' I so vex, if I did have a gun I woulda shoot meself in front a she.

I lef' de house and I tek a bus out to Spanish Town where we keep Marshal. Is a long ride and is night when I reach and the night air cool down me temper. Yes, I getting ole fe true. What I was t'inking, man a my age, to bring racehorse 'cross water? Bible word come hit me all of a sudden — 'vanity.' I never tink a meself as a vain man, but now I see is vanity stop me from seein' what is true. Roy telling me. Cherry tellin' me. Even Rema tellin' me. Me ole. Me finish.

'You was me one dream,' I say, and dis time I talkin' fe true to Marshal Bloom, not to meself.

'Me one dream.'

I keep goin' racetrack every Sat'day. I don't feel no more shame. People stop tek notice of me an' me horse long time.

One Sat'day I place two pounds on a horse name Sky's the Limit, a filly first time on the track. Race start an' I see Sky's the Limit not doin' too bad.

I hear Rema say, 'But see here . . .'

An' nex' ting me hear big shoutin' an' ting. Is Marshal Bloom. I watching Sky's the Limit and not even lookin' which horse winning. Me cyaan believe it. Marshal Bloom, gone like a bullet! Like him jus' mek up him mind to win that day.

Only one human on de whole island put down money on Marshal Bloom. Rema. Every race she still puttin' five shilling on him, fe ole time sake. Ha! She mek a killin'. Roy him laughin' 'bout it fe weeks. Everybody talkin' 'bout it fe a long-long time. And you know, Marshal Bloom do awright after dat. Him don't win every race, but him no lose like before.

Rema, she have a big heart, eh? She never give up on 'im.

After Lim Su pass 'way I ask Rema fe marry me. She say, 'Not a chance.' She say me kill off two wife areddy an' she no reddy fe dead. So we go on same way.

19

'You told Monica?' Paul asks.

'Yes.'

She delayed telling her as long as possible, certain that Monica would scoff at her fears. Monica will never leave Jamaica. In spite of all the difficulties and dangers, her run-ins with the government, and the fact that many of her friends and relatives have left, she has made it clear: 'Come hell or high water, you goin' find me right here a sell bread an' tek breeze 'pon me veranda.' *So we go on same way*. Monica, Jean realizes, is one of those tenacious creatures like Mr Ho Sing, able to withstand tropical vicissitudes. And what about her? There was still time to turn back.

'Monica knows about Alan?'

Jean nods. Yes, she had even told her mother that she was going to live in New York with Alan, a white man twice her age and married. 'It was a bit of a surprise.'

'Monica, surprised?' He considers this for a moment. 'I suppose she never expected any surprises from *you*.'

'That's exactly what she said.' The very words: *Well, Jean, I have to admit, I never expected any surprises like this from you.*

'How did she take it?'

Jean shrugs. 'Like Monica.'

'Still, it must be hard. And now with Lana—'

What about you, Paul, how are you taking Lana's dying, my leaving?

They have an unspoken pledge, it seems, to make this journey across the country as much as possible like the others.

'Look,' he says, pointing.

It's that tree, the flame-of-forest, exploding in orange bloom. A hurricane felled it years ago, yet it continues to grow on its side. The fiery blossoms seem to shoot up out of the ground. She and Paul call it the burning bush.

'You won't see that in New York,' he says.

It's a smarting reminder to her and to himself: this journey is different. The road used to be a refuge for them; now refuge, if it is to be had at all, lies in the destination, not the journey.

20

'Oh, Gawd, only eight days left,' Lana wailed.

'Maybe there'll be a hurricane and the road will wash away,' Jean said, trying to console her.

'Is not hurricane season, Dolly.'

They were in Lana's room at Mercy on a Saturday afternoon, and Lana was filing Jean's fingernails. The other girls couldn't wait for their parents to pick them up for the Christmas holidays. Lana and Jean grew nervous as they counted down the days.

'I wish she would let us stay at Cherry's.'

'Or with Daphne.'

'Never. It not goin' happen. We in fe a hard life, face it.'

There were some nice things about going home: Cherry cooked delicious things for them, and they saw their cousins and their Kingston friends. But Monica's vigilant watch over her daughters grew sharper as they grew older: 'It better not be no boy you dressin' up for,' she would say to Lana as Lana left to go shopping with friends. Monica would find Jean enjoying a quiet moment on the veranda: 'So you have time to waste daydreamin'? That crabgrass growing on the driveway need to pull up.' During the holidays Monica made Jean take lessons every afternoon with Miss Dewey to prepare her for the high school common entrance exams. Miss Dewey, a retired teacher with a reputation for strictness, gave the lessons in her dreary, stifling home; the curtains in the living room were always drawn and the place reeked of Scott's Emulsion, a milky cod-liver-oil tonic which Miss Dewey believed gave children mental stamina. Fortunately Monica had requested that Jean not be given the tonic, her private reason being that she couldn't bear Jean coming home with the smell. Jean was already an excellent student; her grades couldn't be higher. 'Why do I have to go every day?' she asked her mother.

'It's good for you an' it will keep you outa trouble.'

Lana was also supposed to take lessons, but she rebelled and got her way at least in this instance. Every holiday there were miserable noisy scenes between Monica and Lana that had Jean searching for some peaceful corner of the house or garden.

That day in December 1966 when Monica appeared to take her daughters home for the holidays, she arrived in a red Mercedes driven by a man her daughters had never seen before. His name was Dr Delgado. Everyone called him Delly. He was a JLP member of Parliament, and the minister of health. The girls were not driven directly home as usual. Delly had a house in Ocho Rios, so the girls were treated to an afternoon at the beach and a picnic of cold roast chicken and potato salad, which Monica said she had prepared herself. Monica frolicked in the sea with her daughters, a sight that enchanted Delly and stunned the girls. 'What a lovely picture,' he kept saying. 'A wish a had my camera.'

Dr Delgado was married to a woman much younger than himself who ran a baby clothes boutique and who seemed to be perpetually pregnant. She never went anywhere with her husband, not to state functions or to his country constituency, and the doctor was a notorious womanizer. Monica had met Delly before she married Roy, and he had made a good impression on her at the time. He was not very handsome – in fact, his jowls reminded her of illustrations of Lewis Carroll's Walrus – but he was charming and there was something comforting about his large body. They had lost touch, then seen each other recently at a cocktail party. She was pleased to see that he still had a full head of hair, and she was certain that he was flirting with her. She mentioned that she was driving to St Ann to pick up her daughters and by the way, she asked, wasn't his constituency near there? Yes, he was a member of Parliament for that very district and had a home in Ocho Rios – a love nest, he added, laughing.

She had been wanting a man friend for some time. Jean overheard her saying so to Daphne.

'This is not a country for a woman to be alone. People dem start su-su su-su, men dem try to tek advantage a you, an' women dem don't trust you. Is bad business.'

'I don' give a damn what people say, they bound to say something.' Daphne paused a while. 'True, I get lonesome, but come to think of it, I was more lonesome when I was married.'

'I not talkin' marriage, I jus' want a good man by me side. Sometimes I really miss Roy.'

'Delly not a bad fellow.'

Monica learned that Delly had recently moved to a palatial home in Red Hills. So when she ran into his wife, Norma, at Baby World, she struck up a conversation and got herself invited to dinner.

Monica took Jean along. They were greeted at the front door by Norma, a gaunt, light-skinned woman whose only feminine appeal, as far as Monica could tell, lay in her big, dark eyes, which seemed blind to her husband's activities. Monica wondered how a fenky-fenky woman like Norma could run a business. She had given birth to twin girls several months before and was still wearing maternity clothes. The couple now had six children.

'What a lovely place,' Monica said, casting her eyes about the new house and carefully stepping past the assortment of tricycles, prams, and high chairs that blocked the doorway. There was a Winnie-the-Pooh baby blanket draped over the couch. 'Did you do the decorating yourself?'

'Oh, yes, every bit. Would you like me to show you around?'

'Yes, please, but first, I'm just dying to see the two new little ones.'

'Let's start with the nursery, then.'

'The nursery?' Monica was still taking in the living room with its playpen, toys, and crayon drawings. 'That would be lovely.'

Delly joined them in the nursery. Monica picked up each twin in turn and looked intently at their faces, remarking on how the nose resembled the mother's, the eyes the father's, and so on.

'Aren't they cute, Jean?' She turned to Delly and Norma. 'There is absolutely nothing like the feeling of a child in your arms.'

Delly said he would soon be making an official tour of the children's hospital. Would Monica like to come along?

At the hospital, Monica proved to have such a special way with sick children, and she showed so much concern for the abandoned babies that Delly invited her to be on the Ministry of Health's Orphanage Committee. This quickly propelled her into the elite society of charitable organizations, and finally led to her becoming president of WAPC, the Women's Association for the Protection of Children.

Within a year, Monica and Delly had become a popular couple; they escorted each other to public events and entertained together at her house. His former promiscuity came to an end, and he became entirely dependent on Monica. He even said he would divorce Norma and marry her, but Monica didn't want that. She had discovered that Delly was not quite as wealthy as he seemed. He was living on credit and governmental perks, and she had long ago decided that she wasn't going to share her hard-earned money with any man.

He was kind to Jean and Lana and bought them strange presents, completely inappropriate for their ages: large stuffed animals and dolls, and a toy phone for Lana on her sixteenth birthday. Monica came up with a plan for getting rid of these ridiculous gifts. The girls gift-wrapped and presented them to Dr Delgado's own little ones. Norma was delighted, and Delly didn't seem to notice.

With Delly's ongoing devotion, the bakery's increasing profits, and her ascent in Kingston society, Monica was becoming a very happy woman. Lana and Jean discussed the change. 'She hardly ever gets mad at us now,' Jean noted.

'She gettin' mellow. It mus' be love,' Lana said.

Having publicly established herself as a woman concerned about the nation's children, she began to show more affection for her own. One day Jean was reading aloud in her room and didn't hear her mother come in. She looked up and was startled to find Monica watching her. She wondered what she was doing wrong.

'You're a good reader,' Monica said. 'Don't stay up too late.'

Lana and Jean, who had always been proud of her, actually began to enjoy being around her. She was still strict with them, but for the first time in their lives she brought things home solely for their pleasure: goldfish, a Ping-Pong table, and, most memorable of all, a snakes-and-ladders game.

Sometimes they spent the whole evening playing this game, just the three of them. Monica would sit girlishly on the rug with them, having made them all glasses of iced coffee. If not for the chill of the ice against her teeth and the grainy residue at the bottom of the iced coffee to serve as physical evidence, Jean would have thought these evenings the product of her imagination — Monica and her girls joyously throwing dice, sliding the brightly colored discs up the coveted ladders or down into the bellies of the triumphant snakes.

21

A sign says BOG WALK; the letters PNP are scrawled over it in orange paint. Paul honks the horn at some cows walking in the middle of the road and drives slowly through the town.

Bog Walk is hardly a town. It's a wet piece of road and a bridge in a lush valley often in danger of being flooded by rains and by the rising of the nearby Rio Cobre. There are some small shops that cater to the students and faculty of an agricultural college nearby, and country cottages painted bright colors perch on the hillsides; they look like flamboyant trees from a distance.

They cross the bridge and notice teenage girls along the riverbank. She remembers among her father's books one by Trollope called *The West Indies and the Spanish Main*. Trollope had crossed the Bog Walk river on horseback before the bridge was built, and he had complained about the 'copiousness' – that was the word he had used – of Jamaica's rivers and about how difficult it was to get from place to place. He traveled with four horses: one for his native guide, one for his clothes, and two for himself because his weight was too much for one animal to bear through an entire journey. She imagines him 'trolloping' here, a heavyset white man in a white suit and hat, holding an umbrella rather unsteadily in one hand while with the other he negotiates his horse across the treacherous river; securely fastened across his belly is the leather satchel that contains his papers, his account of this unmanageable landscape.

The girls climb up from the riverbank to the road, balancing large buckets on their heads. Water, like flashes of light, splashes from the buckets. There's an Indian girl among them.

Whenever she sees something like this — a blue-eyed boy dressed in rags in some shantytown, stoning trees with Black boys, an old Chinese man with Rastafarian dreadlocks — she asks herself 'What happened here?' Because for all the tourist brochures' claims about harmonious mixing, a White, Indian, or Chinese face among the Black poor is incongruous.

Too much people. Too much story.

Who said that? Sometimes she remembers words spoken to her as if in dreams, as if she left behind an ear in another world. They come to her without solicitation, the sonorous phrases of the dead.

She sees Paul looking at the Indian girl. The girl stares back at him. She wears a worn-out country frock and her feet are bare, but her thin arms are plush with silver bangles.

'Lana went on like it didn't mean anything to be half-Indian,' he says.

'Half Ramcharan,' Jean says emphatically, because Lana's being part Indian wasn't anything; it was being Deepa Ramcharan's daughter and an outside child. Monica hated the Ramcharans so much that the hatred spread to everything and everyone Indian.

'Yeah, but she would just joke about it and call herself Monica's Coolie daughter. What I'm saying is she didn't act like it hurt her. That was her pride.'

He says 'pride' the way he would say 'corn' or 'stone' or the name of some other tangible thing.

'Pride,' he says again. 'She wouldn't ask her father for anything. He sent for her a couple years ago to join him in Connecticut. He was going to arrange a green card.'

'She didn't want to go?'

He shakes his head.

Did you want her to go? she wants to ask. Did it matter to you? Jean knows that it would have mattered to Lana what Paul thought.

Water trickles down the mossy, slippery mountainside from the many secret springs. She listens to this murmuring green, and to the last, gurgling syllables of the Rio Cobre as they leave Bog Walk. She strains to hear, to hear everything beyond Paul's chatter. Who or what is to blame for Lana's death? She wants a confession from this country, from its living and its dead.

She asks him, 'Would you have minded if she'd gone to America?'

'She should have gone when she had the chance. I told her so.'

Not her death but this lost chance seems to grieve him. Then it hits her that Paul has not had time to mourn. The smell of grave dirt is still fresh in his nostrils, in hers too, but unlike Paul she lost Lana long ago.

22

It was the summer of 1967. Jean was allowed for the first time to go street dancing with Lana on Independence night. Paul was to drive them and be 'in charge,' as Monica put it.

They had gone to Paul's apartment the evening before. He had all the latest records and they'd been listening to them and practicing their dancing all summer.

'What you think?' Lana came out of Paul's bathroom in a black-and-white-striped minidress. She had brought a bag full of outfits and shoes to try on. 'Eh, Paul?'

Paul looked up from the turntable: 'Nice. You look like a zebra.' He placed the needle in the groove of the record.

'Boom, boom . . .' Jean and Paul sang and began dancing the rock steady. They knew all the hits by heart, not just the lyrics but every instrumental quirk and ooh and aah.

Lana turned from the mirror and began dancing with them, studying their moves. She noticed that Jean had become a good dancer. 'You been practicing without me,' she said with a tinge of jealousy. 'Learning from the master himself.'

Paul was a superb dancer; he could dance to anything: cha-cha-cha, ska, rock steady.

'She good,' Paul complimented Jean. 'A born dancer. Look how she swing those hips.'

'What hips?' Lana teased. Jean had just started to wear a bra and her skinny body was beginning to fill out.

Jean stuck out her tongue at Lana. Paul saved her: 'She growin' a nice little figure.'

'Lawd, it hot,' Lana said when the song ended. She got some ice out of the refrigerator.

'You eatin' a ton of ice today,' Paul said, putting on another record.

'No, wait. Don't put it on yet. Lemme try on the bell-bottoms.'

They waited until she came out of the bathroom in pink bell-bottoms and a sheer white midriff blouse.

Paul whistled and put the record on.

'Jean, help me zip up me pants. Man, I gettin' fat. Can hardly hold in my stomach.'

'Fat is good,' Paul said.

Jean giggled. Judging from his girlfriends, Paul did indeed seem to find plumpness appealing. Cecile, the longest-surviving girlfriend, was a hefty woman with a huge bottom and hips so wide Jean wondered where she found panties to fit her.

'Chu man. The pants too tight,' Lana complained.

'Wear the mini,' Jean suggested.

'Yeah, wear the zebra dress,' Paul said, grabbing the sisters one in each hand and twirling them round to the song, 'Oh Carolina'.

'Lawd, de heat goin' kill me. Look how I sweatin' in me good shirt.' Lana sat down, fanning herself, breathless. 'Dolly, bring me some more ice, na.'

'After this song,' Jean said, and she took Paul's hand, letting him lead.

On Independence night Jean, wearing white bell-bottoms and a shiny yellow blouse, sat impatiently on Lana's bed. Lana had promised to do her hair in an updo, and Jean had been ready and waiting since seven o'clock. It was nine-thirty and Lana hadn't even started getting ready. She was moving slower than usual, partly because she'd felt ill all day, and partly because she found Jean's readiness irritating. It showed what a baby she was.

'Why you in such a hurry? Dancin' don't start till midnight.'

Jean looked chastised, and Lana changed her tone. 'Come, lemme put some eye shadow on you. Jus' a likkle. Monica won't notice.'

They went downstairs at ten-thirty to wait for Paul. Monica had fallen asleep on the veranda, reading the newspaper.

She heard them and woke up. 'Is what o'clock?' She looked at her watch. 'Lawd, so late.'

She looked at her daughters.

'Wait. You two coming or going?'

Lana tried not to sound nervous. 'Going.'

Monica looked them over and raised an eyebrow.

'Is what that you wearin'?'

'Who? Me?' Lana and Jean asked at the same time.

'You, Miss Ting' – she glared at Lana – 'wid you dress barely coverin' God's wisdom. You not leaving my house dressed like that.'

Jean felt a fight coming on. 'It's a minidress,' she said as if defining the outfit would dignify it.

'Listen, Monica—' Lana began. There was a horrendous moment of silence in which Lana seemed to be building up to some greater impertinence. Jean shuddered.

Paul drove up.

'I'm seventeen,' Lana said. 'I can dress how I want.'

'So you want to look like a whore. That's your idea of how to dress?'

Paul joined them on the veranda.

'Hello, Miss M., Lana, Jean. Ready to rock steady?'

'These girls not going anywhere tonight.'

Monica folded the newspaper and went inside.

Paul sat down. He would wait a few minutes and see how this family squabble turned out.

'You said we could!' Jean shouted after her. She had never shouted at her mother.

'And now I say *no*. Blame you sister, not me.'

'Well, I don't blame her.'

'You gettin' a rude mouth on you. Talk to me like that again an' I slap you so hard you head spin.'

'Jean—' Lana said, the tone of her voice signaling retreat. 'Is not worth it.'

Jean looked at Lana in disbelief. How could she give in so easily?

Monica walked calmly upstairs.

'Lock up the house properly before you come up,' she said.

Lana said good night to Paul and pulled Jean inside before she had a chance to say anything else. 'Trust me,' she said as they obediently locked up the house, 'I know Monica longer than you.'

Jean fell asleep after hours of exhaustive pondering and planning. She thought of running away from home. She didn't understand the recent change in Lana. She was often ill and tired; sometimes she stayed in bed all day.

'Wake up, quick, get dressed!'

It was Lana.

'What?'

'Shhhsh! You want to wake up Monica?'

'Where we going?'

'Dancing. What you think? Jesus Christ, Dolly. You comin' or you staying?'

'I comin', I comin'.'

A car was waiting not far from the front gate. In it was a man Jean had never seen before. Lana got in the front seat with him, put her arms around his neck, and kissed him.

'Gordon, this is my sister, Dolly.'

'Gordon Eales, at your service.' He saluted her.

So this was the boyfriend. He was much older than she had thought he would be; Jean noticed a bit of gray in his hair.

'You two don't look anything like sisters,' he said, studying Jean, who until that moment had thought she looked quite pretty with her grown-up hairdo. He turned to Lana and pulled her to him. Lana giggled and whispered, 'No, man, wait.'

The road around Reggie's Gas Station was all lit up. A band was playing at full volume and people were dancing and hollering. Jean, Lana, and the boyfriend pushed through the crowd and found Paul with Cecile. He didn't seem surprised to see Lana and Jean, and he had already met Gordon the Eel.

'Don't say a word – you never saw us,' Lana said.

'Me? Tell Monica?' he said, 'you mussee mad!'

'It's Byron Lee and the Dragonaires!' Jean shouted, recognizing the band, amazed to see them in person.

It was impossible to stand still without getting shoved or knocked down. Everybody was dancing with everybody and anybody. 'Nice outfit,' a sweaty man said to Jean and began dancing in front of her. The whole crowd was shouting and chanting the calypso lyrics, raising arms in the air, jumping, and grinding their hips. Paul winked at Jean. She looked around for Lana and Gordon.

'Where's Lana?'

Paul shrugged. 'Chu man, don't worry 'bout Lana.' He placed both hands on Cecile's hips and drew her close to him.

Jean was disheartened. She had longed for this night, when she would belong to the older group – Lana, Paul, and their friends – doing what they did, enjoying what they enjoyed. But she sensed that Lana was at that moment doing something secret and compelling and she was excluded from the knowledge of it.

Paul saw the worried look on Jean's face. He touched her arm and said again, 'I tell you, don't worry. Lana awright, man. Jus' enjoy yourself.'

She looked up and saw the sweaty man, her dancing partner, smiling at her in a way that was flattering and made her feel older than she was. She smiled back. Paul said Lana was all right; she tried to believe this, but in spite of her smiling and dancing, she couldn't help feeling somewhat mournful.

There was an unusual gathering of women around the kitchen table a few weeks later: Cherry Ho Sing Landing, Aunt Gwen, Aunt Daphne, Lana, Jean, and Irene. Irene wasn't actually sitting at the table although Cherry had tried to get her to.

'Come, Miss Irene. You part a this family, si' down.'

'No, ma'am, is awright.'

'You mek a good cup a coffee, Irene. You grind the beans?'

'Yes, ma'am. You want a likkle more?'

'Give me another shot, too, Irene,' Aunt Daphne said.

This gathering was all the more impressive because Daphne was there even though it was still morning. Everybody knew she slept until afternoon. Even when she had to do something earlier, like drive Astrid to school, she would stumble into her Volkswagen half-asleep with her nightie on, drive wherever it was she had to go, then go right back to bed. It was eleven o'clock and Daphne was there, wide awake and fully dressed.

'Well,' Gwen said, 'somebody has to tell Monica, because sooner or later she goin' find out.'

'Unless—' Daphne began and looked around.

'Too late for "unless." Is four months,' said pragmatic Gwen. Daphne often referred to her as the white sheep of the family.

'Four months!' Cherry looked at Lana sorrowfully. 'Why you never come to me before, sweetheart? I could a help you before dis ting get outa hand.'

Lana's eyes welled up; then she broke down crying.

'Hush, hush, never mind.' Cherry put her fat arms around Lana. 'Not the end a the world.'

A taxi drove up to the house. Irene went to the front door to greet Mary Darling. Lana had called her the night before, and she had made a six-hour bus journey to get there.

Mary Darling entered the kitchen, looking slightly weary. She had lived in the country all her life and walked, looked, and spoke like a rural woman. There was no urban restlessness about her. Where Cherry was full of quick, efficient movement, Mary Darling was altogether slow and heavy. There was no extra weight on her body, and yet she was not thin. Her straight posture had been inherited by all the Stern women; Jean, most of all, had the stamp of Mary's bearing, the big bones and languid movements. Jean had also inherited Mary's 'bad,' frizzy hair, which, once reddish-brown, was now entirely gray. She wore her hair as she had done for most of her life, in two braids pinned high on her head.

'Mama!' Lana threw her arms around her grandmother.

'Well, well, what we goin' do with you now, eh? Never mind. One, two, three, four, five, six, seven heads better than one.'

The blood raced to Jean's face; she felt proud, almost giddy, because Mary had counted her among the grown-up women.

When Lana had told Jean earlier that morning that she was expecting a baby, Jean's first thought had been, How wonderful, a baby. Then she had asked, 'You getting married? You going to marry Gordon?'

'No, Dolly. I don't think so. Monica goin' kill me.'

Monica! A chasm suddenly opened up before Jean. Monica would probably kill them both: Lana, because she had done something wrong, and Jean, to prevent her from doing the same thing in the future. But she said to Lana, 'No, no. She's your mother. She loves you.'

Mary had brought breadfruit and mangoes from the country and apologized for coming so empty-handed; she had had such short notice. Usually when she visited she brought several parcels of home-cooked food – peppery crayfish, coconut gizadas, plantain tarts, custard-apple pie, bottles of her famous mango chutney, and pickled hot peppers, along with fruit and vegetables from her garden.

Irene brought Mary a cup of coffee. Everybody said how good it was of Mary to come all that way.

'Somebody have to talk to Monica,' Gwen said again. 'Better you, Mary, since she's you daughter. You can reason with her.'

'Me rada try reason wid a scawpion,' Mary said emphatically.

'Let Cherry talk to her,' Daphne suggested. 'Monica usually listens to Cherry.'

'What about Lana?' said Gwen. 'Lana has to face her responsibility. Talk face to face with her mother.'

Everybody looked at Lana. Her face went white; the blood seemed to drain completely out of it. Her eyes were two dark painful holes.

'Oh, Lord, she goin' faint,' Gwen said. 'Put her head down between her knees.'

Mary tended to Lana. 'Come now. Sit up straight an' behave. You a grown woman now!'

Cherry sighed. 'Awright, I will talk to Monica. This evening.'

Lana, not too weak to be alarmed, said, 'This evening?'

'Where?' Gwen asked. 'Here or at your house? Or you want to come over to mine? I could arrange a supper.'

Irene, who was thinking about what it would be like to live and work in that house with Monica over the next few days, made a suggestion: 'Maybe it would be bes' if Miss Lana went back to de country wid Miss Mary. Let Miss Monica cool down likkle.'

'You want to come back to New Hope with me?'

Lana nodded.

Cherry said, 'No, is not a good idea. You need to stay. After I talk to you mother, you go to her and show her that you are very sorry and ask her to help you.'

'No, Cherry,' Lana pleaded. 'You don't know Monica.'

'Trus' me. I know 'bout these things. Remember, I'm a mother, too.'

'But not a mother of daughters,' Mary said. 'Lana better come back to New Hope with me tonight.'

'My daughter is what?'

'Pregnant.'

'This is a joke.'

'Is no joke, Monica.'

'Where is she?'

'With Mary at New Hope.'

'Good. Let her stay there, then.'

'Come, Monica—'

Monica got up. 'Thank you for coming over. At least I can always depend on you, Cherry, to tell me everything plain an' honest. When Lana plannin' to come back?'

'Weekend, I think.'

'I suppose Mary knows about this?'

'Yes.'

Monica fell silent. To Cherry, it seemed a long time before she spoke again.

'And it's too late?'

Cherry didn't answer; Monica knew it was too late.

'Well. That's that, then.'

Lana returned in a few days, sick. She had a temperature of 104 degrees and abdominal pains. Monica was not at home. Irene called Cherry, and Cherry came right over with her brother, Dr

Fred Ho Sing, who said, 'This girl needs to get to the hospital right away. She has acute appendicitis.'

Lana had emergency surgery. Monica was at the hospital minutes after her daughter arrived. Had the baby survived? Everyone wanted to know. 'Lana is fine, and so is her baby,' the surgeon assured them.

She stayed in the hospital for a week. Gordon came to the hospital one day, but Aunt Gwen happened to be visiting so he turned back, leaving the flowers he'd brought for Lana at the nurses' station. He was married; he felt guilty and afraid. He did not try to see Lana again, though Lana cried to him over the phone, and even got Jean and Paul to telephone him.

'I love him,' she bawled. 'I goin' dead if I don't see him.'

Her wailing was loud and ugly; it frightened Jean. Her sister was behaving like a madwoman and seemed not to care about anything or anyone except her married boyfriend.

'No, no,' Cherry said, 'this not goin' kill you.'

'Yes, it will. I goin' dead. An' I don't care.'

Cherry called Gordon. He tried to worm his way out of meeting her, saying he was very busy with work and so on. Cherry said all right then, she would talk to his wife. He agreed to meet her at the Sheraton Hotel bar.

At the bar, Cherry got straight to the point; she didn't see any reason to spend two dollars on a hotel Coca-Cola. She asked him if he had any intention of leaving his wife. He said no, but he loved Lana – 'I really, really love her' – and planned to rent an apartment for her and the child. Cherry told him to go to hell.

Cherry called Monica: 'You daughter actin' like a big fool over that man. You de only one can talk sense into her.'

So Monica began visiting Lana twice a day at the hospital. She did not speak to her about the pregnancy or about Gordon. She was strangely quiet and attentive, setting Lana's pillows comfortably around her, bringing her clean nightgowns and magazines. She spoke constantly with the doctor and the nurses about Lana's condition, and did all she could to make sure that she was getting the best care.

Cherry was right. Monica's mere presence had a miraculous effect on Lana. She was so surprised at and grateful for her mother's attention that she calmed down; Gordon was no longer her chief concern. One day after Monica left the hospital room, Lana, tears streaming down her face, turned to Jean: 'She really loves me, eh Jean. I feel so shame.'

When Lana was fully recovered and had been home for about two weeks, Monica summoned her into the study.

It was Monica's custom to go to her study in the evenings after supper; Irene would bring her a cup of cocoa on a tray. The study was locked during the day when Monica was not at home, and no one ever disturbed her there. To her daughters the room was a solemn, portentous place. Sometimes Monica worked there, but most evenings she settled into the crimson leather chair behind her desk and listened to classical music. Monica had once summoned Jean into the study to question her about some wrongdoing she had been accused of at school. It had terrified Jean to sit across from Monica at that big luminous desk, so well polished it looked slippery, yet she could not help glancing curiously around the unfamiliar room. There was a painting on the wall of Monica's grandfather, Dr John Darling, a handsome, regal man with a waxed, curled mustache. The one photograph on the desk was of Monica and her sisters when they were young, unmarried women. There was a bookcase with some bound business ledgers and several years of *Reader's Digest*, the only magazine Monica subscribed to and the only thing she ever read. Occasionally Monica's business acquaintances met with her in the study; there was a carved mahogany box filled with Jamaican cigars, and a heavy black marble lighter and matching ashtray.

Monica looked across the desk at her pregnant daughter. For a split second an expression of full comprehension and sadness appeared on the mother's face, but it quickly passed.

'It would be best—' Monica began, stopped, and began again, 'I want you to pack your things and leave.'

Lana felt her skin turn cold.

'Where am I to go?'

'Go to your grandmother in the country, or to Cherry. Gwen if she'll take you. For myself, I would prefer if you didn't stay in Kingston.'

'How long?'

Monica spoke calmly: 'I don't want you in this house again.'

Jean saw Lana packing that afternoon. She left the house in silent, stifled anger, without saying anything to anyone, not even good-bye to Jean. Paul picked her up and took her to Cherry's house.

Monica appeared in Jean's bedroom later. Jean was not asleep. She was still dressed in her day clothes and was lying on the bed wondering about the day's disturbing events.

Monica sat down on the bed with her.

'It's late. You should be asleep,' she said sternly but softly.

She continued sitting there while Jean changed into her pajamas and got into bed. She thought her mother was going to explain Lana's leaving. But Monica got up and walked to the door. She turned off the bedroom light, then turned around to look at Jean before going out into the lit hallway.

'You sister is in big trouble. I don't want you makin' the same mistake.'

She left quickly, forgetting to close the door, leaving the light from the hallway glaring into Jean's room.

23

They reach Linstead, and Jean remembers it's Easter. She sees Seventh-Day Adventists walking from church carrying Bibles. The children run ahead in energetic disregard of their washed and pressed clothes. The white shirts of the men and boys are dazzling in the afternoon light. Two small girls, so alike they must be sisters, hold hands as they walk and stop to gaze at the truck as Paul drives by them.

The smell of dried thyme wafts into the truck as they go slowly through the town and stop in front of Linstead market.

'I goin' see if they have breadfruit,' Paul says, stepping out of the pickup. 'Might be a long time before you get to eat that again. Want anything?'

'Guava.'

'Guava not in season.'

'Well, no thanks. I'm all right.'

She hears the general shouting of the market women but not their words. There are coconuts, bunches of thyme, trays of ginger-root, yams, and old, rusty market scales: the real, indecorous colors of food. Things are not displayed to look their brightest. In the country, people know what they are buying, and there's no need, as in Kingston, for the seller to entice the buyer. In fact, the best produce is often hidden away for a favorite customer, and in hard times like these, maybe for the market woman herself. Lately, buyers have become beggars:

'Miss Dulcie, please, you na 'ave a likkle piece a pigtail you can gimme?'

The smells make Jean hungry. She imagines a country dining table offering boiled green bananas, plantain, rice-an'-peas, fish stew – simple country foods cooked in coconut milk and coconut oil.

They leave the town center – market, clock tower, and gas station – and drive past some cottages. A woman who looks a hundred years old sits alone on her veranda, attentive to the road. She calmly outstares history. Smoke rises from the yard behind her cottage, the sweet-smelling smoke of roasting breadfruit.

The violence has not touched them here. No soldiers, roadblock, curfew, graffiti. There is no vigilance or fear in people's faces. In Kingston everyone lives behind iron bars, ever attuned to the sound of intruders and to news of the latest alarming murder. Here the open verandas and unwalled gardens of croton and hibiscus make Kingston seem like some lunatic's idea of reality.

They are now midway between the north and south coasts and about to begin the difficult climb up Mount Diablo. There's still a lot of road ahead of them, treacherous road, and Paul knows every twist and turn. He has been quiet for a while; they have both been. He looks tired, not from driving, but from all the lives he has been trying to take care of – Lana, the people on his farm, the farm itself. Mostly Lana. Jean wants to comfort him. He has always comforted her.

But he's not asking for comfort. Like her, he wants answers.

'You were much closer to her than I was, you know.'

'I don't know,' he says.

'You're the only one who kept in touch with her when she left home.'

'She didn't leave home. She was thrown out.'

Jean can't argue with that.

He relents. 'I not judging Monica. But – Jesus Christ! – Lana wasn't even seventeen.'

They both fall silent again. Jean hears the tires spinning fast against the road, a voracious sound that fills her with a certain panic. They'll run out of road before they find answers.

For eight years she did not see her sister. The women of the family spoke about Lana among themselves but never directly to her. Su-su su-su. She heard them through walls. Su-su su-su. She could tell their voices apart – Cherry, Mary, Gwen, Daphne, Monica—

CHERRY: Lana baby dead.
GWEN: Poor ting.
MONICA: Merciful Father!
CHERRY: She ina state.
MONICA: Tell her to come see me.

DAPHNE: Man, you shoulda hear how Lana carry on when we tell her Monica wan' see her. She say, 'Cooya, so Miss High-an'-Mighty wan' see me? She turn her face 'way when I bawn. She turn her face 'way when I pregnant. Tongue don't have bone. What Monica say today she nuh say tomorrow. She have any right to judge me? I do anyting worse than she?'
I always know Lana have a mouth on her, an' I tell you she raise one hell of a stink in Cherry house.

CHERRY: Monica, Lana ina state. She cyan come see you.
MONICA: Well, you cyan say I neva give her a secon' chance.
MARY: What you expec'? You done break de chile heart. I never turn you 'way, Monica, when you was Lana's age an' you did bring belly into me house.
MONICA: I neva behave like a whore. Look, I offer her a chance an' she refuse.

CHERRY: Miss Mary, sometimes I don't know who to feel more
    sorry for, Lana or Monica. She mek her chile hate her, an' I
    see it comin' long time. Roy, him did see it too.
MARY: History a-repeat itself. Is a cryin' shame.

DAPHNE: Lana's in jail in Montego Bay.
GWEN: Jail!
DAPHNE: Police arrested her at the airport carrying ganja.
MONICA: Let the law teach her what I couldn't teach her.

MARY: Thank God for Deepa. If it was lef' to Monica the chile
    woulda rot in jail.

They're driving through the bauxite-mining area. Every living
thing – river, vegetation, even the goats and pigs – is stained by
the red ore; it's like looking at a scene through red lenses.

'I heard things, all kinds of things,' Jean says, and feels the
old torment and shame.

24

Monica would not allow Jean to see Lana. What began as a rule which Jean, a mere child, obeyed, became a fact of her life as she grew older.

'I not mekin' the same mistake with you,' Monica said to Jean. How many times? 'I not lettin' you grow up like you sister.'

Lana was constantly before Jean: a temptation, a mirror in which she was not permitted to look.

Jean used to sit sometimes in the living room in the late afternoon and wonder about her sister. She tried to fit rumors to first-hand remembrances. Was Lana actually a whore? ('Puta,' the girl had said, the Venezuelan girl at Mercy, or so it had been reported to Jean. The Venezuelan girls kept to themselves. They were sent to Mercy to learn English. Fat chance. They had gotten off on the wrong foot with the Jamaican girls. A case of mutual scorn. No one spoke English to them, and they spoke English to no one, only chattered in rapid Spanish among themselves. But Valerie Del Negro, whose father was Cuban, and who spoke Spanish fluently, told Jean that one of the Venezuelan girls had said Lana was a *puta*, a whore. Faye heard and swept like a hurricane into the Venezuelan girls' room. A fight broke out, with half a dozen girls on the floor clawing and biting, and Sister Pauline had to be called in to break it up. Had she said 'puta' or hadn't she? Everyone at Mercy had an opinion, and the Jamaican girls, who had been so sympathetic about

Lana's pregnancy and who, though they enjoyed the scandal, had not passed judgment on her, now had the word 'whore' to hit back and forth like a tennis ball.) Did men pay Lana to sleep with them?

Was Lana in Jamaica or abroad? Was it true that she had gotten thinner, and did that mean she was ill? Jean would sit alone in the living room in the weakening daylight, her questions unanswered, her hope of ever seeing Lana growing dimmer, until someone — Irene or her mother — would come in and turn on the light. 'What you doin' sitting by you'self in the dark?'

'That daughter of yours lookin' fenky-fenky,' Cherry said to Monica about Jean. 'Something wrong wid her?'

'She jus' idle. Want some hard work.'

Jean felt she was the only one deprived of answers.

'When you're older you'll understand.'

'This is a conversation for grown-ups.'

'You much too young to be concerning yourself with these things.'

Theirs became a family of innuendoes, of hot, unrevealed hurts that spewed out now and then and burned. Lana's disappearance, Monica's hatred of Deepa, Daphne's drinking, Mary's loneliness.

And then, too, there was the mystery of Irene.

Late one night, Jean was in Irene's room listening to the transistor radio. People were saying that the world would never be the same once man stepped on the moon. The radio station was taking calls: 'Man, 'im no God an' 'im no 'ave no right fe walk 'pon moon an' ting.'

Irene was ironing sheets and pillowcases. The room smelled of soap powder and the burning hot iron.

'Where are your children?' Jean had asked Irene this many times before. Irene hardly ever talked about her children.

'In Savanna-la-Mar.'

'Who takes care of them?'

'Dem grandmother.'

'When you going see them?'

'Savanna-la-Mar is a long-long way from here, you know. Seven, eight hours on de bus.'

'How old are they?'

'Lawson fifteen. Philbert thirteen, same age as you. But Philbert not right. Him stay like a baby. Retired.'

Jean knew she meant 'retarded.' She couldn't yet bring herself to ask about the children's father. Irene had never spoken of a husband.

The room was lit by a bare lightbulb hanging from a cord. It made the room intensely hot and bright. Irene's skin gleamed and every oiled strand of her hair was illuminated. She wore her hair in four or five neat plaits. To Jean the outer, physical mystery of Irene was as engrossing as the inner, the life history Irene didn't talk about mainly because she didn't consider it interesting.

Irene had slept in this room for years. It was at the back of the house, connected to the garage. There was a narrow iron-frame bed, a small dresser covered with white contact paper, and a wooden stool. On the dresser there was a tarnished, unframed mirror, a hot comb for pressing her hair, a jar of hair oil, a tin of talcum powder, and a Bible. The transistor radio, which went everywhere with Irene, was on the windowsill. Irene often did the ironing here at night.

Jean thought about the other Irene who once a month pressed her hair, put on her good dress and good shoes, and left to visit her family in the far western part of the country – quite different from the woman she saw every day in housedress and mashed-up slippers, her hair parted in sections, with a comb often sticking out of it as if she were continually being interrupted in the middle of combing and plaiting it.

Irene hid nothing, yet she was unknown to the family with whom she had lived so long. As a child Jean had chatted unguardedly to Irene in the many hours they spent alone together. 'What did you want to be when you were little?' 'A nurse, but me no have money for school.' She saw Jean's concerned look and added, 'Nex' ting me did want to do was look after children.' When she first came to work for them, her main job was to take care of five-year-old Jean. She had been firm but kind. Jean had been an obedient child. They got on well enough.

Monica had gone to bed. She thought that the astronauts would never make it to the moon. When she was told that they had landed, she said that it would be a big mistake if they left their spacecraft; they would fall endlessly into the darkness between the stars. That wasn't how she put it. She said, 'Dem might as well try walk on water. I gone to bed.'

An American voice suddenly came on. Irene stood the iron upright and turned up the radio. Neil Armstrong had opened the door of the spacecraft. There was a lot of static. Irene fiddled with the transistor's antenna. She and Jean stood as close as they could to the radio. The American commentator was counting. Counting man's steps on the moon. At this moment, Jean was aware of Irene's body, the smell of hair oil, the talcum powder on her neck, and her white brassiere strap showing. She was so close, Jean could hear her breathing.

'Him reach,' Irene said. She smiled. She stood listening for a few more seconds, not wanting to miss anything, but there was only the broadcaster's jubilant shouting. She went back to her ironing.

Man on the moon. Man in the moon. One night when Jean was about five years old, she heard a man call her by name. It was during the time of her parents' brief separation, and Cherry was tucking her into bed. Jean thought it was her father in another room calling her. But Cherry said no, Roy wasn't there, maybe it was the man in the moon, and she took Jean to the window and showed her the moon's eyes, nose, and mouth. Then she made her say her prayers before she went to sleep: 'Our Father, who art in heaven . . .' In her child's mind, all three, the moon, her father, and God, became a single ventriloquizing spirit.

25

The day after the moon landing, Paul came to the house. This visit was unusual because it was a weekday and he normally came to Kingston only on weekends. Daphne was there and they were about to sit down to dinner when he arrived.

'Lana's in Montego Bay hospital,' he told them. 'She had a car accident last night. She had a concussion and hurt her shoulder, but nothing serious.'

'Jean,' Monica said, 'go to your room till I call you.'

'Lawd, Monica,' Daphne said, 'she old enough to hear. After all, is her sister.'

'Don't tell me what to do. She not your child.'

Paul turned to Jean, 'You want to go for a drive?'

Once she got in the truck with Paul, Jean sensed that she could ask about Lana. But she didn't know what to ask. She had been fretting over Lana for years and had been in the habit of keeping all this fretting to herself. They drove along in silence; then, at some point, she burst into tears.

Paul suggested that they go to York Pharmacy to buy a box of chocolates and a get-well card. Then they sat at the soda fountain while Jean wrote inside the card: 'Dear Lana, please get well soon. Remember me. Your sister, Jean.'

Paul assured her that Lana wasn't lonely. Geeta, Deepa's sister, who was a nurse, worked at the hospital and she would check on Lana every day. Deepa and Mary Darling were both nearby.

Jean wrote a p.s. to her note: 'All the chocolates have nuts.'

She remembered how at Christmastime when they got boxes of chocolates they would try to figure out which ones had nuts inside, tricking other people into taking the soft-centered ones. And remembering this, she started to cry again.

'Sorry,' she said to Paul.

The waitress came over, and Paul explained that Jean's sister had just had an accident. 'Poor ting,' the waitress said, and brought her another milkshake free of charge, which Jean felt obliged to drink, so she stopped crying.

About a month later, Lana called Jean. She had gotten the note; she had recovered and was visiting Kingston. She asked Jean to meet her for lunch the next day. Jean told Monica that she was meeting Faye.

It was early September, around the time of Jean's birthday, and Lana brought a present. It was a book, *The Romantic Poets: Blake to Keats*.

'I know you like poems. I thought you'd like some *romantic* ones.' Lana's eyes sparkled with mischief as she said the word 'romantic.' 'Lawd, Dolly, you grow so big, you almos' as tall as me.'

Jean had expected Lana to have changed, but Lana was the same beautiful woman. She wore a short empire-line dress and platform shoes, styles that hadn't quite come into fashion yet on the island, so Jean guessed that she had bought them abroad. Her long fingernails were painted frosty pink and she wore the same color lipstick. Her hair was parted down the center and hung straight down her back. Every man who came into the restaurant stared at her. For the first time Jean reflected on how physically different she and Lana were; in fact, Lana was unlike any of the women in her family. Lana was nimble, slender, and small-boned. The Darling-Sterns were large-boned women who gave the impression of being languid. Lana's hands moved constantly as she talked, her eyes darted and flashed, never settling on any one thing for long, and she spoke so rapidly it was sometimes hard to follow her.

While Lana talked, Jean watched and pondered her sister. Lana had given birth to a child. That child had died. She had been arrested. She had almost died in a car accident. Her mother acted as though she were dead. Lana didn't mention any of these things. Her eyes shone the way they used to when they were both younger and she was trying to convince Jean to go along with some prank. Now all she was trying to convince Jean of was that she was all right, more than all right; she was having a wonderful life. She worked for an airline and got free plane trips, and she had her own apartment in Montego Bay. So she wasn't a whore. She wasn't like the women who stood outside the hotels in New Kingston. She talked so rapidly that it made Jean dizzy. The terrible things Jean had heard swirled around in her head with all the pleasant things Lana was telling her.

After lunch Lana dropped her at the bus stop. They kissed goodbye, awkwardly. As Jean got out of the car, Lana said, 'Wait. Dem tell you bad tings 'bout me, na?'

Jean didn't want to answer.

'But you mek up you own mind, eh Dolly?'

Lana promised she would call often, and she invited Jean to visit her in Montego Bay. They would go to the beach. They would go shopping. Monica would not have to know. Jean would tell her mother that she was visiting Paul on his farm. Jean's heart warmed with anticipation; she felt the period of forced separation dissolve, and with it the layer of gloom. But months passed and Lana didn't call. Jean heard that she had quit her job and left Jamaica. No one knew for sure where she had gone. There was talk that she had gone either to Trinidad or

Miami, that she was getting married or breaking up a marriage.

It was only when she won the Miss Jamaica-Miami Beauty Pageant and her picture came out in the *Star* that they knew anything for sure. The newspaper said:

Lana Elizabeth Ramcharan is twenty-one and was born in Westmoreland, Jamaica. She is five feet six inches tall, weighs 120 pounds, and her vital statistics are 36-25-36. Lana is studying beauty culture in Miami. Her hobbies are singing, dancing, and astrology.

Jean thought that Lana was studying art, but Aunt Daphne said no; she was learning how to be a hairdresser and give manicures.

'You think she'll come home for Christmas?' Jean asked Daphne.

'Yes man, Lana no like stay-a-foreign too long.'

26

Lana did not come back that Christmas; she didn't even call, and the holidays were dismal for Jean. Monica and Delly went out every night, and Jean was alone in the big house. It was a great relief to Jean to head north again to boarding school.

Over the holidays Faye had met two brothers, Steve and Rick. The boys were Faye's relatives, second cousins on her mother's side, and had been living in Barbados until recently. Faye continued seeing them after the holidays because they went to Vauxhall, a boys' boarding school not far from Mercy. Steve was sixteen, three years older than Faye, and he became her first boyfriend. That left Rick, the younger brother. As Faye's best friend, Jean was obliged to keep Rick company. He was aloof; she was shy; so they hardly ever spoke. When the boys visited Mercy on weekends, the four walked to the river. Faye and Steve would kiss for hours, forgetting anyone else was there, and Jean and Rick would try not to look embarrassed.

Jean thought Rick was more attractive and certainly more interesting than his brother. Now and then he cracked a smile at something funny she said, and once, he caught her when she almost tripped over a tree root. She wouldn't have minded kissing him, but she had never kissed or been kissed by a boy; she was afraid she would not be any good at it. Lana, and now Faye, appeared to be so confident about such things; Jean sensed there was some special knowledge or technique of which she was ignorant. She asked Faye one day about kissing.

'Pretend I'm Rick,' Faye said, pressing her mouth against Jean's and darting her tongue between Jean's lips. Faye stopped and burst out laughing. 'You not supposed to just stand there with your mouth open and saliva dripping.'

'What am I supposed to do?'

'Push your tongue into his mouth. Let's try again.'

Jean refused. She was hurt by Faye's laughing at her and wished she had not asked her advice; she felt even more awkward than before.

'I hear you have a boyfriend,' Paul teased her one day when she was visiting him at the farm.

They were lying under a star-apple tree. The unripe fruit were small and hard. The morning sky was pale and unripe-looking, too.

Jean decided to let him believe she had a boyfriend.

'Getting to be a big girl with all the boys chasing you.'

She thought Paul was probably a great kisser. 'You still going around with Cecile?'

'Not really. Cecile asking for too much.'

'Like what?'

'You know — wedding ring, baby. Why do all women want to get married, eh? Even you. When you were little, you used to say you were going to marry me when you grow up.'

'You lie.'

'No lie. A true.'

He was wearing a green shirt with the top buttons undone, and she could see his smooth, hard chest. Suddenly she thought him the most handsome man she knew, only it was more than a thought; it was a feeling in every part of her that pricked her with embarrassment. She would not nurture this feeling even in secret; it was a silly mistake.

'Marry you? You have a different girl for every day of the week. Why would I want to be number eight?'

He laughed. 'So that's it? You want to monopolize me?' He grew serious. 'I not marrying anybody I don't love.'

'You don't love Cecile?'

'No.'

'But you together a long time now.'

'Together don't necessarily mean love.'

'Monica says I'm not to have sex with a man before I'm married, or he won't respect me.' She posed this as a question, but Paul didn't reply. 'You respect Cecile?'

'I respect her.'

'So it's all right to have sex before you get married?'

'When you're older we have this conversation again, okay?'

'How old?'

'Sixteen.'

Jean sighed. Monica said she couldn't go out with boys until she was eighteen.

'Was that how old you were when you started having sex?'

'It's different for boys.'

Jean looked up at the star-apple's leaves, which were silky and copper-colored on the underside, green on top. As she talked with Paul, she could hear the legend of Lana being whispered to her. *You sister in big trouble.*

Paul saw Jean frowning. 'You in love or something? Come, we wastin' daylight. You want to go beach?'

There was a hit song on the radio around that time, 'Blood and Fire.' The militant beat of reggae, which had been popular in the slums of Kingston for some time, could now be heard pounding in every part of the country. At Mercy reggae was banned; it was considered as dangerous as marijuana. That the musicians were mostly Rastafarians and that the groups and songs had names like the Liquidator and the Upsetters made the music all the more disreputable in the minds of the nuns. The ban created a huge demand among the students: records were smuggled in by the day scholars, hidden, played, and lyrics memorized. Faye had a stack of Bob Marley singles hidden in a drawer among her underwear.

There was a reggae concert in Ocho Rios one night and Faye decided to go with Steve. She climbed out the bathroom window after lights out, telling Jean she would return by one o'clock the next morning. Jean was to make sure the coast was clear on her return, and if not, to signal by flicking the bathroom light on and off.

Jean did not feel good. Her head ached, and she was dying to sleep. She sat on the bathroom floor in darkness and waited for Faye. She kept catching herself dozing. Shortly after one o'clock she went to the window. There was no sign of Faye. Her whole body ached and her head felt as though it would explode.

She pressed her forehead against the cool windowpane to relieve the aching. She was thoroughly enclosed in darkness. No lights illuminated the countryside. All that separated the darkness inside from the outer darkness was the pane of glass, which seemed fragile and inconsequential. She felt that she probably should not lean so hard against it, but she was too tired to move. Her eyelids were painful and heavy. She closed her eyes.

'Jean. Jean.' She heard Faye's whispered call.

Jean opened the window. Faye stood below, supporting herself on crutches. She needs help, Jean thought; she can't climb up here on those crutches.

A cool breeze swept through the open window and sent a chill through Jean's body. She realized that she had been dreaming and had opened the window in her sleep. Outside, the world of trees and grasses swayed eerily. Why was Faye on crutches in the dream? The vision distressed her. She sensed that her friend was in danger. It was almost three o'clock. Jean climbed through the window.

Her legs felt strange and weightless. Was she dreaming still? She walked among the swaying, whispering trees, heading toward the school gate. Her head throbbed. She began to shiver from the cold, and realized she should have put on a robe or cardigan over her nightgown. Was it foolish of her to be so worried about Faye? What did she know? She had never had a boyfriend. The excitement that had recently absorbed Faye, inspiring her to take risks just as Lana had done, was unimaginable to Jean. But she was worried nevertheless, and could have cried from the weight of worry and helplessness, the ponderous virginal ignorance that held her back and distanced her, first from Lana, now from Faye. She moved like a sleepwalker through the moonless black night. Her feet were bare; the grass was wet and slimy. She bent her head down to see if it really was grass beneath her. *You find something, Jean?* Where was it, the little grave? *Susannah Crawford, beloved daughter and sister.*

'Who dat?'

Jean spun around and saw the night watchman.

'Speak if you is a 'uman.' He shone his flashlight on her.

Jean felt dizzy.

'Gal? Gal, is you? Me tink it was a duppy.' He approached cautiously. 'Wha' you a do outadoors dis time a night?'

An icy coldness gripped her. She fainted.

The local doctor was sent for early the next morning. At first it was thought that Jean had pneumonia, but it turned out to be a severe case of influenza. She was placed in the sickroom, quarantined from the other girls.

'The fever must have gone to her brain,' the nuns said of Jean's odd behavior, walking outdoors in her nightgown in the middle of the night. There was something more alarming on their minds: Faye's absence. Daylight came and she was still gone. Searching through her drawers, the nuns discovered the stack of banned records along with other suspicious articles; a douche kit and a paperback titled *The Sensuous Woman*. The head-mistress called Faye's mother and the police station. The other students knew something was wrong when they saw policemen on the school grounds and the nuns rushing about and whispering among themselves. News of Faye's disappearance spread rapidly and was exaggerated with each telling: Faye had run off with her lover; Faye had been kidnapped.

About eight o'clock that morning Faye arrived and slipped quietly into the dorm. She put on her school uniform and headed for the dining hall, thinking she could walk into breakfast unnoticed. But as she walked through the door everyone stopped talking and stared.

She realized she was in deep trouble regardless of any excuse she could come up with. So she told the truth: how she had met her boyfriend at the gate and driven away with him in a car he had borrowed from a friend; they had left the concert early, had driven out to the beach in Ocho Rios, had fallen asleep on a beach blanket (after having sex and smoking ganja – this part she told Jean later), and when they woke up the car's battery was dead. There was nothing to do but wait till morning for the country bus.

'Where's Jean?' Faye wanted to know.

'Where's Faye?' Jean kept asking deliriously.

'She's in a lot of trouble,' Jean was told.

When Faye learned that Jean was sick she completely disregarded the quarantine and crept into the sickroom at every opportunity.

'What they goin' do to you?' Jean asked.

Faye shrugged. 'Hang me, I suppose.'

There was a huge gong on the school grounds outside the headmistress's office. It was called the Warning Bell and was to be used in case of dire emergencies such as fire, earthquake, or invasion. The bell had been rung once, back in 1938 when disgruntled sugar workers had set off riots throughout the country and policemen had to be placed at the school gates.

On April 7, 1971, two days after Faye's misadventure, Sister Pauline rang the Warning Bell and the whole school gathered in the assembly hall. Jean, who was tossing in bed with chills and fever, was not required to attend but was later given a copy of the headmistress's address.

Sister Pauline reminded everyone of the school's motto: 'Civility Above All.' She reiterated the difficulties endured by the British priests and nuns who arrived at the turn of the century and dedicated their lives to building the school so that the young women of this land might be offered the same advantages offered to Englishwomen. She said that in spite of the changes that had taken place in the island over the years, Mercy had been able to assure parents that here their daughters were protected from the lawlessness, vulgarities, and moral vagaries of the world outside. But, tragically, this assurance could no longer be given because someone, who would remain unnamed, had disregarded 'civility,' had willfully exposed herself to physical as well as moral danger and put the institution in jeopardy. The Sisters of Mercy School for Girls was now in a state of crisis. Sister Pauline called upon the students to rededicate themselves to the founding principles, or else what had been a bastion of civility and refinement would be reduced to bush and ruin. Father Peter, the school pastor, called for a week of penance and solemn contemplation to be observed by the entire school: unbuttered bread and water for meals, silent prayer twice a day in the chapel, no recreation, no sports, no outings.

Faye spoke to her mother. Dr Galdy was concerned about

whether Faye and Steve had used a contraceptive and was relieved when Faye told her they had.

'Your headmistress is a fool,' Dr Galdy told her daughter. 'Talking about closing down the school because one teenage girl goes off on a lark. Not that you weren't wrong, Faye. You had a lot of people worried. Still, it's not as if someone committed a crime. How's Jean?'

'She's getting better.'

'She needs iron. I'll send some molasses. Make sure she takes a tablespoon three times a day.'

Jean seemed to be improving; then she had a relapse and was even worse than before. One evening her temperature rose so high that the nuns circled around her bed and began to pray. This terrified Faye. She was afraid that Jean was dying and she blamed herself; it was because of her that Jean had been out in the cold. When everyone else was asleep, Faye went into the sickroom and stayed with her through the night, cooling her forehead with a rag soaked in bay rum, helping her sip ice water through a straw.

'If you start to feel worse tell me, okay, so I can call Nurse.'

Jean nodded. She whispered: 'Guadeloupe.'

'St Vincent,' Faye replied quickly.

'Dominica.'

'Tortola.'

'Marie Galante.'

'What?'

'One point. Curaçao.'

They had invented this game, Islands, after learning that there were over a thousand islands in the Caribbean. The intervals between the names grew longer until they were both asleep in the sickbed. They were discovered like that the next morning.

Sister Pauline made it seem ugly. In her eyes, Faye had been contaminated by sex and might contaminate others. She had been isolated from the other girls – put in a room by herself, the room usually reserved for novices at the convent – and she ate her meals alone. Now Faye and Jean, both isolated, one for physical the other for moral reasons, had been found sleeping together in a comforting embrace.

Oddly, Faye did not defend herself in her usual boisterous manner; she did not defend herself at all. She seemed perturbed. Her face had the strained expression of her handicapped childhood. And her silence led to further rumors: She was pregnant; she was a lesbian, a drug addict.

Sister Pauline decided to suspend her for the rest of the year. But Faye's mother removed her from the school altogether. She had been thinking for some time about transferring Faye to a better school in Kingston and suggested that Monica do the same for Jean.

'All they care about at Mercy is catechism and tennis. For years I've been telling them to hire a science teacher. Imagine a girls' school these days not teaching science. Jean is a clever girl. College material. She'll fall behind if she stays there.'

'Well, I'll give it some thought over the summer,' Monica said. 'But girls get into too much trouble in Kingston. They meet all kind a riffraff and next thing . . .'

That summer, Jean's cousin Fern Ho Sing got married. It was Jean's first wedding. She was too young to be a bridesmaid and too old to be a flower girl. So she was simply 'in the wedding.' She was to wear the same peach-colored gown as the brides-maids and walk up the aisle behind the flower girl.

While the bride and bridesmaids were getting dressed Jean heard someone mention something about Fern's wedding night.

'Wedding night?' One of the bridesmaids giggled. 'Fern do her homework with Cecil long time ago.'

They all burst out laughing.

'Shoosh,' Fern said, embarrassed, but giggling too. 'Mind you rupture Jean's virgin ears.'

'Bound to happen sooner or later.'

'Shoosh, man,' Fern said again, 'you too crass. Don't listen to dem, Jean.'

At the reception Jean was too old to run around like her little cousins and too young to join Fern's friends. She was as tall as any of the bridesmaids, and she had her hair up in a bun. She had hoped that someone would think her older than she was and ask her to dance, but no one did. It had to be because she wasn't pretty enough, and Monica wouldn't let her wear makeup. Also she knew she looked terrible in that sickening peach color. Everybody looked terrible in it. She despised the bridesmaids for speaking the way they had in the dressing room and making her feel so childish.

Somebody came up behind her and covered her eyes. 'Hi, Jean, guess who.' It was a boy's voice, a boy whose voice wasn't so boyish anymore.

He stepped in front of her. Then he did a very nice thing. He knelt down and kissed her hand. Who was he?

'You don't remember me?' He had an American accent.

She shook her head.

'I used to climb through the fence to play with you at Belmont Road. Then we moved to New York.'

'Trevor! Trevor Blake! You look so different.'

'So do you. Your mother pointed you out. I wouldn't have known it was you. You want to dance?'

She had never slow-danced before. Trevor had gotten very tall. He was even taller than his older brother, who was also at the wedding. His collar smelled wonderful with after-shave.

For the rest of the summer she thought constantly about

him. Maybe *he* would be her boyfriend. Would he wait until she was eighteen?

Everybody was talking about the election campaign and the promise of a new leader: Norman Manley's son and heir, Michael Manley. The regulars at Daphne's voiced their strong opinions as usual.

'Listen. Listen to what I sayin'. Listen—'

'How we mus' listen when you mekin' so much noise?'

'Order! Order, on dis woman veranda.'

'Judge say order on Daphne veranda. Pass de rum bottle.'

'Everything gone from bad to wus since Independence,' Monica bellowed. 'Look at the schools. Schools like Inverness an' St Bede's used to be good schools with English-trained teachers. Nowadays, dem train here at the University an' dem cyaan even talk good English.'

'PNP talkin' 'bout free education an' I feel is high time.' Daphne's voice was like a trumpet. 'Eh, Michael?'

Michael Manley was there on the veranda, eating curry goat from a paper plate. He sat on a bar stool, his head bent over his food. Even when he was quiet, he drew attention. Everyone stopped talking for a moment, waiting for him to respond.

But before he could, Monica jumped in: 'Free education? You mussee jokin'! Nutten no free. Somebody ha fe pay fe it an' dat mean me. Is my tax money goin' pay gi' dem people education an' nex' ting dem turn 'round an' kill me?'

'Chu man, Monica.' Someone said, 'You talkin' ignorance!'

'Me talkin' ignorance? You son of a bitch!!'

'You pussy-clat!'

'Hey! Is me sister you insulting!'

'Order, order!'

Manley remained quiet. Jean watched him. He went on eating his curry and drinking soda. It was impossible to tell if he was following the argument or preoccupied with his own thoughts. Jean remembered that his wife had died recently, leaving behind a baby daughter. Here in Daphne's house she had overheard intimate things about this man. He had loved passionately. Two of his three marriages had involved scandals and there had been this recent sadness. There were people in this country, even people in the opposing party, who adored him. Her father, Roy, had been the same age as Michael and the two had become friends in England after the war.

Michael was head and shoulders above most men (even taller than Fidel Castro, Jean and Faye had noticed on seeing a picture of them together) and his hair had begun to turn gray at the temples. He was undeniably a handsome man, a popular man, a future world leader (you could tell just by looking at him that he had thoughts bigger than an island). But here he sat quite alone. Was he humble or arrogant?

This man wears other faces in other rooms, she decided, and sensed some private need in him, a romantic excess, that made her trust him with the leadership of a country.

To keep herself occupied during the summer holidays, Jean had been taking advanced classes in Spanish. It was a choice between that and working with her mother at the bakery. But when the Spanish classes ended, the summer days dragged. There was a two-week period that was especially unbearable. Paul was away in Florida buying farm equipment, and Faye was visiting her aunt in Mandeville. Jean read three books: a biography of Dorothy Dandridge, *Valley of the Dolls*, and the poetry of Sylvia Plath. She began writing her own poems in which she figured tragically as a passionate, free-spirited woman:

> Mango season, and the beach invites
> forgetting. One is out of season,

wrong, and claiming no responsibility
for the horizon.
Desperate! Desperate! Desperate!

' "Out of season" is interesting, but what's this "Desperate" business?' Daphne asked.

'Don't encourage her,' Monica said. 'She's a dreamer just like her father. All day long she listening to that Bob Manley music.'

'Bob *Marley*, for heaven's sake,' Daphne corrected her.

It was true that Jean was more withdrawn than usual. She had no one to talk to and many things to ponder. The things that had been said in the dressing room at her cousin's wedding still bothered her – 'Fern do her homework with Cecil long time ago'; 'Shoosh. Mind you rupture Jean's virgin ears.' She was fourteen and unable to penetrate the annoying euphemisms and veils surrounding sex. Who would talk with her about sex? Faye had become guarded about the subject since that episode at Mercy. Paul was not around. Fern was too much of a Miss Goody-Good. Aunt Daphne? She remembered spending the night at Daphne's recently when her mother went away. Jean accidentally walked into the bathroom and saw Daphne putting some kind of cream between her legs. Daphne looked up and saw her staring.

'What you looking at? One day you poom-poom goin' dry up jus' like mine.'

Oh, God, no.

There was only one person: Monica. After all, she was the one who kept warning her about boys.

She worked up her courage and went to Monica's room one evening. How would she begin? She realized she was taking a big risk. She might be admonished just for asking, or she might get a trick answer or a downright lie. But the questions had grown so out of proportion and combustible in her that her need to ask was greater than the need for an answer.

As she reached Monica's bedroom door, Monica, who was sitting in front of her dressing table mirror, called to her:

'Jean, come fasten me up at the back.'

Jean zipped up Monica's dress and fastened the hook at the top. She had forgotten that Monica was going to a piano recital that night.

'My hair look all right at the back?'

She had it up in a French twist. A hairpin was falling out. Jean fixed it. Monica dabbed on some face powder, applying an extra coating as usual to cover the imperfections she, and she alone, saw on her left cheek.

Jean glanced at the photograph of Lana and Monica that stood on the dressing table. It was a particularly flattering picture of Monica, which Jean thought was her primary reason for keeping it there. She looked at her mother's reflection in the mirror and remembered how much time Monica and Lana used to spend together at this dressing table, grooming and primping. Roy used to joke about it – 'You two girls married to that mirror?' It occurred to her that Monica must miss Lana.

Monica averted her eyes from her own reflection to Jean's.

'Wha' happen?'

Jean couldn't get any words out.

'Eh?' Monica was insistent.

'When can I get my hair straightened?'

'Next summer. Is not good to start too young. You hair might drop out.'

She saw that Jean looked disappointed.

'You in such a hurry to grow up, eh?' She got up and picked up her evening bag and a red silk stole. 'Don't stay up too late reading. You'll wear out your eyes.'

She pressed her cheek lightly against Jean's and said good night.

'You're a good girl. I'm grateful for that, at least.'

*

You're a good girl.

Where you tink you going dressed like dat?

You don't know better than to stand out a gate talkin' to boys. You look like a whore outa street.

It's not boys; *it's Paul!*

I don't care if is Pope *Paul, it looks whorish!*

The thing about your mother — an' you will understand better when you're older — is she can't forgive herself.

Forgive herself for what, Aunt Daphne?

For what happened to her and Deepa. Not just the way she acted, but the way she felt.

Faye returned from Mandeville toward the end of summer, and Jean spent nearly every day with her.

Dr Galdy had built a house in the foothills of the Blue Mountains. It was a cool, green place, misty in the early morning, where coffee plants grew in the thick shade of taller trees. The girls spent hours at a nearby river, swimming and diving for pebbles in the cold, clear water. Sometimes they sat on the roadside and watched the infrequent car or country bus go by.

One afternoon they walked down the hill to Papine Square for some jerk pork. It was about five miles to town, and walking downhill was easy but coming back they usually hitched a ride. For some reason, that day they decided they would try to walk all the way back up the hill. After their meal of spicy jerk pork and hard-dough bread, they had bought strawberry Sno-Kones to cool themselves down, and their lips were turning bright red as they climbed the hill, sucking on the ices.

The sky was cloudless. There was no breeze. The mountain road was quiet except for their own voices.

'Monica says I can straighten my hair next year. Maybe I'll cut it too.'

'Why you don't get an Afro? I know why. Monica would kill you.'

Jean didn't want an Afro. Ever since she could remember, she had wanted dead-straight hair, as straight as Lana's and Faye's and all the women in magazines.

'Monica think she white?' Faye asked.

'Not really. Just whiter than most people.'

Faye laughed.

A truck dragged itself up the road behind them.

'I tired,' Faye said. 'Let's get a ride.'

'In that ole truck?'

Faye started to wave down the truck.

There were four or five men in the back with shovels and machetes. They were muscular, energetic young men; some of them wore their shirts open, others were shirtless.

'Let's not,' Jean said. 'I don't like the way they look.'

'Chu man, just remember you're Sylvia and I'm Peggy if they ask our names. An' you father is a policeman.'

As the truck got closer, the men called out to the girls.

'Hey, dawta!'

'Sweet ting.'

'What you think?' Faye asked, beginning to have doubts.

'No.'

The truck went by, then slowed down for them a little way ahead. The men continued to make a ruckus: 'Stop, stop de truck, driver.' 'Two gal fe come aboard!' 'Come on, sweet ting.'

Jean and Faye remained where they were.

'Hey! White girl!' one of the men shouted at Faye. 'You 'fraid a me?'

'G'way! You rass-bumbo-clat!' she shouted back.

The other men broke out in laughter. This kind of thing was always happening to Faye. People mistook her for a tourist and she talked back to them in patois, or even better, cursed them in patois. Usually people responded good-naturedly, liking her gumption. But this man felt he had been humiliated by a girl, and a white girl at that.

'See if I don' come down an' buss you pussy-clat—' The truck lurched forward. He continued shouting. 'Dis a Black man country!'

'Facety!' Faye said after the truck disappeared.

'Next time, let's wait for the bus,' Jean said.

'Why? You 'fraid?'

For a few moments Jean didn't answer; then she said, 'I think Jamaica is changing.'

'Places always changing. What that have to do with anything? You think one ignorant loud-mouth butu goin' frighten me?' She paused and sucked her Sno-Kone. 'Is my country too, you know.'

'*I* know that. But,' she added thoughtfully, 'some people don't think so.'

'Well, dem wrong. Michael Manley almos' as white as me. What you have to say 'bout that?'

Jean was about to tease her. No one is as white as you, she was tempted to say. The red Sno-Kone had stained Faye's mouth, and in contrast her face looked paler than ever. But she could tell that Faye had become irritable.

'Don't quarrel with me,' Jean said. 'Is not me you should be quarreling with. Why you don't go and become a politician?'

'Maybe I will. You know . . .' Faye paused in a way that indicated to Jean that she was about to say something more elaborate. 'I think when the earthquake swallowed my ancestor and spat him back up – you know the story – I feel Jamaica was giving white people a second chance.'

Jean was surprised at this bit of fancy. Faye usually saw things quite matter-of-factly. 'You really think that?'

'Yep!' She drained the melted Sno-Kone and wiped away the red juice trickling down her chin. 'Montserrat.'

'Nevis.'
'Bonaire.'
'Barbuda . . .'

Jean asked Monica to transfer her from Mercy to Inverness, the school in Kingston that Faye would be attending. As the summer drew to an end, Monica announced her decision. Jean was to remain for two more years at Mercy, until she completed fifth form.

They were at breakfast. Jean stopped eating and looked down at her plate. 'I don't want to go back.'

'Excuse me?'

'I'll fall behind if I stay there. They don't even teach West Indian history—'

'In case you've forgotten, I pay the school fees.'

Jean muttered, 'I'll go live with Cherry.'

'What's that you sayin'?'

She spoke up. 'I'll go and live with Cherry.'

'But see here, me-dying-trials. This is the way you talk to me?'

'You can't *make* me go back to Mercy.'

'You forget I'm you mother?'

'No—' Jean began to feel desperate. Her mother's tone felt like a beating she could not bear.

Monica's voice rose: 'You forget? You want to see the big ugly scar you left on my belly?'

'I tired a hearin' 'bout the scar on you belly,' Jean burst out. 'If it was left to you, I would a dead inside you an' neva born.'

Monica did not speak. She patted her lips with the napkin and rose from the table.

'So,' she said quietly, 'you already pickin' up bad Kingston habits.'

'It's my education.'

*

For several days, they didn't speak. Jean had made up her mind, and she simply wouldn't allow herself to think of losing this battle. She bought the special red-and-white fabric for the Inverness school uniforms and took it to the dressmaker. Monica saw all this preparation and said nothing.

Two days before school started, Monica summoned her into the study.

'I went to Inverness and spoke with the headmistress. She managed to find a place for you.'

'Thank you,' Jean mumbled. She was thrown by her mother's change of attitude, and not proud of her victory.

Inverness High School for Girls had been founded at the beginning of the century by Scottish Anglican missionaries and was considered one of the best schools on the island. More than half the students were there on government scholarships, so there was a mix of rich, middle-class, and poor girls. Here, Jean and Faye felt like part of something large and important. Along the streets of Kingston, people recognized Inverness girls from their red-and-white uniforms. At the Girls' Championship Games they took up a huge section of the National Stadium and were nicknamed 'red ants' because of the way they looked from a distance all sitting together.

At Inverness, Faye started writing and directing plays. She spent nearly all her free time in the school theater and at the public library, researching Jamaican history, folklore, and folk music. She wrote a play called *The Return* about an old Maroon woman and entered it in a national competition. It won first prize and was produced by the National Theatre company. A newspaper critic described her as 'a strong, emerging West Indian voice.'

Jean continued to excel in foreign languages and literatures, Spanish, French, and Latin, though her passion was Spanish.

'Mind an' don't lose touch with what's around you,' Faye warned. 'You not European, you know.'

'I'm not?' She tried to make Faye laugh.

'It's time for us to pay attention to our own culture. Colonialism is a state of mind.'

Jean didn't respond. She was trying to fathom what lay beneath Faye's decisive tone and sweeping words.

'Well,' Faye continued, 'at least Spanish will be useful. After all, Cuba is our closest neighbor.'

Was Faye changing, Jean wondered, or had she always been like this? Her sense of humor could no longer be relied on; it was all seriousness and urgency with her. Jean was irritated by this kind of talk, but then right away felt guilty because she knew her irritation was caused by jealousy. Faye was involved in something bigger than herself yet not remote from her. She and Jean were both daughters of the nation, born in the morning twilight of Independence, but whereas Faye seemed to be growing at the same pace as the nation, Jean felt that she, herself, was lagging behind. Was something wrong with her? Monica said she was a dreamer, and often she felt like a sleepwalker moving in two worlds at once: here and not here. She looked and listened always from outside. When it came to discussions of the island's politics she felt the way she did around sexually experienced people: self-consciously virginal, inarticulate, incomplete.

By the summer of '71 the election campaign was well under way. Manley took a campaign name lifted from the Old Testament – Joshua – and he promised to lead the people out of capitalist and neocolonialist bondage. Daphne got special invitations to all the campaign events and she often took Jean and Faye along with her. As the election grew nearer the campaign became one long fête; night after night there were bandwagons with Bob

Marley, Burning Spear, and Third World. Diplomats and Rastafarians mingled at poolside parties. African dress was in vogue. To Monica's dismay, Jean, after a few months of straightening her hair, cut it into a close-cropped Afro, or 'natural.' Faye started wearing African head-wraps; her hair was so fine that blond strands escaped from the fabric producing a radiant effect; it wasn't an Afro, it was her 'halo,' she said.

One night at a bandwagon, Jean, Faye, and Daphne were able to stand close to the stage with the VIPs and politicians. Jean noticed June Morgan on stage. She was a popular television journalist and Manley's lover, and she campaigned tirelessly with him.

'Better mus' come!' Michael shouted to the thousands standing there. He waited with actorly timing for the crowd's cheering to die down. 'I say is *time fe a CHANGE!*' These last words rang out in chorus with his supporters who had taken it as their own battle cry. Michael raised his hand in a victory sign: then he put his arm around June. The crowd roared.

Faye beamed: 'The man is a prophet,' she said.

Jean noticed that Daphne was unusually quiet.

'What happen, Aunt Daphne? You all right?'

'I was thinking 'bout you father,' she said. 'How he woulda love to be here. You father, he had a *vision.*'

Lloyd Cole, who would become a minister in Manley's new government, saw Daphne and came over to greet her.

'You know my niece, Jean, Roy's daughter? And this is her friend Faye.'

'Roy's daughter? I knew your father well.'

'I was just saying if only he coulda be here to see this.'

'Yes, man. Is a shame. The best die young—'

'He woulda been proud—'

'Proud as proud-self, yes.' He turned to Jean. 'So, Roy's daughter, eh? You mus' join our youth organization. Hey,

Malcolm! Comrade, come over here. I want you to meet somebody. Malcolm is in charge of youth recruitment.'

Malcolm was in his early twenties and had a mouthful of brown teeth, but it didn't stop a big, ingratiating smile from spreading across his face.

'This is Roy Landing's daughter,' Lloyd Cole said.

Jean could tell that this youngster had no idea who Roy Landing was.

'She wants to join. Sign her up, man. An' her friend, too.'

Minutes later, Jean and Faye were inside a trailer full of orange-colored posters. Faye signed the membership form eagerly. Jean recalled Monica always telling her to read things carefully before signing. The trailer was hot, noisy, and crowded. It smelled of ganja and body odor. She was too distracted to read the fine print. She had a strange feeling about signing, but at the same time she didn't want to appear odd. What could she do – tell them she had changed her mind? This was the party her father had believed in and worked for. She printed then tremulously signed her full name: *Jean Antonia Landing*. She was choosing; she had chosen. She had chosen sides.

27

The entire clan gathered at Cherry's house on Christmas Day, the Ho Sings, the Landings, and the Sterns. Mary Darling went, too; she made the egg punch, a potent mixture of eggs, cream, rum, and cognac with a sprinkling of nutmeg. Cherry cooked everything herself. A whole pig was roasted, but she didn't serve it with the head and feet as many people did. These were put aside and marinated in lime juice and hot peppers to make souse. Every year Jean made sure she was in the kitchen while Cherry was carving the roast so she could get 'a taste' while it was fresh from the oven, the meat juices steaming and dripping. Cherry also cooked duck Cantonese style with ginger and Chinese vegetables. There were platters of baked plantain, roast breadfruit, rice-an'-peas, puréed sweet potatoes, and, because Mary did not eat meat, baked stuffed red snapper.

After dinner, everybody sat for a while on the veranda to rest and make room for Christmas pudding. Cherry prepared this pudding back in September and kept it in a cake tin soaking in rum for four months. It was dense, black, and so rich with fruit and currants that one could eat only a very tiny piece. It was served with a cold, creamy rum sauce.

After pudding, the smallest children sang Christmas carols while Miss Audrey accompanied on the piano. Miss Audrey had been in charge of this Christmas entertainment ever since anyone could remember. She was an unmarried cousin of

Cherry's who lived in the country, and no one ever saw her except at Christmastime. Presents were handed out after the carols. Then the party split up. The adults sat on the veranda; the 'young people' gathered in the Ping-Pong room where they played Ping-Pong and dominoes and listened to music; and the small children ran around the yard.

Christmas at Cherry's was particularly memorable when there was a visitor from abroad. That year it was Astrid, Aunt Daphne's daughter. Astrid, whose father was from Curaçao and who spoke Dutch fluently, was visiting from Holland, where she was studying engineering. She was as unlike her mother as any daughter could be, small-boned and soft-voiced. She regarded her mother's antics with a calm, expressionless face and an occasional smile; mother and daughter had great affection for each other, though it was never demonstrated publicly.

Fern was pregnant and beginning to show. She visited the 'young people' in the Ping-Pong room for a few minutes, then joined her husband out on the veranda. Just a year earlier, Fern had stayed in the Ping-Pong room, and Jean, who was between the two generations of cousins in age, too young for the raucous teenagers, too old to run around in the yard, had sat alone in the quiet hallway reading. But that year she was finally welcome in the Ping-Pong room. However, the real sign that she was no longer considered a child was that Cherry offered her a glass instead of one of the familiar unbreakable tumblers she kept on a tray near the refrigerator for her countless grandchildren. The glass was a rite of passage all the cousins acknowledged.

Trevor Blake was in the Ping-Pong room with his older brother Clive. Clive was droning on in an American accent about acid and 'trips' and buying drugs in New York's Central Park. Fern's younger brothers – Andrew, Brian, Colin – were getting exasperated. They considered themselves rather wild and daring, and he was making them feel provincial.

Trevor, embarrassed by his brother, got up and went outside.

Jean waited a while, until she felt no one would notice; then she went outside to join him.

He was in the garden around the corner from the veranda, hidden from view, smoking a cigarette. Jean sat down beside him looking out across the flat suburbs below. They heard the grown-ups shouting and laughing on the veranda, Daphne's voice, as usual, louder than everyone else's.

'I forgot about the hills while I was away,' Trevor said with misery in his voice.

She sometimes forgot them too; they were so much a part of the city's landscape.

'Look, Jean.' Her father stood with her on the front lawn and turned her around in a full circle. 'Anywhere you stand in this country you see hills.'

'Have you gone to the country since you got back?'

'We went to the beach out by Palisadoes a few times.'

'That's not the country.'

'What the hell—'

Noise and commotion. Louder, nearer. Drums, tambourines. Jean and Trevor, following the sound, came to the front of the house and saw what looked like giant, brightly colored birds.

'Shit!' Trevor said. 'What's that?'

'It's Jonkanoo. Don't you remember?'

There were about a dozen of them, some with tin pans, some with gumbie and dundo drums. Jean had been afraid of them when she was little and used to run to her father and peek at them from behind him.

Don't be scared, sweetheart. They not goin' hurt you.

'They not goin' hurt you,' she said, laughing, and took Trevor's hand, pulling him toward the veranda.

Pa-lang-pa-lang. Pa-lang-pa-lang.

The children stopped playing and stood mesmerized by the noise and costumes.

The Jonkanoo chief loomed in front of the veranda guests. His face was painted hideously white. He wore a headpiece of feathers and animal horns, and had on assorted layers of military garb. He raised a flask of rum to his lips, and this drinking was the only thing about him which appeared human and living. He lurched and swung his arms around like an untamed animal or wild spirit. As he moved closer to them, the children screamed and scattered.

'Tek care, tek care,' the grown-ups shouted, both at the children and at the Jonkanoo chief.

He seemed deaf or stone drunk. He stomped and swayed and swung gracelessly as if he might topple over any second. Hundreds of beaded bracelets rattled around his ankles. Swi-swoosh! He drew out a wooden sword and sliced the air, lunging at the children, who screamed again.

'Give them rum and they'll go away,' someone said.

Pa-lang-pa-lang. Pa-lang-pa-lang. The other Jonkanoo men also wore outlandish garb — military jackets, fancy women's hats with colorful feathers, and strands of beads around their necks. The Jonkanoo women were more subdued, swaying back and forth in the garden, in long patchwork gowns and head ties. Their faces were painted bright colors. Half-peacock, half-zombie, they seemed to be dancing in their sleep. None of the garish masqueraders smiled or laughed; they seemed barely conscious of the spectators.

There was an African named John Canoe . . .

'Spirit ketch dem,' somebody said.

'Turn the hose on dem.'

'Run dem 'way.'

'Is all right, man, is jus' Jonkanoo. Mek dem dance.'

The Jonkanoo chief came up onto the veranda and began to dance lewdly.

'Give them money an' they'll go away.'

'Him look like a big, ugly crocodile.'

'Crocodile!' a child cried, and then the other children chanted: 'Crocodile-man. Crocodile-man.'

Cherry gave the Jonkanoo chief a ten-dollar bill. He spotted Jean and Trevor as he came down the veranda steps, and he began stomping and lurching in front of them. Jean gazed at his white-painted face. She heard the voices on the veranda, full of irritation and mockery, and she also heard her father:

The slaves were given a holiday on Christmas Day and they would masquerade through the country . . .

'Don't give dem any more money!' somebody shouted.

Trevor had taken a dollar bill from his pocket and was handing it to the Jonkanoo chief.

'Shoo!' Cherry said. 'G'wan now.'

Pa-lang-pa-lang. They went away dancing. The Jonkanoo chief kept spinning around to face them as he left, and continued to slice the air with his sword. The pa-lang-pa-lang faded as they went downhill to another house.

The talk on the veranda quieted down. The rowdiness of the Jonkanoo had sapped everyone's energy. Trevor and Jean sat silently in the garden.

'Look, goats.' He pointed to some goats making their way up the stony slope.

He has been away too long, she thought to herself.

'They don't have goats in America?'

'I don't remember goats being here. I forgot a lot.'

He watched the goats for a while, then got up.

' 'Bye,' he said, and headed toward the gate.

The Jonkanoo could still be heard faintly.

'Where you going?'

'I don't know,' he said mournfully, and went through the gate.

*

Lana was back in Jamaica. Her grandmothers missed her terribly. It was Christmas, after all, and family was family. They were fed up with Monica's grudge against her daughter. So they disregarded her and spoke openly about Lana:

'She seems to be doing well for herself these days, eh, Mary?'

'Yes. She spendin' Christmas with Deepa.'

If they had looked at Monica's face they would have seen flesh turn to stone. But no one looked. They ignored her and continued:

'Long time I haven't seen her.'

'Long time I don't see Deepa.'

After her success in the beauty pageant and the completion of her beauty culture course, Lana had returned home with a white-haired, white-bearded white man named Grover. He was obviously her lover though he called himself her manager. Lana had begun a new career, not as a beautician, but as a singer. She had recorded a single that reached the local Top Ten. It was a reggae version of an American hit, 'Tears on My Pillow.' Her recording name was simply 'Lana,' because Ramcharan was too long. Her singing voice was vibrant and girlishly sweet. The song had made her a local celebrity. She got gigs at hotels and clubs, and she was waiting for a songwriter to finish some songs for her so that she could record an album.

The aunts and grandmothers tried to overcome their instinctive distrust of Grover.

'He kinda ole, but maybe he good for her.'

'Maybe that's what she needs, an older man, though him kinda turn me stomach to tell you the truth.'

But they were unanimously excited about her singing career – 'Look like Lana find her true calling, eh?' 'Maybe now she put all her troubles behind her' – and were thrilled to see her picture in the newspaper once again.

Christmas night, Jean went with Paul to see Lana perform at

the Kingston Sheraton. She wore a skintight, gold jumpsuit and a lot of gold makeup. She sang some reggae hits and some Burt Bacharach songs, and then drove the tourists into a frenzy with one ribald calypso after another: 'Big Bamboo' and 'Working for the Yankee Dollar.'

Lana joined Paul and Jean afterward. 'Dolly! What a way you grow big! How you like me show? I look like a Christmas tree up there all light up an' everything, na?' She turned to a white-haired man: 'Grover, this is my baby sister, Dolly.'

'Jean,' Jean said, shaking his hand.

Lana, as usual, talked nonstop, so Jean had an opportunity to study Grover: An old man trying to look young, or a young man who had turned old fast. His skin was red, like a cooked lobster. Jean felt hot and sweaty just looking at him in his cheap, white satin shirt with the buttons open to display a gold chain and the white hairs on his chest. The only difference between him and the gigolos at the hotel bar was that he was old and white. She and Paul exchanged a glance that said they were in agreement about Grover. Fly-by-night operator. Ginal.

What was it about the island, she wondered, that attracted conmen? Any foreigner could come to Jamaica and call himself Doctor, Preacher, Expert, or Lord So-and-So and get away with it.

'I give him two more months,' Paul told Jean on the way home.

Two weeks was more like it. He and Lana got into a fight and he hit her. Jean noted that Lana had the good sense and pride to throw him out. Lana's singing career continued to thrive without him, and she got herself a new boyfriend right away, a Jamaican, more than twice her age and married. He was a member of Parliament and a friend of Delly's. Su-su, su-su: scandal and rumor still hovered around Lana, but didn't seem to affect her at all. There was a popular song from the sixties by Prince Buster, 'A Hard Man Fe Dead'. That was Lana, unsinkable, tallawa.

28

On the last day of 1971, Jean and Paul drove along the Palisadoes road and stopped at a deserted beach. The day was overcast; the sea was rough and dull-colored, and the beach was littered with things that the sea had tossed up like unnecessary sacrifices: driftwood, seaweed, coconut husks, crab shells, dead fish. The sandy wind stung them, and the noise of the wind and sea was so great, it drowned out their thoughts.

They were untroubled. Paul swam. Jean didn't find the water inviting. She took a long, slow walk down the beach, sat down for a while, then walked back, enjoying the water sliding back and forth across her feet.

Suddenly, she was crippled by pain. A jellyfish had stung her. The invisibility of the creature was as alarming as the pain. The sting went deeper than skin and flesh; her bones throbbed. She thought she would faint.

Paul saw her hobbling and was at her side in seconds.

'Jellyfish?'

'I think I stepped on it. My foot—' She couldn't finish.

'Lemme see.' He took her foot in his hands. 'Jesus! Look like you step on two jellyfish. You foot swellin' up like a balloon.'

'Oh, God.'

'Awright. Close you eyes.'

She obeyed. Whatever he did was all right with her as long as it stopped the pain. She was highly allergic to insect stings, and probably to jellyfish, too; this could kill her. She felt a warm liquid spreading over her foot and running down her leg. What balm was this? The pain completely subsided; there was only a residual throbbing.

'Awright,' he said.

She opened her eyes. He was fumbling with his swimming trunks. She realized what he had done.

'Wait a few minutes, then you can go wash off.'

He found a long stick and went poking around the water's edge, looking for the jellyfish.

Later they went to a place in Port Royal for fried fish. It was a wooden shack with red plastic tablecloths and tables by the water. Looking east across the bay they could see the ships and buildings of Kingston's waterfront. In the early evening light it looked to her like a city on a postcard, calm, venerable, and quite beautiful. The fish was spicy, and so crisp they could eat the whole thing, head, fins, and all. She looked at Paul and felt a surge of gratitude for all the vistas and resting places she might not have known about except for him.

'Sting all gone?'

She nodded, suppressed a smile, and asked, just for confirmation: 'You pissed on my foot?'

The people at the next table turned and stared.

'It's something in the urine. Ammonia or something. If it happens again an' I'm not there, piss on yourself.'

'Piss on myself? Suppose is not me foot. How I goin' piss on me own neck-back?'

They suddenly realized they were being overheard and they started laughing, quietly at first, then louder, uncontrollably.

They drove back a little after sunset. Jean loved driving along the Palisadoes road. This long, narrow sandbar had survived earthquakes and hurricanes. They drove with the windows open, with strong sea breezes blowing about their heads. The road, which curved in a perfect crescent from Port Royal to Kingston, led to and from the airport and made a lovely entrance to the city.

But then coming into the city the road cut through a shanty-town and Jean saw the words GO BACK HOAM WHITE MAN painted across a billboard. Underneath this, in red, was the word BLOOD! Very nice. Welcome to Jamaica. She hoped the tourists didn't take this personally. After all, it wasn't meant just for foreigners. (Jean had been with Monica when an old, beat-up car full of ruffians pulled up beside them at a stoplight. One of the men leaned out the window and said 'Pow!' so loudly that Monica jumped. The man laughed and pointed two fingers at her, simulating a gun. 'White lady, I shoot you an' tek you car.' The light changed and the car full of men took off at full speed. 'Ganja mash up dem brain,' Monica muttered, and added that there was not enough rope on the island to hang all the criminals.)

'Want to stop for a milkshake?' Paul asked.

'No. But—' She sighed.

She wasn't ready to go back home. Paul was going to a New Year's Eve party later with one of his girlfriends.

When they came to the road that would take them to Bonnieview, he kept going until they were climbing up to the top of Jack's Hill. He stopped at a favorite lookout point. The city and its suburbs glittered. Kingston looked so welcoming from this height; it was the same pleasant feeling she got after a long country journey and miles of dark, winding roads: lights of the city, home.

'Sorry to hear about your friend,' he said.

Trevor had taken an overdose of drugs on Christmas night. Luckily, he had been rushed to the hospital in time to be saved.

'That New York is a funny place,' Paul said. 'Crazy.'

Like everyone else, Paul thought that Trevor had been

corrupted by the years he had lived in New York. There were real problems: an older brother had been killed in Vietnam; his parents had separated. But Jean thought his was the sadness of someone who did not know which of two worlds he belonged to. She felt for him.

'You ever think about going abroad to study? America, Canada?' Paul asked.

'Yes, maybe,' she said.

The radio was on and they listened to Otis Redding singing 'Dock of the Bay.' It brought to mind their day at the beach, drugs, people dying young, and Lana's effort to be happy. It seemed to be taking more effort than usual for people to be happy.

The country was changing. Cherry had been robbed at gunpoint one evening as she sat on her veranda. On Christmas Day, Jean had heard everyone talking about it and suggesting that she enclose the veranda in grillwork. Jean couldn't imagine what it would be like, to be locked in like that in one's own home.

Ahead of her was the faint line of lights that was Palisadoes. The single, large, sparkling light at the end was Port Royal, or what was left of Port Royal.

Port Royal sank before our very eyes. I believe I heard human cries in the distance.

From here the island was more an island than ever and its inhabitants — herself, Paul — seemed vulnerable in their island isolation. The sea imprisoned them, and the shipwrecks and watery skeletons of the sunken city were their wardens.

'You cold?' he asked. He had seen her tremble.

'No.'

She wanted to stay in the car with Paul as long as possible. She felt safe with him. Safe from what, exactly? She did not know. He had asked her about going abroad to study, and she supposed it would soon be time to start thinking about that. She couldn't picture herself anywhere else. It was not love of country that she felt, so much as simple inseparableness. Wha' fe you, fe you; wha' belong a sea don't fly, Mary Darling once said to her. She thought about the jellyfish; what an ominous, mythical creature it seemed – like a curse, the spit of some god.

Like that legendary garden, ours had a Forbidden Tree.

Once it had just been kuku pods – *Satan's eyeball* – those pods that malevolent children rubbed against their clothes until they became as hot as burning coal; then they would press them like branding irons against your skin – once it had just been kuku pods, cow-itch, wasps, jellyfish; now it was guns. She sensed that they would never spend Christmas like that again, never sit on an open veranda like that, and that was probably the last time she would see Jonkanoo.

'Ready?'

She wasn't, but she knew she shouldn't delay Paul any longer. The day, the year, and the safe feeling were going to end. 'You in such a hurry fe grow up,' Monica had said to her. It wasn't a matter of Jean growing up too fast. Everything that had been worrying her rolled suddenly into the one thought: Jamaica was too young to die.

Part Two

29

Faith's Pen is the name of this scattering of cottages perched precariously on the mountainside. She's never noticed it before, the place or the sign. The sun is fierce here on top of Mount Diablo. They're about to reach the highest point and then begin their descent, not to the plains, but to less treacherous mountain roads. She glances at Paul.

What if she were to stay here with him?

A gasoline truck creeps sluggishly ahead of them. Paul lets his hand drop from the steering wheel. She has an urge to take his hand and press it against her face, and while she thinks about it, he surprisingly reaches for her hand and squeezes it.

Again the thought of staying washes over her.

At Moneague, Paul makes a detour. He wants to visit an old woman who has recently been widowed. Her husband was a poultry farmer, and Paul often bought chickens and eggs from him.

They turn onto a narrower road. Anthuriums flourish along the hillside like red tongues darting out among the ferns and other greenery. There's a strong, comforting smell of earth. They could be driving in an African country. The women's head ties, the abundance of skirt fabric, the baskets and tins of produce on their heads, and most of all the faces themselves, remind Jean that Africa came here not once, but repeatedly.

Yetunde was me grandmother name. It means 'Our mother has come back.'
Yetunde died before I was bawn. But me great-grandmother, Mary, tell me
'bout her — Mary the Yoruba, a pure African; me name after her. She live to
be ole-ole, an' she 'member the ole language.

The gasoline truck is still ahead of them. They follow it
slowly through the arch of an old aqueduct. There are other
ruins among the tall grasses: an old water wheel by a dried-up
river. They pass a large, abandoned house with broken windows
and a gravel driveway overgrown with weeds.

'Is this the old Redfield estate?' she asks.

'Yes. You know the story?'

'Not really. What happened?'

'Well, the Redfields, they weren't the owners. Ole man
Redfield was an Englishman who managed the place. When
slavery ended the real owners abandoned it, and you could say
they abandoned him, too. Things were sold off – carriage,
horse, furniture – but the Redfields went on living here.

'The ex-slaves looked up to the Redfields because they were
the white people in the big house, and they believed they still
needed "Busha." That was how they were used to thinking 'bout
white people. They even sent their children to work for them
without pay because they thought it was something special to
live in Busha's house.

'It went on like that for three, four generations. The
Redfields managed to find other white people to marry, and
they had children and stayed. They couldn't afford to go
nowhere else, and anyway, the black people treated them like
royalty, went to them whenever anything went wrong, disputes
over land, goats, in-laws. Man, they even went to them for
medical advice.'

'But they were as poor as the black people,' Jean says. 'How
did they manage—'

'It was all a façade. The Redfields were poor but they

couldn't live the same way as black people. No, man. They couldn't go to market an' haggle over a piece a pigtail. They would send the "gal" to bring back the best cut of beef, the best tomatoes. They would go rum shop and buy, not just rum, but expensive whisky and brandy, and never pay for it. They had everything they needed, and never, never did they pay for anything.

'I think it was in 1976, three Redfields, a brother and two sisters, were in the house one night watching TV when the gunmen came. It was in the papers. They say one of the gunmen was originally from around here. He'd been in Kingston and gotten involved with a gang. Probably somebody whose mother once sent him to the Redfields to be their garden boy or house-boy or just "the boy," and he brought his gang back to settle some old grudge. Maybe he thought the Redfields actually had some money stashed away.

'The gunmen broke down the front door and beat them to death. The Redfields put up a fight. They say there was blood all over the house, even out in the yard. It was out by the water wheel that they found one of the women, decapitated. They say she was—'

'Stop,' Jean says. 'Enough.'

Paul is quiet for a few moments, then he continues, 'You ever hear people talk 'bout white nigger? In this country, a poor white man is worse than a stray dog. The Redfields knew this, and they tried to keep up a show as long as they could.'

'They still grow cane around here?' Jean asks.

'No.'

'I smell something like sugar cane or molasses.'

'Could be anything. Ganja. Maybe somebody roasting breadfruit.'

'No. It smells like sugar burning.'

*

They reach the little village called Goshen where the poultry widow lives. At the foot of an even narrower dirt road there's a sign with a woodcut rooster:

FRESH POETRY & EGGS.

Jean laughs.

'Wha' happen?'

'That sign.'

'There's a story behind that sign.'

'What?'

'Well, I don't know exactly.'

'Story, me eye. De people dem cyaan spell.'

But she thinks to herself there probably is a story: some misunderstanding involving an English teacher, a rural schoolboy, chickens, and Walter de la Mare.

Paul blows the horn in front of the poultry widow's cottage, and after a few minutes she appears on the veranda. They wait for what seems like an eternity while she unlocks the iron grillwork: unlocking the padlock, then unraveling the heavy chain, and then finally unlocking the door with an enormous, gothic-looking key. The grillwork is new and unpainted.

It's a social visit, but because Paul is not really on social terms with Miss Vera he talks business: Yes, he will take some eggs, and he'd like to take a look at her new chicken coop because he is thinking of building a new one himself; and true, the mesh wire they're selling these days is no good.

Jean follows them around the back to the chickens. The stench from the chicken coops is so overpowering it almost knocks her over. She sees a pretty little river in the distance and heads toward it.

Paul shouts after her: 'Follow the river down the hill an' you reach a waterfall, na true, Miss Vera?'

'Eh-heh. An' a tamarind tree wid a whole heap a tamarind.'

Miss Vera's old voice cracks. 'G'wan, tek you time walk. Is a free country.'

It feels as though she's walked quite far from the poultry farm, and still she hasn't found the waterfall or the 'whole heap a tamarind.' She hears the swift, invisible movements of lizards and suddenly realizes how alone she is. She stops and looks around. Here and there, dabs of sunlight touch the under-growth, creating an eerie glow. A frangipani, pink with wide spreading branches, offers fragrance to the forest. Vines hang, crawl, and clutch the trees and bush together in heavy curtains and spreads of green. Red parasite flowers perch like fantastic birds in the crevices of trees.

This is it, the land she imagined in her childhood games, the undiscovered paradise where Kawara the Arawak boy lived. The river, rushing across ancient rocks, wakes the gutturals of a sunken language. The air is promising and sweet. Tree trunks smell of centuries-old medicine. This is the perfection of the world she was born into.

No one will trouble me here?

She begs to be able to love this place free of fear.

The bushes tremble. She sees the vague forms of men gliding behind the tangled foliage.

Wild-eyed, they emerge swinging machetes. The glint of steel, the slitting blade, blood on the indifferent leaves — she runs, stumbling over rocks and tree roots. Ground lizards part the grasses with their heavy tails, scrambling out of her way. A bird shrieks. What will happen to her body if she dies here?

She reaches Miss Vera's house and enters through the back door. There's no sign of Paul or Miss Vera. All the violence she has recently witnessed spins around her. They have come, the gunmen, and taken them out to the bush to kill them.

The front door opens, and she feels herself falling.

'Jean?'

'Eh! Steady. Mek her lie down on de sofa.'

'Wha' happen?'

'Maybe her sugar low. You want a likkle juice?'

'Yes – thank you.'

Paul feels her forehead. 'You cold like ice.'

Miss Vera comes back with a cold drink. 'Here, drink dis.'

The drink is a translucent ginger-brown color. She thinks it's tamarind juice. Maybe naseberry. It never ceases to amaze her, the sweet drinks country people make out of anything that grows. She swallows; it's cane juice. She heaves.

She has barely enough strength to get up off her knees and pull the chain of the old-fashioned toilet. She sits on the edge of the tub to calm herself, and after a while she becomes aware of a pleasant smell. It's a bar of white soap. She notices how clean and orderly the bathroom is, from the glistening linoleum to the pink hand towel neatly folded on the rack, and it comforts her. There is routine and pride in everything here.

Later, in the truck, she remembers that she used to drink cane juice every day when she stayed with Grandma Darling and that she used to beg for sticks of cane to chew on. The memory of that taste makes her head heavy and lingers with the latent horror of the day: the Redfields' story, Miss Vera's grillwork, the intimations of brutality on the road and in the forest. If only she could find some peaceful place to lie down for a while. She closes her eyes but this offers no respite; the mask of daylight dissolves, revealing the nightmare. There are no more trees. The trees are gone, all the trees; the rivers have dried up, every one. There's only dry bush and dry rock. In the skeletal forest, lizards and birds wait listlessly for the killing blow. There's not even panic left in Xaymaca, 'Land of Many Rivers.'

'Look like you could use some of that bay rum,' Paul says.

Miss Vera gave her a handkerchief soaked in bay rum to dab

on her forehead, and she holds it on her lap along with some eggs Paul bought from the widow, special eggs for hatching, six of them, white, in an old biscuit tin laden with grass.

They leave Goshen and make their way back along the country road, past the Redfield place, past the old water wheel, and back again through the arch of the aqueduct, rethreading the eye of history.

30

She had expected love to appear suddenly, like an act of God, perfecting her.

But she had been warned, also, of how crushing it could be. It seemed there were two ways love could go, just as there were always two possibilities in any fable or parable: the house built wisely on a rock, and the one built foolishly on sand. At seventeen, Jean's heart had not yet been tested. Then she met Mark Silvera.

There are certain times in a young woman's life — at her wedding, or perhaps at someone else's wedding — when she shines, and even people who have known her all her life seem to notice her for the first time. At Lana's birthday party, Jean was radiant. Not that she outshone Lana. But for once she didn't feel she was in the shadow of her astonishingly beautiful sister. Jean had never worn a dress like the one she wore that evening. Lana had helped her choose the slinky white evening gown that covered her like a second skin and bared her long back. Her hair had grown out from the Afro, and Lana had straightened it and put it into a French twist and had helped Jean with her makeup. Monica thought Jean was spending the weekend with Fern. For some time, Fern had been Jean's alibi, and Monica was under the impression that her daughter and niece were the best of friends. Monica had always liked Fern and felt she was a good, stable influence on Jean.

Deepa threw the party for Lana. She had just turned twenty-three and had recorded another hit single. Deepa went all out, renting a penthouse suite at the Pegasus Hotel, hiring caterers and decorators; it was as extravagant as a wedding.

Jean had filled out; her breasts and hips were large and womanly, and the new dress showed her body to advantage. Men sought her out, wanting to be introduced. She felt like a beautiful foreigner who had only just arrived in the country.

She felt a hand on her shoulder and turned around. It was Trevor. She had not quite gotten over the disappointment of his having a girlfriend. There was a big guy standing beside him.

'This is my friend Mark Silvera,' Trevor said.

Mark looked at her as though she were the prettiest woman in the room.

'Hi,' Mark said with a sexy, self-assured smile.

What a conceited guy, Jean thought.

He wasn't interested in what she thought. She was new territory to conquer.

That she was quiet and virginal — as he discovered within an hour of conversation — appealed to him greatly. He was only twenty himself, but quite experienced. It excited him that she had never had a boyfriend. It would be thrilling to teach her things, to get her to depend on him, to be the first man to make her unreasonable with desire.

He was over six feet tall and solidly built, a handsome mix of Creole Lebanese and Portuguese with dark, curly hair and thick eyebrows. He was a typical young man of his class, the descendant of hard-working, affluent immigrants. But being of a new, liberal generation, he enjoyed surrounding himself with people of lesser social standing. He had a companion nicknamed Duck, a street boy from Trench Town who dressed like a gigolo and used filthy language. Duck was praised by all who knew him for his blunt, comical expressions, sort of like a court jester.

Jean made such an impression on Mark that he ignored the girl he had brought to the party, a petite, voluptuous girl who got drunk. After a while Duck escorted her home.

Mark stayed by Jean's side and talked excitedly about himself. He was a guitarist and had recently formed a band. He rhapsodized about his favorite jazz musicians and the kind of music he wanted to compose. She found his monologue bewildering. She'd had a lot of enjoyable conversations with Paul about music, and knew a fair amount about jazz; but Mark spoke as if he were from another planet, full of private jokes, quotations from record covers and from his favorite book, Kahlil Gibran's *The Prophet*, and he made garbled sounds in imitation of his electric guitar. Now and then someone who knew him came along and remarked about what a 'fantastic guitar player' he was.

'Want to dance?' he asked her.

'No. Maybe later.' She liked dancing, but she felt self-conscious and awkward with Mark.

'Excuse me a minute,' she said. 'I have to look for someone.' She went to find Paul. He was the only one who had not seemed to notice how wonderful she looked. When she found him she was disappointed that he did not compliment her, not even silently with his eyes.

'How you like this dress?' she begged, turning around so he could see her bare back.

Deepa came over.

'Doesn't she look fabulous? Like a beautiful white orchid.'

Deepa's voice was gentle and refined even when he was a little drunk, as he was now. He had cultivated a slight British accent, no one knew how, maybe from listening to cricket matches on the BBC. That this kind, affectionate man had once been her mother's lover and was responsible for the bitterness in Monica's heart was a continual mystery to Jean.

Mark joined them, putting his arm around Jean in a proprietary way. 'I not letting you get away.'

Paul looked at Jean to see her response. She felt unsteady and out of her depth.

'Come dance with me,' he said again.

Dancing with him she glanced occasionally at Paul to see if he was watching her, but he was engrossed in conversation with Deepa.

Suddenly Lana got up onto the windowsill and began dancing with the lights of Kingston spread out below her. People began cheering and hollering. 'Sing us a song, Lana!' Someone else shouted, 'Mind you fall!'

'She drunk?' Mark asked.

Jean watched Lana and she watched the people looking at Lana. She wondered what others made of her sister – a self-dramatizing eccentric like Daphne? A bold calypso-reggae queen? The straps of Lana's dress slid from her shoulders until one of her breasts was almost completely exposed.

'Striptease!' someone shouted.

She grinned and rubbed her back against the glass window like a cat.

Jean stopped dancing. There was something odd about the way Lana looked. It seemed to Jean that she was not performing. Her eyes were shining but not with playfulness; she did not seem to see or hear anyone. She spun around facing the window and the lights of the city. Her audience whistled and cheered as she gyrated her hips. She began drumming the windowpane in rhythm to the music; then the drumming turned to banging.

'Hey, mind you break the window!'

'Mind you fall.'

Jean went to Deepa.

'Lana's acting strange.'

Deepa rushed over and saw Lana banging on the window, crying.

'Baby, come—' Deepa held out his arms, and Lana came down from the windowsill and clung to him.

The guests stopped dancing. The room was quiet.

Deepa walked Lana to the bedroom, reassuring everyone as he went by: 'It's all right, she's just tired. Carry on. She'll soon be all right.'

The guests rallied.

'Poor Lana, she overcome.'

'I always feel sad on my birthday.'

Someone joked, 'Come on, Lana, twenty-three not so bad.'

'You sister mad like hell,' Mark said to Jean.

She disliked him intensely for saying this. Without a word she left him and joined Deepa and Lana.

Lana was lying down, and Deepa sat beside her, stroking her hair. Jean sat on the other side of the bed. She remembered another birthday party when she sat worried by someone else's bedside: her sixth birthday, when her father got ill. But she sensed that this was different; this was not a physical aching. Nor could she convince herself that this was merely one of Lana's strange moods; it was acute and disturbing.

'Mark likes you,' Lana said.

Jean shrugged.

'I think you get a boyfriend tonight.' Lana reached out and touched Jean's hair. Who was comforting whom, Jean wondered.

Paul came in. 'You awright?'

Lana nodded.

'Carl is here,' Paul said.

Lana was still involved with Carl Young — a member of Parliament, and married. He tended to turn up late at Lana's events. Jean had heard rumors that he had other girlfriends.

Lana sat up and began dabbing the ruined makeup around

her eyes. 'Daddy,' she said, 'keep Carl company. I'll be there in a minute. Lawd, I mus' look a royal mess.' She got up and went to the mirror. 'Dolly, help me fix meself. Where's my eye liner?'

At the end of the party, as Paul waited around to take Jean home, Mark said: 'Who is this Paul guy, you boyfriend?'

'I told you, I don't have a boyfriend.'

'How about me?'

She wondered if she should tell him she didn't much like him.

He leaned over her in the doorway, bringing his face close to hers. She was certain he was going to kiss her on the lips, but instead he pecked her lightly on the forehead. Oddly, she was disappointed.

'Awright,' he said. 'I know I'm a conceited asshole, but you — are an angel sent by God to change my life.'

He was drunk. She didn't expect to see him again.

But a few days later, he called and asked if he could pick her up after school and take her out for a soda. He spoke over the phone in a nonchalant, weary manner, as if he had either just woken up or was about to go to sleep. She told herself that he was just playing with her, and she half expected him not to show up. But he presented himself at the school gate the next day in his mother's white Mercedes-Benz.

At the soda fountain, he asked her if she would start 'going around' with him.

'My mother won't let me go out with anyone until I'm eighteen.'

This appealed to him: 'When you goin' to be eighteen?'

'In September.'

It was February. 'I'll wait.'

'I hear you give girls a hard time.'

'What you mean a hard time?'

'I hear you're a heartbreaker.'

'Chu, I jus' don't find the right girl yet. Is not jus' a fun time I lookin'. I want to get married.'

They met secretly for several months. Sometimes he picked her up at school, or he met her at Faye's house or at Fern's. She was touched by his little signs of devotion: the way he put his arm around her in public and sought her out daily without fail. He was a braggart, it was true, but, as his girlfriend, she was among the things he bragged about. 'She so sweet and sensible,' he said often to his friends. 'I trust this girl more than anybody in the world.'

Mark had dreams and plans for his music. It was his ambition most of all that appealed to her. He really knew a great deal about music, and spent hours practicing and composing. He had studied classical and jazz guitar and played a number of other instruments. But his real passion was reggae. She began to see that his hanging around with people who were socially inferior to him was not a pretension; he was listening to the language of the tenement yards and using what he heard in his music.

She told Monica she was going to the country with Faye and went with Mark one weekend to his parents' beach house. It was the first time she had ever spent an entire night with him. He knew she was intent on remaining a virgin for a while. 'It's okay. I can wait,' he always assured her. She was not sure if it was the way he said it or the way she heard it, but the word 'can' always seemed to weigh more than the other words: not that he would or should wait, but that he *could*. For her and her alone, as difficult, painful, and possibly even physically harmful to him as it was – 'I can wait,' he would say breathlessly, then hold her in place with a long deep kiss, practically impaling her with his tongue, sliding his finger under her panties and working the wetness between her legs until a single, enormous wave tossed her, mercifully caught her, and let her drift slowly back. Sometimes he would place her hand against the bulge in his pants and grimace and shift about so uncomfortably that she would say, 'I'm sorry.'

That night in his parents' beach house his agony and self-sacrifice seemed far beyond anything that could reasonably be expected of a man, and she decided to give him some relief. It was the first time she had ever laid eyes or hands on a naked, erect penis. He showed her what to do. And then, spent and satisfied, he fell into a deep sleep, while Jean, reassuring herself that she was still intact, drifted into a less profound slumber.

Next morning he played his guitar and sang a ballad he had composed for her. At first she thought she heard him singing 'my Norma Jean,' and was puzzled, then she realized the words he sang were 'my normal Jean.'

Sensible an' sweet. A good girl. No trouble.

31

Saturday was Monica's day of rest. She slept till nine, had her coffee and toast in bed, then she got up and went to the hairdresser for her weekly wash, set, and manicure. By lunchtime she was well rested and well groomed.

It was around lunchtime that Mark Silvera arrived, unexpected.

'Who is that?' Monica asked Jean, seeing the rather handsome young man stepping out of a Mercedes-Benz.

Jean was so shocked, she could barely answer. She tried to sound nonchalant: 'Oh, he's a friend of mine, Mark Silvera.' And then she added the lie, 'I met him at Fern's house a couple weeks ago.'

They had been seeing each other for five months.

Mark walked up the veranda steps with a large bunch of roses, which he presented to Monica.

'Good afternoon, Mrs Landing. Nice to meet you. I picked these from my mother's garden this morning.'

'How nice of you.' Monica looked him up and down. In a matter of seconds she had grasped the entire situation.

'Silvera? Your father is——?'

'Valentine.'

'Oh, Val Silvera. I know your father well. Come in.'

Jean was glad that her mother wasted no time finding out who Mark's parents were. That was all Monica needed to know in order to invite him into her home. He was the son of Carol

Azan, of the incredibly rich Azans, and Val Silvera, the banker Monica did business with. The Silveras were a well-known family — Jamaica-White, meaning there was Black blood somewhere in the genealogy but it didn't show.

Monica looked at her seventeen-year-old daughter. She could not imagine what this good-looking young man saw in Jean and was astonished at her having attracted such a suitable person. Mark, she felt, had come over, in the old-fashioned way, to ask the mother's permission to take out her daughter. She was impressed. No, more than that, she was flabbergasted. She could not believe that Jean had managed this conquest on her own, or, if she had, that she would be able to carry it through successfully.

Jean was on edge for the entire visit. She needn't have worried. Neither of them paid any attention to her. Mark flattered Monica, complimenting her taste in furniture. But he made certain not to be too deferential. He made himself completely at home on the couch and even went so far as to put his feet up on Monica's precious coffee table. This showed he was a person of real class.

Monica treated him like an old friend of the family. She had Irene bring him a cold beer. He must call her Monica, and he must stay and have lunch with them; she added that because it was Saturday they were following 'true Jamaica tradition,' and having only soup. Through lunch, Monica asked a lot of questions — What school had he attended? How many sisters and brothers did he have? — and while she listened, she kept an eye on her daughter.

She observed that Jean had become a fairly attractive woman after all. She was no beauty, but she had a few things in her favor. She carried herself well and had a decent figure. Her bad hair was being properly managed with chemical straighteners and with rollers. Though her skin was dark, it was smooth and flawless. Best of all, there were her lovely eyes — the Stern eyes, attributed to the German side of the family – without which, she felt, her daughter would have been quite ordinary. She guessed that Mark liked Jean because she was a quiet, pleasant, dependable girl who would never cause him any trouble or embarrass him, and she gave herself credit for having taught Jean to be so well behaved. Jean mustn't be too accommodating, though, she thought, or the boy will use her and throw her out like old shoes.

'I have very strict rules about Jean's going out. You know she's only seventeen and still in school.'

'I respect strict rules for girls, Mrs Landing – Monica. My sister, Maureen, has to come home by a decent hour. I wouldn't dream of treating Jean any differently.'

Jean knew that Maureen, who was fifteen, spent most nights at her much older boyfriend's apartment.

'It's one of the things I like most about Jean, you know, that she has such a good relationship with her mother.'

'We're very close.'

'Like mother, like daughter.'

Jean was relieved that Monica and Mark got on so well, though she would have felt better if they hadn't talked about her as if she were not present.

'She's very serious about her schoolwork. She doesn't run around wild like so many girls you meet nowadays.'

After lunch, Monica took Mark on a tour of the garden – the garden Hilston had created from nothing and tended to five days a week – and told him that she, like his mother, was an avid gardener. 'We planted that hydrangea last year,' she said, pointing to a garden bed, 'and it's doing quite well there in the shade.'

It surprised Jean that Monica even knew the names of the plants.

Mark promised to give his parents Monica's warm regards and asked if he could come around later and take Jean to a movie. Jean grew fearful that Mark had now gone too far:

Monica was adamant about Jean not going on dates until she was eighteen. She had said so a million times, and Jean had warned Mark about this.

Of course, Monica said, as long as they didn't stay out late.

Monica stood beside Jean in the driveway, waving good-bye. 'Quite a nice young man,' she said, having strategically decided that it was all she would say to Jean about him for now.

Irene was grumpy for the rest of the day. Jean had noticed her disapproval on seeing Mark's feet on the coffee table that she had spent part of the morning polishing. And it had embarrassed Jean that Mark had not said so much as thank you when Irene brought him his beer. It wasn't long before Irene told Jean what she thought of Mark Silvera. She summed it up in two words: 'No brought-upsy.'

What did he see in her? Monica continually asked herself as Mark's devotion to her daughter remained constant. It was too good to be true. She had the specter of Lana before her, the specter of herself and Deepa. So she became more vigilant than before. She questioned Jean constantly and was not above listening to her telephone conversations. She was alert to every tremor that spoke of her daughter's feelings toward this man and to changes in the relationship.

'How you feel about Mark?' she asked one day. 'You two talk about getting married?'

'All the time.'

'Talk is cheap.'

'Don't be so distrustful. Mark loves me.'

Monica never looked more contemptuous than she did at that moment. 'Do me one favor: don't talk no love-stupidness to me. You think love is something you can live on?'

'I never said *I* was in love.'

'Good.' The lines on Monica's face relaxed. 'Don't let yourself get carried away, you hear, or you regret it the rest of you life.'

'You mean . . . ?' Jean couldn't bring herself to say the word 'sex' in front of her mother.

'The minute you tek off you clothes, everything changes.'

Jean tried not to let it show on her face, that she and Mark had already passed that milestone.

'When you fall in love with a man's body, you start to worship him. An' you put youself at a terrible disadvantage if he don't worship you.'

Mark knew that his parents did not approve of Jean; she was too dark-skinned. He took pleasure in disappointing them. He had not gone into business or law or medicine, but instead had formed a reggae band. He often invited people from the slums of Kingston into the family home. Now to add to his parents' anxieties, he had become serious about Jean Landing.

The first time his mother met Jean, she simply ignored her. When she began seeing Jean regularly with Mark, she was rude to her, especially when Jean phoned: 'Jean who? Oh, you. Call back later, we eatin' dinner.' But then, on discovering that Jean, despite her dark skin, was a person of class – the daughter of Monica Landing and the granddaughter of Cherry Ho Sing-Landing – she began, grudgingly, to accept her, though she never tired of telling her husband that Mark could 'do a lot better.'

Val Silvera pointed out to his wife that Mark could do a lot worse.

Jean became Mark's girlfriend to get out of the house and escape her mother's supervision. It would be some time before she realized that she had exchanged one form of supervision for another. Mark disliked women who wore a lot of makeup or talked loudly or lewdly, and he hated bright, gaudy clothes. She found herself dressing, speaking, and acting in ways that conformed to his tastes. In silent, solitary hours it was his voice, above all others, now inside her head: 'Jean, you have real class, you have sense'; 'You can tell a leggo-beast from a decent girl: one, by how she dresses, and two, by the kind a drink she orders.'

Soon the names 'Mark' and 'Jean' were rarely spoken separately. Jean was described as 'Mark's woman.' Or privately, among the boys, as his 'mattress.' It was assumed that they were having sex. They were all very young, Mark's friends, yet they acted as if nothing was new to them, as if they had been having sex, getting drunk, getting high, and driving recklessly all their lives.

Mark was still bent on getting Jean to give up her virginity, though he kept telling her that he could wait. Meanwhile, she discovered self-pleasing ways of satisfying him. Sometimes she wondered whether she was still technically a virgin; there was no part of his body or hers that they had not explored together. She did not like to admit it to herself, but Monica was right about the risk of falling in love with a man's body: She was in danger of idolizing Mark's penis. It became an object of endless fascination – its unfailing response to the merest brush of her hands, first the slight movement and hardening under his pants, then the rigidity; the way its owner would stop everything and surrender to her. She pondered the pros and cons of letting him do what he yearned to do. He had promised that he would not get her pregnant, and anyway she knew how to take precautions. It was not that. From all she had seen and heard, she surmised that sex was a high-risk game in which there was always a winner and a loser. So far, she seemed to be winning. He longed for her. He did everything he could to drive her crazy with desire, to cause her to lose control and yield to him – which she never did. It would have amazed Monica to learn how far, in this regard, Jean was able to out-Monica her.

But it was not will or guile that mastered Jean; it was fear. There were the constant reminders of Lana. There was the possibility of making some monumental error that would grind her down to nothing.

Then a day came when Monica raged at Jean over a small thing: Jean had accidentally left her purse on a shop counter and it had been stolen. Monica said Jean's head was always in the clouds and that she would never amount to anything. The quarrel escalated and became a quarrel about other things. They flung the names Roy and Lana at each other in the most spiteful and desperate way; Monica said she would have been better off if she had never had children, and Jean wished she could get out of her mother's house for good.

When Mark came by later Jean asked him with a new, defiant tone to take her somewhere where they could be alone. He sensed her meaning, and they went to a hotel room where she drank several glasses of whisky and smoked marijuana – 'to calm myself,' she said. Unbuttoning his shirt and stroking the fine hair on his chest, she told him that at last she was ready.

He began making love to her, and she stiffened.

'If you're scared, we don't have to do this.'

She sat up in the bed and burst out crying. He was right. She was afraid. Between tearful spasms she babbled to him about Lana, about Monica, and about trying to do what was right.

'I don't really understand what you sayin',' he said, 'but is awright. Come, don't cry. Res' you head on my shoulder.'

The sweetness of his words made her cry even more. She couldn't explain the impossible knot of feelings she carried in her, fears that had little to do with her own experience, voices that spoke constantly of effort, error, and regret.

32

Jean Falkirk, 'Doctor Wife'
1871–1936

When my father, the Reverend Falkirk of the Presbytery of Ayr, died, my sister and I left our small village and went to Edinburgh, where we rented rooms in a modest house near Grass Market.

Gillian was twenty, with dreams of marriage and motherhood; I was twenty-four and had no such dreams. We were fairly accomplished women. Our father, having no sons to educate, had employed tutors for us in drawing and music while he himself taught us Greek and Latin. We thought we might support ourselves teaching music and drawing. Gillian, being a competent pianist, would give lessons in the former and I, the latter. But after several months we realized we could not support ourselves this way; Gillian had only one student and I had none, and we were quickly depleting our small inheritance.

I bought the Weekly Chronicle *and studied the advertisements. The types of employment that appealed to me were being offered only to 'young men,' but I hoped by sheer persuasion to transcend the prejudice against my sex. This I indeed accomplished on my first interview.*

A bookseller on High Street needed 'an educated young man' to assist him. The shop was a single, dark, narrow room, and the bookseller, Mr Berry, specialized in medical books and journals. He was old and quite deaf, and his hands shook. Learning that my name was Falkirk and that I was from Ayr, he asked if I was related to Reverend Falkirk. Apparently he had known my father, and so he thought I was paying him a social visit. When I informed him that

I was enquiring about employment, he said he was sorry and that although I was the daughter of his esteemed friend and seemed well-spoken and intelligent, he needed a young man.

I shamelessly took aim at what Mr Berry, like most Scots, held most dear — his purse — and struck a bargain. If he allowed me to work for a month and found me unsatisfactory, he would need only pay me three-fourths of my wages, two pounds six. He said that I was 'a frail lass' and this would necessitate his also hiring a boy to do the heavy work and offered two pounds. I asked him to show me the heaviest book in the shop. It was Hatrick's Encylopaedia of Infectious and Noninfectious Diseases. *I carried it from shelf to counter and insisted on the two pounds six, with full pay if he continued to employ me. He agreed to two pounds three and I was hired.*

I worked in Mr Berry's shop for three years. Often entire days passed without customers. I had to get spectacles as I wore my eyes out reading in the dark shop. One interest led to another — a ship surgeon's journals, tropical diseases — until I arrived at what became my chief interest, botany — in particular, the morphology of plants.

Gillian met and married Mr Cunliff, a professor of moral philosophy, and I was left on my own in the little flat. I was not lonely; city life kept me quite occupied. I joined the Caledonia Horticultural Society and the Society for the Protection of Africans and Asiatics. I went often to free lectures and readings.

I became quite adept at botanical drawing, sometimes copying from books, at other times directly from nature. I began to nurture a secret ambition, that one day I might make a career for myself as a botanist's assistant. The morphologist Dr Calder, a friend of Mr Darwin, saw my drawings when he came to the shop and complimented my hand.

It was while I was thus occupied one afternoon, drawing a species of Erigeron, *commonly known as fleabane, that the bell rang and I opened the door to a dark gentleman, dressed in a black coat with velvet trim. He looked like an Arabian prince. He smiled as though he knew me, and I thought perhaps we had met at the Society for Africans and Asiatics. But we had not. He had come in search of a book on intestinal parasites.*

He introduced himself as Dr John Darling and said he had just completed his studies at the Royal College of Physicians. He was not Arabian but West Indian, from the island of Jamaica. We spoke for some time and discovered that we had a mutual interest in exotic parasites. He had a splendid black mustache and was the most handsome man I had ever seen. I walked him to the door and I, who have never been vain, thought to remove my spectacles as we said good-bye.

We married a month later and boarded the Curaçao *bound for the West Indies. On our voyage, I learned that John's father, Richard Darling, a Baptist missionary, had gone to Jamaica around the time of Emancipation and that he had fallen in love and married John's mother, Yetunde, the daughter of free Africans. She died within days of John's birth, and he had been brought up with the help of his maternal grandmother, Mary, a former slave. John's father was a highly respected educator of the freed Negroes. I learned that John did not classify himself by that term — Negro — but rather called himself a 'Colored gentleman.'*

We arrived in Kingston Harbor in September 1898 and stayed with John's sister, Mrs Peggy Nelson, whose husband, another 'Colored gentleman,' was a coffee merchant. In Kingston, John bought me an unnecessary quantity of hats and dresses. We attended dinners and dances endlessly, and I was introduced to Mrs Peggy's acquaintances. We even went to a party at the Governor's house! John gave me a pearl necklace to wear to these parties. I quickly discovered that Kingston ladies had extravagant tastes. At first, I was coolly received by them. It was rare for a British woman to marry a Colored gentleman; they suspected me of being common. But when they learned that I was the daughter of the Reverend Falkirk of Ayr, I was heartily embraced.

To my great relief, we finally left Kingston, taking the train to Mandeville and then the Royal Mail to Blue Fields where John's father lived. How to describe my excitement on first seeing the tropical countryside! I grew so quiet as we traveled the winding, bumpy roads, that John feared I was ill. I was exhilarated, seeing for the first time the tropical plants I had previously known only from books.

'Is that Hillia parasitica, *John?' I asked, noting an abundance of bright parasitic flowers clinging to large tree trunks.*

He laughed and said that Jamaicans called these plants Scotsman-huggin'-

Creole, and he joked about our marriage being a variation of the species.

When we arrived in Blue Fields, I immediately saw the reason for its name. Stretching ahead of us were not fields but the brightest, bluest of seas. This was the view from my father-in-law's house.

Miss Mary, John's grandmother, was an African woman close to a hundred years old; she was full of energy and exceptionally kind to me, though I overheard her telling John that she found me too thin. She also said I was the whitest woman she had ever set eyes on, 'White fe true.' This, to my amusement, she said to my face.

John's father was not well, yet he insisted on staying up with us on our first night there. He was a great soul, a man with a wicked sense of humor. He liked to take credit for Miss Mary's superb cooking. And though he was very proud of John he teased him, 'I sent the scoundrel away because all he did here was chase girls and get into trouble.'

The house was at our disposal for as long as we wanted. It was a fine country house, and I would have been happy to remain there, but John had something 'better' in mind. I could not help noticing that my husband was extravagant. He engaged builders, and within a year we moved into a new house, a veritable mansion, about five miles from Blue Fields. He sent to England for new carpets, furniture, silver, even though his father was only too glad to part with everything he had.

Richard Darling died a few months before my Mary was born. I missed him and was sorry that he would not know his grandchild. I was sorry, too, because he was the only one who had any influence on John regarding money. It was Richard, I learned, who had kept John's gambling in check. Unfortunately, my husband resumed this vice after his father passed away. He would win and lose hundreds of pounds on horses in a single day. We had been raised very differently, though we both had fine fathers in the abstemious dissenting churches. In my family, frugality was prized, whereas John had been brought up like a prince. But he loved me and little Mary dearly and was so generous that it was difficult to be annoyed with him.

I continued to pursue my interest in botany, learning about the new tropical plants, sketching them and writing notes. In this I was greatly *encouraged by old Mary. Very soon after my arrival she took me on educational walks around the countryside. It was from her that I discovered the healing properties of a type of aloe which grows in abundance on the island and which the country people call Single Bible — a sort of cure-all.*

I had brought two trunks of books with me from Scotland, much to John's amusement, and I also subscribed to the Edinburgh Horticultural Society's journal. But this reading and field work were not enough to keep me occupied, so I began to assist John in his surgery downstairs. He saw patients there in the mornings and spent afternoons at the county hospital. At other times, he made house visits up and down the countryside. His was a busy life. I often envied him. I helped by keeping patients' records, and by such nurses' activities as cleaning and bandaging wounds.

As my expertise increased, I began attending to those patients who came with minor wounds and illnesses when John was away. This began to vex him. In spite of Miss Nightingale's work, nursing was still thought to be an unladylike profession. I assured him that as a doctor's wife surely I could not be seen in a disrespectful light, and furthermore, I pointed out, he needed assistance. He said that he would hire and train one of the country girls to be his nurse.

At this I lost my temper: 'You can't expect me to spend my life dressing up and visiting your friends' wives who do nothing all day but discuss clothes.'

'My wife should not work.'

'What right have you to prevent me from making my life useful?'

He had never seen me so angry. He tried to humor me, saying that he had always heard about the fiery tempers of red-haired women. Seeing that his joke had no effect on me, he finally agreed to let me assist in certain medical procedures, but forbade me to help with the male patients in any way that required the removal of their garments.

'Surely you don't want to sacrifice every vestige of modesty, Jean?'

I was about to ask whether or not this rule of modesty would have been enforced upon the country girl he had planned to hire. But I refrained; I had won the first battle.

So I became a doctor's assistant, and my marriage continued to be a source of great happiness to me. But there was sorrow, too. Our son, John, was born prematurely and died. I was told that my health would be endangered by another pregnancy, and so our hopes for a son were dashed.

After the death of our son there were long intervals when my husband would not come to my room. He was affectionate but, perhaps out of fear of my conceiving again, he withheld himself. I am ashamed to admit that during these abstinences, I grew quite overwhelmed with longing and spent much time daydreaming about his next approach. It surprised me to discover that, although I was a woman, I was the more passionate one, and he the more reserved. In fact, he often appeared disconcerted by our transports.

Months went by without his coming to me. When he did, he would seem captivated — for days — by our lovemaking. Then the hours of pleasure would shame him and he would not touch me for a long time. It became a cycle: During the season of abstinence I grew full with the secret exercise of anticipation, and by the time John next approached me I was ready to meet him with even greater ardency.

He told me one day that my 'masculine appetite' disturbed him.

'It's not right for a woman of your kind.'

The more he withdrew, the more I was drawn forward. Once I forgot myself entirely and instead of waiting for him to come to me, I went to him. Afterward, he said: 'Tell me honestly, Jean. Were there other men who visited you before we met?'

'What do you mean?' I was confused. Did he want to know about Reverend Shaw who came with his sisters once a month for tea?

'Tell me plainly, yes or no, did you have lovers?'

Not a lover, but lovers! I would have burst out laughing if I hadn't seen how agitated he was. I assured him that he was the only lover I had ever had, or ever imagined having. My words did not appease him; he wanted to know 'what kinds of things' I 'imagined.'

I learned to restrain myself, and, oddly, I began to take pleasure in the restraint, in making the act of love an act indeed, convincing John that I was merely accommodating the release of his passion.

How little we really know about each other, we women and men.

For eight years I was in the dark about my husband's true nature, in spite of so many hints and disclosures. And I might have continued in ignorance if that woman had not turned up at my door.

The audacity of Jamaican women! She was a Colored woman by the name of Miss Josephs. She told me that she and John had known each other before he went to Scotland, and that he continued visiting her after our marriage. She also told me, haughtily, as though it were not a strike against her, that she was not the only mistress John kept; there were others in Savanna-la-Mar, Treasure Beach, and Montego Bay that she knew of for certain, and probably more throughout the length and breadth of the island. As she spoke, so many things leapt to mind: the sneers of certain women when they saw me with John; gifts of gloves and silk garments that I'd found hidden and pretended to know nothing about because I believed them to be John's surprises for me — only, I had never received them.

I had been mistaken all that time thinking John overly reserved. He had propensities far greater than my own! Yet he had withheld himself from me, his wife, and satisfied himself with others. Why?

I ordered Miss Josephs out of my house and warned her that if I ever chanced to see her in the vicinity she would meet with an untimely death.

She laughed at me. 'You talk like you have teeth after all.'

Teeth! She soon found out.

A week later, while I was riding my husband's fastest horse, Juno, I saw Miss Josephs leaving the seamstress's cottage with a bundle. I spurred Juno on and we headed toward her at a ferocious gallop. She dropped her bundle and fell into the bushes. I circled and went after her again. She ran, screaming, 'Murder! De White woman goin' kill me!'

I heard that she went to stay with her aunt in St Thomas. Ha! Chased to the opposite end of the island!

One mistress vanquished. Where were the others? I planned to root them out, every one. I would not easily part with my husband!

But God decided otherwise.

John was on his way home one night after days of heavy rain. The river was unusually turbulent. Juno threw him during the crossing, and he drowned.

So quickly then, darkness gave way to darkness. Within weeks of John's death, I discovered another of his secrets: debts. His infernal betting had left us destitute. There were unpaid bills from the builders, butchers, haberdashers, milliners — I would have to pay for his mistresses' hats!

John's sister, Peggy, said we might live with her family in Kingston, but, as they had three sons to educate, it was impossible for her husband to give me any money. She thought it might be best if I took Mary back to my family in Scotland.

Gillian; of course, my sister, Gillian, would help me until I could somehow get on my feet.

Scotland. On my daily walks around the countryside I tried to picture us there. I often took Mary with me to Blue Fields to visit John's grave. She would pick flowers and put them on the graves of all the Darlings buried there. When I first arrived in Westmoreland and saw that church and graveyard overlooking the sea, I had wished that my own body would rest there one day. The view always refreshed me. I imagined, just beyond the horizon, the Tropic of Capricorn and the mountains of Peru. More than any other place in Jamaica this little spot had won my heart.

With reluctance, I prepared to leave for Scotland. Already I missed the island — the brightness my eyes had become accustomed to, the warm nights with open windows and gentle breezes.

Then, on one of my walks, I discovered the little cottage at New Hope. New Hope — the name augured well.

It was the tiniest cottage imaginable. What drew me to the place was the large bay tree at the front, a great shady old grandfather of a tree. There was a FOR SALE sign with an address for directing inquiries. Walking around the backyard, I found an avocado tree, a mango tree, and a pumpkin vine. I thought, what a pleasant, fertile spot, and so near the sea.

I learned that the old lady who had lived in it for sixty years had recently died, and that her son was selling it, with the old lady's bed and coal pot, for ten pounds.

'You can't live here!' Peggy said when she saw it. She had come for us, even though I had told her of my change of plan. 'You can't live in a little shack like the Negroes!'

I told her I had already paid the ten pounds and had thirty left with which to make a new start.

'And what will you do? How will you live when the thirty pounds are spent? Why am I asking? So you have thrown away ten pounds. Poor thing. You're not well. Let's go now, and you'll take the next boat to Scotland.'

'How will I live?' I hadn't given it much thought. 'There are people in New Hope who appear to be living. I'll do what they do.'

'Do what they do? Don't you understand, woman? You can't!'

We moved into the little house with our few possessions — Mary's bed, a writing desk that I was especially fond of, our piano, which needed tuning, and the modern kerosene stove John had bought and actually paid for. I immediately went to work making curtains from some of my gowns; the rest of my clothes, hats, gloves, kerchiefs, I put away for Mary. I kept only the plainest cotton frocks for myself, dresses I could work in.

Work? What exactly would I do? Our thirty pounds was almost gone in six months. We ate the vegetables that grew in our garden, and meager rations of peas and rice. Once a fortnight we ate fish. Fortunately, we had brought some of our chickens with us so for a while we had eggs.

None of our old friends visited us. They thought John's death had unhinged me. But more cruel was the manner in which the country people, our new neighbors, treated us. They laughed at us; their children stoned our trees, and they cheated us at every turn. When I went to the market I was charged twice more than others.

One day, Mary came running home, her face red and flushed, with a pawpaw in her hands almost as big as she was. She had stolen it from someone's farm. I should have scolded her for stealing. But how could I? Hadn't Gillian and I stolen gooseberries from the neighbors' gardens in Ayr? I could only laugh at her little adventure, and we had pawpaw for breakfast for an entire week.

My Mary was a child of the sweetest temperament. It must have been so difficult for her, the change, but she never once complained. She was a plump, *bonny child with John's features, though, as Gillian pointed out (she had visited us before John's death), Mary had been stamped with my expressions. She would raise her eyebrows just as I do when making a point, and she jutted her chin forward when angry or anxious. One thing that she did not inherit from me was her frizzy hair. It was red, like mine, but there all resemblance ended. I never could do anything with all her bush except barber it like a boy's. I tried piercing her ears, so that people would be able to tell that she was a girl, but she developed infections and keloid scars. Without earrings and with her shorn hair, she looked, unfortunately, like a fat boy in girl's dresses.*

I sent her to a school about five miles from New Hope, and she walked back and forth every day. It had occurred to me to tutor her at home, but I felt she needed to be with other children. After her first day at school, some of the children followed her home. I went out to see what the noise was about.

'You an' you mother poor like nigger.'

'You look like a likkle boy.'

'Likkle boy. Likkle boy.'

They tormented her like this for several days. I would reprimand them and they would run away shouting, 'White witch!'

Throughout all this, Mary never cried or asked not to be sent to school. She was braver than I was. I could barely stand up to the women at the market who laughed as soon as my back was turned, and I had not yet found the courage to confront them about their cheating. The only thing Mary asked me during this time was 'Mama, please don't cut my hair no more.' So I let her hair grow, and she took great care every day combing it into many little plaits.

The day came when we had one pound six shillings left and nothing left to eat but pumpkin. I had planted yams, but it would be months before they were ready. There were three scrawny fowls and a rooster living with us; most of the chickens had disappeared. I could not tell if they had been stolen by the neighbors, or eaten by their own hungry relatives or by a mongoose. I decided that we could no longer afford to sustain these poor creatures, and that we should, in all practicality, feed on them.

Needless to say I had never assassinated anything larger than an ant. When I told Mary what I had decided to do she became quite pale. This made me steel myself all the more. 'Go to Mr Jack and ask to borrow his machete,' I ordered her. Mr Jack and his family were the only people who had been neighborly. He had known me in better times. John had saved his little girl's life when she had dengue fever. When we first moved to New Hope, he brought us a leg of pork. Simple, kind people.

I was in the backyard preparing for the gruesome work when Mary brought me the machete. She handed it to me and ran inside. I called her back.

'Do you think you're too fine a person to kill for meat? Stay and learn, because you'll have to do it yourself sooner or later.'

I remembered once seeing a man kill chickens. He had set a box over the body, causing the head to stick out; then he had brought the machete down on its neck.

I tried to do this, but the wretch kept struggling and overturning the box. I had Mary hold down the box. We made a great mess of it! Blood and feathers! I ended up wringing the creature's neck. Mary bawled as if she were the one being slaughtered.

'If you don't stop crying I'll box your ears!' I remember shouting at her.

And then she would not eat the fowl. She never could bring herself to eat meat of any kind again. I realized that slaughtering hens was where Mary's obedience and fortitude came to a full stop, and I never forced her to assist me again. I hardly had heart for it myself.

On Christmas Eve I went to the market to buy kidney beans and a piece of pigtail to make a stew. The market woman poured the beans into a little bag and charged me a shilling.

'You charged that woman before me sixpence for twice the amount,' I cried. 'Shilling fe de White woman,' the market woman said.

I flung threepence onto the ground before her. 'Threepence and not a penny more from the White woman, you rascal!'

They did not try to cheat me after that, but grew no more friendly. 'Go back whe' you come from, White cockroach!'

Poverty was wearing me down, especially the poverty of purposelessness. There was enough to do keeping our little house clean, sewing, mending, tending the yard, but I had until then always felt useful in the world — helping Mr

Berry in his bookshop, assisting John in the surgery. I was becoming dangerously melancholy.

I had purchased a kerosene lamp. To save the oil it was lit for only an hour every night, and it became a ritual, my sitting down and reading for that hour. Of course, reading had become a mere exercise in words; I read again and again the four books I had brought with me: the Edinburgh Almanac *for the year* 1898, Poems of Places, *a little volume that Gillian had given me with poems about Italy, a book of psalms, and* Vanity Fair. *I started memorizing poems and psalms. After a while, like all rituals, this one transcended its hour. During this difficult time I was becoming acquainted with the things that would sustain me through to the end of my life, little exercises of faith and self-encouragement.*

In a sermon once, my father said that one rarely saw results from a single instance of prayer. When we hear about God's manifestations to men like Moses, we often forget that those holy men prayed constantly. Prayer, he said, is to the faithful what daily exercise is to the athlete. One day, when it matters most, we win the race.

I often took walks by the sea and recalled my father's sermons. One day I found myself singing a psalm he had set:

> *Let the beauty of the Lord be upon us,*
> *And establish our work upon us . . .*

I had no work. My daughter would soon go hungry. I finally succumbed and wrote to my sister: Mary and I would return to Scotland.

I hired a man with a horse and cart to take me to the second-hand dealer in Savanna-la-Mar with the writing desk, the piano, the pearls, and — at this I felt great sadness — the gilt-framed portrait of John. I received in exchange enough to get us to Edinburgh. The only things of value that I had left and hoped never to part with were Richard Darling's gold-tipped walking cane and a perfume bottle, painted with tiny violets, which Gillian had brought back for me from Venice.

After the sale of our goods, we rode back along the coast and passed my favorite spot, Blue Fields Bay. I prayed that in years to come, when I was walking along the gaslit streets of Edinburgh, bundled up against the biting winds, my memories of the island would not have faded so as to seem merely a dream.

Mary and I continued to get by in the meager way to which we had become accustomed, while we waited for a letter from my sister. Mary would be eleven soon. I imagined a birthday party for her in Gillian's home with a cake and candles, and suddenly I felt ashamed at all that I had denied her. It was my own foolish, romantic feelings that had kept me here.

It was then, just as I was reconciled to leaving, that Mr Jack took sick and the course of my life changed.

His daughter, Drusilla, came to the cottage: 'Mama say please come quick an' bring medicine or Papa goin' dead.'

I took John's old medicine bag with me and several vials of medicine that I thought might help in case of contagious fever.

When I got to his bedside he was burning hot. Common sense told me that he needed cooling both in the inner and outer body. Fortunately his wife had some pineapple at hand and I made compresses of the fruit for his chest. I made a tea of cinnamon, quinine, and citric acid grains which I administered to him on the hour. At about three in the morning his fever broke and his breathing became regular. He was quite weak, having not eaten for some time, so I prescribed mashed sweet potatoes and a spoonful of molasses four times a day.

Mr Jack told everyone that 'Doctor wife' had cured him. His family gave me a basket of breadfruit and yams in gratitude.

A week later a woman who lived in New Hope — perhaps one of those who had cut her eye at me in months past — asked me for medicine for her sore foot. I washed the putrid foot in permanganate of potash and made an ointment of aloe and camphor. Soon the knocking at my gate became so frequent that I had to put up a small sign saying that I would see the sick only between eight and eleven. I needed the afternoons to study John's medical books and to take walks on which I gathered medicinal plants.

They came, my country neighbors, with tapeworm, gripe, earache, arthritic joints, and every kind of complaint. At first, I did not attempt so much to cure as to soothe. I advised the seriously ill to go to the hospital in Mandeville, and

I also made it quite clear, when one young lady came to me for an aphrodisiac tea, that I was not an obeah woman.

They paid me in food. Little could they have known how much we relied on these gifts. I cured one man's entire family of tapeworm (fern oil expels the worm, and then it is crucial to locate its head and burn it quickly before it grows a new body) and he planted a new row of yams for us.

A new row of yams — yes, I had decided to stay. I had received a welcoming letter from Gillian some time after the curing of Mr Jack. But by then I had become 'Doctor wife.'

I don't have to wonder what John would have thought of my work. I laugh when I think how circumscribed I had been as his assistant, and his agony with regard to my modesty. As 'Doctor wife' I often administered ointments to the pustuled genitals of men. I have seen and smelled everything human.

As my reputation grew, I began to care for more affluent patients — the dressmaker, for instance, and farmers' wives. It seemed improper somehow to take money from them either since I was only 'Doctor wife' and not really a 'Doctor.' Gillian and Frank sent me a little money each year, and Miss Peggy, once she realized I would never return to Scotland, sent a small allowance for Mary. I also made a small sum selling my garden herbs — mint, bellyache bush, and so on. With careful saving I was able to buy back my piano and John's portrait.

My greatest pleasure continued to be the study and sketching of plants. After I had filled several notebooks it occurred to me that I was doing nothing less than creating an encyclopedia of tropical flowers and herbs. I began compiling all my notes and loose scraps into one large volume under the title Single Bible: A Helpful Listing of the Properties and Uses of Tropical Plants, as Recorded by a Jamaican Doctor's Wife. *I thought I might send it to a publisher in England one day.*

On Mary's sixteenth birthday I went into my old trunks. The few dresses I had saved for her were useless, as she was much larger than I, but I found a white hat that I had been especially fond of with pink satin ribbons. I presented it to her for her birthday. Mary was so pleased that she wore it to Easter Sunday service.

I think it was the elegance of the hat that led me to notice how old and worn her dress was. I looked around the church and realized that, compared to the other girls, who seemed to have at least one 'good dress,' my daughter wore rags.

New problems presented themselves. Mary had been out of school for two years and had kept herself busy helping me around the house and in my little clinic. She had only one friend, Drusilla Jack, who was about to marry and move to Montego Bay. What a strange, friendless life I had shaped for my daughter. I felt the disgrace of her faded clothes and impoverished girlhood all the more because Mary had an innate pride and graciousness. Her patchy clothes were scrupulously clean. She spent what was left over of her small allowance from her aunt — after giving the major part to me — on new ribbons for her hair and new stockings.

Mary had no interest in books, so there was no question of her becoming a teacher. Her handwriting was atrocious, so there was no clerical employment for her. Her one skill was housekeeping. She cooked well and kept a clean, tidy house. I began to have a single, great hope for her: that she would have a happy marriage.

Had I lived in Kingston or Edinburgh, Mary could easily have met suitable young men. But in New Hope there was no such opportunity. For her sake, I renewed my acquaintance with estranged friends. I went visiting. This required quite a transformation on my part. I had stopped attending to my own appearance; indeed, I often wore John's old breeches. I could hardly take Mary visiting dressed like that. So I pulled out my old dresses, hoops, hats, and gloves and with a bit of alteration looked well enough for a woman of forty-odd years. I bought some pink organdy and satin for Mary and had the dressmaker make up a dress to match the hat I had given her. We made trips to Mandeville once each month.

On our way, we usually stayed overnight with Miss Dingle, a delightful lady who had been very fond of John's father, and who I believe came closer than anyone else to being chosen as his second wife. She lived in Malvern, near the teachers college. She had been a warden — that is, a housemistress — for the female students for many years. Malvern was beautiful, healthy country. It was inland, and more mountainous and cooler than New Hope. It reminded me of the mountains and valleys of Scotland. There we took pleasant walks with Miss Dingle after lunch, and she talked endlessly to Mary about her grandfather. She delighted in making us homemade sweets, coconut gizadas, custard-apple tarts, and guava jelly.

On one of our visits with this kind spinster, we met Jedaiah Stern. Miss Dingle's drawing room, owing to her former occupation at the teachers college, was a meeting place for young men and women of the parish. She presided over many tea parties, and I felt it highly possible that Mary would meet her future husband at one of these gatherings. I was right, though Jedaiah was certainly not the one I would have chosen for her.

We met another gentleman there, Reverend Robothom, a good deal older than Mary, a widower with three boys, who made a good impression on me. I invited him to visit us at New Hope, and he wasted no time appearing at our home a few days later. His church was at Sandy Ground, ten miles from us. He brought with him his sons, who enjoyed themselves during the visit by playing with our dog, Charley, and I was happy to see that Mary got on well with the boys. Reverend Robothom complimented Mary on her piano playing, which was not really very good, and we apologized several times for the piano, which was out of tune. The piano-playing portion of the afternoon was, in my view, quite harrowing.

He offered to send someone to tune our piano, and a week later, the tuner arrived with his toolbox.

I encouraged the Reverend's visits, and Mary and I began attending his church. I used my credit with the haberdasher, whose sprained ankle I had attended to, and with the dressmaker, a chronic sufferer of flatulence, and had two more dresses made for Mary. The Reverend accompanied us to the church fair at Blue Fields and to the agricultural fair in Clarendon and was extremely attentive to us. After several months of these visits and excursions — which exhausted me — I asked Mary if she liked the Reverend. She said she did and then expressed her wish to visit Miss Dingle again.

I understood at once that she was hoping to see Jedaiah Stern again. So, with reluctance on my part, we visited Miss Dingle. Mr Stern did not appear and

Mary comforted herself during his absence by mentioning his name several times in what I thought a rather obtuse manner.

One day Mr Stern appeared at our door. He was on his way to Savanna-la-Mar and had brought some guava jelly from Miss Dingle. I was quite sure that Miss Dingle, the old matchmaker, had surmised Mary's interest in the young man. We invited him to stay for lunch, a modest meal of beef liver, and Mary beamed from the compliments he paid to her cooking. She made an excellent dessert — the fruit salad that Jamaicans call matrimony, consisting of two fruits, which are 'married' in sweetened milk. In this case, the happy couple were star apple and sweetsop. This dessert gave rise to many improper innuendoes from Mr Jedaiah, and though I am far from prudish, I felt that he showed a want of taste in his conversation.

He was a coarse, conceited oaf, and I could not imagine what Mary saw in him. I suppose it was the fact that he was closer to her in age than the dear Reverend. He also had the distinction of being taller than herself; Reverend Robothom was a rather short, small-boned gentleman. Jedaiah's grandparents were Germans who had settled in St Elizabeth and made a living as farmers. Jedaiah's father had not taken up farming, but instead had kept an inn at Treasure Beach. He was still alive but had left Jedaiah with relatives when he was still a babe and had emigrated to England. On the subject of his mother Jedaiah was reticent, except to say that she had died in a hospital in Kingston. I felt there was something ominous in the mother's story, or lack of story, as it were.

He did not visit again for many months. I was relieved. Mary pined. The good Reverend continued visiting, and in an effort to distract Mary, I encouraged him a great deal more than I otherwise might have.

One afternoon while Mary was out Reverend Robothom came by and said he needed to speak to me about an important matter. I was extremely agitated and at the same time delighted that he was finally going to ask for Mary's hand. He began by saying how comforting his visits with us had been and that it had greatly eased his loneliness. The good man then proposed marriage to me! He saw that I was disconcerted and assured me that he did not need an answer right away.

There was another shock ahead of me.

Mr Jedaiah visited us once again. While Mary was at the stove, he asked me to show him the garden. There he insulted me by making forward compliments about my figure. Me, a woman old enough to be his mother! I did not mince words. I asked him to leave at once and never return again.

I called on the Reverend and told him that although I was deeply flattered by his proposal, I felt that he needed a mother for his children, and I was past the age at which I could devote my energies to such work. I then boldly suggested that my daughter, who was very fond of the boys, would make an excellent wife. He seemed disappointed, but said that he would give my suggestion some thought.

After some weeks absence he began to court Mary in a manner which struck me as quite different from before. He brought her little cakes and sweets and took her for rides in his carriage. They paid visits together to other country clergy. Unfortunately, on one of those visits, they ran into Mr Jedaiah, and this revived Mary's interest once again.

I regret that I never told her about his forwardness toward me. But how could I? I do not know when, where, or how she and Jedaiah contrived to meet and develop affection for each other. After more than a year of the Reverend's attentions, she rejected him and announced her engagement to Jedaiah Stern.

I found it hard to be civil to Mary's husband, and the marriage would have created a breach between my daughter and myself but for the fact that her husband was rarely at home. I tried to find good in him, but was at a loss. Not once had I known him to present her with even the smallest gift. Nor did he ever reach into his pocket to buy her so much as a lemonade at our church and country fairs. On the contrary, she usually paid for him! The few occasions on which I saw him at home, he sat about drinking rum while Mary cooked, cleaned, and fussed over him, and then he had the gall to complain about her cooking. He was a vulgar, unambitious, drunken, red-faced lout.

Miss Dingle thought it her duty to inform me — after the marriage took place — that Jedaiah's mother had died in the lunatic asylum in Kingston. On meeting the other half of Jedaiah's family, the self-important Sterns, I wondered if insanity was not more common among them than the mother's family, as they appeared for the most part to be slow-witted and inbred.

It saddened me to think of Mary's choice. My one wish for her had been that she would always be cared for and loved. I could tell that it troubled her that Jedaiah was away so often. His heavy drinking also troubled her, but it was not like Mary to complain. I realized that he gave her no money, and so I began to give her a few pounds each month — for the babies, as I put it.

After several years of marriage, Jedaiah deserted Mary and their two little girls, Gwendolyn and Daphne. He went to live with a woman who spoiled him even more than Mary did. She was the proprietor of a rum shop and a brothel.

I invited Mary to come back home, telling her I would build an additional room to the cottage, but she preferred to stay in her husband's house. It was, in truth, a much larger, finer home, bought for him by his doting grandfather. But it was not the fine house she cared for; she was waiting for Jedaiah to return to her.

He did return, and his despicable habits grew worse — drinking, cursing, wasting of money. Around this time I decided to write a will so that if life with him became unbearable for her, Mary would have the one thing I owned, the little cottage.

Thank God for my foresight. Jedaiah continued for several years with his unkindness and philandering, while Mary bore two more children. Shortly after the birth of her son, he beat her, not for the first time, but the last. She appeared at my door, the three girls in tow and the baby in her arms. She never went back.

As for myself, I continued with my 'doctor-wiving,' as Gillian called it, and with my botanical writings and drawings.

July 12, 1936
Though not in the habit of keeping a daily journal, I find myself today, for some odd reason, recording these thoughts.

I am sitting in the graveyard at Blue Fields and realize to my shame that five whole years have passed since I visited my husband's grave and my favorite spot in all the world. The scene has not changed. Everything that could possibly delight the eye and imagination is within my view: the splendid flowering bushes of the graveyard, the sparkling, almost motionless blue sea, and, to my right, the dramatic cliffs at Bluff Point, which always remind me of the Scottish coast.

I wonder, if John were alive, would he still call me his beautiful Scottish queen, now with my hair so white? I wonder, too, if he had been taken from me earlier, 'before the years had torn old troths,' how our marriage would appear in my memory. Why did I have to learn about John's infidelity before he died? Couldn't I have been granted an untarnished memory of him? Would I have missed him more? I could not have missed him more.

I look at his grave, and the pleasure I used to feel in his arms returns. Almost.

This 'almost' is the saddest thing.

The greater loss, his passing, followed so closely on the heels of the lesser, his infidelity, that I had not recognized my own change of heart. The passion I thought I still had for him was rage, rage at the world and at him for such a betrayal. How much longer would it have been before that rage turned to bitterness and then, finally, to the lifeless formality I have seen in such marriages?

He would have continued to be unfaithful.

How complicated it all seems. One sorrow has ended: John's body rests here before me in his grave. The other goes on.

Such are my uneasy thoughts as I look toward the Tropic of Capricorn and breathe in the sea air. I hope I do not die soon, as it may be ages before the Resurrection and I would so much miss the view. I have this giddy sensation, which I have had all my life, of waiting for something remarkable to happen. I do not think it will be another marriage, or travel to some new distant place.

Perhaps, like the merchant in the parable who, having found the most precious pearl in the world, sells everything in order to buy it, I, having wandered and sought among verdant landscapes for so long, have a presentiment of getting nearer to that One for which I would give all.

A hummingbird treads the air before me and I see that the scene has changed, after all, in my five years' absence. Here is something new. A lace hibiscus. At least, that is what I call it because the petals give the appearance of lace. And it is the white variety!

A new page, a new entry:

Hibiscus schizopetalus — *Red, pink, and, rarely seen, white varieties. The corolla is made up of divided petals giving a lacy appearance to the flower. An even more remarkable feature of the plant is its long, tubular stamen which hangs several inches below the petals, giving a strange pendulant form to the flower. In plain language: the petals turn inside out as a result of hanging down.*

Remarkably then, the force of light is seen to exert a greater influence upon this plant than the force of gravity.

I will come back tomorrow to do the drawing. It's getting late and it is a three-hour walk back to New Hope.

33

'*Plumeria acutifolia*,' the label said. 'Frangipani, Pagoda Tree, Temple Tree.' She was in the garden at Bonnieview, planting a rare white frangipani Paul had brought her. She had to be careful; the white sap in the stems was poisonous.

'Lana's back,' Paul said.

'When did she get back?'

'Last weekend.'

Lana had been living in the Bahamas for almost a year, singing in hotels. She had decided to go away after a troublesome breakup with Carl. Finding him in bed with another woman, Lana had gone after him with a kitchen knife. His injuries were slight, but that didn't stop the *Star* from printing their story of the member of Parliament who had come close to being neutered by the beautiful singer.

'She's pregnant,' Paul said. 'Any day now the baby born.'

'Carl's baby?'

'No. Some guy in Nassau. But he say is not him pickney.'

Jean sighed, anticipating Monica's response when she found out Lana was pregnant again. There were times when Jean felt it was better, certainly more peaceful, when Lana was away.

'Another thing – she's a Jehovah's Witness now.'

'G'way. You lie.'

'Remember Mrs Cannon? Lana's stayin' at her house.'

Claudia Cannon had met Lana in 1969, when Lana was in a

Montego Bay lockup for ganja smuggling. While other Jehovah's Witnesses went door to door, this zealous lady went from jail to jail. She and Lana had built a strong friendship over the years. Mrs Cannon often let Lana stay with her when she had nowhere else to go. It had surprised Jean at first to learn that Lana, who had mocked the Catholic church all her life, was so receptive to Mrs Cannon's proselytizing. Maybe the reason was Mrs Cannon's warm heart. She was a childless middle-aged woman who had separated from her husband and who, until meeting Lana, had lived for one thing: Jesus' return. She offered Lana motherly care while never judging or denouncing her, and her steady devotion must finally have convinced Lana of Jesus' own unconditional love.

Jean rubbed the soil off her hands and looked at the frangipani. It would grow into a shady and fragrant tree, she thought, and please someone on some hot day.

In July 1975, Lana gave birth to a healthy boy: Claude Roy Dipanjan Ramcharan.

When Monica heard about the baby, she lashed out at Jean: once could be called a mistake, but twice meant Lana was either a fool or a whore; Jean would end up the same way if she wasn't careful; Lana used to have so much going for her, now look at the unholy mess she was in because she couldn't keep her legs closed; Jean didn't have a whole lot going for her except a solid head on her shoulders, and she had better play her cards right or she would end up on the dung heap with Lana. Why had God given her daughters?

Whenever she was this irate, Monica's business sense sharpened. A few weeks after the birth of Lana's child, she performed one of her greatest feats for Island Bakery. She had already acquired all the wholesale business for the southeastern part of the island. She had also begun exporting local bakery items – coco bread, bullahs – to the West Indian immigrant populations of London, New York, and Toronto, and was storing her foreign profits, illegally, in an offshore bank. She had been elected the first female president of the National Tradesmen's Organization. All this was not enough for Monica. She wanted control of the baking industry in the north as well as the south, and was determined to do business with the big beach resorts. For many years these resorts had been supplied by her chief competitor, Hill's Bakery, a small family business in Trelawny. Finally, she got the resort contracts and put Mr Hill and his family out of business.

Faye was appalled. She had been reading Marx and was a member of a radical offshoot of the PNP's youth organization. She and Monica quarreled constantly. Monica called Faye 'Castro,' and Faye called Monica 'the Czarina.'

'What happenin', Castro? Where you cigar?'

'It don't trouble you conscience to think of the people you put out of work?'

'Business is business.'

'People don't forget their oppressors. You reap what you sow. I warnin' you because you're my bes' friend mother.'

'Chu, I no have time fe dis socialist nonsense.'

'It a come, so you might as well prepare.'

'An what exactly is "it," if you don't mind me askin'?'

'Things goin' change. People beginnin' to see the injustices in this country, an' is high time too. It might happen peaceful or with blood but it goin' happen, an' you need to choose now either to hang on to the old way or move forward—'

'Like you? You movin' forward?'

'Yes. I've chosen to move forward with the masses.'

'Then, darlin', is you need warnin', not me. Remember, pretty rose dem got maca. Tek care.'

*

Island Bakery was now a monopoly, and Monica was rich. She had a swimming pool built in the backyard. She purchased a seaside condominium in Ocho Rios and hired a chauffeur for her new Peugeot. She was still thrifty; the small car would consume less petrol.

She sat on the veranda in the evenings with a gin and tonic, taking in the view of Kingston. She could afford to relax a little and ruminate. 'What a long way I come, eh?' She never forgot New Hope. She remembered being an unmarried mother at seventeen in a house without an indoor bathroom; remembered breathing in the stink of cows and hens, and what it was like to own only a single pair of shoes. Discontent, yes, discontent had driven her this far. She still felt its grip on her; even now she thought she could do better for herself. Find herself a better man, for instance.

She was tired of Delly. He was old. He had a heart problem – nothing serious, but it was slowing him down. His party was no longer in power, and even if it returned to power in the next election, he was too old now to run for office. He wanted to divorce Norma and marry Monica, but Monica kept turning him down. 'What I want with that old man laundry in my house?'

She still had affection for him, but he was beginning to seem cloying and bothersome. When he visited, she went to bed early and left him sitting alone downstairs in front of the TV. He would fall asleep there, and Jean would wake him up.

'Oh. Was I sleeping?' he would ask, and chuckle wanly. 'Your mother went to bed, then? Well, I suppose I should go home.'

He would reach for his shoes, which he had taken off for comfort, and Jean would help him put them on, then see him out. He would give her cheek a pinch, as he'd been doing since she was a child, and say something like 'You grow into a lovely girl.'

'You know, is too long I don't get no pleasure outa life,' Monica said one evening.

They were all sitting on the veranda – Monica, Daphne, and their brother, Errol. Jean was in the living room reading, and she heard them talking.

'You talkin' 'bout the "big bamboo"?' Errol asked.

'Big bamboo, or jus' plain ole ordinary bamboo I would settle for right now.'

Errol laughed.

'What happen?' Daphne asked, the topic of sex waking her from her own unsober preoccupations. 'Delly lose him substance?'

Monica tried to recall the last time Delly had made love to her: 'I think it was 'round Christmas, 1973.'

'Dat a long-long time, Monica,' Errol said. 'Find youself a stout young man.'

'Not too young,' Daphne advised.

'No, not too young,' Monica agreed. 'The young ones dem tire you out an' nex' ting you have heart attack.'

They all laughed raucously.

'No, man,' Monica continued, 'I lookin' a man me own age who still have strength in him.' She paused for a moment. 'An' I don't want nobody come love me fe me money.'

'That might be askin' too much, sister,' Errol teased.

'I should look abroad.'

'Europe,' Daphne said. She had had some experience with Europeans.

'No. Too far. Miami.'

'I wish you luck, gal. You deserve a break,' Daphne said.

It was the nicest thing Jean had ever heard Daphne say to Monica. The two sisters were actually very fond of each other though they argued about everything. 'Like cat and dawg,' Mary Darling said of them.

*

One day, there was a terrible fight between Monica and Daphne; it began over Irene's son.

Irene's mother, who had always looked after Irene's sons, died. The oldest, Lawson, called Sonny, was already living in Kingston. But there was nowhere for her retarded son, Philbert, to go. So Irene asked Monica if he could come and live with her in the maid's room.

Monica wasn't too happy about the idea of the eighteen-year-old retarded boy living in the house. In fact, she was always slightly annoyed when something happened to remind her that Irene had a personal life. But Irene had served her well for fourteen years and was irreplaceable.

'Only because he's your son, Irene, and I would prefer him to stay at the back of the house. I don't want him hangin' round the gate. An' I don't want him bringing strangers into the yard.'

So Philbert became a permanent member of the household, a back-door shadow. He kept Monica's car clean and shiny. Now and then Irene sent him on errands to Mr Chin's grocery shop at the foot of the hill. Mr Chin knew he was Irene's son and wouldn't try to cheat him of his change. Most of the time Philbert sat under a tree at the far end of the yard, reading the old comic books Jean brought him. He was skeletal-looking, over six feet, with a big, ungainly head, and he never looked anyone in the eye, not even his mother. He was afraid of people fearing him. Only Jean, when she brought him the comics, began to get a look of recognition from him.

Irene's older boy, Sonny, lived in a tenement yard in Trench Town and was perpetually unemployed. He was always 'lookin' a day's work' cutting grass or doing any odd job he could find. Now and then, he came round to Bonnieview to visit his mother and brother.

One day just before sundown, he appeared at the gate. Daphne was sitting on the veranda reading.

It had come to Gwen's attention that Daphne wasn't taking care of herself and that her drinking was becoming a serious problem. There was never anything in her refrigerator except chasers. After a car accident in which she broke her wrist, Daphne finally agreed that it was dangerous to drink and drive, so she gave up driving. The family arranged for her to have dinner at Monica's on Mondays, Gwen's on Wednesdays, Errol's on Fridays, and Cherry's on those Sundays when Daphne was not visiting Mary Darling.

So it was Monday, just before dinner, and Daphne was reading on the veranda when Sonny appeared at the gate. He was a tall, gangly fellow with a noticeable limp, one leg shorter than the other. The gate was always closed now because there had been several break-ins in the neighborhood. Sonny knocked against the gate with a stone. Daphne took off her reading glasses and peered at him. She didn't know that he was Irene's son.

'Yes? What you want?' Her voice carried down the driveway.

'Please, ma'am, Miss Monica at home?'

'Monica,' Daphne called inside. 'Somebody here to talk to you.' Daphne told Sonny, 'Come in, come in.' She saw him hesitate. There was a BEWARE OF BAD DOGS sign. 'No worry, de dawgs chain up 'round the back.'

He came in and stood in front of the veranda.

Monica recognized him. 'Oh, is you. Go round the back. You mother in the kitchen.'

'Yes, ma'am. But please, firs' ma'am, I come to ask if you need any help round de yard.'

'No, we have a gardener.'

'Then, please ma'am, you need extra help down at the bakery?'

'No, I have all the help I need,' Monica said, dismissing him. She sat down and picked up the newspaper.

He continued to stand there.

She put down the newspaper and looked at him. 'What kind of work you lookin' exactly? You think you can learn how to bake bread?'

Sonny seemed to consider this.

'Speak up, boy. What you can do?'

'I can talk in rhyme, ma'am.'

Daphne put down her book and looked at Sonny.

Monica said, 'Now that is something I could really use – a rhyming man. Boy, go round the back to you mother an' stop waste people time.'

Errol joined them for dinner and Monica told him about Sonny:

'Talk in rhyme! You ever hear anything so? I tell Irene send the boy go JBC, mek him get a job on the radio.'

'That's a good idea,' Errol said with complete seriousness; he had a successful talk show on JBC. 'Maybe I could help him out.'

'But see me-dying-trials!' Monica was astonished. 'Manley tek you people head spin it round till you cyaan tell joke from serious. The boy never do a hard day's work in him life. Jus' idle. Look like me de only sane person lef' in dis place.'

Monica went to bed early, as usual, and Errol, Daphne, and Jean stayed up talking.

Errol shook his head and said to Jean: 'She not easy, you know, you mother.'

'No, Monica not easy,' Daphne agreed.

'Not easy at all,' Errol repeated, opening a bottle of aged single-malt; Monica kept an impressive liquor cabinet. 'Daphne, you remember the time Monica . . .'

Sometimes they told stories about Monica that Jean had already heard, but she pretended she was hearing them for the first time in the hope that some previously forgotten detail might arise. As they said, Monica wasn't easy, and that was why

Jean stayed up late listening to these tales about her mother as her aunt and uncle got drunker, funnier, a little confused, let slip a secret, tried to get it back, made her swear never to tell anyone, drank more, grew quiet, shook their heads, and sighed, moved by their own stories.

A year later Sonny was, in fact, rhyming on the radio and he could be heard on jukeboxes and in record stores. The Reggae Poet, Sonny Law, was hailed as a phenomenal new talent and went on a world tour. Sonny did not write down or publish his poems, he only performed them. One of them, 'Want Smaddy Fe Blame,' became a national cry. Journalists and ordinary, disgruntled people took up the poem's title phrase and aimed it at the politicians; the politicians took up the phrase and aimed it at each other:

> Six pickney me 'ave, gimme
> a day's work please miss.
> Me can cook an' clean chimmy.
> Na bada me, g'wan. Ketch
> a ride back a Trench Town.
> When me reach, riot a g'wan,
> tenement burnin' down,
> me pickney-dem inside,
> Lawd, who do dis? Me
> Wan' smaddy fe blame,
> JLP, PNP, a de same.
> Wan' smaddy fe blame . . .

Jean played a recording of the poem for Monica and Daphne. 'You hear that?' She turned to her mother. 'You never believed he had talent.'

'What mek you think I change my mind?'

'He's reciting his poetry at the Albert Hall, for heaven's sake.'

'These people givin' Jamaica a bad name.'

'How would you know? You never listen to him.'

'All this Rasta dreadluck—'

'Dread*locks*!'

'Whatever, is a heap a foolishness. I suppose nex' ting you goin' tell me Bob Marley is a poet?'

'Yes!'

Daphne said, 'The trouble with you, Monica, is you think only White people can do anything properly. You think anything Black people do bound to turn into a big joke. You brainwash.'

'Is all a you brain wash by that lunatic Michael Manley.'

'That's another thing: You blame Michael Manley for every little thing. If breeze mess up you hair you blame Manley. It tek more than one person to run a country, you know.'

'A bunch of adolescents playin' parliament. Mekin' a big mistake, encouraging these people,'

'Which people?' Daphne and Jean asked in unison.

'Irene son an' all dem boy wha' walk street. Why Manley come mix up everything? The masses! The masses! Me mus' share my hard-earn money wid idlers an' criminals—'

'Jesus Christ, Monica.' Daphne was getting exasperated.

'These people no ready fe change. You g'wan. Invite dem into you house an' before you can blink – *whaps!* – dem chop you up. Look what happenin' over in Africa.'

'Monica you so backward I don't even know what to say.' Daphne's voice was unusually quiet and steady. 'Is hard to believe we come outa the same woman' belly. You forget you own mother had to practically beg food for us one time. Who you calling "the masses"? Is poor people you talkin' 'bout? You don't remember we were in their place once?'

'You maybe. Not me. In my heart I never forget I am Dr John

Darling's granddaughter, and my grandmother was a Scottish lady. A *lady*.'

'Oh yes! A lady!' Daphne stood up and raised her voice. 'An' our mother, Lady Mary Darling, slaughtered cows with her own hands to make a measly living. She pullin' out cow guts all day an' stinkin' of tripe to gi' you piano lessons an' when you move to Kingston you 'shame an' never visit her. You forget, Monica? You forget you mother's trials, an' her mother's trials? An' yet with all they went through they never hardened their hearts like you.'

34

FRESH POETRY & EGGS

Once poetry seemed possible here, not merely elegiac, but in the ancient style of griots, rat-rhymers, and Fools.

'How those eggs doin' on you lap?'

She opens the tin and looks at the eggs. She marvels at how still and perfect they are.

'They're fine.' She closes the tin. 'Is a shame Miss Vera needs grillwork out here in the country, don't you think?'

There's a stretch of dangerous, winding road ahead. She thinks he's busy concentrating and didn't hear her.

'What you really saying, Jean?'

He looks at her for a second, then turns his face back to the road.

What is she really saying? He's right to ask. She's not thinking about Miss Vera's veranda.

But what can she say? This country has forfeited its whole future; it reduces, breaks, kills anyone and anything of promise; there is nowhere else I want to be; but I can't stay here; we've read the signs, for heaven sake; we've heard the lament on one side of the road and the laughter on the other, a continuous exchange of lament and laughter, and we're doomed.

'I'm afraid,' she says. 'I can't stand being afraid all the time.'

'Afraid,' he repeats as if testing the word for accuracy.

Will everything she says today sound wrong?

Is she wrong to be heading north when she should be back in Kingston comforting Faye and lighting candles for Lana? She can't help this looking back as she moves forward, the need to see in its entirety what she's escaping.

35

Jean and Faye both graduated from high school with distinction. Faye began undergraduate courses in social sciences at the University of the West Indies. Jean was undecided about the future in spite of her teachers' encouragement and recommendations that she go to university. She had mentioned to Monica the idea of studying modern languages, perhaps going abroad to get a degree in comparative literature. Monica said if she wanted to waste money doing foolishness, then she would have to do it with her own money.

So Jean got a job at the Peruvian embassy, where she was able to keep practicing Spanish. The Peruvian ambassador and his wife were longtime friends of the island; they had been there since before Independence and had known Jean's father. Jean was put in charge of the small embassy library, which was open to the public. Nothing could have suited her better than spending her days among shelves of South American literature and lore.

Though they had taken different paths, Faye and Jean saw each other often and spoke together on the telephone every day.

One Saturday afternoon Faye drove up to Jean's house; they had vague plans to go to a movie or take a drive out to Port Royal.

'Look like I turn bus driver today!' Faye shouted from her little orange car, the 1963 Volkswagen she had bought from Daphne. Dr Galdy was in the car, and somebody else. Getting into the back seat, Jean saw that the somebody else was Drummond, a friend of Faye's from the university.

'We mekin' a coupla stops. I droppin' Drummond off at the plaza. Mummy's car not working so I tekin' her to see Auntie an' dem. You don't mind?'

'No, not at all. I haven't seen you aunties in a long time.'

Faye's mother visited her elderly in-laws every week in their dilapidated house in Allman Town. When Jean and Faye were children they often went with Dr Galdy and had enjoyed picking and eating guineps in the yard while Dr Galdy sat on the veranda with the old people.

'Haven't seen you in ages,' Dr Galdy said. 'I hear you have a nice job at the embassy. You know Drummond?'

'Yes. Hello.' She smiled, acknowledging Drummond, who merely nodded his head, then stared out the window. Jean had met Drummond several times. He was a short, muscular, unshaven man who wore his scruffiness as if it were an honor he was bestowing on those in his presence.

Jean turned her attention to Dr Galdy. 'I heard about the shooting at the hospital. Thank God you're all right.'

'Well let's say I'm more all right than those people who got shot.'

Jean hoped she would say more about it. All she knew was what she had gleaned from the news: that masked gunmen with automatic rifles had made their way into the public hospital and opened fire in one of the wards. Three patients and a nurse had been killed.

Dr Galdy said no more on the subject. She had a reserve that had always intrigued Jean, like a tightly bound library book, plain-covered, never taken from the shelf. Jean knew that she had suffered and recovered from many difficulties: scandal-ridden marriages to men much weaker than herself, one marriage ending with a death, the other with divorce and bankruptcy. But none of this showed on her. She was a thin, quiet, unobtrusive woman whose outstanding medical career had subsumed her embarrassing personal history.

Faye stopped at the shopping plaza and Drummond got out.

Jean was relieved. Drummond X, as he called himself, was a teaching assistant in one of Faye's political science classes and a professed Communist. He had recently been arrested on a false charge and this had added to his already high opinion of himself, along with making him a campus celebrity. Jean disliked him mainly because he had bad manners. She wondered if Faye had become infatuated with him; she couldn't see them as lovers. But over the last few weeks, whenever she dropped by Faye's house he was there.

'How well do you know Drummond?' Dr Galdy gently asked Faye.

'Why?'

'Just wondering.'

'Look, police planted that gun on him.'

'I didn't say anything about that.'

'No. But it's what you thinking.'

Dr Galdy sighed and did not respond.

'You're a racist,' Faye said.

Jean had to speak: 'That's crazy!'

'I've been living with her all these years. I should know.'

'I'm a racist?' Dr Galdy asked evenly.

'You don't like Black people; you just patronize them. It's neocolonialist.'

'Oh, for heaven's sake,' Dr Galdy said.

All the way to Allman Town, Faye blurted out accusations. Dr Galdy's disdain of Black people was only the beginning; she delved into her mother's marital failures, her lack of a boyfriend, her frigidity, sexual frustration, and selfishness.

Dr Galdy fought back, not with threats or accusations, but

with pent-up anger of her own, speaking the whole time in a quiet, steady voice: she was sick and tired of Faye's bad behavior; Faye had become an unbearable, tyrannical human being, as self-absorbed as her father had been; she wished she had never met Sam Galdy.

The quarrel came to an abrupt end when they arrived. Faye and her mother made an effort to act normally as the aunts made a great to-do of serving cake, marmalade on crackers, and guava juice to their guests on the veranda. But the long-suppressed annoyances and perceived unfairnesses of both mother and daughter had gathered too much momentum. Soon they were quarreling again, with complete disregard as to where they were or who was listening.

'You're pitiful,' Faye spat out. 'I sorry for you.'

'Pity yourself.'

'I do pity myself – for being part of this family.'

'Why are you ashamed of being White?'

'Is this damn prejudice family I'm ashamed of, not my color.'

'What she sayin', Catherine?' Aunt Sylvia asked Dr Galdy.

Aunt Sylvia and Aunt Florence sat on wicker chairs enjoying their cake and visitors and not quite catching the drift of the conversation. Except for Catherine Galdy, they rarely saw anyone. They had been anticipating her visit all week, and today they had pulled up their stockings all the way under their dresses instead of merely rolling them at the knees (which they usually did because the heat was unbearable); they had patted face powder on their uneven complexions – not noticing that the powder had turned slightly orange with age – dabbed cologne on their handkerchiefs, brought out the folding tea table and the good glasses, and placed the embroidered tea cloth on the serving tray as they had been doing every week for twenty or more years.

'And tell me – how am I prejudiced? I work ten hours a day

in a hospital full of poor, Black people. But you wouldn't know anything about it, would you? You've never taken the slightest interest in anything I do.'

'Forgive me, Great White Doctor.'

'How come you not eatin' you cake, Catherine?' Sylvia asked.

'Catherine don't eat a lot a sweet-sweet,' Florence reminded Sylvia. 'Always one piece a cake, no more. That's why she so thin.'

'But she not even eatin' what on her plate. You'd like some more juice, Jean? How about another cracker?'

'No, thank you, Miss Galdy, I'm fine.'

Jean wished she had not come — not because of the quarreling, though that was upsetting; it was the open veranda that scared her.

The Galdys had to be the only people in this part of Kingston who had not put up grillwork. They didn't even have a watchdog. Allman Town had been a middle-class residential area in the early part of the century. Not far from the Galdys' house, Mr Ho Sing had kept a grocery shop, but even in his time the area had already changed, and the better-off families had moved. Shantytowns surrounded the Galdys, havens of gunmen and political gangs. Jean knew that the Galdys' house had been broken into twice within the past year. The first time Dr Galdy happened to be there, and she had handed over her money and jewelry and persuaded the gunmen to leave them all unharmed. The second time the gunmen tied up the old people, made them lie on the floor, and offered them the choice of being stabbed or shot. A neighbor had called the police, and the sirens frightened off the gunmen before they harmed anyone.

Jean kept looking nervously out at the road. She had never had such a yearning for iron bars and gates. She wanted to lock up this vulnerable old White family for their own good.

Sylvia asked again, 'What she sayin', Catherine? What the girl sayin'?'

Florence, at seventy the younger of the sisters, caught the antagonism in Faye's tone. 'Is a shame how you talk to you mother. Personally I agree with her. What you mean bringin' Rasta-man into you house?'

'Who the hell said anything about Rastas?'

'Ras-ta?' Sylvia sputtered. 'Oh, dear.'

'Racist-racist all a you—'

'Do not speak to your aunties that way.'

'They si' down on this veranda all day long sneering at Black people.'

'I don't believe what I'm hearing. Are you on drugs? You smoking ganja? Or you jus' gone completely out of you mind?'

'I've been listenin' to them insult Black people for years. What? I mus' pretend is not true?'

'Stop this right now.' Dr Galdy turned to the old women. 'I'm sorry—'

'They never got married because they couldn't find nobody White enough.'

'I could have married a Canadian once,' Florence said.

Sylvia began to cry softly.

'See what you do now? You make Auntie cry,' Florence reprimanded Faye. 'Shame on you.'

Sylvia suddenly cried out: 'Oh! Let the girl marry whoever she want.'

Willy Galdy came out in his pajamas, carrying a gun. He was now confined to the house, not so much because he was insane but because he was nearly blind and had recently collided with a man on a bicycle while out walking.

He had heard his sister crying.

'Faye want to marry a Rasta man,' Florence explained to him.

'Good Lord.' Dr Galdy groaned and put her head in her hands.

'Obeah-man?' Willy sprayed saliva as he spoke. 'Him put guzu on you?'

'Not obeah-man, Rasta man. She say she don't want nuttin' more to do wid White people.'

'Rasta man put guzu on you?'

'Maybe him brainwash her,' Florence suggested.

'Yes' — Faye laughed — 'I marrying a Rasta an' I goin' have likkle rasta pickney-dem.'

'Not in my house.' He aimed the gun at Dr Galdy. 'I shoot you over my dead body you not marrying no nigga.'

Sylvia stopped crying and started hyperventilating.

'Give her some juice,' Dr Galdy said, keeping her eye on the pistol, which Willy still aimed at her.

'Not Catherine, you big fool! Is Catherine's *daughter* who want to marry Rasta.' Florence pointed at Faye. 'That one right there.'

Willy noticed Jean and pointed the gun at her. 'Is who dis?'

'Gimme the gun.' Faye took it from him and examined it. 'Jesus Christ, it's loaded.' She put it in her bag and turned to Jean. 'Come, we leavin' this madhouse.'

Dr Galdy stood up. 'No. *I'm* leaving. I'm leaving this godforsaken country. Only thing keeping me here was her.' She waved her hand in Faye's direction.

'Where you goin' go?' Florence asked worriedly.

'I don't know, maybe Antigua. Somewhere where they don't have all this violence and — and—'

It shocked Jean to see Dr Galdy on the brink of tears.

'Antigua? What they have in Antigua?' Sylvia asked. She had stopped hyperventilating.

'A hospital where I can practice medicine without people coming in and shooting up the place.'

'Oh, that was terrible, terrible,' Florence said. 'You were there when it happened, Catherine?'

'Go,' Dr Galdy told Faye. 'I'll take a taxi home. Go do whatever you want. It's your life.'

'Gimme back me gun, woman.'

'No,' Faye told Willy. 'People find out you have gun in the house, they kill you fe it.'

'Is my gun.'

'You comin' with us or you staying?' Faye asked her mother.

'Leave me.'

It was understood that Jean would go with Faye, but Jean was so appalled by her friend's behavior that she was loath to get in the car with her. She felt protective toward Catherine Galdy. Yet Catherine Galdy's 'Leave me' had been firm; she had survived bitter partings before; she would be all right. Whether Faye would be all right was the question. Jean got in the car with her friend, and as they were backing out of the driveway she wondered which of the two scenarios was more disquieting: sitting with that old White family on their unprotected veranda, or heading out into the darkening gang-battled streets with Faye, the youngest and perhaps last of the Galdys, who had a loaded gun in her bag and strange anger in her heart.

36

Jean was not comfortable in the smoky, ganja-smelling hotel room. The carpet she stretched out on itched her legs. She was the only woman there. Mark's band had played that night in Ocho Rios and were unwinding with spliffs and beer. Jean did not smoke or drink beer; she wanted to relax, but somehow could not join in their talk and laughter. She always felt like an impostor on these occasions. The best she could do was smile and nod her head.

'What alive, no dead.'

Mark's friends laughed at his words.

'I think you really on to something, Markie,' one of them said.

'Yeah man,' another said, 'that's deep. What alive, no dead.'

'No man. Listen to what I sayin'. I talkin' . . . 'bout – the state of my heart.'

Mark put his arm around Jean and pulled her toward him. He rarely asked her to join him on these out-of-town engagements. 'Is three years I know this girl, an' the love still alive. I tellin' you – de love no dead.'

Someone chuckled.

'So, Jean, I askin' you in front a all dese drunk an' disorderly people who will serve as my witness so help me God – you goin' marry me or what?'

It had come to this: the feeling that some step or other would have to be taken. As the band, Swahili, became more successful, Mark and Jean saw less of each other. He was nearly always on tour. When he wasn't, he slept all day. They had reached the point where they would either split up or marry. She agreed to marry him.

Monica was pleased but still urged caution: 'Remember, you not married yet, not till that ring is on you finger.'

Paul had reservations: 'You so young, Jean. You sure 'bout this?'

What else was she going to do? She was almost twenty-one, and getting bored.

Week after week her life followed the same routine. She drove to the embassy, sat in the quiet air-conditioned building, read one or two of the Peruvian newspapers, and attended to a few tasks. Then she went home, swam in the pool, ate supper — sometimes with Monica, usually alone — went to bed early, and read. On weekends she sometimes invited someone from work to come by for a swim. If Mark was in town they might go to the beach with friends or visit Mark's friends and sit around listening to music.

She saw little of Faye, although they spoke on the phone at least once a week. Faye was doing enough for three people: taking classes at UWI, studying drama at the National Theatre School, and writing a new play. On top of all that she volunteered at the PNP headquarters and went to political meetings.

'You need some interest in life other than you man,' Faye said. 'Come to meetings with me.'

'No.'

'Okay. How about a conventional bourgeois pastime like gardening?'

'I used to do a lot of gardening . . .' Jean sighed.

'Oh, God, you sound so fenky-fenky. You need a project. Something to excite you mind.'

Faye was right. Jean had been out of school for almost three years and had been dithering.

She decided to go through her father's things in the garage. The mildewed cardboard boxes of old books and papers had never been sorted out. Roy had been a collector of antiquarian books, and occasionally she had rummaged through these boxes and been captivated by a first edition of some classic or an obscure nineteenth-century reference book like *The Natural Ports and Harbors of the West Indies and the Spanish Main*. She had now and then come across odd items in these boxes, which put her in mind of her father: a Royal Air Force medal, black-and-white photographs of Africa.

That day she happened upon a leather-bound ledger that she had not noticed before. She opened it and it began to crumble in her hands. She sat down, rested it carefully on her lap, and turned the brittle pages; it was a handwritten journal or notebook of some sort written in Spanish. There was a note stuck between the pages, written by her father on paper torn from a stenographer's notebook. It explained that this was the journal of Don Alejandro D'Costa, his first known ancestor on the island, and that the journal had been given to him by his great-aunt Constance. Jean remembered that it was Constance who had also had the Crawford insignia silver goblets in her possession. A second note on another scrap of paper fell out – 'to translate and publish by August 1960; maybe Daphne can help, and Señor Rodríguez.' Señor Rodríguez, a Cuban-born scholar and refugee from the Batista regime, had been a friend of her father's. He was now the chairman of UWI's Romance languages department. Jean had sat in on some of his courses and they had formed a friendship.

She spent the rest of the day reading the journal. She could not make out every word, and skipped a lot. But she heard the voice. The voice spirited itself from the pages and spoke to her like the others, the dreamed speakers of an earlier world. She read to where the flourishes of gray-black ink stopped abruptly. On that last page was an inventory of his gold, silver, slaves, and horses, and finally the words 'El Inglés, Cromwell!'

The next day, she started again, this time with a dictionary. Don Alejandro, a Spanish Jew, had come to the island in 1638 with his wife, Elisabeta, and thirty-five horses. A daughter, Antonia, was born in Jamaica. He did not write much about his family. He was keen on describing the new country. It was a rapturous exercise, giving names to plants and places. Like other Adams he made myths of intractable forests, epics of rivers. She noticed that he used the phrase 'mi país,' my country, not 'this country' as a new settler would say. And yet, within a few years the country would no longer be his. In 1655 most of the Spanish settlers fled to the mountains and then to Cuba. The Spanish tongue, like the flag, furled, and the names of places were changed by the new conquerors: Santa Lucia became Hanover, Porto de Esquivella Old Harbour. Only a few rivers and a mountain or two memorialized the defeated: Rio Bueno, Ocho Rios, Mount Diablo.

She would take this to Señor Rodríguez and see if together they could make something of the frail, interrupted *historia*.

Señor Rodríguez was enthusiastic but cautioned her, 'It's going to be a lot of work.' They planned to meet every week and he would look over the pages she had translated, helping her with the more difficult and obscure language.

Daphne said she would consider publishing an excerpt in her magazine, and that she knew someone at the historical society who might be of help. There were gaps and errors in the manuscript; Jean would need access to historical records. Monica said, 'Every day that girl gets more like her father . . .'

Irene complained that she couldn't dust Jean's bedroom with all those books spread out and said, 'Me tink you did done wid school.'

There were troublesome moments with Don Alejandro's manuscript beyond translation problems and missing inform-ation. She had expected to admire her ancestor, and he often disappointed her. For several days he wrote of his anger toward one Pedro de Garay for selling him a lame Negress. He did not appear especially cruel toward the Africans, just indifferent; they were his property. In fact, there were times when Jean could not tell whether he was discussing his slaves or his horses, since he gave biblical names to both.

But it was always like this: The voices of the ancestors did not always agree with each other or with her own embryonic voice. Still, Don Alejandro's journal enthralled her; its pages held the dust of that blundered paradise, Xaymaca, whose promise rose before her like the star of a second nativity. And it was her own father who had led her to it.

She was thinking about Don Alejandro's journal and humming to herself when she ran into Lana at the supermarket. The sisters had not seen each other for a long time. What was strangest to Jean about these chance encounters was that Lana would act as though they were not strange. She often asked cheerfully about Monica, and spoke as though all were forgiven. They stood with their grocery trolleys among the cold dairy foods, speaking hurriedly of what was new in each other's lives, more like former acquaintances than sisters who had entered the world from the same womb.

Jean's car was being repaired that day, and Lana offered to drive her home.

Home? Lana had not been home for over ten years. The notion completely disoriented Jean. She looked closely at her sister. Lana was dressed from head to toe in white; her beautiful hair was hidden beneath a white turban.

Lana noticed Jean looking at her clothes.

'Claude was sick with fever, an' I promised God I would wear white for a whole year if He made him better. Look.' She took some photographs out of her bag. 'Cute, eh? And smart. Him – he – goin' brainy like you.'

As they drove to Bonnieview Terrace Lana told Jean that she was saving to get her own home. She didn't like imposing on good Mrs Cannon. 'Jesus stamp that woman passport for heaven. I wish I could be half as good a Christian.' Lana's car was full of Jehovah's Witnesses pamplets. A plastic miniature of Christ hung from the rearview mirror. Jean noticed that Lana was making an effort to speak 'good' English, as though her salvation depended partly on this.

'How is Aunt Daphne getting on? So long I meanin' – I have been meaning – to give her a call. But I am so busy, you know, with the baby and work.'

'Where are you working?'

'Telephone company. Overseas operator. Aunt Gwen looks after Claude in the daytime. When I get me – my – own place I will invite everybody over. How's Mark doing? Are you two still – Wha' de rass! Bitch!'

Lana stepped hard on her brakes to avoid being hit by a woman in a long American car. The woman drove on, and Lana continued to yell at her.

'You no see de stop sign, you ole cow-fart?' She quickly recovered herself. 'You see how the woman have me cursing bad-wud! Chu! Well, at leas' I never call the Lord name in vain.'

As they got closer to Bonnieview, Jean grew anxious: 'I don't want to take up you time. Just drop me at the bottom of the hill.'

'Is awright.'

When they got to the house, the gate was closed as usual, and the dogs began barking, not having recognized the car.

'Cleo!' Lana stuck her head out the window and called to her once-favorite dog, who stopped barking for a moment and looked puzzled. 'What happened to Rex? He died? Is that a new dawg?'

'Yes, that's Cleo's son, Jasper.'

'I hear you have a swimming pool. Go on, open the gate.'

She was coming inside?

Monica's new Peugeot was in the driveway. Maybe Lana didn't realize it was her mother's car. Jean got out and opened the gate. It took all her strength to calm Jasper, who didn't know Lana, and Cleo, who seemed to have forgotten her. Lana got out of the car while Jean held each dog by the collar.

'Sit Jasper, sit. Down, down, good dawg,' Lana said, approaching the ferocious animals. 'Cleo, don't you remember me?'

The dogs continued growling and snarling and now and then tried to leap forward.

This is bad enough, Jean thought. What if Monica comes out? Standing there with a dog on either side, she had an image of herself as one of the three heads of Cerberus guarding the gates of the underworld.

It occurred to her that maybe the dogs could be used to persuade Lana to leave.

'Jasper is vicious,' Jean said.

'Nice puppy,' Lana said, holding her hand out to the one-hundred-and-twenty-pound Alsatian. Jasper frowned and began to whine. Cleo sniffed around Lana's legs, then started wagging her tail with great excitement and recognition.

'Good puppy. Good dawg.'

Jean watched amazed as Lana walked up the veranda steps, both dogs affectionately following her. 'I smell Irene's cooking.'

Monica must have heard the dogs' commotion and seen Lana from a window. She appeared at the front door.

'Monica,' Lana said brightly.

Jean sank into one of the veranda chairs.

Monica stood inside the half-open doorway while Lana rattled on about her baby boy. She told Monica about his recent bout of fever, his first word, how much he loved ice cream. She took a photograph from her wallet and gave it to Monica.

'You can have this.'

Monica studied the photograph for some time. Lana watched her quietly. Jean watched them both.

Monica handed back the photograph. 'I'm glad to hear the child is doing well.' She looked past Lana and said to Jean, 'Dinner is ready.' Then she closed the door on both her daughters.

Lana stood before the closed door. She turned to Jean and opened her mouth as if she were going to say something, and then Jean saw her face crumple, like a face in a distorting mirror.

Jean moved toward her, but Lana held up both hands blocking her.

'Is all right. Is all right,' Lana said. She ran, almost tripping, down the veranda steps, and backed out of the driveway with her foot hard on the gas.

That night Jean and Monica were awoken by the sound of a car crash followed by screams of 'Fire! Fire!'

There was a terrified pitch in the dogs' barking, as if they, or the world, had gone mad.

Monica and Jean rushed out to the veranda.

'What the hell? My God—' Monica gasped.

There was no fire. Lana had smashed her car through the closed gate and now stood on the front lawn screaming:

'*Fire!*'

Monica went back inside. Jean followed her.

'Maybe I should go out to her,' Jean quietly suggested. 'Maybe she hurt herself.'

'Close the door,' Monica said, and sat wearily on the couch.

They heard Lana shouting, 'You're my mother! You're my mother!'

Through the window, Jean saw the lights come on in the house across the road. Other dogs in the neighborhood began to bark. She could hear Jasper and Cleo in a frenzy, trying to break out of their fenced-in sleeping quarters.

'We have to do something,' Jean told her mother.

'Call the police.'

Jean hesitated.

'Please, Jean.'

She went to the phone. 'What should I say?'

Monica didn't answer.

Jean told the police that there was a disturbance at number nine Bonnieview Terrace. The police said someone had already called and they were on their way.

Lana stopped screaming. Jean went to the door.

Seeing someone in the open doorway, Lana began screaming again for Monica. She picked up a stone and threw it toward the doorway. It landed on the veranda steps. Jean went inside. She heard Lana throw another stone, and then another.

Jean sat beside Monica and waited for the police to arrive.

The word 'manic-depressive' alarmed Jean. She had a vision of Lana in a nineteenth-century madhouse among other tormented inmates.

She had called Paul the night Lana crashed through the gate, worried about the confrontation between Lana and the police. He went with Lana to the police station and persuaded them not to lock her up but to let him take her to the hospital instead.

By then Lana had calmed down; Paul said she seemed to be in a kind of stupor. The hospital staff sedated her and kept her overnight.

The next day Monica called the family doctor, and he recommended a psychiatrist.

It was only a matter of time before terms like 'shock treatment' and 'antidepressant' trembled through the family's vocabulary. They – Monica, Gwen, Daphne, Cherry, and Mary Darling – began trying on the idea that Lana was mentally ill. An even more troubling thought lay beneath this: the idea that perhaps Lana had been ill for many years and no one had noticed. Not spoiled, self-centered, bad-tempered, or wayward – but ill.

Lana stayed several weeks in the hospital, then she went to Gwen's house. Jean happened to be visiting Cherry one day when Gwen called in a panic.

'Is Lana. She havin' some kind of fit.'

On the way there, Cherry asked Jean: 'You think we should call Monica?'

Gwen was holding Lana's baby, Claude, in her arms when they got there. He began crying when he saw Jean and Cherry.

'She in her bedroom two days now. Won't get up. She pee-pee right there in her bed.'

Cherry and Jean went to Lana's bedroom. She lay on the bed in a damp nightgown, smelling of urine and sweat; her face was twisted in pain.

'Lana—' Jean went to her. Lana's hair was damp and foul-smelling.

'You in pain, Lana?' Cherry asked.

She tried to raise herself up but her body began shaking with spasms. Her eyes were wide and frightened. Spittle rose to her lips.

'Jesus! Call the psychiatriss,' Cherry said. 'Call Monica.'

Monica met them at the hospital. When she saw Lana's convulsing body and dazed expression, she looked away. Her daughter looked like a stricken animal.

The psychiatrist explained that Lana was having a bad reaction to her medication, and prescribed emergency shock treatment. He asked Monica to wait in his office while Lana was undergoing the treatment. Jean waited with her. Neither of them spoke. After a while Jean asked, 'Do you want a magazine or anything?'

Monica did not respond; it was as if Jean were not there. She did not sit up straight as usual, but had let her head fall back against the chair, and she stared blankly at the ceiling.

Gwen said, 'She can't stay with me any longer. There's the child to think of. It's bad for him to see his mother in such a state.'

'I don't have a car,' Daphne said. 'What if she gets sick in the middle of the night?'

Cherry offered her guest room, but the family decided Cherry was getting too old to take on caring for Lana.

She stayed at Paul's farm for a while, then with Mrs Cannon, and then everyone lost track of where she was.

Whenever her illness was mentioned, the conversation contracted to one or two words, such as 'in therapy.' The family tried not to be afraid of the unpredictable dangers insanity posed, but they were. They knew what all those fancy psychiatric terms meant: Lana was crazy.

For the first time, guiltily, Jean began to believe there might be good reason to fear Lana. Lana's screaming that night on the lawn had been shattering for Jean. She had felt utterly useless and indecisive, not knowing whether to go out to Lana or stay inside with her mother. She had never been acquainted with anyone who was ill in this way; her experience with mental illness had been limited to those people she occasionally saw ranting uncontrollably in the streets.

Deepa placed Lana at a psychiatric center in West Palm Beach, Florida. The family was relieved. She was being 'treated.' Deepa reassured them that it wasn't an 'asylum' – dreaded word – and Paul said he had read that the center used gentle, innovative treatments. No more 'shock treatment' for Lana.

When Jean ran into old school friends and they asked, cautiously, about Lana, she told them what she had heard the women of her family say: 'She's doing a lot better.'

The truth was that neither she nor the rest of the family knew much at all about Lana's treatment or progress. Even Monica seemed grateful to Deepa for handling the situation, though she never said so directly. Seeing Lana's convulsions that day in the hospital had turned something over in Monica, something heavy like a stone. The photograph of herself and Lana that she had kept on her dressing table was put away.

About this time something happened to shift the family's focus from itself. Lana's convulsions anticipated the nation's: There was another election.

37

Nineteen seventy-six was an election year, and it was the year an undeclared civil war began.

The main question in the living rooms and on the verandas was whether Jamaica would now align itself fully with the Communists as Cuba and Grenada had done, or would that 'Communist ally,' Manley, be destroyed? That Manley himself was not a Communist was beside the point.

'Taking over the country' was the phrase on everyone's lips. Something or someone was 'taking over the country.' Every day the newspapers reported rapes and killings by the gunmen. No one knew exactly who or what the gunmen were. At times they were described as 'armed guerrillas' or 'militia groups,' yet they had demonstrated no clear purpose. When cars and their passengers were hijacked, homes burned down, people raped, tortured, and killed, it was the gunmen. Sometimes the gunmen had guns, other times knives, machetes, Molotov cocktails, or simple, ancient fire.

Iron grillwork now enclosed the verandas and windows of suburbia. In addition, people began barricading the bedroom section of their houses with an indoor iron gate, because the veranda grillwork wasn't always enough to keep 'them' out. The gunmen staked out their targets and used every possible tactic to break into homes and torment their victims.

Almost as bad as the violence was the reporting of it. Jean

stopped reading the newspaper, but she couldn't get out of hearing distance of Irene, Hilston, Monica, Faye. The home of Mr Chin, the grocery shop owner, was broken into. After they raped his wife and mother in front of him, the gunmen hacked off a limb from each of them. A schoolgirl who lived across the street from Daphne was at home with the maid when the gunmen arrived, raped them, tied them up, and set fire to the house. It went on and on like this, getting worse as the election drew nearer.

Novels became Jean's only escape. She read constantly, pressing her ear close to the world of fictional characters, like a vagrant at a windowpane. She was reading late one night when she heard helicopters circling and landing. A searchlight lit up the night outside and moved slowly across her bed. Then she heard the rat-a-tat of machine guns.

The next morning, Irene read aloud from the newspaper: The army had raided the shantytown at the bottom of the hill and killed a renowned gangalee called Midnight Rider, who was associated with a member of Parliament. There was a picture of him in the paper and an account of his notorious deeds.

People began leaving the country, even though the government passed laws that prevented them from taking their money with them. Foreign companies had been steadily pulling out because of the violence, and there was little foreign currency except on the black market. Jamaican currency became a joke. Irene complained that a pound of flour had gone from fifty cents to five dollars in less than a year. She asked for a raise.

Monica couldn't argue, not with Irene. She blamed Manley. Irene also brought up the subject of safety.

'Please, ma'am, if you goin' put grillwork 'round de house?'

'Why? You 'fraid a gunman?'

''Fraid, yes. One kick an' dem can bruk down de front door.'

'Is dem suppose to live behind bars, not me. I not turning my home into a prison.'

'I prefer prison than dead, ma'am.'

'We have two big watchdawg. Nobody can pass by the gate much less come into de yard widout dem skin up dem teet'. So no worry youself, me dear.'

'But it does worry me, ma'am.'

'Look. I sittin' out 'pon my veranda same way like always. First dem ha' fe get past de dawg; next, dem ha' fe get past me!'

'I hope it don't come to dat, ma'am. I wi' keep sayin' me priors every night.'

Jean listened but said nothing. Irene was right; the house was not secure. But no amount of arguing or pleading would influence Monica.

After Monica left for work, Irene said to Jean: 'You mother 'come like Clint Eeswood. She a real cowbwoy.'

What Irene said wasn't far from the truth. The guns and violence were reminiscent of Westerns, and Monica behaved like the sheriff in a cowboy town. Especially during the bakery strike.

Naturally, Monica blamed the strike on Manley. The government was asking Jamaicans to become more self-sufficient: Why should the staple food of the poor be bread made from imported flour?

'Is a good point, Monica, you have to admit,' Errol said.

'Get outa my house before I lose me temper.'

The government raised the tax on imported flour; it cost the wholesaler five times more than it formerly had.

Monica was furious.

When her shipment of flour arrived in Kingston harbor, she paid the captain and the dockworkers not to unload it. She used what flour she had in storage to make bread for the north coast hotels, and then she threw her hands up in a gesture of helplessness before the Kingston grocers: no flour, no bread.

A few weeks later, stampedes and riots began in the supermarkets over the rationed, stale bread.

Faye was visiting Jean one afternoon when Monica came home from the bakery. Monica kicked off her shoes and sat on the couch.

'Wha'appen, Castro?'

'I see you playing Marie Antoinette.'

'Marie nothing. Is Manley preventin' the people from gettin' bread. He keep on like this and America will cut us off without a penny. I suppose you think that would be a good thing.'

'We have to suffer before we can thrive.'

'What you know 'bout sufferin'?' Monica left the room, vexed.

Faye spoke to Jean in earnest: 'What goin' happen to her? She not the type to emigrate. I worry 'bout her.'

Jean was getting exasperated with Faye's self-righteous talk. 'Worry 'bout youself.'

The minister of trade telephoned Monica: 'What you tryin' to accomplish, Monica?'

'You want self-reliance. Fine. Call me when the local wheat grow. Till then we jus' have to do without, right? I can't afford to pay dem extra taxes.'

'You sabotagin' de people's government.'

'People government can go to hell.'

She paid her workers a month's wages in advance, gave them a vacation, went to the empty bakery every day, and waited. One day a crowd appeared outside. Monica heard the shouts and the sound of glass being smashed. She looked out and saw men and women with sticks, broken bottles, and rocks in their hands.

The watchman locked the front door and ran to Monica's office.

'Call de police, ma'am.'

'Lemme go talk to dem.'

'No, ma'am. Dem start t'row bokkle. Mek me call police before dem bun down de place.'

'You stay here an' watch. If things get outa hand, then you call police.'

The commotion outside grew louder.

'Lawd, ma'am! Me 'fraid a riot.'

'Then what the hell use you is? You suppose to be a watchman.' Monica took the gun from her desk and went outside.

The crowd hushed when they saw her.

Then somebody shouted: 'Look ya, John Wayne,' and there was laughter.

Monica picked up one of the rocks that had been thrown and the crowd grew quiet again.

'Is this I mus' tek mek bread? I mus' mek bread from stone?'

'She no Jesus,' somebody said.

The words 'Bread outa stone' and 'She no Jesus' rippled through the crowd.

A woman at the front of the crowd shouted: 'I no 'ave no bread fe me pickney. You pickney starvin'?'

Monica shouted back: 'Me, an' me pickney, an' me granpickney. All a we starvin'. Manley say we mus' stop buy American flour. Is him cause me fe shut down me business. Wha' you come bada me fa? G'wan go ask Manley fe bread.'

A man ran to the front of the crowd and hurled a rock. It flew a few inches past her head, shattering a window.

Monica shot the man.

People scattered. They screamed as they ran, some of them with fear in their faces, others laughing as they took flight, as if it were not really happening, as if they were at the cinema watching a movie and couldn't get hurt.

'Suppose you had killed him?' Jean asked later. 'You could have gone to jail.'

'Jail? Me?'

Delly chuckled. 'Monica, I believe you goin' bring down de government all by youself. Heh-heh.'

A week later, the government reduced the import tax on staple foods such as flour. Monica was in business again.

'You prime minister back down,' Monica teased Faye.

'For now. But in the long run is people like you goin' suffer.'

'You dead wrong. You can tek a lot a things from people, but not bread. I didn't have to study university books to learn that.'

Irene brought Monica's gin and tonic out to the veranda.

'Thanks Irene.' She turned again to Faye. 'G'wan invite you Cuban friend-dem. Mek America come bomb we. Bun down de place. You know what?' She settled back comfortably in her chair. 'Me go stay right-ya-so same way.'

38

Daphne still lived at number 10 Jacaranda Road, in the house she had bought when she returned from England in 1954. Very few homes were left on that road. Office buildings had taken over the area. And the house whose doors had been wide open for two decades — a second home to Jamaica's intelligentsia, reverberating with shouts and laughter — was always closed now.

Few of Daphne's friends came by anymore. The brightest and best of them had died — her dear brother-in-law, Roy Landing; the writer Roger Mais; that shining actress and one-woman cultural phenomenon Elsie Benjamin. The list went on, young and old, the truly visionary and the dilettantes. Some had emigrated to escape the violence and rising inflation; and then there were those who had become too busy.

After a brutal killing in the neighborhood, the family had convinced Daphne to be more careful. She refused to put up grillwork, but she put extra locks on the doors.

She rarely went out. Occasionally she ate dinner at Monica's or Gwen's, but often turned down their invitations, saying she was too tired. She walked to the grocery store a few times each week for her staple items — rum, Coke, tea, condensed milk, and saltine crackers. And she walked to and from her post office box every day.

Astrid wrote to her mother regularly from Holland. Daphne lived on these letters. Jean would see them lying open around the house for weeks, and the photographs Astrid sent of her children also lay about. The correspondence had practically come to take the place of fresh air in her stale, reclusive life.

Daphne was a great Scrabble player. When she and Jean played together, it was serious business; they played fast, using a chess clock. Several dictionaries always lay open around them. Between games, Daphne, who was a quintessential performer, pantomimed some of the high and low moments of her life and did hilarious imitations of her enemies. She never repeated the same stories or jokes, as aging or mentally infirm people often do. This, and her formidable play in Scrabble, assured Jean that Daphne's mind was all there. So she didn't pay much attention to the foreboding tones of the family: 'I worried 'bout Daphne, she not eatin''; 'She drinking too much'; 'Mama, talk to Daphne 'bout her drinking.'

Jean visited her favorite aunt once or twice a week. Her house, though it had lost its famous conviviality, was still for Jean the most comfortable place on the island. She was utterly unself-conscious with Daphne, and in that modest, familiar house with its sagging couch and frayed cushions she found relief from Monica and Mark.

Usually she brought over Chinese food, but she had a hard time getting Daphne to eat more than a few bites. Jean often wondered how a human being as big as Daphne survived on such birdlike amounts of food. Her flesh had begun to sag shapelessly around her large bones and she wore the same outfit constantly, a faded red ankle-length caftan. She had stopped combing her hair, but she still enjoyed having Jean scratch her itchy scalp with a long, fine-tooth comb. When Jean was a little girl, Daphne would entreat her, 'Lawd, me head itch me. Gimme a likkle scratch na?' and would reward her with a shilling.

'Watch this,' Daphne said.

They were at the end of their second round. Jean was three

points ahead with only three letters left, all vowels. Daphne had five. There was no place left on the board to make a word. Jean had been waiting for Daphne to stop the clock and admit defeat.

'Ha!'

One by one, Daphne laid down all five letters − FEARN − prefixing the word OUGHT. The E fit neatly in front of STRANGE, the A after CHOLER.

```
                      F
              E S T R A N G E
    C H O L E R A
                      R
                      N
                      O
                      U
                      G
                      H
                      T
```

'Fearnought?' Jean raised an eyebrow.

Every now and then Daphne made up a word, just to keep her niece on her toes.

'That's right.' Daphne's face gave nothing away. Was she bluffing?

'Fear *not*, for I am with thee, saith the Lord,' Jean said. 'Fear *naught*, for I am with thee, saith the Lord.'

Daphne clucked and shook her head: '*Fearnought.*'

'I have to challenge this one, Auntie.'

'G'wan. Challenge me.'

Jean leafed through the dictionary: 'fearful,' 'fearless' . . . Damn. There it was: 'fearnought. I. A thick kind of woolen cloth used chiefly on board ship . . .'

Jean shut the dictionary.

'Age before beauty, darlin.'' Daphne poured herself another drink while Jean cleared the board for the next round.

'I fell down today in front of the store. Look.' She showed Jean a graze on her elbow, which she had treated with red Mercurochrome.

'I walkin' from the supermarket wid me tings. An' me leg dem give 'way like two bruck stick. Nex' ting me feel meself fallin'.'

'You fainted?'

'No, is not faint; is fall I fall down. Tings start slide outa me grocery bag—'

Daphne grappled the air with her arms, comically replaying the scene. 'I grab hold of the rum bottle quick-quick! I say to meself: Awright, the Coca-Cola can go, but not the rum!'

Jean laughed. 'You shameless.'

Daphne threw her head back, laughing.

Her glass fell from her hand; the rum and ice spilled.

'Aunt Daphne?'

Jean saw at once that her aunt was no longer playacting. She went to her.

'Aunt Daphne?'

She touched her cheek, then her neck. Daphne's body was soft and warm with life; her rum breath filled the air; her words and laughter rang in Jean's ears; but she was dead.

Jean tried to call Monica, but couldn't get through. She called Gwen and told her what had happened. Gwen said she would call the doctor and come right over.

While she waited, Jean did what she could for her dear and favorite aunt. No one had ever shown her how to handle the dead, but to Jean, this was not a dead body; it was Daphne. She shut her aunt's eyes and propped up her head on the back of the chair. She ran her fingers along the beautiful high cheekbones.

'Aunt Daphne, Aunt Daphne,' she said softly, like a prayer.

She felt tears coming. No, she would not disturb this peace.

She smoothed back the gray, unkempt hair and began to gently rub and scratch the scalp.

Gwen — boring, efficient Gwen — lost control. She was crying when she arrived and could not stop crying. 'Me sister. An' younger than me. Oh, God. How I goin' tell Mama? Where's Monica?'

Gwen needed to ask questions: 'How did it happen exactly?'

'We were playing Scrabble. She was jokin' around and started laughing. Then she just died.'

'Just like that, no pain?'

'I don't know. It happened so fast.'

'Merciful God. It mussa been her heart. What you mean — jokin' around?'

'You know Daphne.'

Gwen started to cry again.

The doctor came and examined Daphne, and then the mortician took her body away.

Monica drove up just as the mortician's van was about to leave. She insisted on seeing her dead sister. Then she joined Gwen and Jean in the house. Jean dreaded having to go over the story again.

Monica looked around at the disheveled living room, surveying the uneaten food on the plates, the big open dictionaries. Jean braced herself for whatever smarting words her mother was about to speak. But Monica said nothing. She was stunned by this sudden death of her sister.

'Has anyone called Astrid?' she finally asked. No one answered. 'Well, I supposed I'd better.'

Jean went outside. She sat on the sidewalk where a tree had scattered its pods. She could hear her mother and Gwen inside the house, making themselves useful, opening and closing doors and calling to one another from room to room — unfamiliar sounds filling Daphne's house.

Would chance ever bring her back here again, she wondered,

to this place which held so much of her childhood? She remembered the raucous years – how the cars lined up along the road and filled Daphne's yard. The shouts and laughter, the clatter of glasses.

It was her father she was mourning again. With Daphne gone, who would keep bringing up his name? *Your father, he had vision.*

She felt peculiar sitting on this everyday sidewalk with her grief. This was a country of almost blinding brightness. Night, when it came, fell suddenly and heavily, as did the rain. It was not a place of subtle light or subtle reckoning.

'Jean? Where's Jean?' Monica's voice sounded far away.

She picked up one of the fallen pods from the sidewalk; it was so dark, like the dark eye of something.

'Jean!' Gwen called from the door. 'You mother looking for you.'

She got up, reluctantly.

She could hear them, the old revelers, their voices ringing out in that perpetual night, bursts of laughter, ice rattling in glasses, footsteps on the gravel, hands drunkenly fumbling for car keys, for the door.

'Jean. Come help us move these things,' Monica called.

'Coming.'

'What she doin' out there?'

'She say she coming.'

That poet understood, that Irish poet, in his world of lakes, mist, and nuanced light, night often usurps day. She turned to go in to the living, whose voices seemed more distant than the dead.

39

Gwen held the after-funeral lunch at her house. As a tribute to Daphne, the national folk singers came and performed traditional nine-night songs, songs to calm any agitated, hungry spirits that might have been stirred by this new death. Gwen and Monica left a glass of rum out on their verandas every night until the burial; no one wanted trouble between the living, the dead, and the newly journeying soul.

There were many people spilling out of Gwen's house onto the lawn. Those who had neglected Daphne over the last years of her life came now with their remorse and their praises: politicians, performers, artists, writers. Deepa came from Connecticut, where he had emigrated. Shortly after he arrived, Monica left.

Jean went to look for Paul in the garden. But Mark, who had flown in from Montego Bay for the funeral, caught up with her, so she strolled around the garden with him instead. She stopped by a purple bougainvillea hedge, so deeply purple it was almost black. Why it reminded her of Daphne and of her father, she could not say. She leaned against Mark's shoulder and cried.

'There's no reason to be upset, darlin'. Life is jus' a journey—'

'Oh, Mark. Just let me cry!'

'Well, you don't have to bite off my head!' He pulled away from her.

'No, don't go. I'm sorry—'

'You acting crazy jus' like you sister. I beginning to wonder if you whole family mad.' He walked away.

'So when you want to get married?' he asked later as they sat in his car.

It was mid-February. 'How about October?'

'Awright.'

She was a bit perturbed that he seemed so nonchalant.

'The wedding is October thirty-first,' Jean told Faye. They were sitting in an empty theater at the university, after a rehearsal of Faye's new play. 'And you're going to be in it.'

'As long as I don't have to wear no long gown.'

'Wear anything you like. It'll be Halloween. You can come as a pirate.'

'What you going as, Miss Havisham?'

'Not funny.'

'The whole ting sound funny to me. But then, you know how I feel 'bout Big-head.'

After a moment, Jean asked: 'How many men have you slept with?'

Faye grew serious: 'One.'

'One? Just one? Who?'

'Steve.'

'Steve? Steve from way back? You joking?'

'That's the one.'

'That was the last time you had sex?'

'I didn't say that. You asked me how many men I've slept with.'

Faye looked at Jean to see if she understood, but she saw a confused frown on her face. She took a deep breath and sighed. 'I've been meaning to tell you – but then I thought you'd just figure it out by yourself—'

Jean looked at her blankly.

'I'm a lesbian.'

A few moments went by. 'Since when?'

'I don't know. A coupla years.'

'Is there – somebody?'

'Pat Lucas.'

'Pat, the dancer? She's married.'

'Not for much longer. Are you shocked?'

Jean thought for a moment. 'No.'

'Really?'

'Are you happy? I mean – happy with Pat?'

Faye considered the question, then smiled as if it hadn't occurred to her before. 'Yeah, I'm happy.'

A few days later, driving to the country with Paul, Jean asked him the same question: 'Are you happy?'

'What's wrong?'

'You have a habit of answering my questions with questions.'

'Is that a fact?'

'Seriously. Are you happy?'

'How many times you drive in this truck with me?'

'You did it again.'

'I makin' a point. How many times you drive with me?'

'I don't know. A hundred times?'

He studied her for a moment. 'You don't know?'

'How can I know exactly?'

'That's my point. How I suppose to *know* if I'm happy? What's wrong with you, anyway?'

'Maybe it's the wedding. I feel like I'm losing my mind.'

'Maybe you are. You gettin' married to that musician fellow. That's a sure sign.'

✳

She was not losing her mind. She was losing her imagination.

She sat by the pool in the afternoons and often found herself not reading the book in her hands, but staring into the blue water, trying to picture herself married to Mark. There were several pictures, not many and not very different. Something felt wrong.

Mark had another girlfriend. His friends knew, and they knew that Jean wasn't supposed to find out. Long before his engagement to Jean he had started being unfaithful to her. Mostly one-night stands. Then he met Amina in Montego Bay. After a few months, he began paying the rent on her apartment.

He loved Jean and took pride in her calm, sensible nature. He often told people: 'Jean is different. She not no ordinary kind of girl, you know.' She was not the kind of woman who would ever let a man down or embarrass him in front of people. She would make a wonderful mother and see that he had a nice, comfortable home where he could relax and entertain his friends. She would be there whenever he needed her; his own. These were the thoughts of Jean that warmed his heart.

Amina was prettier than Jean and more fun. Everybody looked at her when she walked into a room. The women got nervous; the men couldn't peel their eyes off her. Something about her skin and the way she moved suggested exciting sex. It flattered him when people saw them together and knew he was the man she slept with. The guys in the band liked her. Everybody liked her.

Amina knew about Jean, and there had been fights, which had ended in passionate lovemaking and expensive presents. They spent so much time having sex — he barely had to look at her and he would get an erection — and with such urgency that half the time they couldn't be bothered with contraceptives. Once, she thought she was pregnant, and he realized that if she was, he really wouldn't mind. In fact, it would please him. He daydreamed about keeping her as his woman, the way his father kept Gloria, and their outside child in the country, and his married brother, Peter, regularly visited Lorraine in Miami.

Lorraine had been his brother's high school girlfriend. The Silveras had disapproved of her. She was not from the right kind of family; her father worked as an auto mechanic at a gas station, and she was dark-skinned. Mark remembered the night – it was shortly after his brother broke off with Lorraine – when his father took all five of his sons to the Red Parrot Hotel bar, a place frequented by high-class prostitutes and gigolos. The oldest of Val Silvera's sons was twenty-two; the youngest, Mark, was fifteen. After a couple of rounds of rum, Val told his boys: 'There's a kind a girl a man mus' marry. An' a kind a girl a man can love like crazy but mus' never marry. Jus' mek sure you keep them both happy.'

This was where Mark went wrong. Maybe it was inherent sloppiness. Or maybe, in some deep part of himself, he wanted Jean to find out, needing to know before he tied himself to her for life: How far could he go? How much badness would she take from him?

It was August and the weekend of his birthday. Jean expected him to return to Kingston. But Friday came and went without her hearing from him. She called his mother, who said she didn't know where he was. Jean was so certain he would arrive Saturday night to celebrate with her that she got dressed up and waited for him. Monica saw her waiting in the living room as she left for a concert, and saw her still waiting when she returned.

'Him don't call?'

Jean shook her head.

'There's probably a good reason. Go to bed. Don't sit here all distress'.'

He finally called Sunday afternoon. He was still in Montego Bay and sounded sleepy.

'The guys had a little surprise for me here. I meant to call, but you know how it go. I smoked some weed and it knocked me out. I mek it up to you, darlin'.'

'When you coming back to Kingston?' she said, hurt, but not wanting it to be heard in her voice.

He yawned. 'What?'

She hated repeating the question; it made her seem needy.

'I don't know — a couple days.'

Later, she was distracted from her worries by a surprise: a telephone call from Lana. She had completed her treatment in Florida and was back in Jamaica; she had found an apartment in Paul's building — in fact, right next door. She was with Paul at that very moment and wanted Jean to come over.

They sat in Paul's apartment because Lana still didn't have any furniture. Lana looked vibrant. Her hair was in a girlish ponytail and she had gained back some weight. Most of all, Jean could tell that her sister felt well.

'I'm glad you'll be here for the wedding.'

'I wouldn't miss your wedding, Dolly. Lemme see the ring.'

'Look, if you two women goin' talk' bout weddin' an' ting, I gone.'

'He bad, eh?' Lana said to Jean, and smiled flirtatiously at Paul.

In that instant, Jean felt as if the floor had suddenly disappeared under her. It was something about the way Lana spoke to Paul, the way she sat there as pretty as ever, and the teasing way Paul smiled back at her. A sickening thought darted through Jean's mind — that Lana and Paul were going to have a love affair. She was so disturbed that she couldn't look at either of them. She wanted to leave. It suddenly seemed too plausible, that Paul would like Lana in that way.

'We goin' Port Royal, you want to come?' Lana asked Jean.

'Yes. Come with us,' Paul entreated her.

'No. Not tonight. You go on.' She got up.

She pictured them sitting by the water in Port Royal, at the restaurant where she and Paul often went, and it struck her that she was filled with simple, ordinary jealousy. She reminded herself that she would soon be married to Mark.

'You sure you don't want to come?' Paul asked again, and looked at her strangely, maybe because she had been standing for a while but hadn't actually made a move to leave.

She felt miserable around them.

She talked to herself all the way home: So what if Paul and Lana became lovers? What did that have to do with her? As she waited at a traffic light she looked at her diamond ring. She told herself what a pretty thing it was and how good it would be to get married.

She sat by the pool. *A Room with a View* lay on her lap, but she wasn't reading. It was the end of the week and Mark still hadn't returned. She might have asked herself what point there was in having a fiancé, in getting married, if she was always to feel lonely and miserable. But she didn't ask, because she was used to feeling alone. She opened the book again, began reading, and stopped. Her eyes drifted to the pool's sun-spangled surface through the shallows to its concrete floor.

She knew she should not be marrying Mark. Everything seemed to be telling her not to: her jealousy at seeing something so alive between Paul and Lana; even the book she was reading seemed to repeat to her what she already knew. It was not knowledge exactly, it was a sensation, a wordless brooding in her. She had been with Mark for five years. If she didn't marry him, then what? She couldn't imagine. That was the problem. She couldn't imagine.

Once she had imagined other worlds, places with different palettes, different climates, even different passions. She had been rich with dream sounds and dream sights, day and night. But these things made her feel out of place with Mark and his friends. Dreams, poems, spectacular landscapes, these things that she could happily contemplate by herself for hours, made her quiet and odd.

'Mind you end up a dry-up ole spinster in a house full a books,' Mark had said to her once.

It stung badly, and she never forgot it. She told herself that getting married, living in her own house, and having children would make her feel better. She would see herself differently then, as womanly, not girlish, and would not feel as if she were perpetually waiting, waiting.

Irene called from the kitchen window, 'Miss Jean, telephone. Is Miss Faye.'

Faye was crying. Had Jean heard? Something dreadful had happened. She wanted Jean to come over right away.

Jean asked Irene if she had heard anything on the radio. Irene said yes, and it was terrible; she didn't know how to describe such wickedness.

'Wha' politics ha' fe do wid ole people? Is wicked dem wicked.'

She handed Jean the morning newspaper.

A home for elderly women had been firebombed. One hundred and fifty-seven women had been killed. A few who had managed to get out of the burning building had been shot down. Each party accused the other: The PNP insisted this was another deliberate effort to destabilize the government; the JLP said the PNP were heartless socialists who did not care about the people.

There were women in that building older than the century: legendary singers, beloved teachers, ancient prostitutes, the daughters of slaves.

Irene grated a coconut vigorously as she talked: 'Dem shoot down ole people who too ole fe walk. When God goin' stop dis wickedness?'

'I never thought Jamaicans could be so cruel,' Faye said. 'I feel like it's becoming another country.'

'It is.'

'I could kill them, Jean. Line them up against a wall and shoot them.'

'Who?'

'Somebody gave those people the matches and the guns.'

Yes, Jean thought. PNP, JLP, CIA, somebody.

'I didn't know any of those women, but, Lord God, they were here long before Independence, long before—'

She stopped, confounded, then began again: 'I mean, they were at the end of their lives, in their own country. Old and poor. What gunmen want from them? They didn't have anything. All they had was a little room so they wouldn't have to die in the streets. I know, you see – I know—' Her voice became strangled, cut off, and her eyes welled up.

Jean embraced her, 'Hush, don't—'

'Most of them couldn't walk. I know – what it feels like to be locked up inside you own body, unable to protect—' She stopped, and her voice became a single wailing note: 'They didn't have anything but the little brightness left in their minds, and they took even that from them.'

'Oh, Faye.'

For years, Faye had been full of talk about class structure and revolution. Her talk had been hot, her meanings cold. This atrocity had touched an old wound. It was the bitter help-lessness, Jean thought, remembering when Faye could not walk or stand up without crutches. She was feeling for those old people, yes, but Faye was also feeling again for herself. Here was a new helplessness: a brutal tide that couldn't be stopped, and she was all mixed up in it. She had talked of the necessity for change even if it meant violence; she had believed her own words.

'Oh, God, those poor women, those poor old women . . .' She rocked back and forth, crying.

'I know,' Jean said. 'I know.' Remember this feeling, Faye, remember it's a human hurt that hurts you, not statistics of illiteracy, poor housing, poor health care, but a human hurt.

They went to the river and sat with their feet in the water.

'Man, I remember when we used to come here all the time,' Faye said. 'Not a worry in the world.'

'It seemed safe then.'

'It *was* safe.' She looked profoundly sad. 'You know, my mother's really leaving. Suppose I'm wrong, Jean, about this country, about the PNP, the JLP, everything?'

'Wrong about everything?'

'Who knows? Not even Marx really knew.'

'Maybe it's not so important to figure out who's right and who's wrong; it's what you do, what you keep doing even when the worst is happening.'

'I think that's true. Hey, look.' Faye pointed up the hill. 'We haven't seen that in a long time.'

They watched quietly. The tree that they used to call the evening tree was covered with white blossoms. For a moment neither of them breathed, as though they were afraid the thing that used to happen, would not happen. But all at once, the blossoms rose, flapping, and flew away: a flock of white birds. It happened every day a little before sunset, that tree and those resting birds.

*

Jean called Mark's mother to find out whether she had heard from him. She thought she detected a certain malicious delight in his mother's voice.

'What? He don't call you yet? Poor ting. Hold on, lemme ask Maureen if she knows.'

Maureen was Mark's sister. Jean heard her saying something to her mother in the background, then heard Mark's mother say: 'Come, talk to Jean.'

Maureen had no particular reason for disliking Jean; she just did. She was the spiteful, obnoxious only daughter in a family of six children.

Maureen said: 'I think he's in Mo' Bay. Did you try reaching him at Amina's?'

Amina's? The way Maureen said the name, it sounded like a restaurant or bar.

'What's Amina's?'

'Not what. *Who*. Lemme give you her number.'

Mark returned to Kingston to explain things: Yes, he had been involved with Amina, but it was not serious. It was just sex.

'Just sex?'

'Lemme try to explain—'

'Just sex?' Jean repeated, raising her voice.

'I'm a man!' he shouted, as if he were the ill-used one, the one in need of sympathy.

'Go. Get out of my house.'

'Jean, Jeanie, come now. Don't talk that way. We gettin' married in a coupla months.'

'We're not.'

'Look here, Jean—' He hadn't expected to have to plead like this; she wasn't behaving like the Jean he knew. 'I know how you feel. Sit down, let's talk about this—'

'You know how I feel?'

'Chu! I tryin' to reason with you, but I see you don't want to listen. Call me later, after you calm down.'

The only call she made was to the people printing the wedding invitations, asking them to send cancellation notes instead.

Mark had expected anger and tears, but he'd never believed she would call off their whole future together because of something like this. 'I thought the girl had sense,' he told his friends. Didn't she realize that Amina wasn't a threat?

He called on her birthday: 'Jean, darlin'—'

She hung up on him.

Her behavior shocked him; it was a blow to his idea of himself as a loving person. He complained to all his friends, and even to Jean's friends. He had long conversations with Monica, begging her to 'talk sense into Jean.'

It was not courage that fueled Jean, it was fear: fear of losing this opportunity to change her mind about something that had been feeling like a catastrophic mistake. If she stayed with him there would always be a layer of humiliation, no matter what. Because more than anything else, Mark's betrayal was humiliating. She kept having visions of him having sex with Amina, and it was like being right there in the room with them while they mocked her. One day she came across one of his T-shirts; it smelled like him and she cried. This lingering odor with its hint of sex reminded her of his desire for another woman. She felt as if she had been branded 'unsexual.'

But she would not brood. She fought off humiliation by being unusually energetic. She took an advanced translation course at the university and went back to work on Don Alejandro's journal, determined to finish and publish it.

She changed jobs. She was chosen for an important government position: personal assistant to the minister of national security, in charge of Cuban-Jamaican security. There had long been confrontations and infractions between Jamaican and Cuban fishermen and their respective coast guards. But more important, with the increasing friendship between the two countries, the government was, as the minister put it, 'reconsidering its strategic relations with its closest neighbor.' Jean was required to get police clearance, undergo a lie detector test, and take an oath of confidentiality.

Monica was not happy about her working for Manley's government. She had been so hopeful about his losing the election, what with the violence and inflation and the Americans against him. But what was done was done, and she could see how having a daughter in the government might be useful. She was impressed with how well the job paid. Always looking ahead, Monica told Jean to put some of her savings in an offshore bank.

'The way this government runnin' things, Jamaican money not going to be worth anything.'

Jean couldn't; it was illegal. 'Don't you understand? I work for the minister of *security*.'

'You sound like Faye. Awright, jus' gimme you paycheck now an' then. I'll take care of it. What you don't know won't hurt you.'

About Mark and the affair with Amina, she asked Jean, 'So you couldn't just look the other way? You throw 'way a future with a good man over a thing like that?'

'I wouldn't call marriage to a man like that a "future," Monica.'

'Oh, really?'

Jean didn't feel like quarreling.

Jean heard Monica talking to Errol later that day on the veranda: 'She not no fool, my daughter. She know de man wutless. She fling 'way him ring an' run him ass outa de house.'

*

Lana, hearing about the breakup, took Jean out for lunch.

'You awright, Dolly?'

'Yes,' Jean said, much too quickly.

'You'll meet somebody else soon. I'll pray for you.'

Lana was no longer a Jehovah's Witness. She had been attending an Anglican church, and this meant, for one thing, that she could dress the way she used to. Her arms were covered with the bangles Deepa had given her, and she wore a tight red T-shirt, shorts, and high-heeled sandals. Jean felt dowdy in comparison. She hated Mark at that moment: He had stolen her sexiness.

'You think I did the right thing? I mean, Mark loved me—'

'Did you love him?' Lana continued: 'You have to love somebody more than you love you self to put up with that kind a behavior. You think Amina was the only one?'

'I don't know—' She felt she was going to cry.

'Oh, Dolly. He's a man, not a god. You did the right thing – mek him gone. But you coulda keep the diamond ring, you know.'

They both laughed.

'You going out with anybody now?' Jean asked.

Lana's eyes danced about. 'Not really. This one, that one.'

Jean was relieved. She would not have been able to bear it, especially now, if Lana had told her she was involved with Paul. Thank God, there was still Paul; she did not reflect on what this meant. She simply found comfort in the knowledge that their closeness was intact, that he was there for her as usual, a safe place to land.

She called him one day, lonely; it was the end of October, near the time of the canceled wedding: 'I need cheering up.'

'You still down 'bout that musician fellow?'

'Down but not out.'

He laughed.

'So, what's happening?' she asked. 'Long time I don't see you.'

He seemed reticent. She remembered that he had been having problems with the farm, something to do with government taxes.

'Nothing, nothing much.' He paused. 'So you really broke off you engagement to the guitar man, eh?'

'Why does everybody have such a hard time believing it? You would think I was engaged to Prince Charles.'

'You did the right thing, Jean.'

'Let's go to the beach.'

'I can't today.'

'What about tomorrow? Can I go to the farm with you?'

'That's – that's a possibility.'

'How's Lana? She fixed up her apartment yet?'

He paused. 'You haven't talked to her?'

'About a month ago.'

Again, the reticence: 'She's awright,' he said slowly.

She could sense that he wanted to say something else.

'What?' she said.

'Nothing. Jus' – it's really a good thing – I mean – that you got out of that situation. I didn't too much like what's-his-name, you know.'

She started laughing.

'Maybe you didn't know that?' he continued, deadpan.

She couldn't speak for laughing, and tears ran down her cheeks.

She was alone in the house that weekend, the weekend when, had things turned out differently, she would have begun her married life. In solitude, her anxiety about the future sharpened. She remembered Mark's smarting words about her ending up an old spinster in a room full of books: 'Dried-up,' he had predicted.

Suppose life ended up offering her much less than it did other women?

There was Paul — at least there was Paul. They would drive to the country on Sunday. She wasn't able to reach him by phone on Saturday and began to worry. What if something came up and they couldn't go? She wanted to be assured of this one small activity; she desperately needed something to look forward to.

She lay awake most of the night. Why was it always worse, lying awake at night, the worry, any worry? She kept throwing off and pulling back the light blanket around her. It did not feel like a light covering; it felt like doom. In the last few years with Mark, she had not spent much time with Paul, and she regretted it. She had a sudden, irrational fear that she was in danger of losing him. If Paul should slip away from her for some reason . . .

The next morning he called as he had promised. 'Pick you up at two,' he said.

His phone call revived her. She watered the garden, pruned the bougainvillea hedge, and uprooted a yellow allamanda that Paul had admired; she would replant it at his farmhouse. She washed her hair and sprayed perfume on herself and painted her nails. Paul noticed things like that; he often commented on the beautiful hands of women.

A little before two she sat on the veranda waiting for him. Minutes later she moved down to the veranda steps even though there was no shade there. If he did not arrive soon, she would go down to the gate. She wanted to put the big, empty house behind her.

This waiting reminded her of a day when she had waited for her father to pick her up from school. She must have been in kindergarten, because she was so tiny. Sitting on a bench in the playground, she was aware of the gap between her feet and the ground. She had been told that she would grow, that someday, when she sat on this and other benches, her feet would touch the ground.

'See how the sun makes the flowers grow. In time . . .' her father had assured her. 'In time . . .'

So she had sat there and waited, reassuring herself with her father's words and with the thought that time and benevolent sunshine were on her side, working on her and for her.

One by one, all the other children were picked up by their parents.

When it got dark, she began to cry. Night seemed to her an enemy. It grew darker, and her crying grew louder. One of the teachers who lived at the school found her.

Something had come up at the newspaper that afternoon, and Roy had asked Monica to pick Jean up from school. Monica suddenly remembered a cocktail party she had to attend, so she had asked Errol; Errol had forgotten.

When Roy arrived at the school, he swept Jean up in his arms and clutched her so tightly that she believed she had indeed come close to being devoured by the night.

And now, sitting alone on the veranda steps, she found herself once again fretting that time was not on her side but on the side of the things she feared: sudden violence, the loss of people she loved, death.

I surrendered to that brute unhappiness which had always been at hand.

She felt savage with loneliness.

She waited for Paul.

Part Three

40

There are helicopters at Walker's Wood.

Jean smells smoke. 'What's happening?' she asks Paul.

This roadblock is different, noisier, busier. The soldiers wear combat helmets.

'What's happening, Major?' Paul asks a soldier who comes over.

'Disturbance up ahead.' He looks at Paul with more than official curiosity, and then he smiles. 'Paul Grant? Calabar Cricket Team? You remember me? Sandham Spence.'

'Sandy, what the hell! You turn soldier boy.'

Major Spence turns to Jean. 'This man was one hell of a batter. Man, I still remember the time you demolish Wolmers. You still play?'

'Likkle bit here an' there. Good to see you, man. Hey, Sandy, wha' happenin' here, exactly?'

'Shoot-out up de road.'

'What!'

''Bout eight people dead.'

'What a hell of a ting.'

An ambulance appears, unhurried and without sirens. Major Spence goes over and talks to the driver and sends him through the roadblock. He comes back to Paul.

'Yeah, dem shoot up a PNP man house an' set fire to it.'

Jean sees the black smoke farther up the road and remembers

the fires yesterday in Kingston. *Look like dem wan' bun down de whole country.*

'You can get us through, Sandy?'

'Yeah, man.' Sandy shouts to the soldier at the checkpoint. 'Awright, Paul.' He shakes Paul's hand vigorously.

Paul leans closer to Sandy, his tone more confidential: 'Wha' really happening here, Sandy? We in a war or what?'

Sandy shrugs. 'Right now, I jus' prepare fe anyting.'

Then, wanting to be helpful to his old teammate, he pauses and considers how to put this to Paul. 'You goin' north coast?'

It sounds more like a warning than a question.

'Yeah.'

'Which part?'

'Lucea,' he lies for Jean's sake. Lucea is about ten miles from where she will catch the plane. 'Anyting goin' on up there?'

'Me cyan say exactly wha' g'wan. But if I was you, bredda, I would jus' tek it easy an' stay a me yard de nex' few days.'

'Awright, Sandy. Tek care.' He doesn't seem perturbed by Sandy's warning, and this reassures Jean. She looks at his capable hands on the wheel, the crisp white shirt he put on for the funeral, and thinks, Nothing bad can happen to me when I am with him. He drives on, past the soldiers, the helicopters, and the burning house.

41

He had come for her, as he promised, that Sunday afternoon, the day of her canceled wedding, when she was frightened by her loneliness. And it struck her, as they drove to the farm with the yellow allamanda she had brought to plant for him, that he had never let her down.

How good she felt. How wonderful he was to look at. She glanced at him, then glanced away, knowing well the mouth that always seemed about to smile at some irony, the graceful body, graceful hands. *How many times you drive with me in this truck?* She remembered going to see him play in a cricket match when she was a girl, how the crowd cheered when his turn came to bat. It was like having an older brother who was a matinee idol. She had been his favorite little person in the world. And he still cared for her. She felt saved from the worst mistake of her life, not the mistake of marrying Mark, but of neglecting Paul.

And then, that night on the farm, he told her: 'Me and Lana — we've been going around together.'

She had lost him.

'I've been wanting to tell you, but you were all caught up in wedding plans and all that.'

She tried not to let her disappointment show.

He looked at her, as he often did, to see if she under-stood something important but unspoken between them. *How many times? You don't know?* He said, 'It really seemed like it was going to happen – that you were going to get married.'

'I was,' she said weakly.

'It's strange.' He got up and began tidying things, stacking magazines, putting things back in their right places, anything to avoid looking at her. 'You know somebody all these years, grow up with them, and suddenly they look different.'

'Yes.'

He looked at her. 'You understand?'

'Yes, of course.'

Next morning she planted the allamanda. She patted the dirt firmly around the root. Everything seemed the same, the pale yellow farmhouse and its familiar smells of citrus and all-day cooking, and yet – Lana and Paul: It was momentous; it changed everything. She had always taken for granted her special place on this farm. Paul's other girlfriends had never mattered to her. She couldn't see Lana in the same light as those others.

A few days later, back in Kingston, she went with Lana and the baby to Hope Gardens.

'I know he still go out with other women,' Lana said. 'We tryin' not to get too serious yet. Jean, guess what? I stopped taking my medicine, and I'm feeling really good.'

They sat near the duck pond.

'I tell you, it's like night and day, how I felt las' year an' how I feel now.'

She tried to be happy for Lana, but there was a bitterness in her concerning Paul that made it hard to feel truly happy, and she was sorry that it was so.

Lana went on in a softened tone, 'You know when you called me that day in Florida, something jus' break open, like rain outa the sky an' wash me clean-clean. Everyting start to get better after that.'

It had felt that way for Jean too, the day she had called Lana at the treatment center in Florida. It was Lana's birthday, and Jean had not spoken to her since she had gone away. Nobody had spoken to Lana for a long time — not even Aunt Gwen, who was looking after Claude. The desire to simply call and say 'Happy birthday' made her realize, shamefully, how completely they had all cut Lana off. She remembered how long it had taken Lana to get to the phone and, when she finally did, how far away she had sounded.

'Hello?' Lana's voice had been anxious.

'Lana, happy birthday.'

'Dolly, is that you? Where are you?' she had asked as though she hoped that not only Jean's voice but Jean herself might materialize before her. There was such sweetness in her voice, in spite of the note of deprivation, Jean felt bathed in remorse and forgiveness at once.

She felt it again. What a wretch she was not to want every happiness for Lana.

'I'm not crazy, Jean,' Lana said, and she swooped Claude up in her arms and kissed him.

He struggled to get down, shouting 'Ants, ants!' then ran off with a stick to terrorize more insects.

'It's a physical thing, you know, something to do with the chemicals in my brain.'

'Then maybe you shouldn't stop taking the medicine.'

'*Faith* is my medicine now.' She paused and looked far away. 'I don't trouble myself about Monica anymore. I'm at peace with that, and I hope she finds her peace, too.' She called to Claude, 'Come away from the water!' Then she turned again to Jean: 'I takin' things slow an' easy with Paul.'

Jean wondered what that meant; slow an' easy was not in Lana's nature.

'You know,' she went on, 'I think that man is Jesus' answer to my prayers.'

Jean was about to say something like Don't put all your hopes in one person. But Lana was talking in her old exuberant way that would not allow interruption.

'I don't mean he tek God' place.' Her eyes swept over Claude, over the trees and pond, and fixed for a moment on her red nail polish, as if this, too, were among God's many blessings. She smiled. 'Admit it, Jean, the man is an angel.'

42

'I didn't love her,' Paul says, 'but I cared about her. And I would have taken care of her.'

They're in St Ann. If a country has a heart, she thinks, then Jamaica's is here – verdure in excelsis. There's enough green – rivers, waterfalls, trees, rainfall – for the entire country.

Paul has talked to her before about love, about waiting for love and not having yet loved. This love he speaks of seems as alien yet recognizable as snow on foreign Christmas cards. He is able to both imagine and dismiss it.

Now and then she spots red poincianas, hidden in the overwhelming green of the forest.

Love entered this part of the world centuries ago, not as truth, but as word. In the Great House, in the schoolhouse, and in church; by rape, and rod, and hymn.

Who would tell us that we loved before? Jean wonders. Who would remind us that we loved once in our own tongue, in our own way, long before we crossed the water, we survivors, that there was love once originating in ourselves?

Paul, she realizes, is a man of few words; he says what he means. He doesn't mean that Lana was too crazy to love, or that he's incapable of love. But what is it exactly that he expected to feel and did not feel with Lana?

She remembers Daphne once in an ugly mood telling her: We Sterns have bad luck with love, Jean. Look at us, we mad, we drunk, we lonely. You know 'bout my grandfather, Daniel, and his wife. You know the story. Sometimes I think heartbreak is our inheritance.

43

Daniel Stern
1848–1929

She collected crickets, and kept them in wooden containers made especially for this purpose, with narrow openings between the wooden slats for air. They were kept on the back veranda, where she had potted many lush flowers and trees. I never knew the names of those plants. They were so plentiful that birds constantly flew in and out of the house, and they attracted a good number of lizards, bees, and other troublesome creatures. Sometimes she would take the crickets out one at a time and watch them move among the leaves. When one died she would bury it at sea so that it would return to her as a seashell.

The sound of the waves agitated her at night, only at night. They were messages from men who were trying to seduce her. She accused the boys who worked for us of being fresh with her. I would get rid of one and she would accuse the next one of forwardness.

Adam and Eve lived in the empty house across the road; no one else could see them because they lived there in the form of scorpions. They forced her to do terrible things. Eileen was mad.

If my words appear thick and vague, and if the details of my story seem like distant lights in a northern fog, it is because I have done my best, first to understand, and then to forget. I find it hard to speak about the things she did in the eight years that I remained with her. I was forty-seven when I married her, not a young man by any means, and those eight years bent and grayed me like an old man.

I had never asked that happiness or beauty be part of my life. We were people of hard work and sacrifice, the Sterns, even before we came to the island. That was why the trick they played on us was all the more unforgivable.

My parents had not expected an easy life here. They were not adventurers, searching for the promised wealth of the New World. They had paid for fifty acres of land that no one else wanted, land that they were willing to break their backs working. They traveled for eight weeks on the Cape Verde, a Portuguese freighter, with one hundred and twenty other German families. In Germany they had worked for a pittance, on someone else's land. To finally have land of their own and to make a new start — that was all they asked for. They were prepared to face all the difficulties of the new climate, strange new people, and uncultivated land.

When they reached the island, no one had heard of 'Elsnore Field,' the property they had paid for, and no one had heard of Clegg & Johnson, the Jamaican company that had sold them the land and arranged their passage. About half of the hundred and twenty families remained in Kingston, their hopes shattered, until they were able to arrange for return passage, while the other half made their way into the countryside where the so-called German-towns are now.

Beguiled, not by riches, but by a bone held out to them: That was the story of my parents. They had traveled that far to once again live and work on someone else's land. They became squatters on a farm in St Elizabeth, and saved until they had money for a farm of their own in a place they called West Lacovia. Do you know how hard it is to live by farming yams on someone else's land? Do you understand then, how they must have sacrificed to save enough for their own farm? They were old people and worn out by the time they achieved their goal.

I left home when I was eighteen. For many years I managed a small inn near Christiana. Then I bought property and built an inn of my own at Treasure Beach. As I said, happiness was not something I was brought up to expect. Hard work and keeping out of debt were the simple aspirations of my family.

Eileen O'Meally was beautiful, with a beauty that wasn't of this earth. I used to see her riding by the sea up at Parotee Point. I would raise my hat and she would smile. I didn't have the courage to introduce myself to her. It was she who first spoke to me, and I was so glad to finally make her acquaintance that her forwardness seemed charming. We met frequently after that at her sister's home, where she lived. She was the oldest of four sisters, all of whom were already married. She told me that she had broken off an engagement to an Englishman some years before. This was one of the many lies I was told.

I was enchanted, but more than that, I loved her. I loved her for the opportunity she gave me to love. I had not imagined the word 'love' ever passing through my lips.

She was pale, with long black hair. She told me that her father was an Irishman who had been a plantation overseer, and that her mother was a white Creole. This turned out to be only half true. My family, like most of the German families, married among their own. Both my brothers married cousins, the children of my mother's brother. For many years I had been urged by my family to court my widowed aunt, some ten years older than myself. I was beginning to yield to their wishes and pursue that lady when I met Eileen.

She was not only dazzling to look at, but to listen to. Her voice was sweet, yes, sweet; it was as pleasant as a song when she spoke, and sweet because of the things she said. How she went on about things — fireflies, birds, and the stars, which she called 'God's lacy things.' Our bedroom balcony faced the sea, and she insisted some nights that we keep the doors open for the sea breezes (before the waves started to agitate her with their love messages). I had never thought about things like sea breezes or the blueness of the water or the sky. And she sang, too, so prettily. The sweetest voice!

The crickets, the sea messages, those were early, disturbing signs, but harmless. The accusations against my male servants were wearisome. But the public humiliation of myself and my son, Jedaiah, I could not bear. Humiliation is a violence done, not to the body, but to the soul.

A year after Jedaiah was born, I began to discover unpleasant things about her. She was not white. I found this out when I met her cousin, a Colored gentleman, quite dark-skinned, by the name of Mr Solomon, who owned a rum shop in Balaclava. Do not mistake me, I felt no dislike toward Colored people.

Indeed, what troubled me was her assiduous lying, less about this than about the other matters. Mr Solomon also informed me of the truth about her English fiancé; it was he who had broken the engagement and fled from Eileen. He stopped short of giving me a list of her lovers. Mr Solomon was an old ginal himself and no doubt wanted to make trouble. Jamaica, I am sorry to say, is an Anansi country — a monstrous spider skilled in trickery of every kind.

Eileen began to seem more and more like a stranger to me, and I must admit that, confused, I somewhat withdrew from her. That was when she started her lewd behavior. She did not even try to hide her infidelities. She would leave the inn at late hours of the night with different men. Shame, shame, shame for her and for me. People talked about it for miles around; they mocked us both. I was not a man, but a 'nanny-goat.' Eileen was simply 'Mr Stern mad wife.'

Among the men she went with was a doctor from Westmoreland, Dr Darling. She developed a wild feeling for him which he did not return. Oh, he made love to my wife, I'm sure, but had no ongoing interest in her. When the months went by and he did not come back to Treasure Beach, her passion for him grew out of proportion. You see, she was pregnant with his child. When he found out, he made her take medicine to kill it in her womb.

It was shortly after the death of that child that she lost what was left of her sanity. I had been away for two weeks in Kingston. On my return, the inn was empty and in a shambles; the doors were wide open; furniture and other articles had been stolen. Most of the servants had gone. Outside I was greeted in a peculiar manner by the garden boy and the maid. They laughed insolently when I inquired why the gate had been left open. Inside I was relieved to find Dorcita, our cook. She was a sensible woman who had worked for me in Christiana.

'Masta Stern, sah, me glad you come 'ome. Is a shame before God what 'appenin' in dis place.'

'Where is my wife?'

'She on de back veranda wid Masta Jed. She draw gun 'pon me sir when I try fe tek de boy fe feed him.'

I saw through the back window that Eileen had Jedaiah on the chaise with her; they were both stark naked. She held him at her breast and appeared to be suckling him or trying to do so; Jedaiah was by then three years old.

'I shame fe you sir,' Dorcita said. 'Every man, woman, an' chile, come tru de yard fe look 'pon naked white lady.'

I hurried onto the back veranda, and there I was stopped short by sounds which at first I took to be a croaking lizard. And then I saw them, hundreds of them, the crickets, all over the place. These creatures, with their noise, and infernal hopping, seemed the only beings alive there. They were even on the lifeless bodies of mother and son.

But they were not dead. Shame, that I wished they were. The boy was in shock. Only God knows what she did and said to him. He was ice cold and looked like a zombie. I took him from her and gave him to Dorcita and asked her to fetch the doctor. Then I went back to Eileen.

She lay with her eyes closed, in a deep, exhausted slumber, snoring. Her crickets were crawling from her body onto my hands as I shook her. She laughed when she saw me and began to pull me to her. I asked her what she had done to our boy. She answered with the vilest words. I lost control of myself and beat her; I beat her until she stopped screaming. How I managed not to kill her, I do not know.

Dr Darling came. Considering the atrocious circumstances, we behaved decently toward each other. He acted as though he had not ever been Eileen's lover, and I acted as though I believed that to be so. He felt her case was beyond hope and recommended the asylum in Kingston. And that is where she remained until she died — strangled, I was told, by another lunatic — a few years later.

I left Jedaiah with my brother's family and went to England, where I married a decent woman.

It is not right to speak against a place, an entire people, but I must say: Jamaica is a small, malevolent place. If you have promise of any kind in you, leave before that promise is corrupted. Find the strength to hate what is hateful. The poison of that place, like its beauty, is uncontainable. I saw the poison even in my son.

Perhaps I should reproach myself for these words, poison and hate. I tried not to hate, even in the bonfires of my humiliation. For one thing, I remained, despite everything, grateful for that opportunity she gave me: to love. But there was more to it than that. I kept hoping that if I refrained from hate she would be moved to restore herself and that opportunity to me. I sought foolish shelter in an old-country idea of barter: my tolerance, which I deemed a rare commodity in Jamaica, in exchange for the resumption of her early chaste fervor toward me. I longed for this, and while I could long, I did not hate.

But I was made brutally to understand that her love would never return to my honest house, that such love always flows down to places obscure and inaccessible to him whose life it first made green. She taught me that to have love was to lose it, to others known and unknown. I thought this the careless and regardless way of her love, the way of a pitiable lunatic. I did not understand then what I do now: that the island is peculiarly fitted to teach that Eileen's love is love itself. The vegetation, the rivers, the people do give fruitfully of themselves to civilized commerce with farms, vistas, loyalty, and marriage. But nothing will stay still; rivulets seek new beds, tendrils new hosts, spouses new rooms, new actions. Love is not betrayed but betrayal.

England brought me peace. I lived in the city. No garden, no songbirds, no bright, tropical deceptions. I walked to work every day across the iron bridges, past the shops and factories, and in time my worn spirit was consoled by these new sights. I was given a second chance here, in the smoke and rattle of London. England is not without beauty, as the poets will tell you, but the beauty is circumspect and does not betray men. Betrayal is death. Do not hesitate. Run through the burning gates.

44

'I didn't love her,' Paul says again. It's not a confession, but she feels that it should be.

She hears an older, sadder voice competing with his, and remembers, like words from a dream, *Learn to hate what is hateful.*

She could lose her way trying to understand Paul, following him back to that little-known region of his heart, and she can't risk that. She needs to keep moving. But she can't help thinking that some inscrutable meanness of their history – her history, Lana's, Paul's, missionaries', conquistadores', and slaves' – lies in this fallen notion of love, in some error that can be traced back to those first untranslatable hours in the New World.

I had not imagined the word 'love' ever passing through my lips.

Was love, like spring and fall, something that stopped at the Tropic of Cancer? An attribute, like good English, beyond them?

'What do you mean, Paul?'

'I mean – I didn't want to *promise* Lana anything.'

Why not? Why not promise, if a promise is the only thing on the other side of a nightmare, as it was for Lana, as it is for her?

Where would she be now if nothing had been promised?

'It's still winter here, love. I'll get you some warm clothes.' She remembers Alan's voice, over the phone, brimming with promise. Winter. She's seen photographs of friends who migrated north, in wool hats, coats, and big boots, unrecognizable except for their dark faces. She has an idea of snow from the books she's read: pure and peaceful when it first falls. He says the light is different there. What does that mean? In Manhattan you don't see the stars. If he were to stop loving her, how would she manage in such a cold, starless place? 'You'll be happy,' he told her. 'You'll be safe.'

45

'Don't you think it's time we put grillwork 'round the veranda?' Jean asked Monica one morning after a fretful night. 'I have a bad feeling.'

'Chu! You an' you bad feeling-dem.'

'You goin' wait till something happens to us?'

'You know what your problem is? You read too many depressin' books.'

Jean looked steadily at her mother.

'Awright, awright, I look into the grillwork this week. Everybody wan' prison-up demselves.'

Jean had invited her friend Ines for lunch that day, and so she went to pick her up. Ines was married to the deputy consul at the Peruvian embassy, and though she was older than Jean and had two children, they had quite a lot in common. Both loved gardening, and Ines was a reader, one of the few people Jean could talk to about books.

'It's good to have some time for myself, though I miss the children,' Ines said as they were driving up the hill to Jean's house. Her children were visiting their grandparents in Peru. 'Do you want children?'

'For a start, I'd like a boyfriend.'

Ines smiled. 'I know. This I will keep in mind. Look at those lignum vitaes. Strange trees.'

'You know, the Arawaks used the bark to cure venereal disease.'

'Where are these Arawaks?'

'Dead.'

Ines raised her eyebrows.

Jean laughed, 'Not from VD, and not from the trees.'

Neither of them noticed the car parked by the side of the road, not until it passed them. It was an old gray car, with four scruffy-looking men.

Suddenly it turned and blocked the road.

'What's this?' Ines was more confused than alarmed.

Two men got out of the car and ran toward them.

Jean realized what was happening. She tried to turn around, backing up into the hill, but before she could make the turn there was a man at the window, holding a gun to her head.

'Open de door.'

The men got in the car and ordered Jean to follow the gray car farther up the hill. They came to a vacant lot and were told to get out.

'What's going on?' Ines asked.

The man with the gun cursed Ines.

'She's a foreigner,' Jean said. 'She doesn't understand.'

One of the men – red-looking, as if bauxite had gotten into his skin and hair – raised a ratchet knife to Jean's neck.

'Tek off you necklace,' he ordered Jean. 'An' you watch.'

Jean did as she was told. Her limbs felt limp.

The one with the gun pushed Ines toward the bushes. Ines turned around and looked at Jean, terrified.

'Please—' Jean said to the red-looking man.

'Walk.' He shoved her toward the bushes.

She sprang forward and grabbed Ines's arm. 'Run!' she shouted, and they started down the hill. Ines fell behind and Jean heard her cry out. Jean kept on running. The red-looking man caught up with her. He fell on her and she began screaming.

He brought the knife down to her face and slashed her,

cutting her hands which she held up protectively before her. He slashed her again.

A car came up the hill.

He got up and tried dragging Jean into the bushes with him. She fought him off, screaming, and he ran, leaving her by the side of the road.

'Jean!'

Monica, Irene, and Philbert scrambled out of the car.

'Lord God! Dem cut her!' Irene said.

Philbert went after the man. Jean called out, 'They have Ines! Up the road!'

'Oh, God, Jean, you hand!' Monica bent over her.

'Is it still there?' Jean asked; she couldn't tell – all the blood. She asked again, shouting this time, 'Is my hand still there?'

'Irene, run see if Dr Grant home. Oh, God.' Monica wrapped her scarf around Jean's bloody hand and held it tightly. 'Call police, call ambulance.' She held the cloth against Jean's flesh, trying to stem the blood.

Philbert found Ines by the roadside. She had been hit with a rock, and her head was bleeding. She was dazed but conscious. Paul's father, Dr Grant, came back with Irene and drove them to the hospital. Ines had a minor injury. Jean was rushed into surgery. Her left hand was nearly severed at the wrist.

'This will heal, though you can expect some twinges and weakness over the years,' the doctor said later. 'You probably saved your neck with that hand. You damn lucky.'

'I tell you I sorry I never have me gun,' Monica said later, 'four big men brutalizing two women. That's what this country come to!'

At times, recounting the incident, she grew somber. 'I coulda lost my daughter. Suppose we hadn't come that very instant? Is jus' because I saw Irene an' Philbert down by the shop, an' they ask me to . . .'

The random chain of events that had led to the rescue, the quick decision on Jean's part to run – 'clever girl, because you know, if she went with them into those bushes, we wouldn't have seen her again' – and the viciousness of the men was talked about for weeks.

'And you know the funny thing,' Monica said to Cherry, 'that very morning Jean said how she was having a bad feeling an' asked me to put up grillwork on the veranda.'

'She 'ave sharpenin' powers. I know dis 'bout Jean, from she was a likkle girl. She 'ave – wha' dem call it – six' sense.'

'Yes. She quiet, that girl, but she deep-deep.'

'She awright? She lookin' mawga.'

'She not eatin'.'

'Poor chile, it mus' be draumatic, for her, no?'

'She goin' country fe a few weeks to stay with Mama. Mama will fix her up.'

Jean had now been touched by the epidemic violence. Having seen, up close, the callousness of those men, gave the notorious gunmen a reality and a texture in her mind that they had not had before: the sweat on their faces, the bloodshot eyes, the dirt under their fingernails, their guns, and knives, and clear intent to injure.

She could not think about what might have happened if Monica had not appeared, but it was there, the terrifying might-have-been, like the dark bottom one almost hits in nightmares about falling. Rape had become so prevalent in the island (and horrible stories of gang rape – the girl at the end of the street, the shopkeeper's wife, every day another story of sodomy, burning, tearing women apart; vile, sadistic things that made even policemen cry) it was beginning to seem like a war against women; rape of the nation's women, rich and poor, had become a casual and ubiquitous weapon, like stones in the hands of bad boys.

Strangely, it was her escape, even more than the attack, that left its mark on her, like the thumbprint of God. She had been spared. Why?

New Hope was exactly where she wanted to be. Mary was the most serene person Jean knew. She and her cottage were profoundly soothing: from the cedar smell of the bedroom to Mary's simple, good country cooking: spicy corn fritters, ackee, rice-an'-peas. Fortunately, Mary was a vegetarian, because since the attack, Jean had lost her appetite for meat. Her easy immersion into her grandmother's daily routine made her feel she had wasted part of her life in not having visited for so long.

Mary had a television now and watched it every evening between six and eight, but otherwise the routine was exactly as Jean remembered it. Mary no longer had to work since her children supported her, but her days were fully occupied with cooking, cleaning, and visiting and being visited by her old friends in the district. The girl who helped in the house – whose name was Ena but who was always referred to as 'the girl' – had to be given tasks, grumbled about, forgiven, and taught to do things right. After a couple days, in spite of her injured hand, Jean came under as much gentle scrutiny and discipline as the girl.

'You mean to say you don't know when watermelon ripe? Come, mek me show you.'

Mary had always spoken and moved slowly, but Jean thought she seemed slower than usual.

'You all right, Grandma?'

'Me belly achin'. Everyting me eat mek me feel bad.'

'But you have to eat something.'

'Chu! You the one need fe eat. Look how mawga you get. Jus' mek me up a likkle bush tea fe me.'

It seemed to Jean that bush tea – mint, plantain, cerasse – and sugar were all her grandmother consumed. She loved white, granulated sugar and ate it by the tablespoonful. Also cornmeal dumplings, which, like most country people, she boiled until they were tough enough to bounce off walls.

'No wonder you have bellyache,' Jean said.

'Dumplin' keep you heart strong,' Mary replied.

Nights sank New Hope into oblivion; there was not a light to be seen anywhere. Nothing to do. Jean went to bed early like her grandmother and woke up refreshed at dawn.

The mornings came in stridently, the sun scorching hot almost as soon as it rose. And every morning it rained a little, like a daily 'Our Father.' Sometimes the sun kept shining through this morning shower and then the country people would say, 'The devil an' him wife fightin'.' They said if you conceived when sun and rain were both visible in the sky the child would be bad-tempered.

The village – which was too small and deeply hidden in the countryside to really be called a village – had been settled by newly emancipated slaves in the 1840s. It was a few miles from the main road that ran along the southern coast of the island. There was not even a sign.

About a mile and a half from Mary Darling's cottage was the sea – not the white sand beaches of the touristed north coast, but startling blue water against black sand – and inland, near the cottage, was a river full of crayfish which children caught, boiled with pepper, and sold to travelers along the main road. Jean remembered Lana teaching her how to catch and cook crayfish.

One day Mary gave her an old watch on a chain that had belonged to her mother. It had occurred to Mary that Jean would not be able to wear a wristwatch for some time. Jean

Falkirk's watch was silver and the letters 'J.D.' were engraved on it: Jean Darling. It had been a gift from her husband.

Mary remembered something else. 'You know, I keep meanin' to give you this because I know you like old-time book an' ting.'

It was an old cloth-bound ledger of some kind. The cover, once blue, had turned gray with wear, then crusty after long disuse. The pages were brown with age, and she could see that the ledger had at some point fallen apart and been restitched. She read: 'Single Bible: A Helpful Listing of the Properties and Uses of Tropical Plants, Recorded by a Jamaican Doctor's Wife.'

'She always writin' an' drawin', right up to the day she died.'

'How did she die?'

'Heart attack. Quick. Like Daphne. Strong as a lion, then one day her heartstring jus' pop. You know, she was me bes' friend. I lonely since the day she gone.'

Jean turned to the last page; there was no drawing, just writing:

'Such are my uneasy thoughts as I look toward the Tropic of Capricorn . . .'

'Where is she buried?'

'Blue Fields. The church close down, but they keep the graveyard nice an' clean. Is a pretty place. Walk go see.'

'And she lived here?'

'This was her house. That's her piano there.'

Jean walked the countryside every day, aware now that she was repeating the walks taken by Jean Falkirk, and after her, Mary, Monica, Lana.

At first, she panicked at the sight of any man on her walks, until she realized that no one was a stranger here, that everyone knew Mary Darling. As she passed the same cottages and people every day, her own novelty wore off – 'Miss Mary' grandawta,' they said, as if she had grown up there.

Solitary, but never lonely, in this gentle, neighborly place, she had the chance to reflect.

313

The cuts on her hands still hurt and brought back the day of violence. There would be scars, and, like all scars, they would remind her of her survival. As the doctor said, she was lucky. Something in the attitude of the doctor, the police, and even people she knew felt wrong to her. All the casual talk about survival and recounting of violent details was, to her, as callous as the violence itself ('Dem break ina him house an' tie up him wife an' daughter . . .'; 'Dem line up all de gal-dem in de family an' pick out de youngest . . .'). It revolted her.

Paul had come to see her in the hospital. He sat quietly in the room with her for hours, not needing to say how relieved he was that she was alive, how it would have torn him to pieces to lose her. Then Uncle Errol and some of the Ho Sing boys came with flowers. And stories. First there was the retelling of Jean's assault and lucky escape; then similar stories: 'Remember the time they bruk into that house up Red Hills . . .' And, to her dismay, Paul joined in. She thought of her father; he would have joined in, too. She knew they meant well and that they thought her brave, and this was their way of showing it, but their talk troubled her.

She had always had a daughterly, virginal disposition in relation to the men of this country. At their best, they seemed fatherly; at their worst, predatory. She realized that her feelings were extreme. Her ex-fiance's warning about her becoming a dried-up old spinster burst into her thoughts and felt annoyingly prophetic. She didn't want to be virginal. She wanted to love with ardor, without fear. But the recent brutalities in addition to Mark's betrayal made her recoil. She felt paralyzed, inert. From time to time, faint pangs, mere phantoms of desire, reminded her of that feeling that had been severed as cleanly as a limb. The possibility that she would ever make love to a son of this nation felt more and more remote.

*

Mary liked to have a glass of white rum in the evenings, one hundred and fifty overproof, straight. Rum so strong Jean could smell the vapors clear across the room; the kind of rum country people sometimes used in place of rubbing alcohol.

'You know when I start fe drink white rum? The first day me did ha' fe slaughter cow.'

'How you came to be a cow slaughterer?'

'Heh! That's a long story, too long fe tell one time.'

'You slaughtered them all by yourself?'

'Me one. Blood use to frighten me, you know. Never like to see blood! No sah!'

She closed her eyes and rested a while then looked up suddenly. 'You hear somebody out a de gate?'

'No. Nobody. You were saying how you used to slaughter cows for a living.'

'Yes, fe a living. Me mother she die an' leave me dis house. I did have a roof over me head but no money. Four pickney fe feed. An' no husband.'

'What happened to him?' Daphne had told her, but she wanted to hear it from Mary.

Mary wrinkled her big freckled nose: 'Well, him dead long time an' I don't like speak ill a de dead. But I tell you, him was a wutless, lazy, arrogant son-of-a-bitch. An' a drunkard. An' a liard. Wicked, too.'

'He left you, Granma?'

'He lef' me two times, then I lef' him.'

'An' came here?'

'Came here to me mother house. She died that same year. I didn't have no work. Me friend Drusilla Jack, her uncle used to slaughter cow, an' him sick bad wid art'ritis. Cyan wuk no more. Is him teach me.'

'But what about the blood?'

Mary laughed. 'Blood was de least of it, darlin'. First, you ha' fe find it in you heart fe kill de animal. But wha' me fe do? Four pickney fe feed an' send school. Cow slaughterer, him retire. An' people have cow, goat, an' pig fe kill. So me drink a white rum, put on de apron, an' start chop.'

On the day Jean was leaving, Mary cooked all morning, preparing a package for Lana: coconut gizadas, sweet-potato pudding, plantain tarts. Of all her grandchildren, the dearest to her was Lana – the beautiful and embattled girl who still called her Mama.

Mary Darling told Jean: 'You know, is you mother need the psychiatriss, not Lana.' Mary said she remembered when it happened, the closing down of some part of Monica's brain.

'It was jus' before Lana born. You know, Deepa never mean to leave Monica by herself.'

'Then why did he?'

'Him 'fraid a his father. Everybody 'fraid a him. Anush Ramcharan was ole-fashion. A lot a Indian-dem married colored people, but not the Ramcharans. When Anush hear 'bout Monica, he send Deepa to India. It hit Monica hard. You know how she proud.'

'But' – Mary stopped and considered something, that she had considered many times before, something she was sure of – 'is more than hurt pride that was killin' her.'

She stopped. She would not say what she thought had devastated Monica.

Jean understood. *The thing about your mother . . . she can't forgive herself for the way she felt.*

'She wouldn't even look at Lana when she born. "Tek her, jus' tek her away, Mama," she tell me. I feed Lana cow's milk and tek care of her from that moment, an' I tell you, I want to cry when I look at her face – I never see anything so perfect as that girl.

'Monica come 'round slowly. I tink she cyan help like the

baby, seeing how she so pretty and so good. And everything was fine so long as Lana stay with me. Is after Monica tek over that all the trouble start.'

Mary stopped and looked thoughtful and sighed, remembering.

'I not sayin' Monica didn't love the chile. She love her, yes. But Monica full a spite, an' she confuse Lana. I not no psychia-triss, but I see Lana not awright. She flyin' high one minute, nex' minute she fall. Always so. What goin' happen to her? She cyan get enough love, that chile.'

46

'Lana wanted somebody to save her.'

'You're not Jesus,' Jean says.

They enter Fern Gully. Paul slows down and turns on his lights. She loves this dark, wet road, resting between steep banks of fern and moss-covered rocks.

'For a while things were really good between us, peaceful. We would pick Claude up on the weekends and go to the farm. She could be so much fun sometimes, and then other times—'

He stops and seems to be concentrating on the slippery road.

'I went to see Monica one time when Lana was doing badly. I thought it was time to have a real talk with her, and Monica an' me, we always got on well, even after she knew about me and Lana being together. She fixed me a drink, and we sat out on the veranda. I remember it was right after the grillwork went up. She was complaining 'bout it. She didn't like the idea of living behind bars, she said.

'I told her I wanted to talk about Lana. She asked if something had happened. I said, no, not exactly *happened*, but I was worried because she had been in bed for weeks. I said, "She really can't take care of herself, an' I don't know if I can take care of her all alone."

'Monica said "What you want me do? Play nurse?"

'I didn't know what to say. I wanted to say, "You're her mother," but I didn't. She told me she couldn't do anything for

Lana. That she had given up long ago. She seemed so full of hate when she said that. That's when I realized something.'

'What?'

'Monica was *afraid* of Lana.'

Jean considers this. There is a band of sunlight ahead. They are leaving Fern Gully, and as usual, it seems to her much too soon to be heading back into the bright, dry countryside.

'You expected Monica to start behaving like a mother?' Jean asks him. 'She was never a mother to Lana, Mary Darling was.'

'True. Though even Mary couldn't—'

Help Lana? Could anyone? Jean cannot come right out and ask this, not now, not yet.

47

'No, don't turn off the light. Don't go, Dolly. Stay with me.'

Jean got into bed beside her.

Lana's eyes were closed, but tears leaked down her cheek.

'Lana?'

Lana kept her eyes shut, as if this would stem her crying. 'I want to feel better, so help me God, I do, but I can't. Dolly, I'm afraid.'

'Afraid of what?'

She shook her head, unable to explain, and clutched her abdomen, hugging herself tightly.

'Your stomach?'

Again she shook her head. 'I wish somebody would shoot me and just end it.'

'Don't say that.'

'I know. I shouldn't.' She grabbed Jean's hand. 'Pray for me. Pray, please—'

'Father, comforter . . .' Jean began. She searched for the right words; she wanted mercy and comfort for Lana.

'No. Pray to *Jesus*.'

'Merciful Jesus—'

'I wish I coulda know him.'

'Who?'

'Mr Jesus.'

Lana opened her eyes and saw the flicker of amusement on Jean's face, and she smiled too.

'Seriously, if I have to suffer, why God couldn't mek me born in the same world as his Son? If I was in Nazareth, I would kneel down at his feet like the cripples an' blind people.'

'He hears us, don't you think?'

'Is not the same as being alive same time as him an' havin' him right there in front of you.'

'Eternal life.'

'Yes?'

'You believe in it?'

'Eternal life? I dunno. I so damn mix up. Suppose no. Suppose it's just dark. Nothing at all. Just a grave.'

Jean stroked her sister's beautiful head. 'Don't . . .'

'Where the hell is he?' She started sobbing.

'Hush, sweet. I'm here.'

'Where's Paul?'

'He'll soon be here. Don't cry.'

Holding on to Lana. That's how it felt that night. Not Lana holding on to her.

She stayed with her often at night while Paul was in the country; Cherry visited her during the day. Sometimes Paul took her with him to the farm, but that was hard because he was often out all day and was afraid to leave her alone in the farmhouse too long. She had to be encouraged to eat even the smallest portions of food. And when she was at her worst, Paul would bathe her and brush her hair. He told Jean he was worried that Lana would have to be sent back to the hospital to be properly cared for.

She had become ill again after Gwen took the baby away with her to Canada, following the thousands of Jamaicans who were emigrating. Gwen had looked after Claude like a mother for five years, and didn't want to part with him. At first she had put it to Lana as an offer: He would have a better education in Canada; life was easier there, and he would be near his cousins.

Lana wouldn't hear of it. She was ferocious. She knew in her heart that Gwen took better care of Claude than she did, and she wanted to redeem herself.

'*I* am his mother – not her.'

Mary was on Lana's side and was furious with Gwen; Monica, of course, was on Gwen's side. At first Paul tried to reason with Gwen on Lana's behalf, then he found himself trying to reason with Lana, conceding that Claude might in fact be better off with Gwen. 'The truth is,' he said to Jean, '– and believe me, I hate to say it – Lana doesn't know how to be a mother.' Cherry, like Jean, was torn. It was Cherry who finally talked Lana into letting Claude go.

Lana had to give him up, Cherry said, because she had no other choice. She had signed papers when she was hospitalized in Florida, making Gwen Claude's legal guardian. Gwen would go to court if she had to.

So Lana gave up her son. After Gwen took Claude to Canada, Lana took to bed and grew more and more despondent.

Cherry visited one day while Jean was there. She had just been to the hairdresser; her hair had been dyed jet-black as usual, and elegantly puffed up and styled. Lana noticed.

'You had you hair done? It looks nice.'

'Thank you me dear.' Cherry moved about the room, folding and tidying things and opening the curtains to let in the day. Her fat arms shook, and her expensive gold jewelry glinted in the afternoon sunlight. She had brought lunch and proceeded to warm it up on Lana's stove.

'Come now, Lana. No more of this bed business. Come sit at the table. Jean, help her put on her housecoat. You cyan come to de table in you nightie.'

Jean helped Lana with the red satin robe, and Lana walked weakly to the table. Cherry served the steaming soup.

'This soup gi' you courage,' Cherry said, sitting down.

'I did mek this soup for Lim Su when she first come to Jamaica.'

There were green vegetables — callaloo, bok choy, scallions — in a clear fish broth, and dumplings filled with shrimp and pepper.

'Why Mr Ho Sing sent so far for a wife?' Jean asked.

'Dem starvin' over in China. Mr Ho Sing wan' gi somebody a chance. I was 'bout fourteen an' I have five brothers to tek care of an' dawg an' fowl, so I say, "Good, another woman in the house fe help." But when I see Lim Su come offa de boat, she so scrawny an' fenky-fenky. Me want fe say, "Send her back." She 'fraid a Black people, she 'fraid a everyting. Not one damn use. She won't eat. Won't talk. She cry-cry. One day she start fe look so bad, me heart go out to her. I realize someting did frighten the girl bad. You don't know what go on in dem faraway places, what kind a meanness go on 'pon dem ship. Mr Ho Sing him never talk 'bout it. An him was a man. Lim Su she jus' a poor, mawga gal.

'I mek her dis soup an' she so grateful she come si' down in me lap an' hold on to me an' cry.'

'And she was better after that?'

'She sekkle down. Jus' like a chile. I say to meself, "What a ting, eh? I become me father wife mother."'

'Father wife mother,' Jean repeated. 'That's a new one.'

'What a mix-up family we have,' Lana said.

'Is a mix-up country. But everything have a way a working out.'

48

Everybody expected Cherry to live to be a hundred like Mr Ho Sing. It was Mary whom the family had been worried about: Mary's bellyache turned out to be stomach cancer.

Cherry had never been sick. She was over eighty and as strong and vibrant as ever. A few months before she died, a gunman had attacked her at home. She was outside watering her garden. The gate was open and the dogs were chained up because some of her great-grandchildren had just come and gone.

The man held Cherry at gunpoint and walked her from the garden through the house, stealing jewelry and silver; then he tied her to a chair. She pacified him, talking to him sweetly and offering him something to eat. The maid, who had been hiding in the pantry, ran next door for help. By the time the neighbors and police arrived, the man had gone. Cherry had not been hurt.

'You weren't 'fraid, Cherry?'

'Me? 'Fraid? Chu, gunman come an' gone, an' me g'wan same way wid me life.'

A few months later Cherry was hospitalized with abdominal pains. Within weeks, she had become unrecognizably thin and, for the first time, gray-haired. She was upset at not being able to get her hair dyed. She talked to Lana about it because Lana was a professional beautician.

'You couldn't jus' give me a likkle touch-up, eh, Lana?'

'When you leave the hospital, I promise.'

But she never left alive. Lana told Jean it would always trouble her to think of Cherry going to her final resting place, gray-haired and looking so unlike herself.

Mary died three months later. For Mary, there was a nine-night, except it was actually only four nights. No one could remember exactly what a nine-night was, but Lana had a vague memory of attending one with Mary, and she felt it was fitting. And so it was Lana, surprisingly, who presided over Mary's wake. For four nights she provided food for the visitors: peppered crayfish, deep-fried sprats, mackerel run-down, hard-dough bread, and fruit cake. Deepa brought several cases of rum. Tables, chairs, and candles were placed in the backyard.

At first hymns were sung, and that was felt to be too solemn. So Lana began playing Mary's records and tapes, and that put the visitors in a better mood. The men began playing dominoes; word of Mary's wake spread; the yard filled with people from the surrounding parishes. A cousin of Mary's ex-husband came with his pale-haired, pale-eyed family. Deepa's sister and his mother, who was quite bent with age, came one night; acquaintances and friends of acquaintances all came over the four nights, ate, drank, chatted, grew boisterous; then, as the night deepened and their blood grew heavy with rum, they became solemn, and somewhat fearful, wary of encountering duppies as they took their leave and walked back into the country night.

On the last night an old woman walked into the yard, wearing a white head tie and carrying a crudely carved walking stick. She sat alone eating and drinking all that was offered. Neither Jean nor Lana knew her; they heard people address her as 'Oni.' About midnight she tapped her stick on the ground and began to sing.

'Mash up, mash up, we goin' mash up an' go
Bring more rum or we stay a likkle longer
Bring more bread or we stay a likkle longer
Bring fry fish or we stay a likkle longer . . .'

Someone began beating a drum. Oni stood up and continued singing. Everyone formed a circle around her and began to clap and sing too: 'Mash up, mash up, we goin' mash up an' go . . .'

All the rum was consumed that night. What wasn't drunk by the visitors was poured around Mary's yard into the hungry, waiting mouth of the earth.

Mary was buried in the graveyard at Blue Fields, in the last remaining plot, beside her mother. Gwen came the day of the funeral. She had returned to Jamaica for two weeks but had had too many people to see and things to do in Kingston to attend the nine-night. Monica also came for one day. Both women avoided their childhood home, and Lana avoided them. They sat stiffly in the living room for an hour or so, and talked together about the business of death, the lawyer, the house, the will.

To Jean's astonishment, Monica and Deepa spoke to each other at the funeral. It was a mere 'Hello, Deepa'; 'Hello, Monica,' after thirty years of silence.

Jean drove her mother home from Westmoreland. Monica gave the appearance of dozing, but her forehead was creased and Jean could see that she was restless and perturbed.

Was it her mother that Monica was grieving, Jean wondered, not only her mother's death but also the life Mary had led? Or was it Deepa?

That night, Jean woke up hearing Monica downstairs. After a few minutes she heard piano music filling the house. Monica playing the piano? Jean got out of bed and walked quietly down to the living room. No, it was a recording. Beethoven.

Jean stood in the doorway behind her and could not see her

face. Monica sat with her head bent in an attitude Jean had never seen before. She could not tell if it expressed appreciation, weariness, or regret. How she wished she could see her mother's face.

49

Ines invited Jean to a New Year's Eve dinner party. She wanted her to meet a friend, an Englishman named Alan Weir who was a writer for a New York newspaper.

They were having cocktails in the garden when Jean arrived. She spotted him immediately. He was a tall, heavyset man. His slouching shoulders and loose-fitting clothes obscured his body. His hairline was beginning to recede, but in spite of that, he had a magnificent shock of straight, black hair. His eyes were dark, and she noticed that they moved constantly, alighting thoughtfully on this and that, as he listened. She liked the loose white cotton shirt he was wearing, the sleeves rolled up near the elbows showing his tanned forearms.

'This is Jean,' Ines said to him.

He shook her hand. 'I'm happy to meet you. I read your translation.'

'What?'

No one, as far as she knew, had read her translation of Alejandro D'Costa's journal except Señor Rodríguez.

'It's not exactly a best-seller,' she said.

He smiled and showed slightly crooked front teeth. 'Actually, I read it in the library yesterday. I'm doing some research on the Spanish Caribbean. It was helpful. More than that, it's an elegant piece of work.'

'You speak Spanish?' He smelled wonderful, she thought,

clean and manly without any of that overly sweet cologne.

He answered, yes, in Spanish, and complimented her again on her fine work. Then someone came over and asked him about his recent trip to El Salvador.

He sat beside her at dinner. A woman from the British embassy sat on his other side and engaged him in conversation. Jean talked with a man from the American embassy who introduced himself as Brian Scoley. But the whole time she found herself listening to Alan. She learned that he had stayed with Ines's family on a trip to Peru several years ago and the two had become good friends. He liked speed sailing. He also parachuted.

'For fun?' the woman asked.

'Only when it opens.' He turned to Jean abruptly: 'I hadn't expected you to be so young. Where did you get your degree?'

It was nerve-racking, how appealing she found him. She was afraid she seemed too eager to converse with him.

'I don't have a degree. I took some university courses in—'

'What have you got against a university education?' He spoke with a sudden passion whose source she couldn't locate.

'Nothing. I think about it sometimes, but—'

'What's there to think about?' He looked at her skeptically. 'You translated that book yourself?'

'Yes. My father found the original manuscript—'

'Your father? What does he do?'

'He died when I was seven.'

'So it was a legacy.' He smiled then turned from her and continued talking to the English woman.

Brian Scoley was telling Jean that he was a 'special adviser' at the US embassy. Jean asked him what that meant, but didn't listen very carefully to his reply because she wasn't really interested. She vaguely heard the words 'defense' and 'trade.' He knew her position at the National Security Ministry was not a political appointment and he was curious, he said, to know what her political allegiance was. Was she a member of either party? No, she was not. He thought Jamaica was a difficult place to live in at this time. Had she ever thought about living elsewhere? No, she had not.

'How old are you?' Alan turned to her again and asked.

She was beginning to be annoyed by his tone. He spoke to her as if she were a teenager. 'Twenty-three. And you?'

'Forty-two. Are you married?'

'No. Are you?'

'Yes.'

Ines came down to their end of the table during dessert. 'Jean is driving to the country tomorrow. Why don't you go along, Alan?'

Alan gave Jean a look that said he was interested but did not want to impose.

'It would be nice to have the company,' Jean assured him.

'Well, thank you. I haven't seen much of the country yet.'

Five. Four. Three. Two . . . the year was ending. Champagne was being poured. People put their arms around their spouses and lovers. Alan Weir toasted with the woman from the British embassy, and then turned to Jean.

'Happy New Year,' she said.

'To an education,' he said, clinking his glass against hers.

'He seems not to like me,' she told Ines as she was leaving.

'Don't be silly,' Ines said, and added, 'Alan is not a very happy man.'

He wore white jeans and an emerald-green shirt that was very becoming on him, though the extra weight around his middle showed more than it had the night before. She had put some thought into what she wore – in fact, she had changed several times, wanting to look attractive to him, though wondering why since he did not seem interested in her. And besides, he was married. She had finally settled on a sleeveless pink blouse and white shorts. People said she had good legs. He didn't seem to notice.

They drove along the south coast by Pedro Bay where the cliffs dropped almost a thousand feet to the sea. She explained to him that the south was not considered the beautiful side of the island.

'A wasteland,' he said, waving his hand across the scene.

'I know' — she laughed — 'it's ridiculous.'

'I've spent a lot of time in the Caribbean.' She liked the way he pronounced 'Caribbean,' lingering over every syllable. 'All the islands are splendid, but this one is unusual. So many rivers and mountains. You forget you're on an island.'

'Yes,' she said. 'Trollope complained about the copiousness of our rivers.' He laughed and she was glad to have remembered that about Trollope and to have said something smart. 'But it feels very much like an island to me.'

'You feel cut off?'

'Sometimes.'

'A lot of the time, I should think.' Again he spoke with an edge she couldn't place. Who was he to tell her how she felt?

They talked a bit about the history and politics of the island, and also about some of their favorite books. He was generous with his knowledge, yet mean, or at least mocking, in his tone, like a bored but proud schoolteacher, Jean thought. He seemed uncomfortable and impatient in her little car — and with her.

At New Hope he seemed calmer. He did not ask a lot of questions the way visitors to a new place usually do, but she could see his interest and thoughtfulness. She was sorting out Mary's things when there was a knocking at the gate.

'You Miss Mary granddaughter?' A woman, about sixty years old, stood there.

'Yes. Can I help you?'

'My name is Dorinda, Miss Dorinda Jack. My family know your family from long time.'

Jean remembered her from the funeral. 'Jack? Yes, Mary used to speak of a family named Jack.'

'I am Drusilla Jack's niece. I hear you was coming today so I come down from Blue Fields to see you.'

'All the way from Blue Fields. Come in and sit down. I don't have anything to offer you, only a glass of water.'

'Tank you. Good day,' she said to Alan who had joined them and who was taking in their conversation in his keen, quiet way.

'I was concern as to what goin' happen to de place. You not goin' sell?'

'No, no. The house belongs to my sister and me.'

'Miss Lana? I remember her. I know you family from long time. I did even know you grandmother mother. Well, I don't want tek up you time.'

She didn't get up to go. Jean sensed that there was something more to her visit. Was there something of Mary's she wanted as a keepsake?

'Miss Dorinda, is there anything—'

'Well, since you ask: I don't really come on account a meself. Mary's friends from 'round here, we want to mek sure de place stay nice an' de garden don't spile. Me will only too glad fe look in from time to time. Is not no ardinary place dis.' She turned to Alan to explain. 'Mary mother, you see, the Scottish lady, she was de Doctor wife.'

Alan's eyebrows lifted with curiosity. He wanted to know more about 'the Scottish lady' and about Mary. Dorinda was happy to oblige him.

It grew late. Jean gave Dorinda a key to the cottage. Alan

made himself as small as possible in the back of the car as they gave Dorinda a ride back to Blue Fields.

Learning that Alan was visiting this part of the country for the first time Dorinda suggested places he should go: 'Take him to de Cave, Miss Jean.'

Jean hadn't been to the Cave in many years. It was a place along the coast where seven rivers met.

'Are we still in the uninteresting part of the island?' Alan asked as they sat in the cavernous shelter of the rocks where the underground rivers met and went out to sea. He looked around and said, 'Tell me about this place.'

She liked the way he emphasized the word 'tell.'

'They say that slaves, when they were beaten, used to come here to heal their wounds.'

'Only the slaves knew about it?'

'That's what people say.'

The haunted sound of the place struck her as even more extraordinary than the way it looked: the different currents, rivers and sea, echoing inside the rocks. It was a shelter, but it was not quiet, surging with the unstoppable force of seven rivers tunneling their way through the mountains to the sea. African men and women who owned nothing on the island, who were themselves owned, had made this place theirs and kept it from their owners.

'And now who comes here? Tourists?'

'No. The tourists go north.'

'Ah, yes.'

They decided to spend the night in Negril since it had gotten so late. They went for a walk on the beach around sunset. He asked Jean many questions about herself and her family, still speaking to her in that high-handed, unsettling tone. She thought him a strange and difficult person.

They stopped when they reached the sharp, rocky point. The sun had already fallen beneath the horizon, and the beach had begun its evening life. They watched the deepening stain of night and were aware of the deepening silence.

He spoke first, and she was glad he did. It felt awkward to be quiet like this with someone she hardly knew; he wasn't Paul. At the same time, she hadn't wanted to speak and disturb his brooding.

'It's hard to believe, when you stand here, that there is so much trouble going on here. But then, it's always like that.'

'Why did you move from England to America?'

'That's a long story.' He paused. 'I rather like New York.'

'Is your wife American?'

'Yes, Gail's from Long Island.'

'A writer, too?'

'She writes for a home decorating magazine. Knows a lot about antiques and that sort of thing. She has an exquisite home.'

'You don't live together?'

'What?'

'I'm sorry. You said *she* has an exquisite home.'

'We. We have a home.'

They looked at the sea, but Jean sensed that he was not really looking at anything. He just didn't feel like talking to her. Well, she didn't feel like talking to him, either.

I'm sorry he came with me, she thought, but then asked: 'Do you want to walk on a bit? We can climb over those rocks to the other side.'

He turned and looked at her: 'You're being very gracious.'

She was thrown: 'Not at all, really.'

He continued to look at her with his active, thinking eyes, as if he were perturbed by something, or feeling the need to fix something he saw in front of him.

'Is there anything——?' For some reason she was mumbling.
'What's that?'

'Is there anything else you'd like to see or do? There's a place not far from here—'

He kissed her. It was a pathetic little kiss on her lips.

For some reason, she didn't want to pull away. He kissed her again.

The fragile but cumbersome thing they had been balancing between them – propriety – fell, and they were glad. His lips moved over her face and neck as if he intended to feed on her. She felt his hand moving under her blouse, touching her breasts. She pressed against him. She didn't want this to end. Not until she knew his body like a path that she had walked, walked, walked; she wanted to find out every hidden hardness, heaviness, rise. Her hands moved across his chest and slid down to his thighs. His limbs seemed beautiful to her, things to bend to and entwine. She wanted to strip him and begin the worship of everything manly about him.

'I've never slept with anyone but my wife since I got married.'

'I've never slept with anyone at all until now.'

'Really? And you're twenty-three? Is that common in this country?'

'Highly *un*common.'

He seemed to be letting this sink in.

'I'm sorry I was selfish – it's been a long time.'

They lay there quietly for a long time and he seemed to fall asleep. Jean was wide awake; everything about the night was so new to her. She had never fallen asleep naked with a lover. 'Lover' – the word felt exactly right; she relished the feeling of the sheets covering them and the way he held her easily and affectionately, as if he slept with her all the time.

He wasn't sleeping, either.

'We live very separate lives, Gail and I. It's not easy . . .'

'Living like that?'

'Not easy to talk about.'

'We don't have to if you don't want to.'

'I don't. Let's stay in this room for the rest of our lives. I want to be the next man to make love to you, and the next one after him, and so on, and so on—'

'Horse dead, cow fat.'

'What?'

'It's what we say instead of "so on and so on" or "et cetera."'

'What a great nation!' His laugh filled the whole room.

They spent three more days together before he went back to New York. She went with him to the airport, and it kept seeming as if the subject of their seeing each other again might come up. But it didn't. It was a horrible parting for both of them because it was so awkward and false. The cumbersome thing was between them again, but it was worse now because where before they had imposed it on themselves, now it imposed on them.

50

Brian Scoley called Jean. She did not find him interesting, but out of politeness agreed to meet him for lunch.

They met at the poolside restaurant of a Kingston hotel, a popular meeting place of government ministers and important businessmen. Colonel Waverly Martin stopped by and said hello to Jean. Waverly was a colonel in the Jamaica Defense Force and a special adviser to the prime minister. A tall, gaunt man with an outdated Afro and a goatee, he was one of the young, highly intelligent men that the prime minister had brought into the government. There were rumors of his being a Communist. Some said he was dangerously ambitious; others said he could never make it in politics because he had no charisma. This last thing Jean felt was true. Waverly possessed no charm, but he was clever.

'You're a friend of Waverly Martin?' Scoley asked.

'We've worked together.'

'What do you think about the PNP's close ties with Cuba?'

She told him she had no opinion on the matter, which was not altogether true. Roy had inspired in her an admiration for the Cuban revolution and its heroes. But she sensed that Scoley was anti-Castro and she didn't feel like getting into a political argument with him.

'You don't think it threatens the entire region?'

'Cuba and Jamaica are eighty miles apart; it makes sense to

be neighborly. The red snapper is very good here. I recommend it.'

He took a sip of lemonade and gazed at her. His eyes were translucent blue, liquid. 'What about your own safety? You don't think the association with Cuba might endanger you?'

She was curious now, not about his opinions, but about what was behind his proselytizing. 'In what way?'

'If it leads to civil war. Revolution. The end of free enterprise. The end of free everything. Even free love.' He smiled.

Was he flirting with her? She studied him. He was attractive. A bit younger than Alan, in his mid-thirties, and certainly in better shape. He fit into the category of handsome blond American. His obtuse reference to sex was not very witty, but his attempt to change the direction of the conversation – clumsy though it was – made her a bit more attentive.

She hadn't heard from Alan since he'd left, and this hurt her. She gave Brian Scoley her home phone number.

As soon as she got home, she got a phone call from Paul. Deepa had died of a heart attack. Paul was at his farm and wouldn't be able to get in to Kingston till quite late. He wanted her to check on Lana.

51

'You think Deepa—?'

'Deepa was a disappointment. I liked him. He was good to Lana. Good about giving her things. But he was weak. How could he let Monica do those things to his daughter?'

She remembers the hours Monica and Lana spent together in front of the dressing table mirror; it was extreme, the effort of perfecting themselves, their hair, their complexions, their hands. Monica had seemed loving; so had Lana. But was Lana ever more than a vivid scar on the face of Monica's disappointment? And would that triangle of regret end now that Lana was gone and Deepa was gone?

One day, one day Congotay.

What was that?

She is touched by the notion of reckoning, of the souls of the dead answering to the souls of the living but never to the satisfaction of either, and of the living being burdened by those dead whose remorse keeps appearing like an unwanted child in every generation.

'Want some asham?' Paul pulls up to the side of the road.

'Asham! Yes!' She hasn't had asham in ages and craves something sweet. She and Faye used to love this mixture of ground corn and sugar, which was only sold in the countryside. The asham woman grinds it for them while they wait. She's glad to see that they still sell it in brown paper cones.

Some little girls are playing outside the asham hut, dancing in a ring, singing and clapping their hands. She doesn't recognize the song. Something to do with boys and weddings, with choosing and being chosen.

52

Dipanjan Ramcharan (Deepa)
1932–1979

Maybe two, three years from now . . . That was what I was always saying to myself. It wasn't that I was a dreamer. No, I was a planner. But my plans never turned out.

I never felt with anybody else what I felt about Monica. But we suffered so much because of it — me, her, and me double because I knew she was suffering on account of me.

You could spend your whole life lookin' back and thinking, If I never made that one mistake, life would a been different. But I just didn't have the courage at seventeen. What did I know about loving a woman or having a child? I thought — two, three years, I would go back to Monica and my child.

I used to blame my father for the whole thing. I used to think he was just plain wicked. When I got older and saw more of the world, I began to understand better, though understanding isn't a cure.

His father and mother came from Benares. They came, like all the Indians, to work in the cane fields, and when they finished their term of indenture they were given a piece of land. It was part of the contract; they could get return passages or land — not much land, mind you, just enough to make them stay and go on doing seasonal work on the sugar estates. My grandfather was a great farmer. In the end he owned a big estate in Westmoreland, and my father, being the oldest, inherited it.

My father sent to Uttar Pradesh, in northern India, for a wife. That was my mother, Indra. Just like his father, he made himself another India right here in Jamaica. Everything was Indian — food, clothes, even the cooking pots and brass plates we ate off. He sent me and my sister, Geeta, to Jamaican schools only because there were no Indian ones. Also, his brother's children went to Jamaican schools and he didn't want them to have an advantage over us. But other than that, he wouldn't have anything to do with Jamaica. The day my sister brought home a friend from school, a Black girl, hell broke loose. Food never finished cooking that day; everybody got a beating and went to bed hungry.

My mother knew how much I loved music, and she did this brave thing for me behind my father's back: she sent me to a lady named Miss Simpson for piano lessons once a week. Don't ask me where she got the money. I suspect she sold some jewelry. My mother was an unusual Indian woman with more strength and daring than any of the Jamaican-Indian women I knew. She must have grown brave on the ship coming over, a hard thing when you think about it, crossing all that water to a land and a husband she didn't know. Anyway, I think it really pleased her to get away with something like that, paying for her son's secret piano lessons in defiance of her husband. You see, my father expected me to take over the estate. He didn't want my head full of music and poetry.

It was at piano lessons that I met Monica. I used to walk her home. I fell in love with her mother, her sisters, the whole family. They were different from the women I was used to. No man 'bout the place telling them what to do. Mary, she so softhearted, not a woman who ever raise her hand to her children. Everybody 'round the table in the evenings, chatting and laughing. Poor as they were, they seemed better off than Geeta and me.

But my father had arranged a marriage for me with a girl in India.

I don't want to tell you the kind of things that went on in the house when he found out about Monica. Not only that she was my girlfriend, but that she was pregnant and I wanted to marry her. First time in my life I see my mother stand up to my father. He was whipping me with the switch they use on mules. My mother grabbed the switch from him. He turned on her and started to choke her. He would a kill her that evening if me and Geeta hadn't pulled him off her. Then he turned on Geeta and beat her with the same switch he had used on me. I had to obey him. I was 'fraid if I left and married Monica, he would kill them. And if he didn't kill them, he would make their lives hell.

He sent me and Geeta to India, to our mother's family. I married the girl he picked for me. Yes, I went through the ceremony. But then after the ceremony, that is where I stopped. I said to myself, I'm not Indian, I'm Jamaican, and Jamaica is bigger than my father's estate in Westmoreland. I left my bride in Benares. To this day I don't know what happened to her.

Geeta and I went back to Jamaica on our return ticket, and we stayed in Kingston. I knew if we went back to Westmoreland my father would beat the hell out of us and send us back to India. So I set myself up in a jewelry franchise at Victoria Pier, and then I got into the furniture import business. I was doing well enough after a couple of years to give Geeta the money to study nursing.

I tried to call Monica. She didn't want to talk to me. Finally her mother told me she had moved to Mandeville and gave me an address for her there. I wrote to her and she wrote me back and said not to get in touch with her again.

About two years after I came back, I went to New Hope. It was really my daughter I wanted to see; I knew Monica had left her there with Mary. I bought a present for Lana, a little pair of shoes, they sweet you see, little white shoes. Lana was sleeping when I got there, but I looked in on her. I couldn't believe how pretty she was. Mary looked at the shoes I bought and shook her head. Too, too small.

I left and didn't talk to Lana that day. I didn't want to wake her. And anyway, I felt ashamed of meself.

I used to keep those shoes on a shelf in my living room near the family photographs. When Lana started to visit me, I told her how I had bought them for her but she had grown too big. I don't know, I hoped she would look at them and know I was thinking about her long before I ever saw her. She called them her 'baby shoes,' and she used to put them on her doll's feet when she was playing. Lord, she was a beautiful child.

I realized after a while that Monica was really serious about what she said. She cut me like I never existed, like I wasn't Lana's father. Thank God for Mary Darling. If it wasn't for her I would a never know my child.

Monica, she not like anybody else. What could make a woman that hard? That's not the question to ask. The question is what could have made a woman like Monica so soft? How a toughminded, stubborn woman like her could a let herself get carried away with a man like me? You don't know the girl I knew. That girl, she died; Monica killed her.

It's because she hated her ole self that she gave Lana a hard time. And to make it worse, Lana looked like her. Like a snapshot. Then Lana got pregnant, same way like her mother, seventeen years old and not married. You think Monica could take that?

Monica and I were just fourteen when we met. We were good friends. We couldn't be together enough. She was a big talker and dreamer. She loved music and the cinema, and we used to talk about living in Kingston. We talked like we were always going to be together.

Sometimes when she was having her lesson with Miss Simpson she would look up and see me watching her. It was like she was giving me a special, secret right to her. Young as she was, she decided that about me. You should a see her in those days, her hair in two long plaits with ribbons at the end.

Monica wasn't a wild girl; that's not the way it happened. It was just she really was in love, and she put so much trust in me. It got that we wanted to kiss an' hug-up all the time and couldn't ever find anywhere to do it — sometimes at the cinema, sometimes behind a tree. The harder it got to do — and I mean we were at that age when blood running hot-hot — the more we wanted to do it. We started to talk about getting married. We wanted to be able to lie down in bed in our own house. She knew my father was a hard man and that it wasn't going to be easy. But I told her not to worry — two, three years, I would have enough money of my own and we could live in Kingston.

I wasn't deceiving her. I believed what I was saying.

In the meantime, we found a place, not ideal. Miss Simpson had a garage in her backyard where she kept a car she hardly ever used. We used to sit in the car in the evenings and, well, at some point, one thing led to another, and then — Lana.

I think she gave me her whole, young heart, and that it nearly killed her when I left. I didn't just leave her. I left her in that state, unmarried with a baby coming. I broke her free-given, secret heart, and that way I broke her pride.

Lana — I never understood that girl. Not ordinary. She was like a star in the sky. I loved her but couldn't understand why she felt things so hard. Like Monica, I suppose.

Lana called me one day when she was about fourteen and asked if she could come live with me. She said Monica was going to kill her. I said, Monica not goin' kill you, but yes, come if you want, you can always come here. But she never came. That's Lana — every minute changing her mind.

I suppose I could a' do more for her. The trouble was I couldn't talk to her mother. Monica made me feel so bad, and maybe I was always feeling bad anyway whenever I saw Lana. Poor girl, she in between two sorry hearts.

I never got serious 'bout any woman after Monica. I went out with a divorced lady older than me for a few years, but nothing ever really happened there. I lived alone, and I small-up meself. Not doing much, not having much. Nothing ever worked out all that well, nothing — not woman, not work. The furniture business got tougher with Manley's new taxes. Violence was getting worse. I got held up twice in my shop. My cousin in Connecticut wanted me to join him in his import business, so I decided to go and try that.

I gettin' off track. I have to tell you the truth at last. I hate to say it, but here it is.

I want to say I never stopped loving Monica. But age bring me wisdom. I stopped loving her when I lost the courage to stand up to my father. You understand? The love you have in you heart for somebody — that is not enough. I remember them teachin' me in school the difference between a noun and a verb: a noun is, and a verb does. Well, love don't count one rass unless it's a verb. I stopped loving Monica.

53

They turn a corner and there, spread out before them: the famous white sand and turquoise water of the north coast. They've reached the other side.

These coastal towns – Ocho Rios, Rio Bueno, Seville Nueva – always remind Jean of the early settlers. Bright hotels now stand where forts and cannons had; though recently, the hotels have become forts again, secured behind high garden walls and iron grillwork gates, with security guards patrolling.

She sees the usual north coast activity. Rent-a-car signs, rented men, bead-sellers, Rastafarian roadside artists, and water-sport experts win tourists with their cavalier courtesy; strange, how it is the tourists who become ingratiating, dependent upon the sun, the sea breeze, the rum, and the sex.

They drive past Dunn's River Falls, crashing down to the sea. Land of Many Rivers. Today she is counting. They will cross six more on the way to Paul's farm.

Here, she thinks, are the deltas of discovery and escape. This is where Spain began and ended its reign on the island. They pass Discovery Bay where Columbus first set foot, and other pristine bays where the Spanish settlers, having fled downriver from the British, met the salty current that would bear them to Cuba.

'You remember Lana singing at Deepa's funeral?' Paul asks. 'I almost cried.'

'How was Lana after Deepa died? I mean, she seemed okay to me, but—'

'You were busy in love with Mr Weir. We never saw you.'

'Yes, you did.'

'You mind was someplace else after you went and fell in love.'

'What makes you so sure I'm in love? Did I tell you I was?'

'You not in love?'

'I thought we were talking about Lana.'

Paul suddenly pulls over. They have been driving around a wide crescent-shaped bay, a spot where artists often set up easels. The sea laps against the road and sprays the front of the truck. Paul rubs his eyes in deep weariness – or is it exasperation? she can't tell – then stares ahead at the water. She has never seen him look so overwrought, never.

54

While Lana was sleeping with Paul, she was also seeing a former lover. Jean heard about it from Fern, and was puzzled when she heard who the lover was: Carl Young.

'What's going on with you and Carl?' Jean asked.

'Nothing serious.' She sang out the words nonchalantly. Then her face broke into a mischievous smile: 'Old firestick easy to ketch. The man *hot* for me, you see, Jean. He *hot-hot*, cyaan wait to get me back ina bed.'

'You not going to bed with him?'

'Maybe yes, maybe no.'

'What about Paul?'

'I *love* Paul,' she said with intensity. 'I couldn't live if anything happen—' She stopped and frowned. 'But Paul, he still playin' around wid whole heap a woman. So I goin' have my fun, too.'

'Have fun with somebody else. I don't trust Carl Young.'

'He asked about you.'

'About me? What you mean?'

'"How's you sister?" and he asked me if you still working at the ministry. He was jus' being polite.'

'Polite me rass. The man sly.'

He had seen her at lunch with Brian Scoley. Why was he asking about her?

'He's a snake.'

'Snake, yes. Didn't I ketch him an' Miss Ting in *my* bed?'

'Well, why you going out with him, then?'

'Chu, don't fret-up youself. I know what I doin'. Now do *you* know what you doin'? I hearin' all kind a tings. You goin' out with not one, but two foreigners. Is true?'

'News travels fast in this place, eh?'

She had made the mistake of meeting Scoley again. They went for a drink at a popular bar where she had run into a handful of people who knew her. Later he had taken her to dinner at Blue Mountain Inn, an elegant and very expensive restaurant with an exquisite view. He seemed to know a lot more about her than she had told him, details about her parents and her education. He had checked up on her. Why?

He had talked again about Jamaica's association with Cuba and of an upcoming meeting between government and army representatives of both countries. He wondered about the agenda of that meeting.

'You know I can't discuss that sort of thing with you.'

'Of course not. I'm sorry.' He refilled her wineglass, and his eyes wandered across her body. 'You're attractive and smart. Don't you ever feel you're being wasted here? I can see you in DC or New York. Do you ever think of going to the US?'

'Sometimes, yes. But it's not that easy. I mean—'

'I can get you a green card.'

This seemed an outrageous offer.

'I like you. I – I would like to be your friend.'

She couldn't put her finger on what it was he wanted from her.

'A friend?'

'Yes.' He reached for her hand. She slid it out of his reach as politely as she could and took another sip of wine.

'You don't have friends here?'

'I want a Jamaican friend.'

She cringed slightly. He didn't notice.

'You could help me, and I could help you.'

Was it government information he wanted? It seemed absurd, like something in a movie. He was probably just some crazy American with a grandiose vision of himself. Probably harmless, she told herself, possibly even amusing; she would have fun telling Faye about her date with an American spy.

55

Jean went to the theater to see Faye. She was still in rehearsal, so Jean sat in the back row and waited. She had just gotten her first letter from Alan. She was gratified by its being a long letter. He explained a lot of things, and these things, together with what Jean gleaned from Ines, gave her a much-craved picture of who he was when he was not there with her.

He and Gail had a four-year-old daughter, Emily, and Gail had been pressing him to have another child. He had admitted to Ines, some time ago, that he was not happy in his marriage. Gail, according to Ines, was difficult to visit, much less live with; she was a neurotic perfectionist; the spaces between the hangers in her closet had to measure exactly the same. There was very little intimacy or even conversation between them anymore. He had broached the subject of divorce at one point and Gail had reacted so badly that he had not brought it up again.

Before meeting Jean, Alan had convinced himself that he could endure the marriage if he focused on his work and on his daughter. But what had happened was that, as much as he adored his daughter, he couldn't stand being at home, and so he traveled at every opportunity. Where he had once worried that a divorce would cost him his daughter, he now realized it was the marriage that was coming between him and his child.

He couldn't make Jean any promises.

'. . . That short time with you made a difference to the way I feel about everything. I think about you and imagine what I'd stopped imagining: happiness, even ecstasy. But then I think about how young you are. I don't want to ruin your life by asking you into what might be a messy, wasteful love affair. You deserve a lot more.'

Jean had very little experience with love affairs. To her cautious and worried heart, this sounded like a good-bye letter.

She wanted to be with him again. He was leading her somewhere, to feelings and ideas that were of another, bigger world. But there was the worry, on the other hand, that the affair would lead nowhere, that she would be the prototypical girl waiting on the shore for her lover to return. There were songs she remembered from childhood about such girls – 'My heart is down, I'm leaving my girl in Kingston town.' How pathetic to be in that position, to be the pathetic girl in a song where even the pathos belonged to the man.

What she wanted from him wasn't clear to her. Or why she had fallen in love with a white Englishman twice her age who often spoke to her in an annoyingly paternal tone. He was foreign in every way; she didn't quite understand his moods or his way of thinking.

His body was strange to her too, but that was different, that was an exhilarating strangeness. It was so absurd, really, the act of sex itself; she had imagined that it would be much more balletlike. Not that she was disappointed. No, it was a great relief to her that it did not entail any special talent or refinement. Their twinings, their pinionings, their struggles for footing, their mountings, all seemed continuous, and more eased than harried by desire. She couldn't wait to be in bed with him again.

She had moved slowly and quietly all her life, gathering all this feeling and knowledge. Now she felt that, with him, she had only just arrived someplace where she could see ahead of her.

She didn't want to be left standing there, looking out, the compass shattered, the feeling and knowledge pointless.

'Jean, how you doing?'

She looked up. It was Mark Silvera. He was composing the music for Faye's show. She had noticed him onstage with Faye when she arrived. Sonny Law was there, too, and Faye's lover, Pat.

'Not bad. How are you?'

'Iry-I.' He sat beside her.

Mark had gone through a metamorphosis. He woke up one day and proclaimed himself a Rastafarian. His dreadlocks were now to his waist. He had lost a lot of weight; he could even be described as skinny. And he gave the impression now of being a thoughtful, religious person. One thing had not changed: He still seemed stoned most of the time. His band was now world famous, and she found his success heartwarming. She had forgiven him.

He looked her up and down in a teasing, proprietary way.

'I see you cut your hair.'

She had a very stylish, if severely short, haircut that bared her neck and showed off her best features, her big eyes and prominent cheekbones.

'You looking good, nice earrings, nice shoes.'

Yes: She was Monica Landing's daughter and wouldn't know how to dress badly if she tried. His compliments had a tinge of regret and nostalgia. Amina, she'd heard, had gotten fat and sloppy.

'How's Amina, and the baby?'

'Good. Baby starting to walk.'

Jean was struck by the years and the changes. She never thought she would see Faye Galdy, Sonny Law, and Mark Silvera working together. All three had dreadlocks; even Faye had them — people called her 'Goldilocks.' Jean remembered how annoyed

Monica would get when her father brought Rastafarians to the house. Back then they had seemed like a small, outlandish cult: *'No, darlin', Rastas don't eat children. Nobody eats children. Monica, what kind a foolishness you tellin' the chile?' 'Is it true they believe in Africa?' 'Everybody should believe in Africa. It's a real place.'*

'Awright, Jean, tek care, iry.' Mark left the theater.

Faye came over. 'Going to be one hell of a show.'

The show, a reggae musical, was being sponsored by both parties to promote peace and boost the morale of the nation's disenchanted and fearful young voters. A similar peace effort had been made by Bob Marley in his 'One Love' concert a few years earlier, with Manley and Seaga shaking hands onstage.

'You know somebody called Brian Scoley?' Faye asked.

'Yes, why?'

'He left a message for me sayin' he was a friend of yours and wanted to meet me.'

'Meet you. Why? About what?'

'I figured because you said such *great* things about me. No?'

She hadn't said anything to him about Faye.

A week before the show opened, Jean got a call from Scoley, which she didn't return. He called again and left a rather cryptic message about needing to 'brief' her. It was obvious to her now: He was crazy. Anyway, she didn't have time for him; she was on her way to Montego Bay to meet Alan.

He had stopped over on his way from Peru. She took a couple of days off work, and they spent, a four-day weekend together. They rented a house in the hills above Mo' Bay, the one house in the area that couldn't be called a villa: old, small, without a swimming pool, but with a lovely view.

Talking to him had become much easier now that they were sleeping together, though he still said the strangest things. It intrigued Jean, who at times felt strangled by her roots on the island, that he seemed not to belong anywhere.

'Do you miss England?'

'No. It's there if I want it.'

'Why did you leave?'

'Oh, my leaving England all those years ago probably doesn't deserve as much discussion as your need to get out of here. You'll be leaving a paradise. Where I came from, there was little beauty to leave. I was an aesthetic emigrant!'

'I see, *not* in the great line of starving emigrants.'

'Well, I was starving in a sense. All the men in my dad's family were coal miners, but after the war my dad was able to rise to electrician. That was the government's way of showing gratitude to the lower class for helping them win the war. And that was as far as it would go. My generation saw the lies: We, too, were supposed to know our place.'

'I can't imagine you as a plumber. So you decided to go to the land of opportunity?'

'Well, when I first thought about leaving I was very young and had no idea what was outside England, but I felt it had to be bigger, grander. And for fuck's sake, sexier!'

'You must have learned to make love somewhere other than England. You know what we say about Englishmen and sex?'

'Oh, God, just say it.'

'You do it twice a year, on the feast of St Whichway or St Cuthcod or somebody, and you only do it "backdoor," and that's because you had to learn either by watching livestock on the estate, or by instruction from Senior Best Boy at Eton or Rugby.'

'That's quite true! But only of the ruling class. Actually, my lessons came from a pale blond Englishwoman.'

'No!'

'It's true. My first great love, Ursa. She looked like someone spectacularly down on her luck when she took me in. I was in Soho with my mates looking for a bit. She saw me, or saw the wine I was carrying. I looked so appalling – tall, gangly, with ravaged skin. But she cocked a smile at me, tugged the bottle, and said, "Come on in, lad. Spotty as hell, but you've got fabulous lines.'"

Jean thought it hilarious the way he got so animated and took on different voices when he told stories; it made him seem quite insane. His arm circled her tightly, inviting her into his weird remembrances.

'She was a bit patchy herself, let me tell you. She lived with some other junkies in a crumbling wall in Soho and turned tricks. Later, I found out she'd been back-up singer for a famous rock-and-roll band.'

'Which band?'

'That's not the important part, love. And I promised her I'd keep her secret. I tried to sort it all out while she was still awake and sober enough to hear me: How could I find more of her Gypsyish knowledge in England? She was good; she answered: "Not in England. Go west. East, south. Besides I'm half-Austrian, anyway. You didn't learn it here."'

Jean stroked the fine trail of hair on his flabby abdomen. 'Are you sure you didn't dream this? I think you hear voices.'

'Well, I obeyed hers. I went to New York and got a nonunion electrician job doing renovations at *The New York Times*, and got friendly with an Anglophile editor, who took me on as a researcher. So you see my fucking and my journalism have the same origin. Ursa took my restlessness and set me spinning beyond England.'

'And you didn't stop till you got married.'

'Let's rest here.' He drew her hand to his flaccid penis and she felt it stir.

At the end of their four days together he told her that perhaps she should try to forget about him.

'You're young and free and in the enviable position of being able to do anything and go anywhere you choose.'

'Suppose I choose to be with you.'

Her candor staggered him. He pulled her against his big chest and held her tightly: 'I don't deserve you. I'd like to, but I don't.'

'So I'm just some quickly passing thing in your life?'

'In my dotage, dear, fewer and fewer things pass by.'

'You talk as if you're an old man. You're not.' His defeatism, discernible through all the screens of self-mockery, annoyed her. 'Well, I'm not going to try to convince you. It's not as if I'm sure about anything. I just want to see more of you.'

'That excites me and also scares me, as it ought to scare you. Have you always been like this?'

'Like what?'

'Misadventurous.'

No. It was new. Why did she feel so brave and clear with him? Was it his foreignness?

Jean meant to return to Kingston in time for the opening night of Faye's show, but her flight from Montego Bay was delayed. She went straight home and went to bed early.

Irene woke her around midnight. She had been up late listening to her radio. There had been shooting that night. Gunmen had invaded the theater. Four performers had been killed onstage, dozens of people wounded.

'They want to stop us, but we nah stop,' Faye told Jean over the phone.

'They who?'

'Whoever giving people guns and trying to mash up the country. You're in National Security. You tell me.'

For their own protection, government ministers and politicians began to hire henchmen. These were gunmen, some of them, gang leaders. Jean's boss had several around him. One day Jean thought she recognized one of them and was mortified; she felt it couldn't be the same man, but it was. It was the man with the distinctive reddish tinge to his skin and hair. She heard the other henchmen call him Red Man. He did not seem to recognize her. He had probably been high the day he attacked her; maybe he had attacked so many people that he did not remember their faces. Every day he walked by her office wearing a gun holster; now he had license to do harm.

She told Faye about it. Faye was appalled but not surprised.

'Politicians hiring the very men who've raped their daughters and wives. I tell you, no woman in this country is safe.'

Brian Scoley caught up with Jean by phone and asked her to meet him at the embassy. The day of the meeting, her car battery died, so she got one of the minister's drivers to drop her off, asking him to come back for her in an hour. On the way, she remembered Scoley's call to Faye, and his urgent cryptic messages, and she wondered for a moment – though it was too horrible to imagine – whether he had known in advance about the planned shootings at the theater. She grew nervous and was about to ask the driver to turn around, but it was too late; they had reached the embassy gates.

She went through the usual security check at the front door, but was alarmed to go through an even more thorough search outside Scoley's office. 'Sorry,' he said. 'It's been routine since Springer.' Leila Springer, a vice consul, had been kidnapped several months earlier on her way home from work. She had escaped because of a traffic accident.

She was surprised to see Carl Young in Scoley's office. There was another man there, whom Scoley introduced as being from the US State Department. She kept thinking that she would have a lot to tell Faye later.

'Can I get you something to drink?'

'No, thank you.'

'It's no secret that our State Department is unhappy with the direction your government is going in,' Scoley began. 'I want to help you because I consider you a decent, civilized person in a country on the brink of barbarity.'

'Only on the brink?'

He took her response as encouraging and continued to talk about the nation's security, Cuba, the upcoming meeting in Montego Bay . . .

She interrupted him.

'I'm going to that meeting primarily as an interpreter. I hear things but I don't get around to actually listening and sorting it all out for at least a hundred years.'

Carl Young laughed at this. The two Americans looked perplexed. They looked at Carl as if they needed him to translate what she had said.

'How's your sister?' Carl asked.

She got up.

Scoley looked alarmed.

'Just a friendly question,' Carl Young said, looking at her with calm, serpentlike assurance. 'Jean's sister an' me, we go way back.'

'If there's a point to this meeting . . .' Jean looked at Scoley.

He glanced at the others, then said: 'Thirty thousand dollars and a green card.'

She stared at him, incredulous.

'Play for our team. Think about it and let us know.'

The car was already waiting for her. But there was a different driver; it was Red Man. He looked at her, cocky and insolent.

She could not get in the car with him. But if she refused, he would become suspicious, maybe even remember her. It was hard for her to believe he didn't remember. She walked to the car slowly, watching him as he chewed on a toothpick and stared ahead, indifferent. She reached the car and smelled his sweaty armpits through his cheap cologne, saw the dirt under his fingernails, the ever-present gun holster. She felt nauseated.

'I'm going across the road for lunch. I'll take a taxi back.'

Later, back at the ministry, he walked by her office, giving her again that insolent look, a look that said he was completely sure about his power and didn't think she was worth much.

56

Jean suggests that they stop for a cold drink. They get sodas and sit on a bench in Columbus Park overlooking the sea.

Roy had brought Jean here to the unveiling of the statue of Columbus when she was a little girl. What she remembers most about the occasion was an argument between Roy and a complete stranger. A man who turned out to be a schoolteacher had overheard Roy telling Jean that Columbus hadn't really discovered the island. The man reproached him for misleading the child. It was so important to Roy to set Jean straight on this matter, a matter she didn't have an iota of understanding of at the age of five, that he returned to the statue with her after everyone had gone. He told her about the Arawaks and their peaceful life before the arrival of the Spanish, speaking long into the night with dramatic pointings and sweepings of his hands like a teacher in front of a blackboard.

'You awright, Paul?'

'Yeah. Jus' tired, you know. A lot a things goin' on.'

After a while he says, 'We're almost there, Jean.'

'You going to be all right, after I'm gone?'

He gives her his usual half-smile. 'I'll survive.'

'You know, I never thought I'd be sitting here like this, turning my back on my own country.'

'Don't be so hard on yourself. People leave places. They come back. You would be foolish to stay here right now.'

'You think so?'

'You should do whatever makes you feel safe.'

'It's not a matter of just *feeling* safe. What's going to happen here?'

'God only knows. God, and maybe you father up in heaven. Come, drink up. We cyan stay here all day enjoying the view.'

She suddenly remembers that she recently dreamed about her father. At least, she can only explain it as a dream.

An orange butterfly darts before her, then settles on Christopher Colombus's boot.

'"So rare a wond'red father and a wise, makes this place Paradise."'

'What's that?'

'Shakespeare, *The Tempest.*'

'I remember that play. We read it in fourth form. What was the name of that guy, the savage? Caliban, right? It was his island.'

Jean nods. The butterfly continues to rest on the statue, fluttering its wings now and then but staying in the same place.

If her father were alive, where would he stand in all this violent confusion? She is saddened, but in a strange way relieved, by the realization that Roy's time came to an end with Roy: The early-morning energy of nation builders, the optimism of people waking from a satisfying dream into a satisfying day, just wasn't here anymore. If anyone could convince her to stay, if there was anyone who could assure her that she could and should contend with the violence bearing down on them all, it was Roy.

57

Roy Landing
1918–1963

You went out onto the veranda late-late, long after everybody was asleep. You wanted to be out walking under the night sky, under the bright stars, but you couldn't, not in these times. You stood right up against the grillwork, with your hands on the iron bars, your face pressed against them, looking at the night.

Don't forget that you have the key, not them on the outside.

Once, when you were a little girl, a baby really, I took you to see a street parade. It was V-E Day, and being an ex-RAF fighter, I was in my uniform and medals, up on the platform with some other RAF men and their families.

World War II. What a time! Most of us had enlisted – bursting at the seams – to rescue the mother country. We felt shocked by some of the remarks we heard from other Jamaicans: 'Why you going over there to get your head shot off? What you care if Germany or England win?' We weren't thinking about colonialism an' all that then. We didn't even see the irony of being shipped as fresh recruits to Britain on one of the banana producers' boats. We just wanted to get out and fight, see the world, play our part in the war.

I had my first real taste of racism when I got to England. It was subtle: unhelpful shopkeepers, the drill sergeant's sarcasm. And sometimes not so subtle: 'Oy, blackie, golliwog!' I had been brought up by George Landing and Cherry Ho Sing, bright, proud, enterprising people who never considered color an obstacle. We Jamaican recruits stuck together and listened and learned. But the interesting thing was that, as our eyes opened up to imperialism and racism and as we outgrew our colonial docility, we found other reasons to fight for and alongside England.

We served with great distinction, we Jamaicans, which is a known fact about us. But a fact about the English was their appreciation of our service. And a further fact: From our seeing Englishmen toil in the ways that West Indians always had, from lying with the English in trenches and shelters, and from their ordinary kindnesses, the imperial structure we had just begun to notice, name, and suspect began to show cracks in which something new could emerge.

All right, for a bit longer hear out my optimism.

During the war, I began to feel that a spirit, a guide, had accompanied us to England. Some wayward, mixed-up, and mixing spirit we knew from home, which had long confounded and swapped around the races and colors, using violence, even slavery, business, passion — you name it.

The spirit was not picky, by which I mean it didn't choose either the people or the abominations from which it made its strength. The spirit used whatever was at hand — the Arawaks, the Spanish, me, the RAF, World War II. And it was in that same spirit that I stood with you on the platform that V-E Day.

There was a group of girl cadets, marching with batons and little Union Jacks. You heard the drums and horns and got excited. I picked you up and walked to the front so you could get a better look as they went by. You were enjoying it so much; your little hands were waving up and down and you were making a whole lot of funny sounds. The next thing, I felt your lips on my cheek. You just took it into your little head to turn 'round at that moment and kiss your father. It was the greatest moment of my life.

You carry so much feeling in you, Jean. A little girl who couldn't even talk yet, you said such a lot.

I can't stand to see you tear up like this.

You stayed out on the veranda till you got cold and started shivering. Then you went back to bed.

I came to warn you: terrible things spinning around you, a wheel that isn't stopping. I sat on your bed and watched you sleeping. You opened your eyes.

'Daddy?'

'Leave this place.'

58

'What's this now?' Paul asks.

Another roadblock. This is it. This is the one.

'Is there another way? Can we turn around?'

'It's awright. Just a routine check.'

Routine? This is a tourist town, and there is an army tank ahead. Nobody wants to frighten tourists with roadblocks, much less army tanks. Something is going to happen to us here, she thinks, as two soldiers approach the truck.

The soldiers look them up and down. She avoids looking at them.

'Is your truck dis?'

'Yes.'

They look the truck over again, noting the license plate, and ask, skeptically:

'Fe you own?'

'Yes man. Me buy it, me no tief it.'

'Papers.'

Paul hands him his registration and license.

Jean reaches for Paul's hand in a jerky motion.

'Awright, g'wan,' the soldiers say.

'What's the matter?' Paul asks as they drive on. 'I told you it's routine. Jean, you goin' to get out of here. Awright?'

He says this, but he looks nervous. After a while it occurs to her that his anxiety is not about her safety; he's anxious to talk about what happened to Lana before she goes away, before distance breaks the truth in half.

59

'A married man! Jean, you of all people should know better.'

Monica had found out about Jean's affair with Alan.

'How she found out?' Jean wondered.

'Bush have ears,' Faye said.

'That's all I need,' Jean said, 'on top of everything else, to have Monica's tongue let loose on me.'

Jean hadn't heard from Alan for weeks. It didn't help, having her mother watching and interpreting the impasse.

'Tek my advice. Forget him. When a man don't call you is because he don't *want* to call you.'

The Sterns have terrible luck in love . . .

Monica looked at Jean, who was at that moment sitting quietly on the veranda steps, and in a rare moment of sympathy said: 'Why you don't come with us to Ocho Rios and stop moping 'round the place.'

Jean declined, and Monica went to Ocho Rios for the weekend with old, ailing Delly. After years of neglecting him, Monica had recently reclaimed him.

This is how it happened.

Delly's wife had divorced him and married someone else. He asked Monica to marry him, and she turned him down. Delly, twice spurned, started going out with a younger woman. Monica heard rumors that he was thinking of marrying this young upstart.

'The old fool think he goin' marry Miss Hurry-Come-Up. Over my dead body.'

Jean hadn't told her mother that she actually knew Miss Hurry-Come-Up: Delly's younger woman was Cecile Knight, Paul's on-and-off girlfriend. She didn't tell Paul or Lana either, and if distressing things had not been happening in her own life at the time, she might have relished being the conveyor of this delicious gossip. Imagine, Monica and Lana sharing a rival.

Cecile Knight had been trying to get Paul to marry her for the longest time. She was a successful anesthesiologist, and it had always seemed to Jean that she was wasting her time trying to marry the island's most unmarriageable man. 'She must be in a trance or something,' Jean once said to Faye. Now she was attempting to ensnare Dr Delgado, a man who had once been her teacher, and whom she had idolized in medical school.

But Cecile hadn't reckoned on Monica.

Jean was out on the veranda with Monica, Errol, and one of Errol's lady friends, when Monica told how she had triumphed over Cecile.

Cecile had taken the first step toward moving in with Delly: she had hand-picked a maid to look after his house.

'You know what that mean?' Monica raised her eyebrows.

'Housefly,' Errol answered. A spy in the house; fly on the wall; ears in the kitchen.

'I kept wondering how come Delly not returning me phone calls, and how Miss Hurry-Come-Up seem to show up everywhere. Delly come one time out to Ocho Rios to see me, an' she call him say she 'round the corner an' her cyar bruk down.'

'Housefly,' Errol repeated, knowingly. 'What a way she bold an' brazen.'

'I decide is time fe show de likkle wretch whose lawn she waterin'.'

'But, Monica, you have to be careful who you cross nowadays,' Errol's lady friend said. 'Life cheap. Gunman fe hire. You hear 'bout the woman out a Harbour View the other day who pay a man fifty dollars fe chop up her boyfriend wife?'

'Chu, me no 'fraid. Is *she* fe worry 'bout *me*. Well, I hear dem gettin' married, an' I say to meself, no way that goin' happen. The girl jus' after him house an' him money an' ting. Na true?'

'True-true.'

'So wha' you did, Monica? How you did hangle her?'

'Me tek Delly on a cruise – Puerto Rico to St Lucia. De gal cyan walk 'pon water. Wha' she goin' do? She cyan do a ting.'

When they got back, she got rid of Delly's maid, the one Cecile had installed, and replaced her with a country girl whom Irene recommended.

'I say to Delly, If I ketch you wid another woman again, I goin' shorten you ole age.'

In spite of their teasing and cajoling, Monica would not admit that she genuinely cared for Delly. 'Chu, dat ole fool?'

So Monica and Delly went to Ocho Rios, Lana and Paul went to the farm, and Jean was spending yet another weekend alone at Bonnieview. Solitude was beginning to feel like a curse. Even when she had a boyfriend, a lover, she was alone. The vistas opened back one upon the other – the same scene, different times – of herself sitting in the house alone.

As she was locking up to go to bed, Faye arrived. Jean could tell it was going to be bad. Faye collapsed onto the couch and sat with her head in her hands. 'Sonny's dead.'

'What happened?'

'They stoned him.'

'Stoned him?'

He had been walking in West Kingston, near a JLP constituency office, though even Faye, who hated the JLP, would not say they were responsible. Some men recognized him, taunted him with lines from his poems, and started an argument with him – what was he doing in their part of town? Sonny, who was adamantly nonpartisan and who was known for speaking out against party violence, had answered, 'I man bawn in dis country, an' I free fe walk anywhere.' Someone hurled a stone, and the rest of the gang followed. Sonny ran, jumped over the wall of a churchyard, and the men chased after him, stoning him. A taxi driver passing by saw them and tried to make them stop. By then Sonny was on the ground, unconscious and bleeding to death. The men started stoning the taxi driver too, but he had a gun. So they ran off. The man put Sonny in his car and drove him to the hospital; he died on the way.

Jean went to the back of the house and looked out. Irene's light was off. She was sleeping. 'We have to go wake Irene,' she told Faye.

The next day's newspaper headlines said: Sonny Law, poet, stoned to death.

Some of Irene's relatives came from the country the next day. She seemed to not really understand what had happened to her elder son. She clung more than usual to Philbert, who appeared to understand and accept much more quickly than his mother that the brother he had idolized had been killed. Jean tried to comfort them both, but she felt somewhat in the way. She decided to give the house over to Irene's slowly dawning grief and her relatives, and go to Trelawny to be with Paul and Lana.

Out in the quiet countryside, she felt even more stunned and perplexed by what had happened. She wondered what Daphne would have said about this stoning of a man, a poet. She remembered in her high school English class being moved by the scene in *Julius Caesar* where the angry mob kills Cinna. 'I am Cinna the poet!' he cries in vain. And there was the stoning of St Stephen in the New Testament. 'Oh Jerusalem, Jerusalem, thou that stonest them which are sent to thee ... behold thy house is left desolate.' That was ancient Rome, Jerusalem. This was now and her own country. And she had known him. 'Speak up boy. What you can do?' 'I can talk in rhyme, ma'am.' She heard Sonny's voice — *Wan' smaddy fe blame* — and then heard him no more.

Lana kept saying she felt 'down.' Paul had two unhappy women on his hands, and he tried his best to cheer them, cooking for them, playing music.

While Lana was taking a nap in the late afternoon, Jean and Paul played chess.

'Is Lana upset because I'm here?'

'No. She's been like this for weeks. Tired, complaining 'bout everything.'

When Lana got up from her nap she said, 'I sick a de country, nothing to do but sleep.'

Jean and Paul went on playing chess. He suggested things they might do later — go for a drive, go to a club in Montego Bay.

She wanted to go back to Kingston.

'But we just got here,' Paul said.

'Let me make you some hot cocoa,' Jean said.

'Lemme mek you some hot cocoa,' Lana mimicked Jean in a high voice. 'You sound like somebody old auntie.'

'Come on, Lana, it's so peaceful here,' Paul said.

'Peaceful me rass. Chu, if you and Dolly want to stay, you can stay. I'll take a taxi back.'

'Taxi? You goin' tek taxi hundreds of miles?'

'I want to go back *now*. If you don't want to take me, I find me own way.'

So they all went back to Kingston.

Jean's phone rang about an hour after she got home. It was

Paul. 'Princess Lana is asleep. I tell you, it's easiest just to give in.
I know she not in her right mind when she acts like that.'

Jean wondered how long it could last between Paul and Lana.

'Sorry we had to leave. That was a good game.'

'Want to come over and play another one?'

They opened a bottle of cognac.

'So I hear you goin' round with a Mr Weird.'

'*Weir*. Alan Weir.'

'American?'

'English.'

'Oh, the motherland. What-ho, bloody, beastly bollocks!'

'Actually, he's married – but not happily married.'

'I suppose that's an important distinction. On the stove, but
not actually cooking.'

'Have a heart, don't make fun of me.'

They talked for hours, flitting from one thing to another,
putting music on the stereo, dancing to one of their old
favorites, Paul teasing her about her Englishman and reducing
her to uncontrollable laughter; they never got around to chess.

It had been a while since they had spent time like this
together. As they sat talking and laughing, she realized how
immensely happy she felt with him. He must have been thinking
the same thing because he suddenly said: 'We get on so well.'

There was a lull after he said that.

Jean heard a moth hitting the lampshade. She watched the
moth for a while, then stared down at her glass; she couldn't
look at Paul. She wasn't sure, but she had the feeling that he was
looking right at her. She looked up. He was.

Her throat felt heavy. 'For a long time now.'

'For a long time now – what?'

'For a long time now, we've been getting on so well.'

He put his arm around her and she put her head in the crook

of his neck and shoulder. So familiar, so dear. He placed his hand under her chin, raising her face to him.

It was the first time they had ever kissed like that. She didn't know, until it happened, that she had been waiting for it to happen. This was not an approximation of something she longed for; this was it exactly.

60

They sat together for a long time after that kiss, Jean and Paul, worried but also strangely wishful, like a couple waiting for a ship that would take them to a new country. He fell asleep for a few minutes, and she sat awake, watchful. When he woke, he held her tightly, then said he had to go home. She walked him to the door. He kissed her again, this time on the cheek, in the old way.

She closed the door behind him, and stood for a moment with her back against the door, listening to his truck drive away.

Alan called to say he was coming. His visit coincided with the meeting she had to attend in Montego Bay, so he agreed to meet her there. He sounded distant and slightly agitated on the phone, and she wondered if he was still uneasy about their affair, or perhaps had come to the conclusion that it could not go on.

She was uneasy herself, tossing about and getting nowhere in determining what she felt since that night she'd kissed Paul. She didn't dare scrutinize her actions, the precariousness and folly of being involved with two men both of whom were tied to others.

On the way from the airport he blurted out: 'It's clear to me I've got to end my marriage. And I will, Jean. But I haven't worked out when, how.' He grabbed her hand and searched her eyes for a sign of doubt, but it was his own eyes that were filled with fear. 'Will you risk loving an old, weak-kneed, married man until he can sort himself out?'

'If you keep calling yourself old I'll start to believe it.'

'When you're forty and in your luscious prime, I'll be almost sixty and bald, if I'm alive.'

'Are you looking for more reasons for us not to be together?'

He laughed. Then, to throw a blanket over his terrifying mix of emotions, he started to tell her about his recent trips and what he was writing.

There was a strange moment while she was sitting beside him in the car when she thought, Who is this? That Alan was driving made it seem all the more jarring: Alan, not Paul, driving her along this familiar coastal road. She stared at his large, white, freckled hands on the steering wheel and almost shuddered at the strangeness of the man, her lover.

'So there we were, the chap from the BBC, the driver, and me, walking up to the customs post . . .'

In a matter of months she might be with him in New York, Guatemala, Colombia, in that much greater world that was part of his work; it was daunting.

But sex with Alan was not daunting. They took the same little house they had stayed in before. The moment they got inside he began pulling off her clothes.

'I hate not fucking you and I promise never not to again.'

'Do it here, now.'

'Wait – naked – I want you naked.'

'There – old man—'

'On top of me – crawl – up the front of me. I want to feel your nipples drag across my balls. Bring them up to my chest. Oh, your face, your beautiful face. Let me fuck your face – feed you.'

Somehow his need for her to do certain things felt, not like the tyranny she feared in other men, but like license to expose her own wants, her own fierce phrasings of yearnings.

As they drifted off to sleep she drew closer to him, wedging herself between his arm and chest. She thought: Paul and Lana are together, and I am to Paul what I've always been, that indefinable thing, not nothing, but not anything either. I am here beside Alan's warm, large, breathing body; this is something.

'Waverly Martin broke up the meeting,' Jean told Alan.

'The JDF colonel?'

'He said the government should prepare to defend itself against a CIA-backed coup within the army. He said he had proof of CIA involvement in recent violence.'

He stroked the back of her neck. 'Not surprising. Is it?'

'I suppose not. But this was: He asked the Cuban delegates if they could be counted on for military support.'

Alan's eyebrows shot up.

'The minister looked like he was going to have a fit. He called for a recess until he could reach the prime minister.'

'Did he?'

'Yes. The prime minister had a long telephone conversation with Waverly. Waverly came back and tried to cover his blunder by rephrasing what he'd said to the Cubans. He said the government hoped it could count on Cuba in a worst-case scenario, but that for now the prime minister was in favor of extensive negotiations with all parties. It was quite confusing, believe me; I was the one translating.'

Alan sighed. 'Waverly and Manley are splitting into separate camps. "Negotiations" means negotiating with the US.' He looked at Jean. 'Leave.'

'My job?'

'If I were you, I'd leave the country for a while.'

She told him about her peculiar meetings with Brian Scoley, and the offer of money and a green card.

'In exchange for what, specifically?'

'Information, photographs, documents. You know how paranoid people are about Cuba. Some of the things that have crossed my desk would make anybody paranoid. There'd be another Bay of Pigs.'

'You're too close to all this. It's people like you who get hurt in these situations. Come back with me.'

'I don't have a visa, and— Come with you where?'

'I have friends in Miami who can get you a visa, passport, whatever you need, in a matter of days.'

'What kind of friends? Drug lords?'

'Utterly reliable. They'll even fly you out of the country in one of their planes.'

'If things get that bad, I have a friend in the country I can stay with.'

She felt strange mentioning Paul, and it must have shown.

'Someone I should know about?'

'Just an old friend.'

'If this country splits in two, there won't be anywhere to hide.'

A week later the deputy minister of national security, who had worked at Jean's side during the Montego Bay meeting, was gunned down by his own security forces. It was the first of several assassinations set up to look like an accident or blunder. The minister of security resigned a few days later, and Waverly Martin replaced him. Some of the former minister's henchmen stayed and attached themselves to Martin. To Jean's dismay, Red Man stayed.

Waverly asked her to remain. The day after he took over, she went with him to a section of West Kingston where, hours earlier, sixteen people had been killed, some of them children on their way home from school, in a shoot-out between PNP and JLP supporters. It was the first time the word 'bloodbath' had seemed accurate to her. The victims were still lying in the street, drenched in their own blood, the children in school uniforms with their school bags beside them.

Alan sent her a New York newspaper story on the incident, including a photograph of the gunmen in paramilitary outfits firing automatic weapons. With her own eyes, she had seen the bloody aftermath; that had been upsetting enough. But to see her city under siege in a *foreign* newspaper – the newspaper there, she here – and in a photograph as true as the ones she'd seen of Cambodia and El Salvador, locked her inside the horror.

'Sixteen people were killed as warring political factions opened fire on a busy street in Kingston. The guerrilla warfare has claimed over 600 lives in the past few weeks . . .'

There was a brief note from Alan: 'I've contacted those friends I told you about. Trust me in this, at least.'

61

'Either I'm a duppy or this is another country,' Jean says.

There are army and police vehicles along the coastal road. People, children especially, stand around gawking at the tanks and trucks. This is strange to them, too.

'You think it's going to be like this the rest of the way?'

'Jean, it's the north coast. If anybody's getting in and out of the island safely it's the tourists and the ganja traders. That's probably why the army's here, to protect them. You'll be safe in your little ganja plane.'

They make a turn and drive through the center of the old seaside town of Falmouth. It's a poor town; the two-story Georgian houses are neglected but intact. The tidy streets are broken by glimpses of the sea. Falmouth is her favorite north coast town; tourists do not come here; it is proud, bright, and ghostly. After Falmouth they turn inland. She glances at the silver watch that hangs around her neck by a chain – her great-grandmother's, one of the few possessions she has brought with her. If all goes well, they will reach Paul's farm in about an hour.

'I have one more stop to make,' Paul says. 'But we'll make it before dark.'

They drive up a steep dirt road, a road so narrow there is barely room for Paul's truck. Leafy branches brush Jean's arm through the window. She has not been here before but knows this is the Trelawny rain forest. Here are some of the tallest, thickest trees in the land. Bright-colored forest birds fly from branch to branch in alarm. They are practically in the Cockpit country, the mountainous country where African runaways hid and built towns. The road continues steeply with sharp, abrupt turns; it is at times like these that she realizes Paul is no ordinary driver. It seems impossible for anything without wings to climb at such an angle.

She sees smoke rising ahead, and they reach a clearing with a small wooden house. The smoke is from yams being roasted outside.

'Kofe is a Maroon,' Paul says. 'He picks bananas for me from time to time. I asked his wife to make something for you.'

Kofe comes over to the truck. Yes, this man is African. He is dark as night and has a youthful, unlined face despite his gray hairs. He wears his khaki shirt open and carries a machete. He greets Jean with a gruff good afternoon and doesn't make eye contact with her. He and Paul talk about the farm. His wife comes out of the house. 'Hello. Good afternoon.' She also does not smile. This is not surliness but a particular kind of country politeness and deference. She remembers a few years ago on a country bus, a little boy smiling shyly at her and his mother reprimanding him: 'What you doing smilin' at big people?'

'Adina is a great-grandmother, you believe it?' Paul says.

Adina has the slim, firm body of a thirty-year-old. Her hair is covered in a red-and-yellow head tie. Her skin is taut over a high forehead, and her cheekbones seem uncontainable. In this face, tight as a drum, her mouth stretches full and broad from one side to the other. She is the most spectacular woman Jean has ever seen. It is hard not to stare at her.

'I jus' mek some dukonoo,' Adina says.

'We cyan really stop, you know. We jus' came to pick up the package.'

'Awright, but mek me wrap up some dukanoo gi' you.'

Jean and Paul follow her into the tiny house. Kofe stays outside. The wooden slats of the floor and walls seem as if they have been scrubbed and polished mercilessly every day, and the house smells of dukanoo – sweet mashed cornmeal and coconut rolled in banana leaves and boiled.

She hands Jean a package and says, 'Linens.'

It's a set of handkerchiefs, not linen, but extremely thin, white cotton with a delicate lace tacking around the edges.

'They grow the cotton themselves,' Paul says.

'You want to see the tree?' Adina asks.

They walk about a quarter-mile; at one point Jean thinks she sees a green parrot in a tree. The land is noisy with the long-drawn-out cries of birds, and the air stings with the sharp odor of things ripe and ripening, fallen, smashed oranges, and the sap of green mangoes.

'It's not actually cotton,' Paul explains. 'But similar – what it call, Kofe?'

Adina answers. 'Ceiba.'

The ceiba tree is almost a hundred feet tall, with a massive trunk. It is full of oval pods with cottony seeds.

'Some people call it cotton, some call it ceiba, some call it duppy tree. You not 'fraid a duppy?' Kofe asks Jean.

Paul laughs and says, 'Jean and duppy good friends, man.'

'Spirit-dem ina dis tree 'bout two hundred years. Is dis tree dem used to tek fe mek boat an' coffin, na true, 'Dina?'

'Boat, an' coffin.'

'Is not no ordinary hankie Adina mek give you,' Paul says. 'Is a piece a history wha' you goin' tek blow you nose.'

'Maroon history,' Kofe says adamantly.

'Come mek me fix up de dukanoo gi' you,' Adina says.

They leave with the handkerchiefs, the dukanoo, and some ackee, which at the last minute Kofe picks so Jean can have it for breakfast tomorrow.

'Do Kofe and Adina know what people in Africa they come from?'

'Mando – Manda – something like that.'

'Mande?'

'Yeah. You never hear Adina and Kofe talk 'bout slavery, you know. They don't consider themselves descendants of slaves the way we do. Is a spirit thing. The slave ships had their bodies for a little while, but their spirits were already waitin' for them in these mountains and guiding them here.'

He looks at her and smiles. 'You didn't know you were goin' to get a history lesson today, eh?'

A history of spirits, Jean thinks.

She is the descendant, not of runaway Africans, but of African slaves. And not only of Africans but of English, Irish, Spanish, Jewish, Germans, and Chinese. Does this motley ancestry make her spirit a less able traveler? Does confusion of the blood cause the spirits to flounder and lose their sense of direction?

Some wayward, mixed-up, and mixing spirit.

Her old Cuban friend, Señor Rodríguez, of African descent, told her about *egun iponri*, ancestors coming and going, living in and around a person. He showed her an altar in his house dedicated to Yoruba gods and Catholic saints – Shango, Ogun, St Christopher. 'No conflict,' he told Jean. 'It's all the same, all one spirit world.' But they're not all the same, Jean thought, that's the glory. She realized then that she had always believed in *egun iponri*.

The vastly differing voices are not a floundering but a steadying influence.

'Jean always lands on her feet,' her mother often says.

Always landing with her, perhaps, are the resilient *egun*.

62

Mary 'Iya ilu'
1798–1904

I see sun shine an' rain fall on t'ree centuries.
When I tun a hundred, Queen sen' me letter.
I tun a hundred an one, Governor sen' fruit basket.
One hundred an two, Governor sen' him wife.
One hundred an t'ree, antropologist an' history teecha come.
One hundred an four, magistrate put plaque 'pon me house front.
One hundred an five, me get certificate write-up in gold letter say me a ole, ole
  'ooman.

Ha, one day, one day Congotay!

I no bawn here. I come from Ife.
Ife ondaye, ibi oju ti i mo wa.
Me out in a forest pickin' bisi when dem ketch me,
Tek me 'pon ship. Me an' me sister. Dem tek her one way,
Me anada way. We a Yoruba people. Yoruba.
I mussee twelve, t'irteen when I reach ya. I go wuk
In Masta William house look after him pickney.
Him free-up plenty slave-dem. Him free me husban', Dayo,
An' him free me. Him no 'gree wid slavery. Congotay!
You see picture ina history book, you

Hear story, an you ask how we let
Dis ting happen to we.
I tell you: On dat ship
I did tink me was dead-o.
I tink me in anada life-o.
Who can fight Ara Orun?
Plenty people tek sick and dem trow dem a sea.
I tink every day me fe fall a sea. Me neva know
So much water exist. Yes, I did tink a dead. True-true.
I did tink spirit ketch me tek me 'way.
I must be ina spirit world fa all me see is water an' white people.

Me cyaan see me muma nowhere. O-day Congotay!

Me reach Jamaica an' come a plantation,
Yoruba slave explain me say — me nah dead —
Me nah in spirit world — me wus than dead! Fa
Call as loud as me can call, me muma na hear me.
Walk as far as me can walk, me na reach home. Africa gone.
O-day, o-day Congotay!

When you add-up an' subtract-down all dem people,
You ha' fe wonder when Africa' go' stop wail.
One day, one day Congotay.
Fa dem no know say we tuff it out here an' mek it, dem no know say we
  survive-o.
I want to tell me muma — Look ya, me no dead-o.
One day, one day Congotay.

Africa. Me know dat is a real country. But how dem goin' know
We ina real country. Fa we jus' disappear. Orun!
O-day, O-day Congotay.

Me husband, Dayo, him muma was Yoruba like me.
When I reach here she 'com me muma.
After she dead, me chile born.
We name her Yetunde. Omolokun ogbolu,
Oba leni, oba lola, ola nigba kugba
Ina ori omi kuku gbona ku. *Muma come back.*

Wha' g'wan now in Jamaica is a sin.
Rain a-fall, but dutty-tuff. Me glad fe dead-o.
River dry, wheel a-stop, tree cut down, belly bawl.
Dem burnin' an' killin' baby. O day!
Everywhere me see black people' bone.
How come no white hand on de knife?
We come all dis way fe slaughter-o!
One day, one day Congotay.

Dem carry Israel pickney go Egypt. Dem carry
Africa pickney come ya. So much people
cross water, cyaan be God mistake.
God cyaan shut him eye fe four hundred years.
Four hundred years mus' mek sense.
One day, one day Congotay.

Listen, Jean-eleye, no matter wha' you do,
survive-o. Go back a Ife, go tell me muma
Hush now. Tell dem we did mek it cross de water.
Mek dem know. Mek dem know we is here.

63

The Martha Brae is calm and glistens like green satin. This is the last river today. She knows the legend. The spirit of Martha, known as River Muma, lives in the water. People are afraid to swim, afraid they will be pulled down into one of the secret holes where the gold lies hidden. Martha was an Arawak woman, the wife of a cacique. The Spanish conquistadores, after killing her people, forced her to lead them to the gold. She brought them to this river and the water parted, revealing an Arawak tomb, which drew her in and closed around her. The Spaniards fled in horror. Because the river loved her it made her a golden comb, and very early in the morning – 'soon-a-mawnin' – you can see her sitting on the rocks combing her long hair.

Coconut trees fringe the water. It's a dense, opaque landscape in the late afternoon. The silence is solid like something that can be dredged up from the bottom of the river. They are very close to Paul's farm now. What happened to Lana?

'Last time I spoke to her,' Jean says, 'she was about to paint your apartment.'

'Yes, she had the idea of painting the walls yellow, golden yellow, sun yellow, something like that. She started to—'

He stops. Too much has happened, she thinks.

'That was the thing about Lana,' he says. 'She kept picking herself up. Finding new ways. Believing if she tried this way as opposed to that way she would be happy.'

Nothing stays still here; rivulets seek new beds, tendrils new hosts . . .

The question rises in her again about her and Lana. They are daughters of the same rank tropical growth, daughters of the same history, backed up against the same walls. Will the waters close around her, too?

Tell dem we did mek it . . .

She knows now why she is taking this journey.

64

Jean called Paul's apartment. Lana answered.

'Hi, Lana, is Paul there?'

'Paul, some bitch want talk to you.'

Paul came to the phone.

'Doesn't she recognize my voice?'

'Is you sister you callin' a bitch, you know?'

Jean heard Lana burst into laughter.

'Sor-ry Dol-ly,' she sang over Paul's shoulder.

'Did you hear?' Jean asked.

'What?'

'The Peruvian ambassador and his wife were killed last night.'

'Jesus!'

'I can't believe it. They were lovely, lovely people.'

That was why it shocked everyone, not just that they were diplomats, but a couple well known and loved by many Jamaicans, a couple, near retirement, who had lived here so many years, killed in their home by gunmen. The diplomatic corps were naturally alarmed and were considering evacuation. American expatriates and Jamaicans filled the American embassy and stood in waiting crowds outside its gates.

Jean's secretary interrupted her. 'The minister would like to see you.'

She said good-bye to Paul and went to Waverly's office.

He no longer wore his army uniform, choosing instead one of the local 'caribas,' a collarless shirt-jacket. It was more casual than the traditional jacket and tie and was considered a kind of anti-imperialist statement. Waverly had learned about her visit to Scoley and wanted to know what it was about.

She found herself lying: 'It was a personal visit.'

'You're friends?'

'Well, not exactly. Is there a problem?'

'No problem. But we're in the business of national security.'

'I assure you—'

'Yes, try to assure me, Jean.'

There was silence for a moment; then Jean said, 'I doubt that I'll be seeing any more of Mr Scoley.'

'So he's *not* your friend?'

Why not tell Waverly about Scoley's offer of a visa and money in exchange for information? Wasn't it the patriotic and right thing to do?

'He's just an acquaintance.'

She had already done the right thing by not accepting Scoley's offer; she had not done anything wrong. 'I understand the nature of my job, and I'm dependable.'

'I hope you'll be able to prove that.'

The remark sickened her. She heard it as a threat.

Scoley, Waverly. She felt as if she were walking through a narrow corridor between two grimy walls.

Two days after the killing of the diplomats, the prime minister announced that the country was in a state of emergency.

Jean drove to West Kingston, to visit Faye at the little theater she had rented. Faye had started her own theater company. After the burning of the home for the elderly, the idea had come to her to write a play based on some of the women who had died in the fire. She got together a group of untrained actresses, women from poor areas like Trench Town, and she had each woman research and write her own role. The play was brilliant and enjoyed great success in Jamaica and on tour. Afterward, Faye decided to continue working in this kind of experimental theater, focusing on the nation's women.

Your father, he had a vision. Faye had a vision.

Jean did not consider herself a visionary. Born in British Jamaica just as the colony was drawing its last breath, she had entered a place of waiting. It was not an exceptional place – the waiting rooms of history were full of people like her – but it was a place of wonder. As she drove, she had a flash of memory: She was standing on a hill, holding her father's hand while he pointed below showing her something that dazzled in the distance.

The memory left as suddenly as it had come. She saw the police barricades, and her heart sank.

Driving past the graffiti'd walls of West Kingston, she had huge misgivings. She was crazy to drive through these streets during a state of emergency, and it was even more crazy of Faye to work here. But Faye reasoned that this area was safer than the rest of Kingston because here they were fully prepared. Soldiers and policemen patrolled; barricades had been set up; no one dared cross partisan lines for fear of snipers or execution by political gangs. There was a deadly quiet to the place that afternoon. A police car pulled up beside her at a traffic light. The policemen looked her over briefly, then drove on.

Faye's theater was a small barnlike building with a corrugated tin roof. Outside she saw the broken windows and graffiti Faye had told her about. A gang had thrown rocks in the windows, entered, and fouled the theater with urine and garbage. There was writing on the outside walls, the usual party slogans, threats against white people. And there was another thing that caught her attention, written in red:

BURN ALL LESBIAN

Faye's lover, Pat, opened the door. She was in her late twenties, dark-skinned with laughing brown eyes and a contagious chuckle. On stage she was a regal, powerful dancer; offstage, a quiet, almost giggly girl.

'You don't have grillwork or a watchman?' Jean asked. She knew that Faye had been getting threats.

'We have a watchman at night now, since the break-in. Come on in. Faye is with the lighting tech.'

She chatted with Pat as colored lights beamed on and off the bare stage. She heard the offstage pulling of levers and Faye giving directions from some omniscient perch. Pat had been living with Faye since Dr Galdy had emigrated to Antigua. She was telling Jean how much she loved the house, the old wooden floors and veranda, the nearby river. It was so peaceful up there, she said, there was no need for grillwork; sometimes they didn't bother closing the windows at night. 'It's like being in the country.'

'But it's not. At least close the windows at night.'

Faye was as stubborn as Monica about safety precautions. 'I won't be a prisoner in my own home,' they both said, again and again. The fact was, like it or not, they were prisoners. For several nights in a row, Jean had been awakened by the dogs' barking. One night she thought she heard footsteps and whispering outside. She had mentioned it to Irene and Monica. Irene said that she had noticed a strange car parked across the road. Even Monica seemed concerned at this and told Irene: 'Make sure you keep the place lock up during the day, an' be careful when you go outside.'

While she and Pat were chatting, Jean watched Faye, who had come out on stage. No one would believe she had endured so much physical pain as a child. She seemed so happy in her body now. In fact, Faye seemed altogether happy.

'Jean.' Faye came over and hugged her. 'Remember that imaginary island game?'

'Curaçao—'

'No, not that.'

'Robinson Crusoe?'

She laughed. 'No, the game you told me you used to play when you were little – how you used to imagine Jamaica before it was discovered, and that Arawak boy?'

'Kawara?'

'Yes!' she shouted. 'I have an idea for a new play.'

'About Arawaks?'

'About recovery.'

'Discovery?'

'*Recovery.* I'm starvin'. Mek we go eat some food.'

They went to Golden Dragon for Chinese food. Faye was in high spirits. Jean brought the conversation around to the question of safety. What were these threats Faye had been receiving? Did it have anything to do with her involvement with the party's youth organization?

'I don't think it's directed at me, exactly.'

'You don't think somebody writing "White Girl" across the wall is about you?'

'It's men trying to intimidate women. They know this is a woman's project.'

'And the writing on the wall about lesbians, that's nothing to do with you?'

Faye threw her hands up: 'So, what I goin' do?'

'Be careful.'

'She's a worrier,' Faye said to Pat. 'Worry, worry, worry.'

Golden Dragon was an old favorite of Jean's family. Cherry had celebrated her sixtieth birthday there, and the owner was related by marriage to the Ho Sings. It served spicy Jamaican-Cantonese food; the tastes and smells made her miss Cherry.

Faye nudged her. 'Eh-eh! Look who a come.'

It was Lana and Carl Young. Jean felt her stomach clench.

'Dolly!' Lana came over to the table, hugged Jean and Faye, and introduced herself to Pat.

'You know my sister,' Lana said to Carl Young.

'Yes, yes. You're at Ministry of National Security, right?'

You know I am.

'Tough place to be these days.' Words slid from his mouth like worms.

Lana and Carl Young went off to their own table.

'What she see in him?' Faye asked.

'I don't know. But he can't do her any good.'

'Chu, him too big a fool to cause any harm.'

She remembered a cautionary proverb Daphne had been fond of, 'Yuh nuh know which way wind a come from fe blow fowl tail.'

Lana called Jean the next morning in a temper. 'You tell Paul you saw me and Carl yesterday?'

'Of course not.'

'Then is who?'

'Bush have ears.'

'We had a big fight last night.'

'Over Carl Young?'

'Chu man! Paul came in from country just to see me, and him mad as hell because I wasn't here.'

Jean figured that Lana had probably planned it that way: 'What you doing, trying to make him jealous?'

'Oh, Jean,' she said, agonized. 'What I goin' do? I want to marry him so bad.'

'Then jus' tell him how you feel.'

'Chu, you no understand de supplety a de situation.'

'Subtlety,' Jean corrected her.

'Nutten between man an' ooman is straight or simple.'

Maybe she did mean 'supplety,' Jean thought. She changed the subject: 'How you feeling these days, Lana?'

'I prayin' every day to keep me balance. Some days better than others. Anyway, I goin' out now to buy paint. Did Paul tell you I paintin' his apartment. I don't know how him can live with all that black. Like him in mourning. You prayin' for me, Dolly?'

At work the next day, there was talk of bad blood between the prime minister and Waverly.

'Who leading the country?' People in the office whispered.

All morning, Waverly had been in a meeting with Cuban delegates and the Jamaican foreign minister. Jean, who normally attended such meetings, had accompanied the Cubans into the conference room, only to be told by Waverly that she wasn't needed. In a way, she felt relieved; if she was excluded from meetings and uninformed, all the better. Obviously, Waverly no longer trusted her. She had come into work one day and found some confidential files missing. Since then she had begun to feel as if she was being watched. Waverly's hostility made her uneasy. She remembered what Alan said about people in her position getting hurt.

Within hours of his meeting with Waverly, the foreign minister resigned, announcing that he had 'health problems.'

They were on the veranda: Monica, Errol, Faye, and Jean.

'Look like a sinking ship,' Monica said. 'Wha you think 'bout Waverly, Faye?'

'Wavering Waverly. At first, he seemed to be far right, then he shifted left. Now nobody knows.'

'Waverly is for Waverly,' Jean said. 'Manley should leave him parked outside.'

'Manley not no fool. Him still in control of the country,' Errol said. 'But it look like him not in control of other tings.'

'What you hear?' Monica asked, anticipating sex gossip.

'I hear girlfrien' not too happy,' Errol said.

'Why not?' Monica asked. 'She have her man, an' she a smart-smart woman. She not no flim-flam. Me would vote fe her before me vote fe Manley.'

'She's more radical than Manley,' Faye told Monica.

'True?' Monica was surprised.

'She's a Marxist.'

'You lie.'

'You think the marriage fallin' apart because of her politics?' Jean asked Faye.

Faye shrugged.

'No, man, that's not the reason. I hear Manley's weldin' tools need sharpenin',' Errol said.

'Is jealous you jealous, Uncle Errol?' Jean teased him.

Monica said, 'Chu, all men ever tink 'bout is dem cock.'

'A true,' Irene agreed, coming onto the veranda with some codfish fritters. Irene was grieving bitterly over her son, trying to come to terms with a death she still could not comprehend. She blamed the entire nation for Sonny's death, but most of all, the men of the nation. Her anger had been channeled into daily battles with shopkeepers over food shortages.

Everybody began raving about the codfish fritters.

'Flour so hard fe get now,' she complained, 'me ha' fe mix in some cornmeal.' This was her way of accepting a compliment and at the same time showing contempt for the national state of affairs.

'You tink politics can mash up a marriage?' Errol asked Faye.

'I jus' sayin' I think June Morgan is a Marxist and Manley isn't.'

'I wish all a dem would go to hell,' Irene said, leaving the veranda. 'I wish de queen would tek back de country.'

'Har, har!' Monica raised her glass to that.

Jean missed Daphne. She missed her shouts and laughter, her outrageous remarks. 'Don't you wish Daphne was here?'

They did. They refilled their glasses and toasted her.

'I want to repaint this grillwork,' Monica said. 'White, maybe, then the veranda wouldn't look so much like a prison. What you think?'

Errol would not leave the matter of the prime minister's potency alone: 'I tellin' you is his *powers*. Him losin' him fire.'

'No way,' Faye said.

'How you know, Miss Ting? You sleepin' wid de prime minister?'

'I would sleep with him in a minute,' Jean said.

'In a second,' Monica topped her. She put her long feet with their painted toenails up on the chair opposite her. 'I don't like him policy, but I always like the way him look. Him wouldn't even ha' fe come right out an' ask me. Jus' crook him likkle finger.'

They all laughed.

Monica had been showing more of the raunchy, raucous side of herself that was so much like Daphne. But unlike Daphne, Monica was as fastidious as ever about her appearance. She still went to the hairdresser every Saturday; her nails were always perfect. She might throw off her shoes on the veranda, but the shoes were expensive. Monica was deeply committed to stylish shoes. She had two closets with nothing else in them.

She sat now in the tailored white pants suit that she had worn to work, with a heavy gold necklace around her neck, gold bracelets, and diamond earrings. Her hair was becoming quite gray, and she used a rinse to achieve a striking platinum effect. Yet she was getting old, Jean thought.

'When I see him 'pon TV representin' Jamaica abroad,' Monica said about the prime minister, 'I feel proud. Him is a prince.'

'Monica, if I didn't know better I woulda say you votin' PNP,' Faye teased her.

'No man, dis is strickly a sex ting me talkin'.'

Jean saw Faye's face crinkle with amusement; for all the arguments she'd had with Monica, Faye liked and admired her. It was heartwarming to notice that the two had not let their political convictions overcome their natural good feeling for each other. Jean had been worried for a while. Harsh words had passed between them. The first time Monica saw Faye with dreadlocks, she had ordered her out of the house. And now here was Faye, doubled over with laughter at something outrageous Monica had just said.

Shortly before Jean went to bed, the phone rang. She picked it up. There was silence for a moment and then a man spoke: 'Gun, knife, or fire. Choose. You dead, girl. All a you dead.'

She went straight to Monica: 'I can hardly sleep anymore, I'm so scared.'

'They do this all the time. Jus' tryin' to frighten people. Everyday at the bakery somebody callin' 'bout how dem goin' bun down de place. Don' worry. The house lock up good.'

The next day was Palm Sunday. Jean and Monica went to a morning mass.

'Christ the Savior entered Jerusalem knowing he was to suffer and die ...' The microphoned voice of the priest boomed through the church, jolting Monica every time she started to nod off. Jean couldn't keep her mind on the service. She was troubled by the dream she'd had the night before:

She was sleeping over at Faye's house, along with Pat, Lana, and some of their former school friends from Mercy. Faye was 'swooning,' performing the little melodrama she used to do at school.

'Oh me 'eart! Me 'eart gwine bus'!' Faye clutched her chest. 'Pish! You jeer? I stagger. I swoon. Smelling salts! Antonia, smelling salts!'

She fell to the floor, dragging everything in sight with her, pulling the curtain and curtain rod down, knocking things off the coffee table.

The girls howled and cheered.

They fell asleep, some on the couches and chairs, some on the floor. Jean was sleeping by an open window. Someone crept in through the window and placed a knife at her throat . . .

Jean sprang out of bed, knocking over the lamp and other things on her dresser. It wasn't until she reached the door that she realized she had been dreaming. When she calmed down, she went to the window and looked out. The dogs were not barking; all was quiet. There was broken glass at her feet, the broken pieces of the perfume bottle Lana had given her long ago, the one with painted violets that had belonged to their great-grandmother.

The Palm Sunday service ended, and Jean and Monica left church, carrying their palm leaves. They drove along Trafalgar Road, a stately road with a row of poincianas on either side. It was a typical quiet Sunday morning, not much traffic.

Suddenly, Jean heard sirens behind them. Monica pulled over. Motorcycle outriders and a polished black state car passed by.

'Who dat?' Monica asked, 'Manley?'

'Waverly Martin. On his way to see the prime minister.' Jean knew Waverly was urging the prime minister to take more aggressive military action against the threat of a CIA-backed coup. The army was on the verge of splitting in two; Jean had seen the memos.

'Well,' Monica said, 'better him goin' to see Manley, than Manley goin' to see him. At least we know who still in charge.'

'Manley not goin' let Waverly Martin take control.'

Monica looked at her with interest. 'You seem to have a whole lot of faith in your prime minister. I hope he don't disappoint you.'

Jean thought about this. Faith in the prime minister? No. She admired him, liked him, and had grown up with a romantic notion of him as the passionate husband of the nation. But she had no faith in his office or any political office.

When they reached home, Irene rushed out to meet them.

'Dr Galdy phoned. Is Miss Faye, she in de hospital.'

65

'I have confidence in Dr Bissoondath.' Catherine Galdy was struggling for composure. 'We have some fine surgeons here.'

Faye was in the operating room. The doctor was trying to save her left eye. Earlier a bullet had been removed from her spine.

'What happened?' Jean hated having to ask at that moment.

'Jean—' Monica said, softly admonishing.

Jean looked at Dr Galdy, who turned to her sister: 'Cynthia?'

'Let's go outside.' Cynthia led Jean out onto the waiting room balcony. 'You know how far that house is from anywhere. How many times I tell Faye to get grillwork.' She sighed hopelessly. 'A man was driving up the hill and heard gunshots coming from the house then he saw some men driving away. He drove up and found Faye on the veranda, the other girl—'

'Pat?'

'She's dead. The gunmen came through a window while they were asleep. Beat them. Police said blood was everywhere. All over the house they draggin' them an' beatin' them. They—'

She stopped for a while, then went on.

'The police found Pat tied up in the living room. Faye's arms had rope marks. Whether she talked them into untying her or managed to do it herself, God only knows. Faye is such a fighter!' Cynthia's voice shook. 'I think she must have been trying to get away, because they shot her in the back.'

'They said her eye was damaged.'

'They beat her in her face. Dislodged her eye.'

Faye's surgery lasted till late afternoon. The surgeon told them that he had managed to save her eye. Her jaw had also been badly broken and part of her ear torn away.

'God, have mercy—' Catherine collapsed into a chair.

'What kind of savages . . .?' Cynthia began to cry.

The doctors were uncertain about Faye's survival; she had lost a lot of blood and suffered so much trauma. But, they pointed out, she was young and her heart was strong. That was the better news. The worse was that she might be left partially paralyzed.

Jean stayed at the hospital the rest of the day and through the night. Paul came with food and a bottle of cognac. Waiting became their small world, because they were helpless to do anything else, go anywhere else. Now and then when one of the nurses came out of intensive care, Cynthia or Jean would ask about Faye. Why more morphine? What did those numbers mean? Eighty-five? Was that normal? Why did she need oxygen? Was it her heart? Dr Galdy was too close to the patient and to the procedures for Jean to gauge her responses to these questions. By nighttime Jean had a new vocabulary of medical and pharmaceutical words, words to which all hope was attached.

Paul stayed awake with Jean while Dr Galdy and Cynthia dozed on the waiting room couches.

They spoke quietly so as not to wake them.

'I can't help wondering where God is when something like this happens,' he said.

'Not in the earthquake . . .' Jean recited softly. She leaned back and let her eyes close for a moment. She had not cried. She was not afraid. Her faith did not waver, and she was determined that it would not waver as long as Faye was alive. To lose faith for an instant, she felt, would threaten Faye.

'. . . not in the wind,' she continued murmuring, 'not in the fire . . .'

'Well, where, then?' Paul asked.

Not in the barbarity that shakes the foundations of the house, nor the savage tearing of flesh.

66

They continue driving alongside the smooth river, getting closer to Paul's farm.

'That night I stayed with you at the hospital, I got home about six the next morning. Lana was in one hell of a temper. She knew where I'd been. I called her from the hospital. But she was jealous like crazy . . .'

'Which one a you woman-dem keep you out so late?'
'I was at the hospital all night with Jean.'
'All dis time wid Jean?'
'Have some pity, Lana. You sister's best friend almost dead tonight. You know I was with Jean.'
She was silent, and he could tell she was softening. He walked over to the bed and caressed her.
She pushed him away. 'You smell like pussy. Leave me alone.'
'Okay. You want to know the truth? After I left the hospital, I went to Africa. I went to Zaire to look for a diamond big enough to satisfy you.'
Her eyes became narrow slits when she smiled. She reached for him, and began to unbuckle the belt of his pants.
'Big enough to satisfy me?'
He woke up a few hours later to find Lana, stark naked, energetically moving furniture away from the walls and getting the place ready for painting.

'It goin' to be bright like sunshine when you come back from the farm. When you comin' back anyway?'

'Thursday.'

'Thursday when?'

'I don't know. Morning. Probably around eleven.'

'I'll fix lunch for you.'

'What? Paint walls and cook too?'

She slid back under the sheets and climbed on top of him. He groaned with pleasure as she ran her hands down his chest, toward his groin. 'Don't bother go lookin' for no more big diamond. I have everything I need, right here.'

Jean stares out the window at the Martha Brae.

'I kept thinking,' Paul says, 'lemme try make things work out with Lana, because it seemed to me I was never goin' know anybody else like her. She was all heart, Lana, but no softy. An' Lana — well, it was unbelievable. She was so damn good . . .'

'In bed.' Jean finishes for him.

'Outstanding. That matters if you thinking about spending the rest of you life with someone—'

'You were thinking that?' Jean looks at him. 'I thought you said you didn't love her.'

'I cared enough, Jean, I cared enough to try being faithful.'

He stops for a moment, and she sees him frowning darkly.

He isn't looking at the road, and Jean thinks it's a good thing he knows the countryside well enough to make it home blindfolded.

She senses that he wants to tell her everything, but she has seen and heard so much in the past few days it is a wonder she has not gone insane. 'You don't have to . . .' she starts to tell him.

'I left her in the apartment, busy, painting. And I was

planning to go back Thursday morning. I had every intention of getting back in time.'

'Then I turned up.' Jean remembers.

'In one hell of a state.'

67

It was Tuesday of Holy Week. Jean sat in the dark corner across from Faye's hospital bed. On her lap was a missal she had picked up in the hospital chapel, with a picture of the crucified Jesus on the cover and the caption 'Life More Abundant.' She had been sitting for a good part of the morning in the chapel, not praying, just sitting there. Also on her lap was a book of stories, *Dubliners*, which she had been reading to Faye.

She wasn't reading to her now. She just sat and watched her.

Faye was connected to an IV. Her uninjured eye was barely visible in her swollen face; her battered mouth drooped to one side. There were bandages across her left eye and around her head.

In silence, Jean raged: pure, hot, and formless. No words, no thoughts, and no sense could be made of what she felt when she looked at Faye.

When Faye had woken after surgery and looked at Jean, the best Jean could do was try not to let her own face mirror what she saw. But Faye knew how bad she looked. She knew, too, that Pat was dead.

A nurse came in with tiny sponges on Q-tip sticks like lollipops, and a bucket of ice water.

'You can hold the sponge up to her mouth if she gets thirsty,' the nurse told Jean.

The nurse stood still for a moment, looking at Faye. She

spoke quietly, just above a murmur: 'I see a lot of terrible things. But this one wrench me heart.'

'She's my best friend,' Jean said. 'I've known her since I was seven.'

The nurse patted Jean's hand and left. Faye woke as the nurse closed the door.

'Thirsty?' Jean asked.

Faye nodded.

Jean dipped a sponge into the ice water and held it to Faye's mouth. She sucked on it eagerly, then closed her eye, seeming to return to her medicated slumber.

'I'll let you rest.'

Faye shook her head.

'My mother?' The words came out with difficulty.

'She's with Cynthia. Don't worry about us, just get better.'

She seemed not to want Jean to go just yet. She reached out her hand. 'I heard Pat screaming.'

Jean searched for something to say to her friend, anything at all to keep herself from crying.

'Remember when I had that bad flu at Mercy, how you stayed with me?'

Faye winced. She seemed not to remember.

'You fed me ice water through a straw.'

Sitting with Faye these last few hours, Jean had been thinking back on their school days, how inseparable they had been, how exhilarated and out-of-control. She had been remembering too the girl on crutches and the transformation of that girl.

Tears slid down Jean's face; she could not stop them; they ran down to her lips where she tasted their salt.

Faye patted Jean's hand. 'Jean, have faith.'

'Have Faye?' Jean managed to smile at this left-over silliness from their childhood, but she wanted to beat her fists against the door of heaven, cry loudly, beg God: Don't let her die.

Faye let go of Jean's hand. It was all right for her to go now. 'You'll be out of here soon, working on that new play.'

Faye's expression became strained. Jean felt she had said the wrong thing.

But Faye nodded and mumbled, 'Yeah. You'll hear from me.'

She would stay and help Faye to recover.

As Jean drove home, her mind plowed across the idea.

She would not leave. This was her country. Rage had replaced fear.

Don't forget that you have the key, not them on the outside.

Jamaica was at war with itself. But there were many people like Jean who wanted no part of this war, who wanted life here.

The history of our island is a history of hell; it is also a history of Grace terrestrial.

Red poincianas blossomed by the road. Goats wandered along the suburban avenues in front of house gates and barking dogs. Every day the mild goats wandered along avenues like these, and every day dogs like these barked at them. The air was becoming cooler. Evening began to dim the gardens and avenues. She saw housemaids walking home, walking in groups of three and more, chatting with an ease they had suppressed all day. The street life that had moved in stunned languor in the earlier heat now settled into a different kind of languor, anticipating relief and rest.

Jamaica is our country.

A mango tree in someone's garden caught her eye. It was full of early green mangoes. She turned the corner.

She didn't see the roadblock ahead, or the car that had stopped in front of her. She rammed into the back of it, hitting her brakes too late. It lurched forward on the impact and knocked down the soldier who had been standing in front of it.

He was not hurt. There was not a scratch on him, but he was

outraged, first at the driver of the car that had knocked him down – a woman about Jean's age who looked as if she was on her way home from the office – then at Jean when he realized that she had caused it.

She got out of her car and saw the soldier, his helmet askew, picking himself up and dusting himself off. And that was when everything inside her turned over, and she lost control.

She burst out laughing.

The absurdity of it all – soldiers who had no idea what they were looking for in these roadblocks, the sight of them in their helmets ready for combat on these otherwise quiet suburban roads, and the fact that the most dangerous thing they had encountered all day was her bad driving. There was something truly slapstick about the soldier's fall and his recovery from it.

Jean found herself surrounded by soldiers, some staring curiously and others shouting and questioning her. They were irate, not so much because of what had happened, but because she was not showing enough respect for the increased import- ance and authority given to them by the state of emergency.

She tried to stop laughing – she realized no one else was – but she couldn't. Her whole body was shaking and tears were streaming down her face. She sat on the sidewalk and gradually began to regain composure. She heard the soldier who had been knocked down bellowing at her and saw him pointing his finger close to her face.

He pulled her roughly to her feet, handcuffed her, and pushed her toward the army truck.

'Hey! Wait! Soldier! What you doing to that girl?'

A man got out of the car that had been brought to a stop behind Jean's. He had been sitting in the car with his wife, a man in his mid-thirties, dark-skinned, with a neat mustache and a wiry body. He wore a tie and white dress shirt. Jean had noticed the couple at the beginning of the incident; they looked like decent, understandably harried people trying to get home after work.

The man seemed not so much to have lost his patience as to have simply felt the need to bring back a measure of sanity to a situation getting out of hand.

He came over to Jean and the soldier. The soldier relaxed his hold on her.

'Come on, soldier, what is this?' he said in a reasonable and relaxed tone. 'You roughing up this girl over a little traffic accident?'

The soldier shoved the man with his rifle, pushing him back against Jean's car; then he raised the rifle and shot him in the chest.

The sound of gunfire brought the other soldiers over, soldiers who had not seen what had happened. In an instant they all stood around the car with their rifles drawn.

The man's wife was by him, crying, and crying out.

Jean, with her hands bound behind her, fell to her knees on the road.

Soldiers were pulling away the one who had shot the man.

Jean gazed at the man in the white shirt, who had done nothing more than come to her aid in a situation that had gotten out of hand. He lay dead with blood seeping from the bullet wound in his chest, his eyes open, his arms flung wide in alarm.

It was almost midnight when she got home. Monica picked her up at the police station, then took her to the hospital. Jean kept bursting into tears. Every time she tried to speak, a flood of tears. The doctor prescribed sedatives to help her sleep over the next few days.

Irene brought hot cocoa up to her bedroom. At the sight of Irene, Jean's tears began flowing again.

'Poor ting.' Irene tried to console her and seemed also to be consoling herself. 'Enuff happen dese las' few days fe mek de hardest heart break.'

Monica came in and sat on the bed. She gave Jean a sedative. 'Try to sleep, darling.'

The sympathy in her mother's voice caused another spasm of crying. Her entire body lurched and sank in spasms.

'Eh-eh,' Monica said and her voice regained some of its normal severity. 'All this crying. You crying enough for all of us, eh? You goin' wake the dead with this crying.'

'She ina state. Mek me stay wid her tonight, ma'am.'

'No, is awright. The tablet will mek her sleep good.'

'But if she wake, an' it dark, an' she don't see nobody, she might 'fraid an' go ina shock.'

'I'll keep the light on and my door open. You go to bed, Irene. Lawd, what a worl'.'

She woke up after Monica and Irene were asleep, woke with a strange, almost painful clarity that made her aware of every muscle in her body and every sound, the rustle of leaves outside, and her own footsteps as she walked down the carpeted stairs.

She opened the front door and stood on the veranda. The night seemed so soothingly dark and quiet. But she knew that it was not peaceful out there. She would not dare go out into it.

She stood up close to the grillwork, her hands gripping the bars, her forehead against the wrought iron.

I can't stand to see you tear up like this.

She still could not believe it, the sudden fatality. None of the things that had happened over the last terrible months shook her as deeply as this unnecessary killing of that man whom she had never seen before.

Run through the burning gates.

She remembered how she had collapsed in the middle of the road, handcuffed, not knowing if she was next to die, caught in the screaming chaos of soldiers and ordinary people — *this helplessness, history* — and realizing he would never, ever get up again, that man; it could have been her; it could have been any of them.

The grillwork was cold and painful against her forehead.

She went back to bed. Exhaustion took over. She closed her eyes and when she had almost fallen asleep, she thought she heard someone come into the room. The sedative and the turbulent events of the day weighed her down; her eyelids were too heavy to open. She felt someone sit on the bed beside her.

Leave this place.

The next day she drove to Trelawny. It was night by the time she got there. Paul woke up hearing her loud knocking at the door.

'Jean? What the hell you doing here?' He saw her car. 'You drove all the way here by yourself?'

She couldn't speak. She tried to and started crying.

After a shot of cognac, she calmed down enough to tell him about the man killed at the roadblock, about Brian Scoley, Waverly, Red Man, about being watched, threatened, and about her decision to leave.

'You should have called me. I would have come for you. I can't believe you drove all this way in such a state.'

He poured them both more cognac and put on some soothing music.

As the frenzy that had gotten her there drained away, she realized how odd it was for her to have come. She could easily have spoken to him about these things on the phone. But then her being here was so like one of their many spontaneous drives together, when one or both of them had been in dire need of sorting out.

They listened to music and eventually began to talk as though nothing extraordinary was happening in their lives. She drank quite a bit and took her sedative so that she would be able to sleep. She started to doze off on the couch, and he woke her.

The events of the last few days and the effect of the drugs and cognac shifted things around in her mind. When she woke and saw his dear face, it was apparent to her that this wasn't an ordinary evening, and they were not an ordinary couple. She took his hand and pressed it, needfully, against her lips.

'I would be such a lonely person if I didn't know you,' she said.

'We've always been good friends.'

'It's more than that, isn't it?'

He patted her hand. 'You're exhausted. Get some rest.'

The next morning she woke up gripped by terror. She was afraid to leave the farmhouse. She began to cry again, uncontrollably.

'What's happening to me, Paul?'

'A lot. What's going on now isn't like anything that's ever happened before, not in our lifetime or our parents' lifetime. It's enough to make anybody crazy. Bad enough that you feel bad. Don't make it worse by worrying about feeling bad.'

They went for a drive around the farm. He showed her the new pimento field he had planted. The trees were still young and the berries unripe. He got out of the truck, picked some leaves, crushed them in his hand, and held them up to her to smell.

'Tell me what you smell.'

'Cinnamon, clove, nutmeg.' It was all these and distinctly itself, which was why the plant was also called allspice.

She loved him. He made her feel safe. Why couldn't she stay here with him? She wanted to live with him and spend the rest of her days within the foundations of this honest love. This was what she had always wanted, so secretly that she had not even admitted it to herself.

Paul was a true son of the land; he would never leave Jamaica.

But she felt she could live in the Jamaica she had always inhabited with him, within the pastoral confines of their drives, their talks, this farm.

'Oh, hell!' he said suddenly. 'I told Lana I was coming back this morning. She cooking lunch for me.' He looked at his watch. 'If I leave now, I can make it before dark.'

She felt this was her last chance to ask him: 'Are things all right with you and Lana?'

'All right? Not really.' His eyes rested on her for a moment; then he looked away. 'But – I feel I'm getting old, and maybe it's not going to get a whole lot better than this.'

The smell of allspice filled the truck, and she thought, I will always remember this disappointment whenever I smell this.

She loved him with all her heart, but she realized that he did not deserve all her heart. For some unfathomable reason, he would never see her as part of something hopeful that could be sought after and fulfilled. He did not want to, or could not, hope in that way. He offered solace from the various worries and loneliness of her life. But worry and loneliness could not be her life. His was not a healing love but a consoling one, and theirs was not a hopeful bond with each other and the land they loved, but a fey paradise.

68

They are descending into the valley, where the river branches into an enormous Y with Paul's farm resting in the center. To the south of the farm is the thick mountainous forest of the Cockpit country. For centuries, first the Spanish, then the English, tried to penetrate the forests so they could capture and subdue the Maroons. The Maroons evaded them so skillfully and the European soldiers were so bewildered by the landscape that it began to seem true that only Africans could inhabit the region because they had powerful African sorcery on their side. In 1738, before the American War of Independence, before the Haitian Revolution, these Africans won their autonomy and a peace treaty was signed with the English. An island within an island, fortified by untamed forest, they were free Blacks in the New World whose hidden villages, with names like Accompong and Look Behind, were lighthouses in the minds of desperate slaves. *If this country splits in two, there won't be anywhere to hide.* People escape, she thinks, people survive.

Lana had weathered so many catastrophes that she seemed indomitable. She was oblivious to the increasing violence around her; her self-made chaos seemed to offer her a kind of protection.

'She was tough,' Jean says. 'She was tallawa.'

'Lana didn't want to die.'

'What happened?'

✻

'I was late, already late,' Paul tells her. 'And it was my bad luck to reach Kingston during rush hour. Traffic was crazy, and to make things worse there was a roadblock at the corner of my street . . .'

A huge crowd had gathered, and there were ambulances, police jeeps, and a Red Cross truck. A minibus had been firebombed. Some of the passengers had been pulled out. There were no fire trucks because of the firemen's strike, and people stood and watched the bus burning in the middle of the road. The fire and smoke made the air swim in front of Paul. He felt queasy.

He did not normally believe in premonitions, but that day, during the whole drive back, he could not rid himself of the feeling that something was wrong with Lana and that he had to get to her as quickly as possible. Yet it was as if something kept pressing him backward in the opposite direction, keeping him from reaching her. He was, in fact, proceeding with great difficulty against the tide of onlookers and emergency vehicles. Cars were turned in every imaginable direction as people tried to head back out of the confusion of the roadblock, and barely moving because the onlookers kept getting in the way. The higglers and cartmen who usually ran a makeshift market near the intersection were in the middle of the road, too, selling refreshments. A cattleman suddenly loomed toward Paul, pulling a steer by a rope. In the smoky, wavering air the steer seemed for a moment to be disembodied and all he saw was its horned head. Paul understood for the first time the panic Jean had described to him: Kingston was a nightmare.

When he got to his apartment, the door was open. The room gaped dark and quiet as a grave. He thought, She's left me.

He turned on the light and saw Lana sitting on the floor in the corner. The tins of paint, paintbrushes, and a bottle of turpentine were beside her. She had started painting and had stopped.

'Lana, why you lef' the door open?'

'Dem comin' fe me.'

He realized that she had probably heard the sirens up the road and that maybe she had become distraught and confused.

'Who?'

'Gunman.'

She looked at him accusingly, as if he were part of the conspiracy. 'The bitch is pregnant,' she said.

For a moment he was so taken aback that he thought she was, in some convoluted way, referring to herself. She had been talking about wanting to have another baby. Then he realized:

'Cecile came here?'

'You goin' marry the bitch now.'

'You telling me to?'

'Don't joke wid me.'

'What Cecile want? Why she come here?'

'She say gunman comin' to kill me if I not outa here tonight. How *you* could lie to me?'

'Lie to you?'

'I thought you stop sleep around.'

'Cecile is four months pregnant. Me and you weren't serious back then. Anyway, I don't know if the baby is mine.'

'Who the hell answerin' you phone outa country? I call today an' some bitch answer.'

'You don't recognize you own sister's voice?'

'Jean?'

'Yes. Jean came to the farm las' night.'

'What she doin' there?'

'What? You jealous of Jean now?'

Lana stood up. Her voice became shrill. 'Cecile tell me everything. Everything.'

'What is everything? Tell me.'

'She pregnant an' – you gettin' married – an' is only me in you way. An' I goin' sorry this very night if I don't go.'

'Cecile crazy like hell comin' here to threaten you.'

'You not the kind a man fe leave pickney all 'round the place. Is you chile. Oh God—' She broke off. 'If you ever know how much I wanted – how I pray—'

'What time Cecile came here?'

''Bout twelve-thirty.'

If he had only remembered and been there on time. He pictured Lana sitting alone, afraid of being murdered, and not knowing where he was. He wanted to kill Cecile for doing this to her.

'She cyan mek me go. I na leave you.'

He put his arms around her, and she clung to him. Then suddenly she pushed him away.

'I not good enough to be you baby mother?'

'Don't talk foolishness, sweetheart.'

'Don't "sweetheart" me. You damn liar.'

'I not—'

'Liar!'

'Lana—'

'You never love me.'

She ran out of the apartment into the hallway, screaming, 'Mek dem come! Mek gunman come kill me! See me here!'

He caught her in the stairwell, and she struggled with him, screaming 'Mek dem come! I want dem come!' She bit his hand so hard she drew blood, and she ran back into his apartment, slamming the door in his face. It locked.

'Lana. Open the door.'

He heard a clattering sound and then complete quiet. He banged on the door. 'Lana, open the door.'

Then he realized that he didn't need to beat down the door: It was his apartment; he had the key.

When he opened the door, he saw her pouring the turpentine on herself. She looked at him and lit the match.

It was the look she gave him lighting the match that made him say to Jean, 'She thought I'd save her.' And he might have. He ran out to the hallway for the fire extinguisher, and when he tried to use it he found it didn't work. He threw a rug over her and began beating the flames. He didn't hear any sound from her; he feared that it was too late, that she was no longer Lana. But he kept on beating at the flames until they were out. She was there. She was conscious and breathing.

She remained conscious while they waited for the ambulance. He filled the bathtub with cool water and gently lifted her into it. He cupped the water, carefully wetting her ghastly, swelling skin. Her eyes were bright and demanding.

'I hot, Paul.'

'I know, darlin'. This will cool you down.'

She raised her hand from the water and reached for his crotch.

'No, I mean I *hot*.'

'It never occurred to me that she wouldn't make it, even when they told me she had third-degree burns. She was jokin' with the ambulance guys. She didn't act like somebody who was dying.'

69

It's dusk when they reach the farm. The sun has left red traces like abrasions in the sky. The air is still, the orange trees fragrant. They walk around the garden, inspecting and admiring, as they often do, though this evening they are quieter than usual; their hearts are not in it. Jean notices that the alamanda she planted is growing into a hedge of perky yellow flowers.

'It's been a long day,' Paul says. 'I well tired.'

Jean makes some hot green tea with condensed milk, a comforting drink of their childhood.

The lights go out.

'Power cut,' Paul says, looking out and seeing no lights in the surrounding valley. He lights a kerosene lamp.

They sit together in the lamplit room. Without the usual humming of the refrigerator and other appliances the silence seems bottomless. He looks at her in the semidarkness. She can't tell if he has something important to tell her or if he just wants to look at her uninterruptedly. She's tired, too, but cannot see herself going to bed anytime soon. She still feels the restless spirit of the day's long drive.

Some wayward, mixed-up, and mixing spirit.

Did they fail Lana, she and Paul? Does Paul feel that he failed, that he is failing even now? He's no longer looking at her; he looks at nothing in particular, and his tired body slouches. He hasn't finished telling her everything he has to say, but he has retreated. He can't speak about Lana or her death anymore.

Paul, Jean reminds herself, is a farmer. The day's work has ended, and the work of tomorrow waits. When Jean is gone, he will continue to go back and forth between his farm and the city, asking himself in loneliness the same questions he asked today, looking for some consolation which might in time turn into a conviction. He has ashes to make sense of.

She cyan get enough love, that girl.

Lana had wanted to be saved. She felt it her right to ask for redeeming love — with screams, sexual offerings, prayer, *Pray for me, Jean, pray to Jesus* — and when all else failed, she tried to prove love with fire.

'So — you're really going?'

'Yes.'

'That's good, good. I suppose.'

She is sorry for his complicated burden of grief and love.

'Will you be all right?'

He rubs his eyes and thinks for a while. The silence around them is powerful and daunting, but not as daunting as the hesitation they both feel and have felt all these years.

'What about you?' he asks.

She nods.

'If you change your mind,' he says, 'you know where to find me.'

Her heart could burst. Anything she says in response will be painfully pointless.

He gets up. 'Well, good night.'

'Good night.'

She watches him go.

Mixed-up and wayward is the grace that keeps them friends.

✻

She remembers talking with Monica a few nights ago on the dark veranda, with the lit doorway of the living room behind them.

'You mean you jus' goin' leave everyting an' go?'

'I'm not thriving. I'm dying here, Monica.'

Monica sighed, but didn't interrupt; for once, she listened.

'The brutality is killing me. If I stay any longer, I'll have to accept it, and I can't accept it. I find the acceptance brutal.'

Monica looked at her daughter in the half-light and heard the courage and good sense in her words. This girl, this young woman before her, had turned out well after all. She wanted to tell her – but no, she couldn't say it, it was too prideful. Maybe one day she would tell her what she thought at this moment, maybe she would write it to her in a letter: Good, bright, sensible Jean was her daughter. She praised her in her heart.

Then again, so many people had disappointed Monica; she did not expect much from anyone. She wondered if Jean would really thrive in the bigger world. Was she really strong enough, or was she too much of a dreamer and fancy thinker like her father? Well, it would be interesting to see.

'So you not takin' anyting?' She repeated her question, her concern. 'You just goin' get up and leave, jus' so?'

Jean nodded.

Monica took off her diamond earrings and placed them in Jean's hand. She had bought them for herself on her fortieth birthday.

'Take something of mine, something of value.'

Jean smiled at Monica's sending her out into the world with diamonds. It was so thoroughly her mother. She will be alone now, Jean thought, but as tough as ever. She didn't have to worry about her. Strange that it was Monica, not Roy or Daphne or

Faye or Jean herself, but Monica, who never professed any love of country, who had what it took to endure here. Monica, selfish and adamant, would be the last drum left beating. God, she was tough. What was she made of? Jean smiled inside herself as her mother went on to advise her about what to do with money in her new country, and how to ensure that she always had enough saved. Savings gave a woman courage, she said, 'because a woman widout money — money she earn fe herself — is nutten but grass fe man to walk on.' This brave, vain, pragmatic, ferocious, hurt, and hurting woman was her mother.

'You listenin' to me? I don't know why I bother talk. You head soft, jus' like you father. Sometimes I think feelin' goin' mek you fail in life.'

You carry so much feeling, Jean.

Feeling. Failure. Courage. These were tender, complex abstractions, but she had grown up hearing such things talked about as though they were, in fact, things — things that could be picked up and weighed in one's hand. She had not dared to think about tenderness until now, tenderness itself, or the tenderness implicit in feeling, failure, courage.

She walks out into the country night, trying not to give in to fear. She wants to stand in the open night air of her own country. Above, the stars are so many and so close together that they almost drain the sky of night. But around her is pure, distilled darkness. She is, in fact, afraid.

To leave one's country. It is not a complete sentence, a complete anything. Its infinitive possibilities leap from loss to promise and back again from promise to loss. She will have to try to reconcile the two.

Escape, live, and be silent among the migratory.

She has stood close to the fires. Will they burn this hot in her memory? Will she forgive herself for leaving?

Mek dem know we is here.

She didn't dream them: Roy, Monica, Paul, Deepa, Moses, Daphne, Lana, Rebecca, Mary Darling, Cherry, Mr Ho Sing, Jean Falkirk, Daniel, Mary, Irene, Faye. They are here.

70

Jean stops, out of breath.

She can see the whole valley from here: the Martha Brae, the church's silver steeple, visible through the dawn mist, the silvery corrugated roofs of cottages separating the thick vegetation. Green hangs on green in every conceivable shape and at every angle, domes, fringes, vines. She continues climbing.

Footsteps. A boy and a goat appear. The boy wears a spotless, white shirt. In one hand, he carries a Bible, and in the other, the rope to which the goat is attached. He is obviously on his way down to the valley, to church.

'Good morning,' she says, startling him.

'Good morning,' he mumbles quickly and shyly. He does not stop or stare, but continues at a brisk pace down the hill.

She looks back and sees that he has turned to look back at her. She knew he would. She will soon be a stranger everywhere.

Church bells ring. *He is risen!*

Her eyes sweep the valley and she sees it waking, stirring. The country people proceed to Easter Sunday service. She imagines, because she can't see them clearly enough from this distance, that their white dresses and hats are new. She remembers, once when she was spending Easter holidays with Mary, being taken to the dressmaker for a fitting; the dressmaker's house smelled of fabric freshly unrolled from the bale, and while they waited, others came for their dresses, all white, yet all different.

She turns hearing footsteps. The boy and goat coming back? She sees no one, but feels someone nearby. She continues up the hill until the path ends at a small gurgling rivulet feeding into the Martha Brae, shallow with large rocks, the kind of river she liked to play in as a child. She throws a broken twig in the water and watches it spin around, then disappear.

The church bells ring and ring.

And now the sun rises above the hills, unsealing the horizon, spreading uncontainable brightness. Spears of sunlight strike the steeple and corrugated roofs, turning everything in the valley into a dance of lights, dazzling her.

The river heaves; pebbles turn and turn again in the swirl and flow, and she looks through the transparent shallows for what the river bottom might reveal. *Kaíma águyu namúlalua.* She hears the first language of this place, and feels him there beside her. Kawara? The spears of light dazzle him too.

Namúlalua. Have we been discovered?

71

Jean Landing
1956–

I am leaving the island.

The taxi driver goes sedately through the countryside as if he were taking someone from rather than to the airport. We turn onto an impressive, wide street in Montego Bay with a traffic island of pink oleanders. Century palms line both sides of the street, palms that blossom every hundred years; my father was the one who told me that. None blossom now. I look among them as I pass, like someone wanting an artifact, something to link the land's memory to my own.

I won't forget the beauty or the violence of this place.

But does it have a remembrance of me? I can't help hoping there might be some vestige of my own voice here. For Paul, maybe, as his tires tread the road back and forth past the broken flame-of-forest, over the Bog Walk bridge, in the whispering dark of Fern Gully. Or a stranger might one day hear what sounds like the voices of two friends, one dark and placid, one pale and stirred, in the swift river or flapping ascent of a flock of birds.

We drive through Montego Bay's hilly suburbs where the avenues are wide and graceful, overlooking the sea. Inside the garden gates the spry tropics — bougainvillea, bird-of-paradise — have become pruned borders, tamed hedges; they are beautiful nonetheless.

Descending into the busy town, I'm surprised to see so many soldiers and army vehicles; after all, this is the tourist capital. The driver tells me he knows a shortcut and can avoid the roadblocks.

We drive through a settlement of half-built concrete houses, an abandoned government project, the driver says. Wood shacks have grown helter-skelter among the neglected modern foundations. Goats pick over stones and garbage. A child sits at the steering wheel of an ancient, stripped-down car — his artifact; and a man leans against the wall of a rum shop, listening to the reggae pounding from a jukebox: Bob Marley's 'Coming in from the Cold.' Except for this blast of pounding bass, it is a quiet place, paralyzed by want and burning sun. Nobody wants to be here.

Leaving the settlement, we come to a traffic light. Some soldiers up ahead seem to be taking a break. They stand around their trucks drinking sodas. This is nothing to worry about.

A woman saunters up to the street corner and stands there, drinking a beer. I realize — with a shock — that she is practically naked. Her bare breasts hang almost to her waist. She wears only a pair of men's underpants tied around her belly with a piece of electrical cord. I look to see if the soldiers across the road have noticed her; they haven't.

She begins crossing the road in front of us, stops halfway, and starts to argue with herself.

I look at the driver.

'She panic,' he says, shrugging.

The driver presses hard on his horn.

The woman with a hundred devils in her, or 'panic' as we say here, staggers toward the car. The driver shouts something obscene, swerves around her, and drives on. The soldiers, hearing the commotion, look across the road and see the half-naked woman waving her arms and cursing. They shout and move as a group toward her. I turn around to look, but it's too late — the blinding sun, the speed of the car. Panic and history are mine.

Glossary

anada	another
Anansi	mythic trickster spider, confidence man
bad-wud	curse-word(s)
bawn	born
bukra/busha	white overseer or estate owner
bun	burn
butu	a good-for-nothing person
bwoy	boy
chu	expression of impatience or scorn
chupid/ness	stupid/ness
congotay	future reckoning
crawny	scrawny
cyan/cyaan	cannot, can't; 'cyaan' is more emphatic
de ya	there or over there
dem	them; suffix forming a plural, e.g., cow-dem (cows)
duppy	ghost, spirit
dutty	dirty
face boy	gigolo, a man vain about his looks
facety	impertinent
fe	for or to
fenky-fenky	weakly, faint
gangalee	gang leader
ginal	trickster, con-man
g'wan/g'way	go on/go away or get out

hangle	handle
iry	good, excellent, a form of greeting
ital	right, righteous, wholesome
leggo-beast	a loose or promiscuous woman
liard	liar (emphatic)
likkle	little
liming	gathering for the purpose of chatting
maca	prickle, thorn
mawga	skinny, meagre
mek	make
mussee	must be
na/nah/nuh	no, not
nine-night	a funeral wake that goes on for nine nights
nyam	eat
obeah	voodoo
'ooman	woman
pickney/dem	child/ren
priors	prayers
quattie	quarter-penny
rada	rather
rass	derisive, curse word
smaddy	somebody
spile	spoil
su-su	whispered gossip, behind one's back
tallawa	tough, spunky
tek	take
tief	thief
tink	think
wus	worse

MARGARET CEZAIR-THOMPSON

The Pirate's Daughter

When legendary swashbuckler Errol Flynn washes ashore in his yacht in Jamaica, teenaged Ida Joseph makes it her business to meet him. For Flynn, Jamaica is a revelation: a tropical paradise that promises adventure and a fresh start; when he and Ida do meet, he is intrigued by her poise and singles her out for attention. Soon Flynn has made a home for himself on Navy Island where he entertains the cream of Hollywood, and Ida has set her heart on this charismatic older man.

Ida's child, May, will meet her famous father only once. *The Pirate's Daughter* is a tale of passion and recklessness, of a mother's battle to protect her child, and of a nation struggling to rise to the challenge of hard-won independence. It is a story as spellbinding as even the richest haul of pirate treasure.

'An unabashedly frangipani-scented – and wholly satisfying – armchair holiday of a read' *Vogue* (US)

'A love song to a slice of paradise that's teetering on the edge . . . A complete joy' *Daily Mirror*

'A heady mix of love and loss, treachery and post-colonial politics' *Guardian*

'Sparkles with characters real and imagined . . . A surprising yard that is rich, salty and ultimately satisfying' *Washington Post*

'A joy to read, at once humorous, touching and poetic . . . *The Pirate's Daughter* charms as surely as any dashing film hero' *Sunday Telegraph*

978 0 7553 4359 1

headline
review

MANETTE ANSAY
Vinegar Hill

'A place for everything; everything in its place. The house is as rigid, as precise as a church, and there was nothing to disturb its ways until three months ago when Ellen and James and the children moved in because they had no place and nowhere else to go.'

When Ellen Grier's husband loses his job, she has little choice but to agree to his suggestion that they and their children move in with his parents on Vinegar Hill. Their new home is more stifling than she feared – a loveless place where dark secrets lurk behind a façade of false piety, and calculated cruelty is routine. Ellen's spirit is close to crushed: how is she to protect her children from their grandparents' bitterness and disapproval? Will her love for little Amy and Bert give her the strength to find a way for them to escape?

'Magical . . . A satisfying journey to freedom . . . Ansay writes in a lovely voice' *Vogue*

'One of the best books of the year' *Chicago Tribune*

'Ansay transcends both feminist epic and midwestern Gothic to achieve, finally, the lunar world of tragedy. This world is lit by the measured beauty of her prose, and the book's final line is worth the pain it takes to get there' *New Yorker*

'A modern-day *Little House on the Prairie* gone mad . . . Manette Ansay is a powerful storyteller with lyrical gifts, and a wry, observant eye' Amy Tan

978 0 7553 3548 0

headline
review

ANITA AMIRREZVANI

The Blood of Flowers

'I would never have imagined that I could lie . . . that I could betray someone I loved . . . that I would nearly kill the person who loved me most.'

A village girl's dreams of marriage end on the death of her father. Cast on the mercy of relatives in fabled Isfahan, she and her mother are reduced to servitude until she reveals a talent for designing carpets – an invaluable skill in seventeenth-century Iran. Hope is short-lived, for a disastrous, headstrong act results in the girl's disgrace. Caught between forces she can barely comprehend, she faces a life lived at the whim of others – unless she is prepared to risk everything and choose a future based on her own strength and will.

THE BLOOD OF FLOWERS tells an unforgettable story: a tale of sensuality, of the treachery of friendship, of the power of love, and of the fragile possibility of finding happiness against all odds.

'A stunning debut' *San Francisco Chronicle*

'Amirrezvani . . . infuses her heroine with lilting eloquence' *Washington Post*

978 0 7553 3421 6

headline
review

You can buy any of these other **Headline Review** titles from your bookshop or *direct from the publisher*.

FREE P&P AND UK DELIVERY
(Overseas and Ireland £3.50 per book)

The Pirate's Daughter	Margaret Cezair-Thompson	£7.99
The Vanishing Act of Esme Lennox	Maggie O'Farrell	£7.99
Towelhead	Alicia Erian	£7.99
Then She Found Me	Elinor Lipman	£7.99
Reading in Bed	Sue Gee	£7.99
Villa Serena	Domenica de Rosa	£6.99
Wives of the East Wind	Liu Hong	£7.99
The Ingenious Edgar Jones	Elizabeth Garner	£7.99
Red River	Lalita Tademy	£7.99

TO ORDER SIMPLY CALL THIS NUMBER

01235 400 414

or visit our website: www.headline.co.uk

Prices and availability subject to change without notice.